GREEN APPLE HARVEST

Green Apple Harvest

BY

SHEILA KAYE-SMITH

AUTHOR OF "TAMARISK TOWN," "A CHALLENGE TO SIRIUS,"
ETC., ETC.

NEW YORK
E. P. DUTTON & COMPANY, INC.

TO
MY FATHER AND MOTHER

CONTENTS

PART I

GREEN APPLE HARVEST

§ 1

THE Fullers of Bodingmares had lived in the parish of High
Tilt for nearly three hundred years. They had come into the
neighbourhood as Forest Squires, impoverished by Royal
Charles, to eat the bread of poverty and retreat during the
days of the Commonwealth. They had sunk into the country
of their seclusion—when their Cause revived they did not re-
vive with it. The concerns of a Sussex village received their
souls just as its churchyard soil received their bodies.

The Fullers mixed no more with prelates and nobles, but
with country parsons and small squires. Then, as Bodingmares
sank from manor to farmhouse, so their company sank to
farmers and marsh-graziers; and, as time went on and the
big farms of the Rother Valley grew and exalted themselves
over Bodingmares, to the small men among these, the tenants,
the copy-holders, the fifty-acre men. Slowly yet remorselessly
the country of the Rother Levels was eating up the Fullers.

Bodingmares stood close to where the River Rother and the
River Dudwell flow together in the flats beneath Haremere
Hall. The dwelling-house, spiked about with Lombardy poplars, stood among its barns and oasts on the high ground by
Bugshull Wood, but the Fullers' land—their fields of skinny
oats, their sheep pastures, their acres of turnips and wurzels—
sloped down to the brookside, and found shelter there for a
loop-shaped hop garden, in summer a place of green twilight
and scented, steaming air.

The Fuller in present occupation was James Fuller, lately

3

from Bulverhythe, where he had managed a fairly prosperous market-garden till the death of a childless uncle put him in half-reluctant possession of two hundred acres. He was town bred, though not town born, and this may have been one reason why he broke the long tradition of the Fullers and worshipped at the Primitive Methodist Chapel instead of at the Parish Church. The Fullers had long forgotten that they owed their mean estate to their allegiance to the Church, but it was a convention in High Tilt, indeed in most agricultural parishes, that a yeoman farmer could never go to chapel, and by outraging this convention James earned a mean opinion from his neighbours.

Many a man on discovering his blunder would have rectified it, but not so James. To the Methodists he owed the wonder of his conversion, his place among the elect, the occasional raptures that broke the chill cloudiness of his experience. He even waxed bitter in his constancy, and spoke hard things to his children about the Church which had departed from Apostolic tradition and compromised with the severer dogmas of grace.

He had two children by his first wife Susan Sharman, who had been very like him in temperament, though she had always set more store than he on respectability and the neighbours. She died before he left Bulverhythe, and he had gone into the country as a widower with a boy and girl. Then one market day in High Tilt he had met Elizabeth Bourner, driving her father's trap behind his cattle; and her soft face, with deep dimples in the hearts of the roses on her cheeks, her round, sweet mouth like another rose, and her hair flying dustily golden like pollened anthers, had stirred in him feelings which he had thought would never stir again. They did not belong to his memories of Susan, whom he had married from practical motives, so much as to the memories of a past put away and wished forgotten, of the days before the Lord changed his heart. But he could not think them evil, linked as they were with the flower of Elizabeth's face, with her sweetness which seemed to hold the dew on it still. So he had yielded to them, after much prayer; and as she was sorry for him, with his eyes

both sad and triumphant and his tongue both kind and sour,
she had married him and become the humble successor of those
Cavalier ladies who had submitted too well to their seclusion.

§ 2

One evening in October James Fuller stood in the yard,
waiting for his two sons by his second wife. The elder children
were already at tea with their stepmother in the kitchen, but
these boys of Elizabeth's were late, as usual. He was vexed
and irritated, for that night he was taking his family to a
Revival Service at High Tilt. His mouth stretched into a
line which might have been a smile if it had not been so thin
and tragic. If anything was left out of the evening's pro-
gramme it should be the young men's tea. Then the line of
his mouth sagged towards his chin—he remembered that he
could not make Robert go without his tea if he wanted to
have it. Robert was grown up, twenty-two at Michaelmas,
and for five years at least his father had been incapable of
making him do anything he did not like. Clem he could still
force a bit, for Clem was only seventeen and vulnerable; but
he did not care so much about Clem, whose docility had never
challenged his weakness. It was that big, heavy, bounding
Robert—all health and sin—whom James would have liked to
subdue. Sometimes in dreams he took it out of Robert.

"Mäaster!" His wife's voice came from the house, calling
him in to his heaped plate and cooling teacup. He turned
away, a broad, stooping figure in his chapel blacks, and passing
through the outer kitchen, with its wash-copper and bricked
floor, entered the warm room where Elizabeth Fuller ate bread
and butter and cheese and onions with Susan Sharman's children.

Jim was like his father, but just lacking in those qualities
wherein James redeemed himself by weakness. He had his
father's hard, thin mouth, but without its rather sorrowful
flexibility, he had his father's eyes without their light. For
the rest, he was a well-built man of thirty, and he seemed
to James to have grown up like a tree, from a fixed root. He

had never seen in his son any of the shifts and stresses common
to young men, such as had formed so unforgettably a part of
his own youth—no more than he could detect in him any
warmth or flicker of his own spiritual fires.

Mary was not unlike her brother, two years younger, with
bright, active eyes. She did most of the talking during the
meal, for Elizabeth was planning a gown in her head, to be
made out of the gown of the last five summers, with some new
stuff, and James was brooding, and Jim was hungry.

"I'm middling tired of waiting my meals for them boys,"
said Mary; "only last Sunday the meat was spoiled because
of them, though, I mun say, Mother, as you'd got the oven
too hot . . . it's a waste to heap a fire these days, and the
meat cooks all the better if you cook it slow. You cud see
as that bit of loin wur cooked too quick as well as too long.
Howsumdever, it mäade it a wuss job waiting for them two as
ud never bin to Church, but gone roving in the fields lik
heathen, never thinking as they wur spoiling good meat."

"We haven't waited our tea fur them, anyhows," said Elizabeth mildly; "reckon it'll be tedious cold by the time they
git it."

"Sarve 'em right. I can't abear wud them wot never thinks
food has to be cooked as well as eaten."

"Here they are," said Jim, with his mouth full.

A quick step sounded in the yard, the outer door crashed
open, someone said "Shoo!" to the cat, then the kitchen door
burst in with the same violence as the other, and an atmosphere
of vitality and disruption seemed to enter the room with Elizabeth's elder son.

"Where's Clem?" asked Mary.

"I dunno; I reckon he's out wud Polly. Hi, Mother, I'll
täake a cup of tea."

"If you're thirsty I guess it äun't from want of drinking,"
said Mus' Fuller, sniffing at the strong smell of beer that had
come into the room with Robert.

Robert leaned back in his chair and stuck out his legs before
him. He looked older than his years. His face was florid, and
there was a little dark moustache on his upper lip, shading

without hiding the full curves of his mouth. His eyes were blue, and also rather full, his hair was dark and carefully oiled. He was dressed after the manner of the exquisites in High Tilt—in a fawn coat and checked riding-breeches, with leather gaiters and boots.

"I had two Basses wud Pix and Boorman at the George, and a Barclay Perkins over at the Woolpack wud old Pepper. Otherwise it's bin a dry afternoon."

James Fuller groaned.

"That's how you git ready for Meeting."

"I'll sing all the better wud a wet throat"—and still tilting backwards in his chair, his blue eyes fixed on the ceiling, Robert began:

> "There is a fountain filled with Blood,
> Drawn from Emanuel's veins."

"Höald your tongue, you blaspheming sinner!" cried James. But Robert, who enjoyed the hymn, sang on in his lusty, untrained voice:

> "I do believe, I *will* believe
> That Jesus died for me,
> That on the cross He shed His Blood,
> From sin to set me free."

James shot up with a clenched hand.

"Mäaster dear," broke in Elizabeth.

"Döan't meddle, Eliza. You've a-done enough harm in giving me such a son as him here, who spends his afternoon in drinking and his evening in blasphemy——"

"Why is it blasphemy fur me to sing a hymn at my tea, and all good and holy if I sing it in Church?"

"You wur singing it to mock."

"I wurn't."

"Git on wud your tea, Fäather," said Mary briskly, "or there'll be no chapel fur none of us."

James turned with a grumble to his food. Robert's behaviour annoyed him even more than Clem's, though he knew that the latter was trying to dodge chapel, whereas the former was

willing enough to go. Curiously enough, in spite of his uncouth spirits and regrettable behaviour, Robert had always
enjoyed going to services and bawling hymns, while docile
Clement had in this matter shown himself truant and intract-
able.

To-night he might altogether have escaped his obligations
had not Robert's late arrival and hearty, impenitent tea de-
layed the setting out of the others. They all came out with
a scurry, dark shapes tumbling into the thick autumn dusk,
and startled two figures just coming in at the yard gate.

"Oo-er!"

"That you, Clement?"

"Yes, Fäather—me and Polly."

A faint yellow moon had swum above the stacks, and put a
honey-coloured stain on the mists of the yard. In the thick
radiance the shapes of the boy and girl were smudged together
as they stood hand in hand.

"You tedious young vagabone!" cried James Fuller. "I
know you! Sneaking in after you thought as we'd gone to
chapel. You thought as you'd pick a valiant supper off the
plates. But you shan't have a bit, surelye. You'll come along
wud us to the Prayer Meeting this wunst. . . . And you,
Polly Ebony, git höame to your folk. I'm hemmed if I'll see
you spannelling over the parish wud my boy, kipping him
from his salvation. Git you gone!"

Polly Ebony stared round at the dim faces; then she put
out her tongue at James Fuller, and, suddenly diving in an-
ticipation of the sweep of his hand, turned and ran away.

"She's lik her folk," said James, glaring after her. "That's
valiant company fur Clem to kip—reckon she comes of no
class of people; they're a black lot over at Orznash, and
Polly's naun but a lump of reprobation."

"I'm unaccountable sweet on her," muttered Clem.

"Höald your licentious tongue, and step out beside me."

Clem threw an entreating glance at his mother and Robert,
but found that no help was to be had from that quarter. It is
true that Elizabeth came forward with her gentle "Määster
dear——" but James told her not to meddle—quite gently,

since he was not afraid of yielding to her. As for Robert, he only laughed immoderately, thinking how jolly well Clem had been had.

§ 3

Clem was not angry because Robert laughed at him; indeed, he felt a vague satisfaction in having contributed to his entertainment. He plodded on meekly enough through the thick yellow twilight, every now and then blowing on his cold hands. He was of a very different build from his brother, being short and lightly made, though sturdy enough. He had queer, woolly black hair, curling over his head like a lamb's fleece, and his eyes were a clear brownish yellow, like pools in a lane. Otherwise his face was just the face of a common Sussex boy, with wide mouth and short nose, and a skin of Saxon fairness under the summer's tan.

The moon was climbing up above the mists, and among them huddled the still shapes of the sleeping country, dim outlines of woods and stacks and hedges. Here and there a star winked across the fields from a farmhouse window, or a pond caught the faint, fog-thickened light of the moon. There was no wind, only a catch of frost on the motionless air, and the mist had muffled all the lanes into silence, so that even the small sounds of the night—the barking of a dog at Bantony, the trot of hoofs on the high road, the far-off scream and groan of a train, the suck of all the Fullers' feet in the mud—were hushed to something even fainter than the munch of cows on the other side of the hedge.

The Methodist Chapel stood at the Throws just beyond the village, where one road goes to Mountpumps and Little Pix Hall, and another goes into Kent by Switesden and Merriment Farm, and a third goes adventurously and ultimately to London, though the sign-post refuses to see it further than Ticehurst, five miles. The door was open, and the lamplight and the smell of lamp oil came out together. Mus' Fuller took off his hat, and shook hands with Mus' Cox of Haiselman's and Mus' Bream of Little Moat, who were standing in

the entrance with hymn-books. Mus' Cox said that the Missioner had been much favoured in his discourses elsewhere,
and he hoped that the High Tilt Revival would be equally
blessed; Mus' Bream said hoarsely that it was valiant weather
fur roots.

The Fullers sat in a pew very near the front, only at a
third remove from the towering, pitch-pine pulpit with its
cushion and sounding-board. Everybody stared at them,
partly because they were the aristocracy of a congregation of
tenant-farmers and tradesmen, partly because it was the custom in those parts to stare. The Fullers stared back—all
except James, who opened and read his Bible. Clem sat next
his father, which was unfortunate, as no amount of spiritual
concentration seemed to make James insensible to his son's
many lapses from decorum. Robert, at the end of the seat, was
in happier circumstances, being free to ogle Janie Luck, the
grocer's daughter, who sat in the gallery.

Soon there was a whispering and scuffling at the back of
the church, and a murmur went round: "It's the gipsies,"
"The gipsies have come."

The gipsies lived in a big old cottage called Blindgrooms,
at the beginning of High Tilt Street, and were represented to-
night by old Leonora Iden and her daughter Hannah, with two
young men in corded velveteens. It was not really surprising
to see them, for they often came to chapel, or even to Church,
if they thought anything was to be got by it, and old Leonora
always said she loved a holy place. They were not pure-bred
gipsies, or they would not have lived in a house—they were
off-shoots of the big Ripley family, who had somehow found
their way under a roof. They owned Blindgrooms, and one
or two other cottages in High Tilt and the neighbouring parish
of Salehurst, and were obviously well-to-do, though that did
not keep the men from poaching, or the women from selling
clothes-pegs and baskets.

Clem felt the charm of their outlawry, and craned round
in his pew to see them better. Old Leonora was hideous, with
her wrinkled face and unvenerable black hair, but the men
were handsome, dapper little fellows, and Hannah was lovely.

She was the colour of a hazel nut, with dark red lips. Clem
stared at her fascinated, but she would not look at him, and
he realized that she was answering the stare of his brother
Robert, who had taken his eyes off the too responsive Janie
Luck.   Clem was shocked—no one in High Tilt ever had
anything to do with the gipsies, and by ogling Hannah, Robert
was flouting convention more boldly than he had ever done
before. . . . Then, to his surprise, he saw that Robert had
flushed and turned away, and was staring at the pulpit, where
the Missioner now stood.

The service began with the hymn "Rock of Ages."   Clem
enjoyed the hymn, and sang it nearly as loud as Robert,
though no one could sing a hymn quite as loud as Robert
Fuller, standing there with his chest thrown out and his legs
wide apart and his eyes fixed sentimentally on the ceiling.
He sang so loud that when he went wrong, which happened
once or twice, all the congregation lapsed with him, ignoring
the efforts of Miss Bream at the harmonium or the minister's
hand beating solemnly up and down.

When the hymn was finished, they leaned forward over
their knees, with their handkerchiefs up to their mouths, while
the minister said a prayer.   Then they all settled themselves
for the sermon.   Experience told Clem that this might last
very nearly an hour, and he looked round for ways of making
the time pass pleasantly.   One good way was to exchange
winks with Robert, but Robert was always odd and unre-
liable in church, and to-day he sat quite unsusceptible to
winks, with his arms folded across his chest and his eyes fixed
on the preacher.   Another good way was to suck a peppermint,
and Clem accordingly took one out of the corner of his handkerchief, sucking it meditatively and not quite noiselessly,
while he stared at the pitch-pine front of the pulpit.   He
thought about the lane outside, how it lay in the thick muffle
of the fog, with a sweet, moist smell of mist and mud rising
up from it. . . . It was queer that thinking of the lane outside
made him feel good, while chapel did not make him feel good
at all.   Other things that made him feel good were little new-
born animals, the red sky-rim at dusk, and suet pudding for

dinner. Bob was different, he knew. Bob always felt good in church, even when he was making eyes at girls. . . .

Clem made himself a little island with his thoughts, and took refuge in it away from the stuffy chapel and the pitch-pine pews and the congregation that smelt of moth-killer and peppermints. The preacher's words seemed to batter like waves round his little island; he heard them moaning and droning round him like the sea; they could not come near him, they could not reach him. The moon hung very dim and flat over his head—it was like a smoky plate, there were shadows on it. The sky was red at the rims, for the frost was out and had frozen the rims of the sky and the water in the chickens' trough and all the thick brown puddles in the lane. . . . The stars were flashing as they always flashed on frosty nights— they jumped and jigged to keep themselves warm. There was the dipper—you always knew the old dipper by the way it swung from its handle, slowly round, all night. It was funny to think of pots and pans in the sky. . . . The sky seemed full of homely things—all glittering and gleaming. Why couldn't there be some of them in Church? Why must everything lovely and homely be left outside? Inside here there were no stars—only God, shouting at him. That was God shouting: "Turn, sinners, turn to Me!" He felt all the sinners scrambling over him as they jumped out of their pews and rushed to God. They were trampling on him, smothering him; they were kicking him in the ribs. . . . Oh!

He sat up, choking, and wriggled away from his father's elbow. It was not the first time he had fallen asleep during a sermon, but custom had not yet staled the sense of guilt. He must be quite unconverted; only unconverted people slept in sermon time—with a peppermint in his mouth, too; that was what had made him choke.

The sermon was now flowing on with the same peaceful strenuousness as before. Indeed, he could not really tell if it had been interrupted. He tried to atone for his lapse by listening to the rest of it. Fortunately it was nearly over. He saw with shame that no one else had fallen asleep, not even Leslie Dunk. On the contrary, several leaned forward in their seats, with their eyes and mouths wide open and other symptoms of profound attention. Robert was among these. He sat with his eyes fixed on the preacher's face, his jaw dropping towards his flashy tie, a few beads of sweat on his forehead.

"Now, brothers and sisters," said the Missioner, "before I sit down there is something I should like to ask of you here. Will those who have felt the grace of God in their souls stand up and be witnesses to the congregation?"

He had a pleasant, persuasive voice, with a west-country accent, and Clem was smitten with renewed penitence. He would have stood up himself if everyone had not most likely known he had been asleep. He looked round to see the effect of the minister's words, hoping for a good response. One or two old men and women stood up, and a young man with a turned-down linen collar. The gipsies were also standing up, their eyes fixed intently on the preacher. But no one took any notice of them, for they always "testified" at every meeting. Clem turned back in his seat, and then was utterly confounded, for his brother Robert was standing up, breathing very hard through his open mouth.

There he stood, a great hulking, strapping creature—the most conspicuous object in the room in his fancy waistcoat and check breeches. His face was crimson, and he looked half dazed. Clem felt a thrill go down his backbone. Robert was Saved. Robert was a Believer—he who had been brought home drunk only a week ago. Would he never get drunk any more? Would he never play "crown and anchor" at the pub? Would he never have any more girls? Would he . . . Oh, how Clem wished he had listened to that sermon and heard what it was that had so powerfully moved Robert's heart. Had God really said: "Turn, sinners, turn to Me"?

There was a faint scuffle and mutter in the church. Some people were angry to see Robert Fuller standing up. "Reckon he döan't know what he's doing—reckon he döan't mean naun, no more'n the gipsies." . . . "Bob Fuller's got salvation," young Tom Shovell whispered behind his hand in the next pew. And, "Bad days fur the Royal George," came the ribald

answer of his brother Stan. Clem glared at them. He felt
proud of Robert, standing there among the Elect.

§ 4

He was surprised to find that none of the family seemed
to share his pride and deference. Both on the walk home
and at supper afterwards their words and behaviour expressed
doubt if not condemnation. Mary was vexed because Robert
had made a gazing-stock of them all. Jim said it would have
been well if Robert had managed to keep sober for a month
before he got converted, and he'd point out to him that it
wouldn't be a bad idea to keep sober for at least a month
afterwards. His mother was perplexed and a little worried
because she thought he must be feeling poorly. As for his
father—that was Clem's greatest surprise, for he had thought
his father, that pious, religious man, would be full of delight
at his son's testimony. But Mr. Fuller seemed positively
annoyed by it, and thought that, like his singing hymns at
supper, it was done to mock.

"I wurn't mocking," mumbled Robert. He spoke very little
at supper, though he ate a great deal.

"Then you mean to tell me as you're präaperly saved?"

Bob wriggled in his chair.

"I dunno."

"Wot d'you mean— You dunno as you're saved? I tell
you as there äun't never no mistäake about that. As the
lightning shineth from one part of heaven to another. . . .
Wot did you stand up for if you didn't know as you were
saved?"

Robert filled his mouth quite full of pudding, and was
silent.

"Are you convinced of sin?" asked his father solemnly.

Clem felt quite sorry for his brother. He looked so utterly
sheepish, and sat there swallowing painfully—cramming in
fresh spoonfuls of pudding before he had swallowed what he
already had in his mouth, till he nearly choked. He was

quite unlike the cheerful, swaggering Robert who so often put the table in an uproar.

"You're a fool," said James Fuller. "You're that if you're no wuss, surelye."

At half-past nine Clem and Robert were alone in their large low room at the back of the house, looking out on Bugshull Wood. It was a very big room and their beds were at opposite ends of it, so that a whole country of shadows divided them. But to-night they drew together at the window, whose top reached only half-way up the wall and whose sill was plumb with the floor. They crouched down by it together, looking out at the web of moonlight and fog that the night had spun round the Bugshull trees.

"Well, Robert?" said Clem rather diffidently. He hoped his brother's silence was not going to spread over the hour generally devoted to confidences. At this hour Robert would tell him all sorts of things—strange things, wonderful things, scaring things, beautiful things, bad things.

Robert sighed, and stretched out his arms, tilting his head back against the framework of the window, so that Clem saw all the soft, strong muscles of his neck.

"Robert, wot mäade you stand up lik that in Church?"

"That's just about wot queers me."

"Bob!"

"Döan't look so sorrowing at me, young 'un. I tell you it äun't my fault. I'm queered more'n you."

"But wot mäade you stand up?"

His brother edged closer to him on the window seat.

"I'll tell you, lad—but it queers me. Now döan't you go telling Fäather."

"I wöan't, surelye."

"Nor Mother, neither. Promise me solemn."

"I'm solemn."

"Right. Well, it wur middling sträange. I wur listening to the sermon and I heard him telling us to come to the Lord. And I thought to myself—'that's good words.' Then when he asked us to testify, I no more thought of standing up than you did. But all of a suddent, something says inside

me: 'Bob Fuller, stand up.' And up I jumped as if I'd bin
shot, and then I felt too big a fool to sit down agäun."

"But, Bob, maybe it wur God speaking to you."

"If it wur, reckon He's played me a trick, fur I feel no
more sääved than a potato-trug."

"Maybe you can be sääved wudout feeling it."

"Not you! You feel all your böans praising the Lord.
If it ud bin last week I'd have known wot to think—sometimes,
when I'm a bit on, I hear voices hollering all sorts o' things
at me, some of 'em middling pious too. But to-night I'm
sober as a pump. I tell you, young 'un, it queers me. And
I reckon I feel a fool too. To-morrow all the plääce ull
be laughing, and asking me how I lik Salvation!"

"Döan't fret, Bob. Reckon you can soon show 'em as you
äun't sääved."

"Reckon I can, and reckon I will. I tell you if it wur
God wot spuck to me last night, He's played me a blasted
trick, and I'll sarve Him out."

"Tääke care how you talk. It äun't right to say such words."

"I tell you they're true. God's angry wud me because I
lik enjoying myself and loving girls and drinking at pubs and
doing all the things as He döan't hold with, so He's a-done
this to sarve me out. Howsumdever, I'll show Him as I äun't
beat as easy as that. If anyone here abouts thir.ks as I'm
sääved he'll soon think different, or else he'll think as a child
of God can have as valiant tough a time as any ordinary
sinner."

Clem looked scared, as if he expected the skies, or at least
the roof, to fall on such blasphemy, but the universe and Bodingmares stood equally firm.

"I'll learn 'em," continued Robert, working up his rage,
"reckon I'll learn föalkses around here all that Robert Fuller
can do when he's sääved. I'll show 'em some tough salvation!
I'll tell you wot I'll do—I'll go to the gipsies and I'll have that
girl Hannah Iden. I'd never touch her before, but now I
reckon I döan't care wot I do."

"Oh, döan't go after Hannah, Bob. She's a tedious lot I've

heard. And the gipsy boys reckon they'll have all your money off you."

"Not they! I know them and their tricks—they're silly swine. But I'll have Hannah, fur she's a valiant girl, and I'd have had her before if she hadn't bin a gipsy. But now I döan't care—it's naun to me if I shame myself, seeing as God has shamed me before everyone."

"Täake care, Bob, or maybe He'll mäake a bigger fool of you yet."

Bob swore, and his anger showed signs of diversion towards Clem, who smelt his brother's fist within an inch or two of his face.

"Git to your bed and kip your mouth shut, or reckon I'll start my way to glory by breaking your böans."

So they went to their wide-set beds, and the shadows divided them.

§ 5

The next morning broke in the clearness of October sunshine. The mists had sunk into the earth or shredded into the sky, and the distances that had been blurred since twilight were now almost frostily keen of outline and colour. The air was thinly sweet—scented with the sodden earth, with the moist, golden leaves, with the straw of rick and barn-roof made pungent by dew. At Bodingmares there was a sound of singing, Robert's voice raised in happy unregeneration as he took the horses to the pond:

> "As I was sitting by the fire
> Winking my eye at Reilly's daughter . . ."

Mary in the kitchen set her arms akimbo and said to her stepmother:

"Thur's Robert singing his ugly, rude songs agäun, and fur wunst I'm thankful to hear him."

"Poor lad," said his mother; "reckon as he wurn't himself last night."

Mary sniffed.

"If you wur to ask me I'd say as how he'd got more drink in him than he'd tell. He'd never go and disgrace us all lik that wudout summat stronger than the Gospel inside him. He's a larmentable, drinking feller and ull come to no good end."

"And whose fault's that, I'd lik to know? From a child you've all bin set agäunst him, giving him a bad näum, till reckon one day you'll mäake him what you think him."

"He's bin bred in a Christian house, and shown präaperly how to mäake himself useful. So thur's no sense in blaming others fur his ways. Maybe I haven t allus bin as soft wud him as some, but, then, I never wur one to stand a bad smell and not wrinkle my nose. . . . Thur's the kettle boiling and I've never hotted the teapot. Carry them pläates in, Mother— not the liddle ones, but the deep ones wud the flowers on 'em."

The Fullers had no servant at Bodingmares, whether indoors or out. Indoors Mary and Mrs. Fuller did the work between them, out of doors the four men cared for the yard and fields. The farm had not always been run so meanly. Before James Fuller's time there had been one or two hands employed, and at the corner of the street-field (as the field next the lane was called) stood a tumble-down old cottage, where generations of ploughmen had lived till now when it was let for two shillings a week to the drover at Bantony. James did not see the sense of employing a man when he had three lads of his own. He refused to listen to Jim when he urged him that if only they had more help the farm could be expanded in various directions which were at present closed. He was not an enterprising farmer; for one thing he had been bred to different ways, for another his heart was set on that treasure in heaven, which though it might be safe from moth and rust, yet demanded all his anxious guard, all his careful holding. Jim often chafed at his father's methods, and spoke enviously of the enterprise of other farms, of their stallions, their catch-crops, their machinery, but James, in spite of his absorption elsewhere, would not let another man be master of the mammon of unrighteousness, and Bodingmares jogged on ingloriously from day to day, just solvent, just in repute.

This meant hard work for everyone. James hated to see his sons idling, and Jim was ruthless in the matter of doing all they could. Robert often rebelled and went after his own devices; Clem submitted with cheerful docility, and milked and groomed and fed and drove and dunged and dug from five in the morning till seven or eight at night in apparent contentment.

To-day he was busy carting roots. Robert should have been helping him, but he had gone to market—he never could resist all the joy and jostle of market day, with the strings of horses, and droves of sheep and cattle, and all the drinking of jolly farmers at the George and the Woolpack. He had gone off to enjoy himself and spend his money, leaving Clem busy with spade and aching back and a few resentful feelings. Clem liked market day too, and rather wondered how it felt to get drunk . . . it must be pleasant or people would not do it so often.

He looked up and saw a bright patch of pink on the rim of the field. It stood out against the hedge, moving towards him down the field, and suddenly he was glad that Robert was not with him. He put up his hands to his mouth and called softly:

"Polly."

The answer came, a faint "Hallo!"

He left his spade and his cart, and went up the field to meet her, his feet heavy with the thick clay that stuck to his boots.

"That you, Poll?"

"Surelye."

"I wurn't expecting you so soon after yesterday."

"They've all gone to the market, them at höame. Let's go to the market, Clemmy."

"Reckon I can't leave my roots."

"Thur's a show wud roundabouts, and swings, and a shooting gallery. Why wöan't you come?"

"I wur out gadding yesterday—all the afternoon. Fäather wur larmentable sorry about me when I came höame."

"So wur my Dad. Says he'll täake a stick to me if I do it agäun."

"Then wot d'you want to go to the fair fur to-day?"

"Reckon I döan't care wot becomes of me. Reckon it's all one to me wot happens so long as I enjoy myself a bit fust."

Clem looked at her little sharp sorrowful face, and a soft look of pity came into his eyes.

"Come up and sit wud me at the top of the field and talk to me whiles I work."

"That'll be a valiant way fur me to spend my marnun. Reckon I'll git some other boy to tääke me since you wöan't."

Her eyes blazed at him, but her lip trembled as she met his deep, troubled stare. She suddenly sprang forward and threw her arms round his neck, kissing his cheek.

"Forgive me, Clemmy; I didn't mean it."

He returned the kiss.

"Of course you didn't, Poll. Reckon you'd never go wud them other boys. And I'll tell you—it's a promise—I'll tääke you some day. The swings will be here a week, and Fäather ull give me five shillun on Saturday, so we'll have a valiant time."

Polly crimsoned with delight, and they went up together to the top of the field, where Clem took up his spade again and she sat down on the sun-dried clods and watched him. They did not talk much, for he was working hard, and she was con-templative, in the peace that often came to her when he was near. She sat with her elbows on her knees, her hands sup-porting her small, elfish face. She was nearly sixteen, and scarcely pretty, with her large mouth and narrow eyes, and her hair which hung in long hanks, grooving with shadows her cheeks already too thin. But the whole face was alive, sharp and imaginative as the faces of the Rother villagers sel-dom are. In some ways she seemed older than her years— her voice was old; in others she seemed much younger, and her clothes were those of a girl of twelve—a short pink pina-fore over a still shorter stuff skirt, which showed graceful legs in ragged stockings and hideous, clumsy boots.

"Clem, Betty wur at me agäun this marnun."

He stood leaning on his spade, his eyes fixed on her sadly, as the sweat ran down his arms.

"Wot about, this time?"

"Oh, she says I'm dirty, and I spannell up the house—and I should ought to go to work since I'm over school age. Oh, Clem, I'd just about hate to be a sarvent."

"And I'd hate to see you one—it äun't the life fur you. Your Dad ud never send you—it ud shäame him."

"Sometimes I think he'd sooner be shäamed than kip me aräound. You see, there's näun particular to do in the house now we've got Ellen. If Ellen went maybe Betty ud mäake me help her, since we'd never git another girl, since everyone knows now as Dad äun't married to Betty. Ellen ud never have come to us if she hadn't got her baby, so as no respectable föalks ud täake her."

"She äun't lik to go then, I reckon."

"Not if Betty kips her tongue and her hands off her. But the temper she has, that Betty! She threw a boot at her Tuesday, and maybe she wöan't stand much more of it. I'm sure I shouldn't, even wud the baby. I hope she'll stop, though, fur reckon I'd sooner be a sarvent in a stranger's house than a sarvent in ourn. And, Clem, I do middling love Ellen's baby."

"Do you, then?"

"Oh, she's a liddle soft thing as it's joy to kiss. Her hands —you shud feel them höalding you! Reckon I'll break my heart if she täakes her away."

He was sitting beside her now, unfolding a checked handkerchief on his knees, and carefully taking out of it a large hunk of thinly buttered bread. He broke it in half with his dirty fingers.

"Have a bit o' lunch?"

"I döan't lik to täake any of yourn."

"Why? I'll have my dinner soon as I git in."

She hesitated a moment longer, then a new impulse seized her, and clasping in both of hers the hand that held out the food, she pulled it to her, dragging his arm across her breast.

She was struck by the contrast of the white skin of the under-arm with the hard brown skin that had caught the sun through-out the summer. A blue vein in the midst of the whiteness seemed to her peculiarly refined and beautiful. She put her lips to it, and they both laughed.

"I wäonder wot your fäather ud say if he wur to see me setting wud you here. Reckon he döan't lik fur you to be kipping company wud me."

Clem laughed.

"It all sounds so grand and growed up—'kipping company.'"

"Well, we are that, äun't we?"

"Reckon we are—and we'll be married some day, when I'm öald enough and have put by a bit o' money."

"And you wöant let your fäather mäake you give me up?"

"Not I, Poll! Wot d'you think of me?"

"No, I knew as you wudn't; only sometimes, Clem, when I think wot poor shabby trash I am, and coming from a house where there's shäame . . ."

"Hold your tongue," he said almost roughly, and, to enforce his words, he suddenly, and for the first time, pressed his mouth on hers. She gave a little recoil, then yielded, her arms twining round him and holding him close, though he was all hot and dirty from his labour and smelt of earth and sweat.

§ 6

Early the next week Clem was able to fulfil his promise to take Polly to the swings. Work was already beginning to slacken for the winter, and the dim rose-coloured evenings brought men home from the fields between four and five. As soon as he was free that Tuesday, Clem ran upstairs and cleaned himself and put on his Sunday clothes, and went to meet Poll at the end of the drive, for it would never do if his father saw them start out together. Polly had known that her boy would be smart, and had done her best to make her-self presentable—in which she had had a certain amount of help from "that Betty," who was sometimes known to be sympathetic where boys were concerned. So Polly wore a big, straw hat set round with moon-daisies, and a pair of fawn cotton gloves that nearly reached the bottom of her sleeves, while round her neck was hung a diamond heart transfixed with a turquoise arrow. Her feet were squeezed tormentingly into a pair of Betty's cloth-topped boots, and altogether she was a good match for Clem, with his hair all oiled and plastered out, and his black coat and high white collar, above which his chin twisted and craned in discomfort.

She took his arm, and they set out in their pleasure and constraint to where the flares of the booths had already caught the darkening sky. A red glow hung over the festival, rising from the midst of a circle of tents and caravans, which huddled round it, mysterious and unilluminated. In the middle the merry-go-round trundled to a strident tune; the swings were just behind it, and all round were the stalls of sweets and ribbons and lace collars and false jewellery and flowery chinaware. It was one of those innumerable travelling shows which grind and rattle through the lanes behind stinking engines one day a week, hire some unvalued field or pitch on the village green, display their goods and their fun, and make a whole neighbourhood happy for a few coppers a head.

Clem paid two pennies at the entrance, kept by an imposing lady in diamond ear-rings and a fur coat, and then two pennies more for their ride on the roundabout. They always had just one ride on the red and blue spotted horses, but their greatest delight was in the swings. It was a wonderful thing to sit in a swing-boat together, and fly up into the darkness hanging above the show, and then rush down into the light again. They hardly knew which they liked best—that mysterious ascension towards the cold, wonderful things above, or that swing back to the warm, human, noisy things below. They had to swing very high to get right out of the glare and to see the stars hanging there big and untroubled above the misty redness of the show; it sometimes took Clem five minutes to work the swing up to the necessary height, and Polly found herself biting her tongue to keep down her screams as all the lights of the fair swung away from them, and the red glow rushed down, and they flew up for just one instant into the cold, still darkness, which seemed to stroke their faces like a wing. . . . Then down again! The sky with its myriad stars heeled over and was lost—the red ground roared up to meet them, and all the stalls with their shuddering candles; it seemed as if they would strike the bottom, but they just skimmed instead, their shadows running ahead of them over the crimson ground . . . and then up again, with breath almost gone and hearts in suspense, seeking once more the adventure of the dark. . . .

You had ten minutes on the swings for twopence, and Clem had counted to spend a shilling in this way. Eightpence would buy their supper in gingerbread and apples, he had already spent fourpence, so exactly sixpence would be left to buy Polly her traditional fairing. For though Clem had had five shillings given him on Saturday—as a sedative to his father's conscience for making him do a man's full work seven days a week—he had brought only half a crown to the show. He always put by half a crown a week, and had calculated that he would have saved enough to get married by the time he was twenty-one. The trouble was that he did not always succeed in keeping his hoard inviolate. Bob had a great deal more than five shillings a week—he said he'd be hemmed if he'd work for his father for less than a man's full wages—but he had an expensive life, standing drinks all round at the pubs, and taking girls to the pictures, and going by train to distant markets and football matches, so that he was sometimes obliged to borrow from Clem, not always the whole five shillings, but often part of it.

Clem suddenly caught sight of Robert on a downward sweep of the swing. He saw him standing in the glow of the houp-là stall, beside a shawled figure whom he did not recognize. He had expected to meet his brother. Robert had been out when he went up to their room to dress, but he had been to the show nearly every evening of its visit, and would most likely be there to-night. He craned to see what sort of girl

Bob had got this time, but before he could do so the swing
had rushed up with him into the darkness, and when it came
down again they had moved on.

But when the shilling was spent, and Clem and Polly stood
rocking and rather sea-sick on the solid ground, Robert and
his companion came once more into view round the corner
of the shooting gallery. This time Clem knew her at once,
and made a face of disgust. She was Hannah Iden, the
gipsy; after all, he might have recognized her by her bright
shawl. None of the girls in the neighbourhood wore a shawl;
only the gipsies did so. Above her shawl was tilted her crazy
hat, full of great feathers, and her eyes looked out from under
it black and smouldering, and her red mouth laughed in her
brown face.

Clem was shocked. Never before had his brother been seen
about with Hannah Iden. Local convention was strong on
the matter of the gipsies. Bob had now and then gone with
a low girl, but never with a girl from Egypt. Clem thought he
saw judgment written on every face. He was ashamed for
his brother—who was, for that matter, ashamed of himself.
Clem read the secret of his swaggering gait, his hands thrust
deep in his breeches pockets, his cap pushed back from the
great curl on his forehead. . . .

"Wot wud you lik, darling?" he said to Hannah in a loud
voice; "I'll buy you wotsumdever you please."

"I'd like you to treat me as a young gentlewoman," came in
Hannah's soft, humming voice, so unlike the drawl of the
Rother villages, "and not call me darling without acquain-
tance."

Young Pepper of Weights, who stood near, burst out laughing.

"That's präaper," he said to Hugh Willard of Boarsney;
"that's teaching him manners."

Robert turned crimson, and the way he looked at Hannah
was not pretty.

"Then wot am I to call you, ma'am, since I've the honour
of täaking out an Egyptian?"

"My name is Hannah Iden, and was given me in a good way in Church. So you can call me by it."

Robert made her a low bow—it struck Clem that he must be a little drunk. His brother suddenly caught sight of him, and nodded in a way which said plainly, "Döan't you come nigh me," so Clem walked off, with Polly holding sedately by his arm.

But all the joy of the show was spoiled—even the supper which they ate standing side by side at the refreshment stall, in the midst of a great, happy sound of strong teeth crunching apples. Clem could not forget Robert, even when he did not see him swaggering along beside gipsy Hannah in her wicked, outlandish shawl and hat. He had disgraced himself, outlawed himself by his behaviour to-night. No decent labourer—let alone a yeoman farmer's son—ever went with the gipsies. They were thieves, they were furriners, they sold low things like clothes-pegs and kettles when everyone knew they had plenty of money; they poached and were never caught, they stole horses and could never be brought to justice, they had cunning hearts and dark faces and ate hedgehogs. . . . Yah! they made decent folk sick.

Everywhere he went the little brother seemed to hear echoes of Robert's shame: "Thur goes Bob Fuller—him wot got säaved on Thursday." "He's wusser than ever now—he never used to go wud gipsy trash before." "He's a dirty dog!" came harshly from a young farmer at Etchingham. "I'm hemmed if I ever täake another pint wud Bob Fuller."

Clem felt utterly miserable. He could not enjoy the show, even for Polly's sake. Once in his desperation he thought of trying to make Robert go home with him, but he knew the folly of such an idea—Bob had drink in him and might make a scene. So they wandered forlornly among the glittering stalls; Polly recognized and shared her boy's depression, and had scarcely the heart to choose a sixpenny bangle richly set with rubies and emeralds. She was pleased enough when she woke up the next morning with it under her pillow, but that night she shared her lover's melancholy, and felt a little of the throbbing shame of the heart against which her hand was pressed.

§ 7

They left earlier than usual, for the glory was departed and they were tired. About a quarter of an hour before they went, Robert and Hannah disappeared, and Clem's trouble was increased by miserable conjectures. Had Bob gone back with her to Blindgrooms? However, when in the slow, cold midnight he came to Bodingmares, having seen Polly to the bottom of Orznash drive, he found his brother lying fully dressed and face downwards on the bed. He did not move when Clem came in, and for a moment the boy stood looking helplessly at him, wondering whether he was drunk or asleep. At last he said:

"Can I do anything fur you, Bob?"

There was a heave of the strong shoulders, and Clem drew back, when Robert's voice came suddenly and huskily out of the pillow:

"You might täake off my boots."

Clem had performed this office before, and did so now, fumbling in the darkness with the laces and legging-straps.

"Robert, you shudn't ought to have laid down wud your boots on the counterpane. Reckon you've spannelled things up unaccountable."

"Wot's that to you? Höald your tongue!"

Clem said no more, merely tugged and hauled till the boots were off, and then brought his brother some water. Bob wetted his head and drank the pitcher dry, after which he felt better and rolled over on his back.

"Clem, äun't she justabout beautiful?"

"Who? Hannah Iden? I reckon she's got a fäace lik the bad girl on the Pictures."

"You saw us, didn't you?"

"Surelye."

"Clem, she's a bitch."

"No need to tell anyone that."

"But, listen here," and Robert raised himself excitedly on his elbow. "Wot d'you think, kid? *She wöan't have me.*"

"Not have you?" Incredulity, indignation and relief struggled together in Clem's voice.

"No—that she wöan't. Spuck me short 'cos I called her 'darling,' mäade me täake her höame at ten o'clock, and then wouldn't so much as give me a kiss at the door. She's a bitch."

"Maybe she's got another boy."

"Wot's it to me if she's got a dozen? I said I'd have her, and have her I will."

"But since she wöan't have you. . . ."

"She's got to have me. Wot's she that she should choose?"

"Bob, can't you let her alöan' now? Reckon you've shown everyone as you äun't säaved."

"But I äun't shown myself."

"Wot d'you mean?"

"I döan't mean naun. But if I can't have Hannah . . . I tell you, youngster, I've a tar'ble sort er feeling as by standing up that time I've gone and put myself among the Elect wudout knowing it and I've got to be säaved whether I lik it or not. And then I say as my only chanst is to go straight to the devil, and reckon Hannah Iden ud show me the way better'n most."

"But, Bob, you wudn't lik to go to hell?"

"I dunno. Wot do I know about hell? All I know is that it's just about scaring to have a trick played on you lik that. Besides, I want her, Clem. She's lovely . . . her mouth makes my mouth ache . . . she smells of grass . . . and her eyes in the shadder—they mäake me want to drownd myself. I wish her eyes wur water and I could drownd myself in 'em."

He was sitting up on the bed, and looked sick and excited.

"Döan't 'ee vrother," said Clem soothingly; "she äun't worth your thoughts—and reckon you döan't look säaved ever such a liddle bit. Think of something nice. I heard Mary say as she wur mäaking a blackberry puddin' to-morrow."

"I guess I'll be sick to-morrow. Not that I've took much,

but I feel unaccountable bad. Oh, Clem, I wish as I'd never
been born!"

§ 8

The next day Robert was, as usual after such outbursts,
inclined to be sulky. But in course of time his spirits revived,
and Clem's mounted with them till they reached at last the
level of contentment which was their natural state. Polly
Ebony, his mother and Bob, the succession of October days
and nights, his work, and what there was for dinner, became
once more the happy realities of his life.

Even Robert's evening confidences ceased to obtrude dark
things. It was not till later that he came to realize that this
was not normal, and to suspect that these confidences were no
longer real confidences, but were tainted with the reserve that
seemed to have passed from Bob's general conversation. Also,
in time, he began to notice how often he came up to bed to
find his brother apparently asleep, and very nearly as often
Robert was out and did not come in till Clem himself was
sleeping.

Once more his mind was shaken out of the joyful common-
places in which it lived, and began to ask questions which he
found at last on his tongue: "Whur's Hannah Iden?" . . .
"Have you see Hannah Iden agäun?" . . . "Has she still naun
to say to you?" Once Bob answered that Hannah had gone off
basket-selling into Kent; another time he told Clem to hold
his tongue. Both were bad answers, since one showed a suspicious knowledge of her doings, and the other a suspicious re-
luctance to speak of them. But though Clem asked no more
questions out loud, he could not stop asking them in his
thoughts. For it was queer to have Robert silent with him
like this. Robert had told him all about his other girls.
Clem loved hearing about Robert's girls. But now he scarcely
ever opened his mouth—you would really think he hadn't got
a girl; though that, of course, was impossible.

The farm was still slowly settling down into its winter quiet
—it was like some old thing falling asleep. The autumn

ploughs dragged over the brown, ribbed fields, while yellow rags of leaves fluttered on the hedges and on the trees of Bugshull Wood. The Rother mists rose very high at night, right up to the gable windows of the farm, and all the valley of the river, stretching away to the north, was full of mist for half the day. The mist seemed to penetrate everything: it covered the grass with white, half-frozen pearls; it draggled the leaves till they were limp; it made the earth soggy, so that there was a poach of mud and yellow water at every gate.

Clem found it very cold rising in the dark, muffled mornings and going out with his lantern to the milking. But the cows' udders were warm, and their sweet-smelling flanks, in which he could hide his cold nose—and breakfast was good, with his big plate of porridge—and at ploughing he'd sweat nicely. . . . He liked the autumn work, with its care of the ewes, which would have lambs before long; and he was proud of having saved a heavy field of roots from the damp. His only trouble, and it was serious enough, was that the shortening days did not allow him to see much of Polly Ebony. His father did not like him to bring her to the house, and her father would not have him at Orznash—and the lanes at night were cold, even for lovers.

Sometimes she would come and stand for a minute or two beside him at his work, blowing on her fingers, or stamping her sodden, mud-caked boots. But she could no longer sit and watch him while he worked; and though in his free time they often found a barn full of straw or a warm corner among the stacks, they both regretted the summer days, with the streamside rambles and the sanctuaries of shade which the great woods gave them both from prying and from heat.

Clem wished he could have persuaded his father to approve of Polly and let her come to the house, for he knew that his mother liked her, and they could have sat together in the warm, red kitchen, so peaceful of an afternoon, and his mother would have given them cakes, hot out of the oven. But though James did not actually forbid his son to associate with Polly Ebony outside the farm, he would not allow her to cross its respectable threshold, because of the "goings on" at Orznash. To have suffered her would have been in some manner to countenance sin. She was part of the shame of Orznash, where the farmer lived with a woman who was not his wife. In this attitude James was not singular—his neighbours would have done the same; and a sense of injury and injustice made Tom Ebony retaliate with an equally strict and far more wide exclusion, since he shut out all those who would have shut him out, and Clem, in other respects a desirable match for Polly, was forbidden to enter her home just as strictly as she was forbidden to enter his.

This state of affairs made him all the more anxious for their marriage, but he failed to see how it could take place for many years yet—partly on account of parental opposition, which he believed could not be successfully withstood till he was twenty-one, partly on account of money difficulties. He had now left school four years, and had saved about twenty pounds. In four years more, at the same rate, he would have saved another twenty; but he hoped that his father would soon see fit to raise his wages, since he was really no longer a boy—he had asked him once already, but James had sternly bidden him be contented with his lot. It is true that he could have taken himself off and found work on some other farm, but then he would have had to pay his own board and keep, so that the advantage gained would not be substantial enough to make up for the breach with his family and the loss of any chance of concessions from his father. Also he would probably fail to get employment anywhere in the neighbourhood, where James, if not liked, was considered and respected, and would have to endure separation from Polly and the prospect of her being left without his comfort and protection. So he plodded on, doing all he could, and hoping almost more than he could.

Then one day, towards the end of the month, Robert suddenly asked him for the loan of a couple of pounds. It was a shock. Robert had never borrowed more than shillings before—after all, the dissipations of village life are generally matters of pence. But here he was asking for two pounds, and asking as if he expected to get it. Hitherto Clem had never made any difficulty—Bob's fingers had always been free of his treasure. It had never struck him that it was a shame that, with fifteen shillings a week and no marriage to save up for, Bob should take the fruits of his young brother's sacrifices—that, on the contrary, he might have helped him out of his own abundance. He had always excused his brother to his own qualms, stressing the demands of that glorious life which he was naïvely proud that Bob should lead, though he never had any temptation to lead it himself. Robert, in his check breeches and leather gaiters and rakish cap, driving his gig, or drinking at a pub, or twirling his little clipped moustache at some girl in a street window, was a Man. Of course he wanted money, and it was only right and natural that he should go in his embarrassments to his brother Clem, who was not a Man, and would have had no use for his money had he not been rashly contemplating marriage. . . . But to-day he suddenly felt moved with anger against Robert; he suddenly saw the cruelty as well as the injustice of his demands. Two pounds—a four months' saving—it wasn't fair. . . .

"But I'm not asking you to give it to me," said Bob when he had recovered from the shock of a scowl and a short answer; "I'm only asking you to lend it."

"Wot d'you want it fur?"

"That äun't your concern."

"It is my concern, since it's my money."

Robert was positively startled into an explanation.

"I lost more'n that to Darius Ripley at Catsfield räaces."

"Räaces—you dudn't use to go to räaces."

"Well, reckon I've bin now."

"Wud the gipsies!"

"Wud Darius and Ambrose."

He stood glaring at his brother, his angry blue eyes meeting defensively the stare of Clem's round golden ones.

"Döan't git thick wud them gipsies, Bob."

"I'll git thick wud whom I please."

"Then döan't come asking me fur money."

Robert bit his lip.

"Reckon you're a tarble chap, Clem—you've chäanged unaccountable—ordering me about and grudging me money. You never used to grudge me."

"I döan't grudge you naun."

"Yes, you do. You've got a dunnamany pounds in that box of yourn, and yit you wöan't let me have as much as two— only for a week. I'll pay you back—honest I will."

Robert had not always been immaculate in the matter of repayment.

"You git fifteen shillun a week of your own, and it äun't fair as you shud come to me and täake the money as I've put by to git married, and spend it on a gipsy baggage."

"Who says I spend it on a gipsy baggage? How dare you say it? I tell you I lost it to Darius Ripley at the räaces."

"You wudn't go with Darius if you wurn't after Hannah."

Robert flushed, and his fists clenched at his sides.

"I äun't so much as seen Hannah fur a week—she's over at the Fivewatering picking oziers."

"Bob, you döan't tell me as you äun't doing it all on account of her. You dudn't use to go wud the gipsies, you dudn't use to go to räaces—and now you do both, surelye. Wot am I to think?"

His anger was weakening and the tears came into his eyes.

"Döan't think no harm of me, Clem—but let me have that two päound. I'll pay you back in a week—honest—I swear."

"How are you going to pay me back?"

"Thur's räaces at Plumpton on Friday, and I know . . . well, never mind wot I know—but I tell you as it's präaperly säafe. I'd never täake all that amount of money from you, kid, if I couldn't pay it."

Clem was relenting—he could not withstand the pleading of Bob's eyes, that look as of a hungry dog which was hidden under all their cunning and guilt.

"Döan't think as I grudge you aught, Bob—it's only—it's only as I do so unaccountable want to git married."

"Of course you do, young un, and I tell you as you shall— soon. Reckon I'll help you after this—I'll see if I can't put a bit by fur you; and I tell you I've had a tip fur Plumpton as'll——"

"Oh, Robert, fur marcy's säake döan't put any money fur
me on a horse. It'll be lost fur certain sure . . . and the
railway fare to Plumpton's something tedious."

"Döan't vrother—I'll git back my fare and a bit more too.
If only you'll stand by me now. . . ."

His case was won, and Clem, with a sigh which he tried in
vain to suppress, unlocked his hoard, and counted two pounds
in silver and copper into Robert's hand. As he counted out
the last sixpence he suddenly lifted his eyes and looked straight
and pleadingly at his brother.

"Bob, döan't kip things hid from me. . . . Wöan't you tell
me about Hannah—after this?"

"Höald your tongue!"

Robert's voice came angrily, as his hand closed on the
money and plunged it with a jingle into his pocket.

§ 9

He paid back Clem one pound five at the end of the week,
apologizing shamefacedly for having no more; but his luck,
though good, had not been so good as he had hoped. He
promised the rest in a day or two—there were räaces at Lingfield. . . .

Clem, whose sense of injury had long ago given place to
shame for having grudged him anything, gratefully reassured
him of his patience, and felt thankful and undeserving. He
was glad to have such a lot as twenty-five shillings back so
soon, and accused himself of having misjudged Robert, till
one day he overheard Pont of Udiam say in the village:

"Reckon as Bob Fuller's through wud all that money he got
at Plumpton."

"He can't be," said Willard of Boarsney. "Reckon he mäade
more'n five paound out of Market Garden and that selling-
steeplechase outsider."

The words came to Clem passing by on the road, and they
went into his heart with a sick stab. But it couldn't be true—
it was only talk. He was treacherous even to think of it. If
Robert had come back five pounds the richer from Plumpton,

he would certainly have repaid his whole debt. But the words thus blown to him on the highway irritated his heart like dust. . . . After all, men like Willard and Pont were more likely than he to know the extent of Robert's poverty or wealth —and he knew that Willard had been to the races. . . .

The next day he was in the post office, buying a stamp for a letter to Polly, when Stan Shovell came in for a postal order. He nodded to Clem, and they exchanged remarks about the weather and ewes and roots, and then, just as young Fuller was going out, Shovell asked him if Bob would be at Lingfield for the races.

"I reckon so."

"I wäonder if he'll have as stout luck as he had at Plumpton."

"Did he have stout luck at Plumpton?"

"Reckon he did. He put his money on that hemmed outsider what won the selling pläate. A tip the gipsies guv him, I calculate."

"He never töald me naun."

"Ha! ha! He's got some know! And all the money's a-gone by this time, I'm certain sure. Huwsumdever, I'm sorry as he dudn't tell you; I'd a feeling as maybe you cud give me Bob's fancy fur the Lingfield Cup."

Clem shook his head.

"Oh, he's close, is our Robert—he knows how to höald his tongue. But I thought maybe he'd guv you a tip, being his brother. He gits his tips from the gipsies, I reckon; and though a gipsy's a louse, he knows an unaccountable lot about horses and rääcing."

Clem went out, feeling troubled and heartsick. So it was true that Robert could have paid back the whole two pounds. He had lied to his brother, he had cheated him. The angry, shameful crimson gathered on Clem's cheeks. He felt outraged and disappointed, not only because of the money, but because of Robert's reticence, the arch-secrecy which had enabled him to win and spend five pounds without his brother knowing it. Why had he never told Clem of his luck? Because he wanted to keep four pounds out of the five? It could not have been only that. And why did he want to keep so much?—spend it, rather, since all the village was agreed that he had nothing left. It must be Hannah Iden, that outlandish Egyptian. She had power to tie Bob's tongue which had wagged so roguishly about his other girls, she had power to extort pounds where her predecessors had had to be content with shillings. Robert was mad for her, and he was buying her; he was buying her with pounds and with the fellowship of her low relations, all the Ripleys and Rylys and Bosvilles and Hearnes, that poaching, thieving, welshing lot that hung round Blindgrooms. . . . Clem hated her, because she was making Bob miserable and because she would one day (he knew instinctively) make him happy, when he had paid her price.

For the length of his walk home he thought of telling his brother what he knew, and pleading with him at least for open treatment. But by the time he saw Robert he had decided to hold his tongue. Bob would not bear remonstrance—he was crabbed—and after his last explosion of wrath Clem dared not speak again of Hannah Iden. He must wait for a while, and see what would come of Lingfield races.

Nothing came but silence. Bob did not pay the fifteen shillings he still owed, or even speak of them. Perhaps he had forgotten his debt, but that was hardly likely with such an unprecedented sum. It was more probable either that he had had bad luck or that his winnings had been spent on Hannah. Clem was beginning tragically to acquiesce in the reserve between them. Their talk was now all of trivial, outside things. When they were alone together they talked of crops and stock and fairs and food, and such things as they talked of to Cox of Haiselman's or Dunk of Shoyswell or Pont of Udiam, or anyone else who didn't matter.

§ 10

Early in November Mus' Fuller fell ill. At first it seemed to be only a cold; he sat shivering over the fire, and drank a great many cups of hot tea. But suddenly a fierce pain took hold of his side and his breath became sharp and noisy. It struck the family that here was a real illness, and that they had better send for a doctor.

The doctor came and looked grave, but he said, "He'll pull through . . . he'll pull through." He said it for three days, and at the end of the fourth Mus' Fuller was dead. The doctor seemed to think that he ought not to have died, that he might have lived if he had not suddenly tired of his fight for life and wanted nothing but rest.

Clem helped to nurse his father. A streak of capable gentleness made him useful at the bedside, while Robert sulked miserably outside the door, and Jim found practical distraction in hard work. He could not help being a little surprised at the small interest Mus' Fuller took in spiritual matters, now at the very time they would be expected to concern him most. The years of his health had been spent in brooding on heavenly things, but from the moment his last illness began his mind seemed to concentrate on the small affairs of his sick-bed. His fight for life was entirely a matter of dose and diet, and his final surrender was not to the Everlasting Arms, but to his own fatigue. Clem had not expected this; he was so used to his father's religion hanging like a cloud over his most earthly concerns that he would not have been surprised if the Four Last Things themselves had stood at the four posts of his death-bed. Now and then he read the Bible to him, but the sick man would constantly break in with, "Has the time gone by fur my medicine yit, Clem?" or "Reckon there's an unaccountable draught from that winder," or "My poultice is turning cöald." He did not even think of sending for the minister, and his last words were about a wagon whip he had left behind on a visit to Mountpumps.

Clem shed many tears for his father, but his grief was nothing to Robert's. For a day or two Robert would not eat and would scarcely speak. He cried a great deal and accused the others of being unfeeling because they were able to live their daily lives. He said that Jim was glad 'his father was dead because he could now do as he wanted with the farm. Considering the way Robert had treated Mus' Fuller during his lifetime, it was scarcely to be wondered at that he now found his family more resentful than sympathetic. "I always knew as Bob wur low," said Jim one day, "but it äun't till now I've larned he's a hypocrite."

The funeral came, and Robert was a little comforted. He found a certain relief in driving behind the hearse in a new suit of blacks. His attitude at the graveside was almost childishly solemn; he knelt and prayed over his folded hands. A large company watched him, half contemptuously, for all knew how he had behaved during his father's life—farmers who had come from many miles round to do honour to a man whom no one had liked. There was Cox of Haiselman's, and Pepper of Weights, and Bream of Little Moat, and Dunk of Shoyswell, and Willard of Boarsney. No wonder that Mary Fuller could hardly fix her mind on the prayers, for thinking of the funeral tea awaiting the company at home, and now of necessity in charge of a hired girl—"and everyone knows as they äun't to be trusted."

Clem did not find the same comfort as Robert in his father's obsequies. He was struck by the chill of that black procession—the hearse with its lumbering horses, and the mourning coaches with horses gradually lightening from black, through brown, to the last bay pair, which was also the last pair at weddings. Even the wreaths of white flowers, with all the inscriptions that had been written and read so proudly—"With deepest sympathy from Mr. and Mrs. Pont and little Reg," "In memory of an old friend, from Mr. and Mrs. Tom Bream," "From all at Little London," "In everlasting remembrance of our Dear Father, from Mary, James, Robert and Clement. Not lost, but gone before"—even these now struck him as a little repulsive, with their miasma of white smell and the brown smirching of petal-edges.

When his family stood round the grave, their backs to the Martinmas sunshine and the white clouds that sailed through it on a sea of shallow blue, they seemed to him almost strangers, as unreal as the long black shadows that lay on the grass before them. Mary looked strange and stout, and Jim looked strange and worn, and Robert looked strange and childish, and his mother looked strange and comely, with a queer youthful freshness in her eyes and skin, and at the corners of her lips. . . . Even he himself seemed strange to himself, with the new bowler under his arm, and on one broad red hand the black kid glove which was the sole survivor of the pair he had spent half an hour trying to force on after dinner.

One joy of all this strangeness was that before the funeral was over it had extended to the central piece of realism. That dead man in his coffin became a stranger too; he was no longer Mus' Fuller of Bodingmares, Clem's father, human and loved and pitied, who had lived in futility and grace and died in pain. He was just the ballast of that shiny wooden box, buried in the earth, with wilting flowers to hide the scar. . . . He had no more connexion with the real Mus' Fuller than he had with Mus' Cox or Mus' Pepper or Mus' Bream. He was a sign that had lost its significance, a dream of someone now awake, a nothing. . . . The sun did not shine upon him, the minister did not pray for him; he was no concern of those present, a dead man out of mind. . . .

Such cold comfort Clem got from the burial of a Christian man; at least it was something to have ceased to identify his father with the contents of that shining box—an elm coffin. Twelve pounds it had cost, "but folk ull expect us to do things präaper." . . . On the way home the horses trotted, and the hedges went by in a soft powdering of light. At Bodingmares there was a substantial tea—with brawn and cheese, and tinned salmon and tinned peaches—and if it was not seemly to talk much, one could eat the more.

§ 11

It was curious to feel the change that had come to Bodingmares. As soon as the funeral cloud had passed the sky was sunnier than it had ever been before; an oppression was gone, a misty gloom, it was easier to breathe and act and see. James Fuller had never been a tyrant, he had ruled chiefly by interference, by the spoke rather than the whip, nevertheless he had been a clog on growth and freedom. The progress of Bodingmares had chafingly dragged, and all Jim's enterprises had been fretted and peeled into ineffectiveness. Now the eldest son was master, and free to develop the farm beyond his father's market-garden standards. Bodingmares should be great and prosperous and worthy.

Jim's emancipation would have had its effect even without the general lightening of the atmosphere, for he was expansive in his new satisfaction, and liked to see himself doing the generous thing by his brothers. The day after the funeral he sent for them both, and told them that he was now going to run the farm on sound business lines. It was not sound business to have forced or unwilling labour, so he offered Robert twenty-three shillings a week, and Clem thirteen, both of them to pay a fixed sum weekly towards their food; their lodging, since he was not out of pocket by it and most yeomen lodged their hands, should be free. Clem was quite bewildered by this generosity, and could hardly find words for his acceptance, which it seemed strange that his brother could doubt. Robert was not quite so overwhelmed, but he accepted all the same.

Clem calculated that he could save quite seven shillings every week. He was blissfully happy, and his gratitude to Jim involved an immense amount of hard work, a spending of himself in his brother's service. He would be up before daylight, and in bed long after everyone except Robert, trying his hardest to deserve that Saturday morning's mercy of thirteen shillings. This kind of life did not allow him to see much of Polly, but the drench and draggle of November did not offer the same temptations to lovers' hedgerow meetings.

Besides, his work was giving her to him more surely than any caresses, bringing nearer the day when she should belong to him, when they should share together food and house and work and sleep. That day need not now be much more than two years ahead, for fifty pounds would furnish their house and pay their first year's rent, and buy them something in the way of pigs and fowls to set up stock with. It is true that he would still be under age, but he did not expect the same opposition from Jim as from his father. Like any decent yeoman, Jim disapproved of the "goings on" at Orznash, but as his disapproval was uncomplicated by religion there was every chance of its being overcome. Besides, it did not extend—at least in the same intensity—to Polly, who was now, at Elizabeth Fuller's invitation, occasionally to be found in the kitchen at Bodingmares.

Poor little Polly did not quite see her lover's new remoteness with her lover's eyes. She could not share his abasement of gratitude towards Jim—"done no more fur you than he shud ought" was her comment—and she found an honourable hour with Mrs. Fuller in the kitchen a poor substitute for those uncovenanted wanderings by field and stream.

"Reckon you äun't näun of a sweetheart to me now, Clem," she said one day when, having lugged Ellen's baby all the way from Orznash, she found him absorbed and sweaty in the oast-barn, slicing roots.

"Reckon I'm less of a sweetheart so's I can be more of a husband."

"I'd sooner have a sweetheart to-day and a husband two years after next."

"It ull be sooner'n then, I guess. I'm putting by seven bob a week regular."

"And if Jim says 'No'? And if Fäather sends me away to be a sarvent?"

"Jim wöan't say 'No' when he sees what a stout bit of money I've säaved; and if ever you're a sarvent, I'll come and fetch you out that wunst."

"I'd die if he mäade me a sarvent—even fur one month. And now he says it oftener and oftener—that Betty's going to have a child, you know."

"All the more reason fur him to kip you to help look after it."

"Betty says she'll look after it herself, and it ull be better if I äun't around eating idle bread."

She looked infinitely pathetic as she sat there on the straw, clasping another woman's baby. Clem stooped and kissed her, for a moment holding both her and the child in the crook of his strong, weary young arm. Her eyes lightened, and taking a handful of his thick, woolly hair, she pulled down his head between hers and the baby's. . . .

Suddenly he straightened himself and stood up.

"I mun git forrard wud them roots. Stop and have a cup of tea wud us, Poll."

"Wot'll your mother say?"

"She'll say näun but wot's kind."

"And your brother Jim?"

"He mun be civil to my young lady."

Perhaps it would have been as well if Polly had not gone to her first meal at Bodingmares hugging part of the shame of Orznash. But everything passed off better than she and Clem had any right to hope. The family was still in its reactionary state of good humour, and though at first Mary was a little antagonistic in her bustling, and Jim, for want of a remark neither cordial nor offensive, said nothing for a quarter of an hour, the meal soon became friendly. Mrs. Fuller had always been compassionately disposed towards the poor little girl from Orznash—"not but it wur silly of Clem to talk of marrying her and him näun but a boy"—and Robert, with vague ideas of gratitude and atonement in his heart, was almost embarrassingly amiable. Polly did not talk much; she sat quite humbly between Clem and his mother, conscious—as her lover was not—that the friendliness of everyone, save Robert's, was largely due to the fact that she was so reassuringly little, only a bit of a child, and now that they had properly seen her and spoken to her they were sure that there could be nothing serious between her and Clem.

The loud yells of Ellen's baby made it necessary that Polly should take her back to her mother directly tea was over.

"I didn't bargain to kip her out so long," she apologized; "you've bin middling kind to me, ma'am, asking me to stay."

Clem walked with her to the bottom of Orznash drive. He felt exhilarated at this new prospect of toleration. His boldness had been justified; if he worked carefully, fifty pounds and the family's goodwill ought to be his at the same time. In that respect it was providential that his father had died

. . . the hard young thought scarcely woke a reproach in him now. He had ceased to be ashamed of his relief. At first it had caused him some pangs—poor Fäather, whom he had always pitied. . . . He did not pity him now, and that was perhaps one reason why he could not feel ashamed of his happiness and sense of freedom. He had once or twice dreamed very comfortably of Mus' Fuller, dreams in which the dead father was free and happy too. That was what seemed to take away the feeling of treachery. His father had been unhappy while he lived—though he had then, as Clem knew well, hidden springs of joy which ordinary people could not understand—but now he was dead the joy had come up from the hidden springs. . . . So he was happy, and free among the dead—as the Psalm said.

He had had one dream which was so peculiar that he had not told it to anyone, even to Robert. He dreamed that he saw his father eating his supper in the kitchen, and wearing that bright and contented look which he always wore in Clem's dreams. Clem was with him, and said, "You feel better, döan't you, Fäather?" Mus' Fuller said, "Yus—now that the Flaming Judgment is täaken away." Clem looked up and saw floating in a corner of the room a Bible with flames of fire running out from under the covers. He was so frightened that he woke.

§ 12

Robert had quickly and unaccountably, almost absurdly, recovered from his grief at his father's death. His attitude confirmed the general impression of hypocrisy. He seemed the only one of the family who felt no secret shame at the new lightheartedness. During Mus' Fuller's lifetime, his exuberance had been often sharpened and smitten into hostility; now, without discipline, it functioned as riotous good-humour, which seemed positively indecent under the circumstances. No longer soured by conflict, he filled the house with a sense of outrageous heartiness.

Clem alone of the family did not put down Robert's good spirits entirely to relief at Mus' Fuller's death. He breathed the general atmosphere of lightness, it is true, but there must be deeper causes for his new ease. Bob had had other griefs than his father's repression; he had been consumed with his desire for Hannah Iden, for the gipsy rubbish who thought herself beyond the price he paid for decent Sussex girls. For him to be so happy now he must either have forgotten her or he must possess her.

The first was unlikely, for though Robert easily forgot, he did not forget till after he had gotten; besides, if the Iden episode were over, the details of it would now be in Clem's possession—the baffling, humbling secrecy would be gone. Nothing less than Hannah's witchcraft could tie Bob's audacious tongue. He must have won her, bought her at last. And he was happy; his conquest made him tolerant and good-natured to everyone. Just as she had been harder to get than other girls, so she was better worth having. But it was queer that Robert should still keep silence like this, that he should not tell Clem of his rapture, as he had so often done before, of his kisses and roamings and treatings, of his power over smiles and tears. For Robert had always been a boaster in conquest. He did not boast now; he was just happy and noisy and satisfied.

Then at the end of January Robert borrowed another thirty shillings off his brother, making a debt of two pounds five in all. Clem had expostulated and pleaded, but he had no power against Bob's disgust at his meanness, and ended by handing over the money, though he had small hopes of its being repaid, even partially.

He tried hard not to think about it; he didn't want to become the sort of chap who always thought about money. Yet how could he help it? It wasn't only for his own sake; there was Polly too. It was middling hard. . . . Of course it was a bit his own fault; he ought to have said "No" to Bob. He would say it next time; but habit and affection made it almost impossible for him to deny his brother.

One evening as he was passing Weights' farm, which stands back a furlong from the street, Bill Pepper of Weights called to him from the drive:

"Seen Hannah Iden's watch-bracelet?"

"Wotcher say?" asked Clem, not understanding quite.

"I ask you—have you seen Hannah Iden's watch-bracelet, wot your brother Robert guv her?'

"Robert äun't guv her näun of the lik."

"That's queer, seeing as she's got a beauty—a gold un."

"Reckon Hannah Iden's got a dunnamany ways of gitting a watch-bracelet if she wants one."

Pepper sniggered.

"Reckon she has. Howsumdever, Robert Fuller's her main way of gitting things at present."

"Bob äun't got the cash to give anyone gold watches, surelye."

"Not after wot happened at the Woolpack last week?"

In the misery of realizing that he had not the slightest idea what had happened at the Woolpack last week, Clem lost the conviction of his defence, and began to plunge.

"Bob—wot shud he give aught to Hannah Iden fur? She's näun to him."

"Ha! ha!" laughed Pepper of Weights.

"I tell you Bob he döan't care two moldy onions fur Hannah Iden."

"That's odd, seeing as he goes to Blindgrooms regular every evenun, and many a time I äun't seen him come out till the night's turned."

"That's odd too, seeing as I sleep wud Bob and he's a-bed in our room at ten o'clock punctual every night."

"You liddle liar," grinned Pepper.

"I äun't liddle"—Clem was sensitive to his height.

"That's all right, so long as you döan't say you äun't a liar. You've gone a bit too far in sticking by your brother, young Clem. You äun't so durn innercent as all that."

"I äun't innercent at all, and if you go on miscalling me, Bill Pepper, you'll find as——"

"Kip your fistses down, young feller. I äun't miscalling you. But I've just one bit of advice to give you, as coming from a man wot's seen life and earned his living into the bargain, which äun't always done. You kip clear of dirt, and döan't git in wud any lazy, lousy, loose-living set. I'm sometimes afraid fur you—that you'll go your brother's way—you seem to turn natural towards wot's low. You stick up close to your brother Robert, wot's a bad character, and you stand off your brother Jim, wot's a good 'un—and you're thick wud them at Orznash, wot's——"

A mouthful of Sussex clay prevented any definition of Orznash, and by the time that Bill Pepper had choked and spat his way to utterance, Clem was half-way out of the village.

"Liddle gutter chap—that's wot he is, that Clem Fuller. No better'n a street boy. . . ."

As a matter of fact, Clem had his own doubts as to the effectiveness and dignity of his conduct. Close on eighteen and going to be married . . . he ought to have grown out of throwing things at people. However, he guessed rightly that the present was not the suitable moment to return with apologies, so put them off to some future occasion when they might be better received.

§ 13

He reached home late for supper, and Jim grumbled at him for "spannelling araound" when he was wanted for the ewes. Mary grumbled, too, because she wanted to clear the table. They found their culprit silent and without excuses—his one wish seemed to be to eat his supper and go to bed. Therefore Jim kept him working at the corn accounts till it was nearly ten and any more of Clem's arithmetic would have made book-keeping impossible for at least a fortnight; and Mary insisted that before he went upstairs he should go into the scullery and wash up his own plate and cup, since he had made more trouble by being late. Then their punitive instincts were satisfied, and they forgave him.

Clem went slowly up to bed, dragging his feet from stair to stair and spilling grease from his candle. He felt very tired, and muddled with the sums. But his chief feeling was one of thankfulness that Robert had not yet come home. Clem had effectually missed him by being late for supper; when his brother returned he would be asleep.

But he had reckoned without the thickness of Robert's boots, which it never occurred to him to take off on his brother's account. His elephantine tread broke into Clem's sleep, which the sums had made lighter than usual. At first he fought against returning consciousness, but he was too restless and Bob was too noisy for sleep to be easily won again, and in a moment or two he was broad awake.

The window was uncurtained, and showed a deep sky dazzled with frosty stars. Outside lay the great stillness of midnight; inside the room the boards creaked as Robert moved to and fro, undressing himself. His candle stood on a chair by his bed and lit up his side of the room, while Clem lay in darkness. He lay quite still, not wishing Robert to know he was awake, but as he watched him he felt love and compassion rising up in his heart. There was something about Bob, as he laboriously and creakingly undressed himself, sitting on the bed to unstrap his gaiters, or stooping and fumbling with his braces, while his big shadow stooped and hung on the wall behind him, something about his bigness, his unawareness, the half-satisfied, half-sheepish look that his face wore when he thought himself unwatched, that melted away Clem's annoyance, that made him lift himself on his elbow and call gently:

"I'm awake, Bob."

"Go to sleep, then," was Bob's discouraging reply.

But Clem was now definitely, if unconsciously, aware of an advantage over his brother, so he did not lie down obediently under the bedclothes, as he would have done the night before; instead, he raised his voice a little and said

"I want to speak to you."

Robert swore, but made no other objection.

"I want to ask you why you've guv Hannah Iden a gold watch wud my money."

"I äun't guv her näun wud your money."

"That's a lie. You know as you've got thirty bob of mine,

besides wot you didn't pay, when you said you hadn't got it, though I know now as you had."

"You're a mean liddle devil if you can't give a loanst to your own brother."

"It äun't that I mind so much—it's your telling me lies about it and spending it on her."

"I'll spend it on whom I choose."

"Not my money."

"Adone, do, wud your everlasting money. You talk as if your money ud have bought Hannah a gold watch. That watch cost me more'n five paound, so hold your tongue about your thirty shillun."

Clem felt rebuked.

"I shudn't have said näun if you'd told me things out. But you hide everything from me and go your own way like a cat on the tiles—you never tell me a ward."

"Why shud I tell you? You're only a kid."

"I äun't a kid—I'll be eighteen by the spring sowings, and I'm booked to be married as soon as you'll let me säave the tin. Anyways, you've always töald me things before. Why should you stop now?"

"There's never bin anything lik this."

The two pairs of eyes—Clem's round, alert and yellow, Robert's bulging, heavy and blue—met across the room, and held each other in a characteristic stare.

"Wot d'you mean?" asked Clem.

"I mean as Hannah's not lik the other girls, and I'm not going to tell you aught about her, surelye."

Clem felt a sudden nervousness; he seemed to lose his advantage over Bob.

"I—I——" he stammered. "I thought as how you'd only täaken her on to sarve out God."

"Wot shud I want to sarve out God fur?"

"Because he mäade a fool of you."

"Oh, that!" and Robert grinned. "Well, wotsumdever I meant by it wunst, I've helped myself to the finest woman south of Kent Ditch."

"Is she sweet to love?"

"Is she sweet! Is the fire sweet? Is the winter sweet? Reckon you don't know näun of love. There's hard and soft love, säum as there's hard and soft kisses . . . there's a kind wot mäakes your heart like a bröaken stoan."

He was sitting on his bed, and he lifted his chin with a queer, rapt look—very much like what Clem had sometimes seen on his face in chapel, but not so foolish. In his eyes was a strange new wisdom; the younger brother felt himself silenced.

"I love her," said Robert, "not because she's sweet, but because I can't help it, surelye."

"And does she love you?"

"She'll let me love her—that's all I ask. All I ask is fur her to tääke me and let me love her. Reckon she's been hard to win, but then she wurn't a-going so cheap as other girls."

"Shud you want to marry her?"

"Want? Of course I want. But we come of different folk, and she can't abide our ways."

"Reckon we'd never abide her'n. Wot ud Jim say if you brung her home fur his sister-law?"

"You'd better mind wot *you* say, anyways."

"I äun't miscalling her. You're tedious short wud me, Bob. It's only natural as I shudn't git things clear at fust, seeing as you've kept me in the dark this two month."

"Thur you go wud your everlasting grumble—'kept you in the dark,' 'not töald you aught'—you mäake trouble lik a straw-rope twister. Wot's the sense of my telling you about Hannah Iden, seeing as you döan't know naun about love? Oh, you needn't fire up and say as you're booked to be married. That döan't show you much. You're but a white boy, wot's never known a woman . . . never known love in your body. And I tell you as my Hannah äun't lik your Poll. Reckon your Poll's 'sweet to love'—Hannah äun't sweet. And she döan't give herself fur näun. And she döan't want a boy to love her—she wants a man . . . and I'm that man so long as I'm man enough. You marry your Poll Ebony, and she'll mäake you happy. Hannah wurn't born to mäake men happy —she wur born to mäake them men."

He stood in the middle of the room, his head flung up, his

eyes unusually awake and aware. He looked enormous in the shifting light of the candle, which, as the draught shook it, sent his shadow heeling over wall and rafters. His bare arms were folded over his chest, and the play of light and darkness on their muscles, and on the big muscles of his back and neck, gave a glowing impression of beauty and strength.

"Reckon you *are* a man," said Clem admiringly.

Robert was pleased.

"You mustn't think as I've turned agäunst you, young 'un— only I'd sooner you didn't meddle wud wot äun't your concern."

"Reckon my money's my concern."

"If you say another word about your money I'll smack your head."

"It's only because I want it to git married."

"Well, you'll have it—and years before you're ever lik to git married, liddle boy. So höald your tongue."

§ 14

Clem found that he had to change his attitude towards Robert and Hannah—it became more humble. He could not treat his brother the same as when he thought he was just being lustful and obstinate. The fact—which he received and believed—that now, for the first time in his life of squandered experience, Robert was truly in love, filled him with deference, but not with rejoicing. In spite of all that Robert had said, he could see nothing but sorrow in his love for the dark, outlandish woman. He felt sure that Hannah did not love Bob, or, by his simple calculations, she would never have taken so much from him. What would Polly say if Clem were to spend five pounds on her? Reckon she'd have a fit!

There was no doubt but that Hannah was a bad lot, and not merely a bad lot as they go in the Rother villages, but with all the deeper dye of Egypt. It was true that Clem had hardly ever spoken to her, but there was a definite tradition about her in High Tilt—and about her mother Leonora and her cousins Ambrose and Darius Ripley and Jerome Bosville.

Polly shared, or rather concentrated, the local points of

view. She was also extremely annoyed about the money. To
hear her talk one would think that Bob's two pound five was all
that stood between them and their marriage.

"Reckon you wur a gurt owl to have let him have it, Clem.
And it wurn't seemly, nuther—you must have known how he'd
spend it. Reckon you love him more'n you love me."

"Poll, you know as that äun't true."

"How am I to know it, wud you letting him spend our
marriage money on his fancy girl, buying her brooches and
rings and bracelets, wot all the pläace talks about. Reckon
your brother Jim wöan't have any call to be ashamed of your
marrying up at Orznash, seeing as thur's wuss shäame in your
own house."

Clem tried to soothe her with caresses that were now growing bolder. But Polly was sore and sick, and he was bound
to acknowledge that there was much to be said for her attitude. Moreover she was going through a bad time at home.
Betty, whose kindness had always been erratic and occasional,
was turning more and more against her now that her time was
near. She was jealous of her man's child by another woman,
and morbidly afraid that the child she was about to give him
might suffer as the second-born. During the languor and
inertia which the later months had brought it had seemed to
her that Tom Ebony had come to rely more on his active daughter—Poll had acquired a value in the house. So Betty vowed
that she should go out of it—into service, or—since Betty
was not really ill-natured—with some boy who would take her
away at once, and not go hanging around waiting till he'd
saved enough to be married, like Clem Fuller.

"Oh, Clem—let's do summat quick. It's tar'ble waiting
lik this and feeling as I döan't belong to näun but them wot's
set to git shut of me."

"Wot can we do but try and sääve, and try and git araound
Jim? We can't be married wudout any tin, surelye, and till
Jim turns friendly we can't be married wudout one of us is
twenty-one."

"Reckon Jim's beginning to git friendly."

"Aye—he's beginning, but he äun't done it yet. I spuck to

him about marrying two days agone, and he töald me to wait till I wur growd up"—and Clem spat.

"Reckon it's a pity you're so middling stuggy, or maybe we could have gone to one of them registers or pläaces where they marry you wudout a parson, and then you say you're twenty-one. But you look no more'n a lad of sixteen, surelye."

Clem was a little huffed. "Wot you want is some more of patience, my gal. I tell you as I'm warking steady and sure to git us wed, and, if you trust me, reckon I'll have done it before the year's out, fur all I look but sixteen."

"I dudn't mean to mock at you, Clem. But reckon as it's unaccountable fretting being as I am, and never knowing as one marnun they wöan't say: 'Pack your box, my gal, fur I've fixed fur it to be fetched from somewheres over at Berrish—or Wadhurst or Bulverhythe, maybe—and off you go and earn your own bread instead of eating ourn.' And then Steve Alce from Nineveh, he come a-vrothering me, saying as he'll tääke care of me if I go to him, and that Betty fur always trying to mäake me go. . . ."

"You tell me next time Steve Alce he asks you that, and I'll go over to Nineveh and break his fääce and his jaw and his head and everythink he's got on him, fur all I look no more'n sixteen."

"I know as you would, Clem, and that's why I never tell you. I döan't want you to git fighting, fur all as I know you'd win. Fur Steve's a low kind, and ud mäake trouble. Dad wur saying only t'other day as you can't bash a feller the ways you could wunst. Fur Ellen's got a new boy, and he's jealous of Dad, and he mäakes trouble by telling Betty as Dad's after Ellen now. . . ."

He drew her to him, and kissed her, as if he would kiss the defilement of her home from her lips.

§ 15

One day early in March, when he was walking home from High Tilt, smoking a cigarette which Cox of Haiselman's had

given him, he unexpectedly encountered Hannah Iden. She
seemed to blow up the lane before the spring wind, her brown
dress swelling like a sail, all the wicked feathers of her hat
flying out together in a thin blurred line like a cirrus cloud.
Clem looked straight ahead of him as she passed, his chin
high, his teeth so firmly clenched on his cigarette that to his
chagrin he bit it in half. He heard her go by, then was
irresistibly impelled to turn round and gaze after her. To
his disgust he saw that she was looking back too.

"Are you going to speak to me?"

He blushed furiously, and would have walked on if it had
not suddenly struck him that here was a chance of finding
out more about her and Robert, and if she really loved his
brother. He stood hesitating, and she strolled back towards
him, her eyes slanting in a laugh that was not on her lips.

"You've gorgeous manners, passing by a female without taking off your cap."

Her voice accented the "furrin" note struck by her appearance. It lacked both the local drawl and the local idiom, and
yet it was not a genteel voice. Clem's heart hardened against
her.

"I äun't awares as I've got your acquaintance, miss," he
said loftily.

"Then it's time you got acquainted with your brother's
female friend. Now let us begin to get acquainted. You
takes off your cap and you says, 'Pleased to meet you'; and
I says, 'You're a gorgeous young gentleman—too gorgeous to
be enemies against me.'"

Clem stood before her as stiff as a rake.

"I äun't enemies agäunst you. But reckon I äun't friends,
seeing the ways you've sarved my brother."

"Have I served him badly, then? He's never been happier
than he's been with me."

"But you täake his money—you mäake him give you things
wot cost more'n he earns."

"If the sweet gentleman likes to give presents to the poor
person's child. . . ."

"You know it äun't that. He'd never have guv you all them things if you hadn't mäade him, surelye. Reckon you led him on and promised him näun säave he paid fur it."

"Mind your manners, young chap. I ain't used to being spoken to disrespectful. If your brother loves me and gives me presents, it's none of my doing. I don't go out after men; they comes after me."

"But you mäade him come. And now he's come he can't go wudout you let him."

"You talk as if I was chohawnee and knew spells. No doubt there's females among us what knows more than the moon knows. But they ain't taught me nothing—I've no need. I've got my own spells. Shall I show them to Bob's little brother? No—he's too young a child. But I'll tell you, little brother, I've got spells in my eyes and my fingers and my lips and my throat and my breast, what no wise female has never no need to show me."

She stood before him hugging her red shawl round her shoulders, her hands hidden in its folds, as with her crossed arms she held it over her breast. Her attitude was all reticence and veiling, yet Clem suddenly felt his throat thicken with the sense of her beauty. He had never before been so deeply affected by a woman. For a moment he felt her power, crude, physical, yet with an almost mournful appeal to his higher senses, to all in him that was stirred by the scudding March day, and the grey, tumbled sky that hung low over the fields. . . . She seemed to make that appeal and fail to sustain it, dropping back to lower, physical inspirations. He found himself stepping backward, as a man would step out of a shadow.

"Don't be afraid of me, little brother; all prickles like a hedgehog. When I saw you coming along the road I says to myself, 'Here's my chance of getting to know my pretty brother with the woolly hair. It's a pity he should be set against me just because I'm kind to his brother Robert.'"

"If I thought as you really wur kind and ud always be kind. . . ."

"And what makes you think different?"

"I dunno . . . it's your looks and your ways . . . and your

täaking so much . . . and wot Bob's töald me, and the way he's turned all secret. . . ."

"But he's happy now. Your own eyes can see how happy he is."

"I've a feeling as it wöan't last. How can it last when he says as he knows you döan't love him? And he says his heart's lik a bröaken stöan. . . . Reckon one day he'll want a bit of love back fur all the love he's given . . . and then I hope as his bröaken heart ull be lik the stöan in the Bible, and ull fall on you and grind you up to powder."

"You talks gorgeous and terrible. I likes to see you angry— your eyes shine like a cat's when she's in the dark. You've shining eyes and a mouth to give joy, and yet you're afraid of love. You're afraid of me because I've taught your Bob how to love, as none of the silly, fat young girls in this place have taught him. I loves Romanly, not like the silly rawnees— laughing with their big mouths out of their red faces. I could teach you how to love, little hedgehog, if I hadn't your brother for scholard. There's my cousin Yocky Lovell that ud teach you, if one night you'd come along with your brother to Blindgrooms. Why don't you go with him where he goes instead of whining after him? There, you needn't blush. I haven't said nothing unfit for a female's tongue or a young chap's ears."

But Clem, calling her a name unfit for a female's ears or a young chap's tongue, walked furiously away, and left her standing like some dark image in the lane.

§ 16

For long afterwards her shadow seemed to lie on the dusk —on the wet gleam of the road, on the twigs and spines of the thorny hedges, on the clear sky with its spatter of yellow rain. Yet it was not her beauty which defiled, but the cruelty in which it was rooted like a rose tree in dung. She was cruel—he saw now that the stain was not in her loveliness nor in her "furrinness" nor in her coarseness, but in some under-lying and perverse depth of mortal cruelty.

He could not tell how he knew this—her voice had been soft, her words caressing, and her eyes both merry and sad. But she had left the taste of cruelty—the conviction that she had spoken to him only that she might torment him, punish his dislike of her by showing him her power over Bob. Her crude physical power would not have disgusted him if it had had its accustomed growth out of a healthy instinct. He was not the type easily revolted by such things. But she was like the bitter kernel of a ripe, sweet fruit—she was the hard stone in nature's heart. . . .

By the time he reached Bodingmares he was tired and depressed, and nothing happened there to lighten his heart. Robert was not in for supper, and did not come in by the time the family went to bed. It was not a local necessity or custom to lock up house at night, but Robert's absence at this hour never failed to provoke some sour comment from Jim or Mary.

"Whur's your brother to-night—d'you know, Clem?"

"I dunno."

"Maybe he'll have gone to the Oddfellows' smoking concert at the George," said Mrs. Fuller. "Harry Wheelsgate's a-going, and Mus' Willard and Mus' Pepper. I hear as Jerry Pont's to sing."

Clem was grateful to his mother for having suggested such a respectable engagement for Bob, even though he was well aware that no one, not even herself, believed in it. But her step-children were vexed at her.

"Adone-do, can't you, Mother, wud sticking up fur Bob. Leave that to Clem," said Mary; "he'll tell all the lies any-body wants."

"Well, why shudn't he have gone to the George? Reckon half the parish is going."

"When Bob goes to the George, he döan't go to listen to songs and speeches, but to drink spirits and play billiards, or to make bets on horses, or to borrer money off the landlord."

"And we all know where Bob is to-night and every night," said Jim, "he's at Blindgrooms."

They all, even Jim himself, stiffened at this blunt mention

of the family's shame. It was the first time it had been spoken of so openly.

"You shudn't ought to say such things," murmured Mrs. Fuller.

"Why not, since everybody knows 'em? And it's time as summat wur done as well as said."

"We can do naun."

"We can mäake Robert know as how we've had enough of his ways; either he can mend 'em, or he can go off to whur we're clear of the splash of his muck."

"If Bob leaves this plääce," broke in Clem, "reckon he'll go straight to the bad."

"Höald your tongue, Clement," said Mary, "as if this wurn't some of your doing, wud your helping and sticking by him."

"If I wur you, my boy," said Jim, "you'll kip a little furder off that brother of yourn. It's like one bad root in a sack, that'll rot the lot if you give it time."

"I'm sure, Mäaster, I wish as you'd git shut of Bob," continued Mary, "you've no notion how their talk goes up at the Street. It äun't seemly to kip on a chap wot gits us all talked about. If Clem married Poll Ebony there'd be naun to compare . . . and it äun't as if Bob wur much use on the farm, always out from his tea forrards, and caring naun if we goes to the Auctioneer's next week, so long as gipsy Hannah ull let him run after her. Maudie Pont wur a-telling me only yesterday as how she saw him carrying a basket of her beastly clothes-pegs after her down Salehurst Lane. A valiant sight!"

"If you wudn't shut your hearts agäunst him, maybe he'd mend," said Mrs. Fuller. "We all know as he loved the gals from a young boy upwards, and this ull just pass like the rest, if you döan't fix him in it by shutting your hearts."

Mary rejoined with a sniff. She considered that in this matter Robert took after his mother, for there was beginning to be just a little talk in the village about the frequent visits of certain farmers to Bodingmares now Mrs. Fuller was a widow. Jim was silent for the same reason; and Clem, also aware of the situation, took advantage of the lull it brought to slink away to bed.

He wished Robert would come home. Apart from the scandal of his absence and the painful knowledge that he was with Hannah Iden, he badly felt the want of companionship. The big, low room looked desolate—the candle lit so small a corner, and flung so many shadows in comparison with the comfort of its little flame. The dark sky seemed to press against the windows—it was a relief to take the candle to the sill, and shed a faint red glow down into the yard, showing the cobbles and the midden and the big weather-eaten door-posts of the barns.

Usually Clem felt very sleepy at night—hard work and the fresh air made of him between nine and ten a groping automaton, which stumbled out of its clothes and was asleep almost before it had huddled the blankets over its head. But to-night he was restless and unhappy. He did not want to lie still. It must be that woman—drat her! He wished that he had never met her. Why had she upset him so? Was it just because she had shown him how hard and cruel love can be? He had looked upon love as all soft and all sweet, and here were Robert and Hannah showing him the love that strikes and burns and kills. . . . "Lor, she gives me the shudders."

§ 17

However, he must have been sleepier than he thought, for he fell asleep while he was saying his prayers, and woke up to find himself lying, still dressed, in a heap beside the bed. The candle was burning, so he could not have slept long, but he was already cold and stiff with the draught that ran along the boards from under the door. Footsteps sounded in the house, and a lifted latch. Robert must have come back. The door opened at the foot of the stairs leading to the bedroom, but no one came up—instead a voice called, "Clemmy!" It was Polly's voice.

In a moment he was up, and had run down to where she stood in the entrance to the scullery. He was hardly awake, and therefore hardly surprised to see her as she leaned against the doorpost. Her hair and clothes dripped with the rain which he could now hear falling with a steady hiss into the yard.

"Wot is it, duckie?"

"Oh, Clem—I've runned away."

Then he realized how strange it was to have her there in the middle of the night, and his sleepy embrace became suddenly awake.

"Wot's happened—wot've they done?"

"Oh—oh—oh," she burst into tears. Clem put his arm around her and guided her through the scullery into the kitchen, where a few red gleeds still smouldered on the hearthstone. He sat down on a chair and took her on his knee.

"Wot is it, my lovey? Tell me now. Tell Clem about it."

"I can't—it's tar'ble. It's that Betty . . . and Dad . . ." She sobbed into his neck, and he sat there silently, rocking her against him, while bit by bit her tale was gulped and stammered out: "A tar'ble row. . . . Alce, he wur rude . . . and Betty she töald Dad I'd brought him on, and as I wur as thick as I dare wud boys . . . and Dad he knocked me down . . . and said he'd git shut of me—I'd given him trouble enough. . . . And I smacked Betty's fäace—reckon it wur all her doing . . . and Dad he threatened he'd lay me open, so I runned and locked myself in . . . and he comed up, and I jumped out o' the winder . . . fell and cut my leg . . . it wur all her doing . . . she's bin trying to git shut of me since the New Year . . . and now she's a-done it . . . and I'm glad I smacked her fäace."

Clem cherished her sorrowfully.

"Reckon you can never go back after now."

"I döan't want to go back—I wudn't go back if she cäum on her knees from Orznash."

"Not to Ellen's baby?"

"Oh, adone-do," she cried fretfully—"wot's the sense of my thinking of Ellen's baby or any woman's baby? . . . I've myself to think on, and wotsumdever shall I do?"

"Reckon it's fur me to think of that."

Something in his patience calmed her, and she nestled up against him, quiet as her heaving breast would let her be.

"I'm glad I came to you, Clem. I run here straight—I thought as maybe you wurn't all in bed yet; but my leg mäade me go slow."

"I wur disremembering your pore leg, duckie. Let me see it——"

They stooped their heads together into the firelight, and she pulled down her stocking which was caked with blood and dirt. "Reckon some glass fell into the yard when I bruck the winder, and I jumped on it."

The cut was long, but not very deep. Clem fetched water from the scullery, and then went upstairs for his three white handkerchiefs. Polly was shocked at such a use for the linen that made it glorious for Clem to wipe his forehead in Church on Sunday—she would have torn off the hem of her ignoble petticoat. But he was firm, and not too polite to tell her that nothing of hers was clean enough for bandaging.

Polly leaned back in the chair while Clem knelt at her feet, and when he had finished tying his clumsy knots, he crouched down beside her, resting his head against her knee. For some moments they did not speak. Her sobs were quiet now, and he was busy with many preoccupations.

"Is Bob upstairs?" asked Polly, at a sudden, restless movement of his head.

"He äun't."

"Then can't we stop here together till he comes in?"

"You're tired, girl. You shud ought to go to bed. Let me täake you up to mother—she'll mäake room fur you, surelye."

"Clem, wull your mother let me stop here?"

"She mun let you stop."

"But your sister and your brother?"

"Döan't vrother about 'em. We'll hear to-morrow wot they say."

Polly began to cry again.

"I döan't want to hear wot they say—reckon it'll be naun good. They wöan't let me stop. How shud they, seeing as my own fäather wöan't kip me? They döan't höald wud me nor wud you loving me . . . they'll send me off . . . and wotsumdever shall I do?"

"They wöan't send you off." He put his arm round her and gently pulled her off her chair to the floor beside him. They crouched together on the rag mat, and for a moment held each other closely, cheek to cheek, their hearts beating together. Her heavy heart-beats seemed to break up and stifle him—he felt a queer suffocation in his breast.

"Reckon we mun git married, Poll—wudout waiting any longer."

"Oh, Clemmy——"

"I've got near thirty päound put by, and maybe when Jim knows it and finds you're on the loose lik this, he'll give over."

"And if he döan't——"

"We'll have to manage wudout him, surelye."

"How'll we do that?"

"Somehows. Anyway, it's mother's business too, and reckon we'll git aräound mother easier than Jim."

She crept closer to him, and his arms once more came round her, meeting behind her back. He slowly pulled her against him, his eyes fixed upon her tired, soft mouth, drooping open like a child's who has been hurt and craves for tenderness. Then suddenly he took fire, and his own mouth closed upon it. He held her against him with a strength that seemed to hurt them both. All his body felt bruised as he held her to it. At last she cried, "Döan't, Clemmy, döan't!" But he only held her more tightly. She struggled, but he did not care—her resistance gave him a queer delight. . . . He was a man, loving her like a man at last. "Don't be afraid of love. . . . I could teach you to love, little hedgehog. . . . I loves Romanly."

There she stood, with all her wicked draggled feathers, like an image in the lane . . . the hard stone in love's heart.

He suddenly released Polly, and she seemed miles away. He crouched on his heels before her on the rag mat, his cheeks burning with shame.

"Wot's the matter, Clemmy?"

"Forgive me."

"Wot fur?"

"Fur being rough."

"That's naun, my dear."

"I've loved you cruel instead of kind."

"You dudn't love me cruel. Döan't talk so sträange."

"I dud—I loved you just lik *she* loves Bob."

"I dunno wot you mean."

She began to cry again, and he took her back into his arms. This time her warmth and weight as she lay heavily like a child in the crook of his elbow, her helplessness and surrender, roused quite a different response in him. Her abandonment both physical and moral to his power and mercy stirred in him a depth of compassion and protective tenderness.

"Döan't cry, Poll," he soothed, "döan't cry, my duckie. It'll soon be over now—all our waiting and trouble."

He stood up and pulled her to her feet.

"Whur are you täaking me?"

"To mother. She'll let you sleep along of her till it's morning. . . . And I'll tell her as I'm marrying you this day month."

§ 18

By the evening of the next day the family had more or less come to the conclusion that Clem was "growed up." Jim and Mary had woken that morning to the news that Polly Ebony was in the house, having run away from Orznash, and had been received by Mrs. Fuller, who now supported Clem in his insane resolve to marry her without delay.

Elizabeth had been won over by the persuasions of Clem and Polly, sitting on her bed in the darkness for nearly an hour—by the plight of poor little Polly, ragged and soiled and homeless—by the love of these children which answered the dayspring that was beginning to visit her own heart. Five months of widowhood had brought a strange flowering to Elizabeth. Once more she had learned to sit and watch the sunset like a girl, to breathe in the first scent of spring on the February wind. Hopes that had lain asleep and half stifled for twenty-three years now began to stir and whisper, and these the love of Clem and Polly now called out of their graves.

"Reckon it's true," said the mother, "as they're naun but two children. But children can love, surelye, and these two have loved faithful sinst they got acquainted three year agone. Let Clem have the keeping of Polly, and you'll see as he wöan't be a liddle boy no longer."

"Clem's more of a boy than most lads of his age," said Jim.

"I äun't," said Clem, "or I wudn't be courting."

"And wot are you going to kip your wife on?"

"I'll wark, säum as I do now, and I've säaved more'n thirty päound fur the furnishing."

This was news to the elder brother, and did not fail to impress him.

"Wot! You've säaved it out of your wäages?"

"Surelye."

"Even when poor fäather wur paying you five bob a week?"

"I säaved half a crownd then."

"And he's loanst me four päound since October," broke in Robert, "or he'd have säaved more."

"I döan't doubt it," said Jim sarcastically. But Clem threw a grateful look at his brother. Robert's championship might do more harm than good, still it was comforting to feel that Bob was on his side.

"Thirty päound wöan't furnish a house nowadays," said Mary.

"It'll furnish all they want," insisted Mrs. Fuller; "they döan't expect to settle in Buckenham Pallis."

"You can't live on furniture," said the practical James, "and even if you stop on as hand at Bodingmares, thirteen shillun a week wöan't give the two of you bread to eat, and I can't run to more."

"You wur talking last week of gitting a gal fur the chicken," said Clement boldly; "why döan't you set Polly to look after the chicken? You'll be bäound to git somebody, wud all them new Wyandottes. Polly knows fowls, and did valiant wud 'em at Orznash."

"I know calves too," said Polly, wishing her terror of Clem's relations would let her voice sound above a whisper.

"It'll have to be pigs and dairy as well, fur the gal I git," said James.

"Then you'll be bäound to give her seven shillun a week and her board, and Polly ull do it wudout board. I'll answer to kip the two of us on twenty shillun a week and a house."

"And whur's the house? I've got but the one they call Pookwell, and the Bantony man's in that."

"You can git shut of him. He pays but two shillun a week, and you'll be säaving my board. Reckon I eat more'n two shillun a week."

"Reckon you do," said Mary, "reckon you eat twelve. You'll have to be unaccountable less greedy if you set to kip yourself and a wife on twenty."

"Why not Clem and Polly stop on here?" said Mrs. Fuller, "they cud have the room where Clem and Bob is now, and Bob cud go in wud Jim."

"You talk as if it wur all settled," said Jim, "but it äun't. It äun't sensible as Clem shud marry at his age. He's but a boy; I'm mäaster here, and he can't git married wudout I let him."

However, though no further advance was made that day, fresh ground was gained on the next and the next. Jim was kind-hearted in the main, and he felt he could not turn out Polly to fend for herself, nor could he force her to go back to a home where she would be ill-used, and from which she might again be driven. Also Jim was fond of his young brother Clem, whose hard work and docile nature had touched his heart through their service to the farm. Clem was just that steady, gentle sort of chap who would work none the worse because he was married, nor assert his independence and give himself airs. Of course he was over-young to settle down, but he was quiet enough to be trusted, and he certainly was in love with Polly. The mating with Orznash was a blow to the self-esteem of Bodingmares. But had not Robert long ago scotched that self-esteem, so that it could no longer be any real stiffening? Robert had more to do with the settlement of Clem's difficulties than might have been thought. Certainly his championship was no use. But the fact that Bodingmares already shared in a measure the guilt of Orznash—that men shot out their lips and shook their heads as much at the one as at the other—weighed with Jim in his balancings and ponderings of considerations.

"Reckon as it's only fair to the boy as he shud have his way," he said to Mary. "Bob's gone his a dunnamany year, and not half such a good 'un. The gal's no class, but she's got decent yeoman blood in her, and it äun't her doing as her folks have gone wrong. She's a stout liddle warker—helps us präaper in the house—and quiet as a mouse and respectful-spoken. If she'd täake on the chicken fur seven bob a week, and Clem täake his thirteen wud Pookwell instead of board, then I guess we'll säave money on the business."

"But it wöan't help us set ourselves up wud them wot spik agäunst Bob if we go and have low truck on Clem's side too. Two rotten eggs döan't mäake one fresh 'un, and I can't see how we're to mend Bob's bad wud Clem's wuss."

"Clem's äun't wuss. You shudn't ought to say that."

"But he's marrying her—at least Bob hasn't had the wickedness to do that."

"Bob's is different. It ud be shäame if he married her. But Clem's is a decent, quiet gal, for all she comes from a bad höame and äun't bin taught clean ways. And Clem's a decent, quiet young chap, and has warked hard and säaved money. Reckon we shud ought to let him have his way."

"He's naun but a child."

"I've töald you he's on the quiet side, and that döan't count in years. He's säaved money, too, and it täakes a man to do that."

§ 19

With Jim converted to his hopes, Clem had nothing more to fear. He did not, however, exactly fulfil his promise to Polly, for the marriage did not take place till the beginning of June. By that time Clem was well past his eighteenth birthday, and Polly had learned some household wisdom as the pupil of Mary and Mrs. Fuller. She did her best to show her gratitude for the kindness of these people, whose ordered ways perplexed her, and to prove her fitness to be Clem's wife and to keep the little house of Pookwell for him. She submitted to Mary when she told her that only the "lowest sort" put china and glass on the same tray—she learned the iniquity of setting the pudding on a table which had not been cleared of meat and vegetables, of making a bed "all of a lump," instead of drawing on and smoothing each sheet and blanket separately, of dusting a room without opening the window, of laying a fire without first drying the wood in the oven. She was taught to cook, too, and in three months could tackle the dozen of dishes which make up a yeoman's fare. From Mrs. Fuller she learned a sweeter knowledge—which pudding Clem liked best, how much milk and sugar to put in his tea, how to make him cocoa for a snack, when he ran in to her during the morning, how to darn his socks and shirts, and to polish his boots for great occasions.

Polly's family left her more or less alone. Jim and Clem had together interviewed Tom Ebony a few days after her arrival at Bodingmares. But Tom, pipe in mouth, had little to say about his daughter. Let 'em keep her if they wanted her—he was shut of her. She'd given him trouble enough. Did young Fuller want to marry her?—he wished him joy. She'd treated his own wife shameful, and she wanted a lot of looking after. Yes, he gave his consent—after a fair warning. He was glad to see her so well settled.

Jim was pleased that Ebony did not care to play his part in the match. It made things better for Bodingmares if it was known that no social link with Orznash had been forged by Clem and Polly. The attitude he found best to assume was one of charity—charity to the girl in her homeless state, charity to the love of the young people. In time he came to see himself as a magnanimous man—receiving the poor orphan into his house, bringing her up with his own family, and finally bestowing her in respectable marriage on his younger brother, whose worldly circumstances he had advanced so as to enable him to meet the occasion.

Some of the village saw the affair in the same light as Jim, and he was praised for a decent chap. Others, however, in-

sisted on regarding him as the victim of pressure. Mrs. Fuller
had approved, and she was joint guardian with him of young
Clement; of course, he couldn't risk losing his brother's services on the farm—if Clem had threatened to go away, Mus'
Fuller couldn't very well help himself . . . he'd never get
such another hand for what he paid the lad.

There was a great throng of people at the wedding, for
everyone, whether they had come to show their approval of
Jim Fuller's conduct or to enjoy the spectacle of his discom-
fiture, felt curious to see the young bride and bridegroom, little
more than children. Polly was not well known in High Tilt,
which she haunted only occasionally; Clem was known to
everyone and also, it was now discovered, generally liked. True,
he was queer in some of his ways, and a bit common, and
stood by that Bob of his till it made you think he couldn't
be quite straight himself, but everyone declared him a quiet,
obliging, stout-hearted little chap whom folk couldn't but wish
well.

The ceremony took place in High Tilt church, which, un-
dismayed by any thoughts of "pore Fäather," Jim and Mary
both decided to be more aristocratic and suitable for a yeoman's wedding than the Throws chapel. There had been great
anxiety among the more responsible Fullers as to who was to
give the bride away. Tom Ebony might have done it, but Jim
felt that Polly was best as an orphan, rescued from ignoble
surroundings by Jim Fuller of Bodingmares. Besides, Tom
had taken his Betty and her child for a fortnight to Brighton,
and would not be available on the only date that fitted nicely
between the hay-making and the sheep-shearing. So Polly,
having no other kinsman, was given away by Dunk of Shoyswell, who considered a certain relationship established by the
fact that he had bought roots from Orznash for a dunnamany
years, and had always said as Ebony's roots wur good roots
no matter wot other folkses might say of his goings-on. The
best man was, unfortunately, Robert—Clem had insisted on
having him, with an emphasis of ingratitude which disgusted
Jim. Robert with his sensual face and roving blue eye, with
his thick oiled quiff and little clipped moustache, with his

swagger and his check breeches, would spoil the look of the wedding—he would bring the shame of Bodingmares into the foreground from which Jim had so successfully banished the shame of Orznash.

Robert was now once more difficult and moody. That burst of animal spirits and animal strength had died down in the spring. He seemed to have lost confidence in himself. Clem wondered how Hannah was behaving, but Bob seemed to be with her as much as usual. Was it possible that he was sorry for his brother's approaching marriage, for the breaking up of that comradeship which of late months he had hardly seemed to value. It did not seem so, for Robert's attitude towards Clem's luck was a delightful one of sympathy and enthusiasm—and he had bought him a beautiful silver-plated cruet, quite the most handsome present the young couple had received.

When, on the wedding day, after his usual morning's work, Clem went upstairs to clean himself and dress for the ceremony, he found Robert in the bedroom, already dressed in his wedding garments, but in a scarcely bridal attitude, for he sat bolt upright on a chair beside his bed with a large Bible on his knees.

"Hallo! Wot's happened?" said Clem, tearing himself out of his corduroys.

"Summat tar'ble."

"Wot's that?"

"I've had a warning."

"Out of the Bible? Wot are you a-doing wud it, Bob? You're a middling queer chap."

"I saw it a-lying there—I found it when I wur a-getting out my shirts, and I says to myself, 'Let's see wot it's got to say.' So I opened it, as they do, and it said, 'It's a tar'ble thing to fall into the hands of the living God."

"Well, wot of it? You can't go reading the Bible lik that."

"That's the präaper way to read it—then it tells you things."

"I never heard of a more outlandish, heathen notion. Reckon it's wot folkses dud a dunnamany years agone, when nobody had any know or sense."

"Döan't you go telling me as I äun't got no sense."

"I never said it. I only say as it äun't a sensible thing to do."

"You think you know a lot about religion just because you're going to be married in the Parish church. The church can't do naun fur you, but the Bible can—the Bible's a Good Book. Listen here, I opened it agäun, and it said, 'They shall cry, but I shall not hear.' "

"But, Bob——"

"Höald your tongue. You döan't understand naun about religion if you döan't see the Finger of God plain here. I tell you I döan't care naun fur your parish church—my religion's the Bible, säum as my fäather's wur."

"But, Bob, I dudn't know as you had any religion."

"Thur you go, as I said, mocking and disbelieving my religion because it äun't the säum as yourn."

Clem swallowed the retort on his lips. The bridegroom and best man must not quarrel on a matter of theology just before the wedding; besides, poor Bob looked so abject and scared. Clem took the Bible into his hands and opened it at random:

"Thur, it says, 'Three bowls made like unto almonds, with a knop and a flower in one branch'—wot d'you mäake of that?—it's naun."

"It wöan't answer you, because you disbelieve, but it'll answer me. Give it me here—no, kip it—put it away—I mun't scare myself wuss."

When the two young men were ready they went down to the four-wheeled cab which was waiting to take the bridegroom's party to church. Jim had rigidly followed the local etiquette, even to the point of sending Polly for the night to Shoyswell, so that she should be brought to the ceremony by her "father." Jim and Mrs. Fuller sat facing the horse, and Mary with her back to it. Bob climbed in beside her, and Clem was going to take his place on the box when Jim suddenly realized that it would be more seemly for the bridegroom to ride inside. So Bob had to go up beside the coachman, much to his own annoyance and Clem's vexation.

The bride had already been waiting at the church a quarter
of an hour, all the clocks at Shoyswell being fast. Clem at
first hardly recognized her in her dress of bright saxe blue
with cream lace trimmings. She had done up her hair, too,
which gave her an odd, grown-up appearance. It was only
when she turned her eyes to him with a look that had grown
in them of late—a queer look of appeal and submission, lit
with a flame—that he seemed to recognize his own little Polly,
the black lamb of Orznash, now to be taken upon his shoulders.
She put her hand into his arm as they walked up the aisle,
the whole party together, and he pressed it tenderly against
him in its tight kid glove.

He had forgotten to put on his own gloves, and the first
part of the ceremony was almost obliterated by his earnest
attempts to do so. He decided to be content with one—after
all, it was almost impossible to hold a small object like a
ring with gloves on. Both he and Polly had studied the marriage service very carefully, so that neither of them made any
mistakes, though every now and then Polly threatened to
become speechless. Mus' Brackpool, the Rector, galloped them
through their vows, and soon they were holding the big splayed
ends of his stole while he irrevocably gave them to each other.

It was all very quiet and very quick. Clem liked the priest's
soft gabbling voice—so unlike the accustomed voice of prayer
at High Tilt chapel—but the rest of the family were annoyed
because they could not find their places "wud him muttering
lik that," and Robert missed the bit about Abraham, to which
he had been especially looking forward. Altogether they were
rather disappointed in the resources of the parish church, for
after the ceremony the organist lost his place in Mendelssohn's
Wedding March, and Clem led his bride down the aisle in a
naked silence.

The ceremony had been so quick that the bridegroom's
coachman had not yet come back from his refreshment at the
Royal George, and Clem and Polly had to wait for two or
three minutes in the scent of a warm, spattering June shower
while he was fetched back to his duties. The congregation
crowded out and round them, and those who had waited out-

side in the churchyard assaulted them with confetti. A thousand coloured disks fluttered in and out of the shining rain, and spangled the blue of Polly's dress and the black wool of Clem's hair. They were too shy, too bewildered to defend themselves, but dipped their heads together as they stood hand in hand, and giggled as the fluttering rainbow blinded them.

"Here's luck to you, little brother!" and Hannah Iden suddenly pushed her way to the front with her cousin Darius Ripley, and threw a handful of rice in his face.

The rice was different from the confetti—it hurt and stung. Clem ducked away from her, and Hannah laughed.

"I've frightened the pretty bridegroom—but then I knew he was easily frightened. I've frightened him before."

For a moment she stood in front of him, swaying against Darius, whose arm was round her waist. Then to his horror Clem realized that Bob was coming forward to speak to her, pushing his way through Ponts and Dunks and Peppers and Shovels. . . . Bob did not care for anyone, he would speak to her before them all.

But she did not wait for him. She laughed again, flinging back her head against Darius's shoulder, and then she turned and ran off, still laughing, with the neat little gipsy man beside her.

For a dreadful moment Clem thought that Robert would go after them, but the crowd swaying round and knotting to condemn her, thronged him back into the porch; and the next moment the coachman arrived, running desperately, and showing himself a coachman only to the waist, below which he was a labourer in corduroys and clay-thickened boots.

The Fullers and Dunks piled into the first cab, leaving as many as possible to follow in the other. Polly sat on Clem's knee, very quiet and scared, and sticky in her thick dress and the hot, tight clasp of her bridegroom's arm.

§ 20

A large company sat down to the wedding breakfast at Bodingmares. It was laid in the dining-room, which was not

used above once or twice a year, except as a waiting-room
for those more genteel visitors who sometimes fetched their
own eggs and butter from the farm. The walls were green—
unfortunately, quite a different green from the serge curtains
looped across the window—and adorned with cases of stuffed
birds. There was also a coloured picture of Queen Victoria,
an engraving of Frith's railway station, and one or two Ger-
man prints of fat children and angels. The window was
crammed with plants, mostly ferns and cactus, which tempered
still further the greenish light that filtered between the curtains. A dining-room was a distinction owned by few of the
neighbouring farms, and gave an almost manorial dignity to
Bodingmares.

The table nearly filled the room, and the guests had to
squeeze carefully round it to their places. In the middle was
the wedding-cake, masterpiece of a Bulverhythe confectioner,
who had also supplied tarts and jellies and meatpies and wine.
But in spite of the two decanters full of a pale shade of
antipodal burgundy, the teapot still dominated, towering over
concentric rings of teacups. Local trade, also, had not been
entirely shoved out by the Bulverhythe interloper, for plates
of tinned salmon and tinned lobster from the High Tilt gro-
cery stores quenched even the flaming colours of the jellies
and tarts.

It was nearly five minutes before everyone was seated. At
one end of the table sat Jim Fuller, the Mäaster, with his
mother at one elbow and his sister at the other. At the opposite end the little bride and bridegroom squeezed shyly together and eyed the display. Down the sides piled farmers and
their families—Pont of Udiam, Willard of Boarsney, Dunk of
Shoyswell, Cox of Haiselman's, Pix of Little London, and
Pepper of Weights—the latter a widower, and as close as he
could to Elizabeth Fuller, with her soft throat and face, and
her eyes that were wide and young under her fading hair.
There were also one or two friends from Bulverhythe, linked
with the family's town days. Among them was the confectioner who had supplied the meal, and his daughter Mabel.
They contrasted rather sharply with their neighbours—Arthur

Powlard in his town suit and soft collar among all the black coats and chokers, Mabel in her smart coat and skirt, and little hat on one side, among all the silk blouses and lockets and big straw hats trimmed with daisies.

She was a pretty girl, and would have liked to flirt with Robert, who sat beside her. But the best man was in a state of restless gloom, and had few words to bestow apart from the thoughts that followed Hannah Iden as she ran off laughing with Darius Ripley's arm round her waist. The picture of her rose between Robert and the invitation of Mabel's lips, between him and the glories of the table, between him and the younger brother whose happiness should have been his to-day. Ripley's bold, careless hug which would have meant absolutely nothing with any High Tilt or Salehurst girl at a wedding, was full of suggestion and omen in the case of Hannah, whom no man touched in friendliness or jest. "She wudn't have let him do it, if she wurn't meaning aught. She's on wud that liddle gipsy mäaster—though she swore to me——"

Mabel came to the conclusion that the big, handsome Fuller was just a bumpkin.

So the shadow of Hannah Iden lay over Clem's wedding feast. The general atmosphere of labour and silence that affected the guests was not due entirely to the shyness of the married pair, who would scarcely open their mouths except to eat their wedding cake. The gloom seemed rather to radiate from Robert, where he sat with his hands ungraciously in his pockets, staring at the food on his plate which had never been suffered to lie there so long. Clem watched him anxiously—he guessed his trouble, he knew that he was jealous. Of course, Hannah might have been free with Ripley just to whip up Bob's emotions and spur him to a more sacrificial wooing . . . but it was just as likely that she had got tired of him, and turned to a man of her own people . . . she had certainly looked very spitefully at Clem . . . his face still seemed to tingle with the handful of stinging rice she had flung in it.

The Australian burgundy was potent enough at last to put a little life into Robert. He hated the rough, sour taste of it on his tongue, but it had the powers of an unaccustomed drink, and in time the vision of Hannah blurred a little. When he found this out he drank more, and was able to return thanks quite genially for the bridegroom's mother when her health was proposed. Dunk of Shoyswell spoke for the bride, and Clem was left in the coils and tangles of his own speech, still further and most horribly confused by half a glass of wine. However, everybody wished him well, and received his remarks with a noisy good will in which they were most of them lost. He sat down, feeling very scared, but comforted by the sight of Bob laughing loudly at him.

The honeymoon being limited to thirty-six hours it was imperative not to lose any of it, and as soon as the healths had been drunk, Clem asked Jim if he and Polly might go at once to Pookwell. There was no reason why they should not—the days were past when weddings worked up through hours of eating and drinking to the climax of a dance. Most of the guests were beginning to feel sleepy after their wine, the table was once more dropping into silence, and Clem was afraid that if he waited he would see the shadow of Hannah Iden fall over it again.

So he and Polly climbed, this time mercifully alone, into the old cab with its stuffy smells of stable and leather, and leaving the wedding party obscured by a languidly eddying cloud of confetti, drove solemnly down the drive and along the thirty or forty yards of road between the drive gate and Pookwell.

But though the cottage was so near, it seemed very far off when they were left together on the doorstep, and the cab was grinding and clopping its way back to the inn. A clump of yew, blotted against the side wall, hid Bodingmares three fields away, and at the back a ring of alder pierced with two aspiring darts of Lombardy poplars shut out all the familiar tillage. Only in front the little house lay open to the south-ward sun, which had warmed its plaster walls to the brownish-yellow of a well stood cheese. Across the hedge and the lane fields of tall, unripe corn sloped to the marshes. The river Dudwell crept shining at the foot of the meadow hills of Sock-

nersh, where the black oasts stood like steeples, and the pollard
willows swam in the mirror of stormy light. The same light
wavered angrily on to Clem's face as he lifted it from his
struggles with the door key. Then, as he flung the door open,
it poured over him into the house, illuminating the steep ridiculous little staircase that shot up almost from the doorstep to
the floor above.

Polly followed him in with a queer stiffness, and they went
into the kitchen which seemed very tidy and bare. The light,
now definitely kindled into sunshine, poured over the scrubbed,
deal surface of the table.

"That'll mean more rain," said Polly.

They faced each other awkwardly across the strange table,
in the strange, bare room, with the unfamiliar pots and pans
hanging round it, and all the new china on the dresser. They
looked strange, too—Clem in his black coat and high, stiff
collar, and Polly with her tight blue dress and coiled up hair.

"I dudn't marry you fur you to talk to me about the
weather," said Clem slowly at last.

Then suddenly they both laughed, and he ran round the
table and took her in his arms.

"Oh, Clem, it's all bin so sträange," moaned Polly.

"But it äun't sträange now."

"No, but it's bin tar'ble . . . all the company . . . and you
lik a sträange young gentleman——"

"Is this how you go on wud sträange young gentlemen?"

"No, Clemmy, not now—but, oh, leave them pins in my
hair."

"I döan't lik your hair all piled up—it looks furrin."

"Now I'm married I mun't have it hanging down."

"You can do it to-morrow, when folkses are about. But
now thur's only you and me."

Polly let him caress her, submitting to, rather than accepting,
his love. She was not so used to happiness as he, and still felt a
little scared in her new surroundings. The strange, bare
kitchen, and the new ardour that was creeping into her boy's
voice and touch both made her ill at ease. But as the evening
passed her sense of the abiding sameness in him grew and cast

out fear—he was her dear Clemmy, even in that strange house and transmuted by passion. His sweetness and gentleness were fundamental—a deep gratitude stirred in her heart, making her take his dark, woolly head in her hands and kiss it with the slow, reverent kisses of a thankful child, and then suddenly find herself the mother with that head upon her breast.

§ 21

Three fields away at Bodingmares Robert watched the feast expire. Traps and gigs lurched off with yeomen, stragglers gossiped round the door, in the dining-room the guttered meal grew hard and stale. The kitchen seemed full of dirty plates and the whisking skirts of Mary and the hired girl. Mary wished to goodness the men would go, instead of hanging round mother—then she could begin to think of getting straight. It was hardly decent to see them like that, fooling round an eight months' widow. It was a pity mother didn't see it herself. . . .

So she hurried meaningly to and fro between the kitchen and the porch, where Mrs. Fuller stood smiling and flushing as she spoke to Pepper and Cox. Pepper had given her his wedding buttonhole, and both men were making use of the licence that weddings allowed. Mary was shocked, and Robert himself felt a little disgusted. His mother ought to remember that she was the mother of grown up sons. . . . Here she was actually smiling on Wheelsgate the postman when he came up with the letters. "Good evenun, Mus' Wheelsgate. I'm unaccountable sorry you cudn't be at the wedding, but I'll see if thur's a bit of cäake left."

This was too much. "It's gitting cöald fur you, Mother," said Robert, "you mun't be out in the swale lik this at your age."

"Lor, child! I haven't come to an age when a June swale ull git my böans. How you talk! Howsumdever, I mun go in and fetch Mus' Wheelsgate his cäake."

"It's all gone," shouted Mary from the passage.

"That's queer. I thought I saw a good lump on the täable.

Howsumdever, Clem and Polly may have took it wud 'em, surelye. I'm sorry, Mus' Wheelsgate, but if Clem's got it you shall have a bit läater, fur we're meaning to send räound bits to friends—we've got dentical liddle boxes wud lace on them from Mus' Powlard. You shud ought to see them."

For one of the few times in their lives Mary and Robert exchanged a look of sympathy. Mother was incorrigible—she needed poor fäather to look after her. Jim, who alone had authority, was busy in the yard. All they could do was to hang uneasily and embarrassingly round her and her friends till at last the men went off and Mrs. Fuller with a placid smile turned back into the house.

"There's naun lik a wedding fur pleasure," she remarked.

"Maybe," said Mary, "but it's a pity when it comes too soon after a funeral."

Relieved of his charge, Robert set off about his own affairs. He knew that he ought to go and help Jim with the milking, but he felt that he could not settle down to work. So it was the women who had to change quickly into their oldest gowns and take their places on the milking stools, while Robert, still in his wedding finery, walked off to Blindgrooms.

It was rather early to be sure of finding Hannah, but her mother would be there, and Robert felt that he would not be wasting his time if he could get himself into the old woman's good graces, for to her mother's dislike of his "gorgeousness" or Gentilehood he attributed Hannah's occasional withdrawals. But, contrariwise, it was the daughter and not the mother that he found in the big dark kitchen of Blindgrooms. It was an enormous room, probably two knocked into one at some forgotten date, and very damp, for the cottage was built below the level of the road—one went down to it by a moss-grown pathway slanting through a garden of thistles and derelict vegetables. Hannah was busy with a large bundle which she was tying up in the corner.

"So you've come, child," she said without looking round. "You didn't think a blasted wedding ud kip me away."

"Weddings are fine things. Did you dance?"

"Not I! We döan't dance at weddings."

"When my cousin Yocky Lovell was married we danced till the stars went out; and we dances at funerals too."

"Wot are you a-doing wud that sack?"

"I'm packing for a journey."

"Where are you going?" Almost a falsetto note of anguish came into his voice. Hannah answered quietly:

"I'm going bikkening into the hop country."

"Döan't go answering me in that outlandish speech. Tell me wot you mean."

"The hop country is Kent, as you might have known for yourself, and bikkening in our outlandish speech is selling clothes-pegs to Gentiles."

"Nannie—döan't go."

He had come swiftly up behind her and put his arms round her as she knelt fastening the mouth of her sack. She pushed him away.

"Don't come troubling me now."

"But you mun tell me—you mun answer me—why are you going away lik this?"

"Haven't I been away before?"

"Yes, you have, and be hemmed to you. But this is all of a suddint."

"It ain't. I made up my mind last week."

"You never töald me naun."

"Why should I tell you? You never asked."

"Döan't you belong to me?"

"I belongs to no one."

"Nannie, you're cruel—I can't määke you out. You let me love you and I'm full of heaven, but in between whiles you're no more'n a lady acquaintance. You'd think to hear and see you now as we'd never bin thick in our lives."

"I'm not one of your Gentile rawnees who's love and kisses all day and half the night. If you want that sort of thing you shouldn't have taken up with me. I love when I feels like it, and I bet I give you more to remember than any silly fat girl in these parts; but when I doesn't feel like it then I doesn't love, and I expects you to behave yourself."

"How long ull you be away?"

"Maybe a couple of weeks."

"Who'll you be travelling with?"

"I shall travel alone."

"Darius Ripley wön't go wud you?"

"Are you jealous, gorgeous Bob?"

"Tell me—tell me straight, is he going wud you?"

"He is not—as I'd have thought you'd know; I travels alone. But Darius has his cart, and sells horses to Gentiles, and the roads is free to all poor people."

"Nannie, Nannie, dön't go hitting at me like that. I can't abear it. Tell me—promise me as you wön't täake up wud Darius."

He could keep his craving hands off her no longer. They came down on her shoulders, and, bending her back, he sorrowfully and passionately kissed her mouth. She twisted herself out of his grasp and scrambled to her feet.

"Leave me alone, will you? I won't have your hands on me. You ought to learn how to treat females."

"You let Darius put his arm aräound you at the wedding."

"Darius is my kinsman."

"And I'm your lover—which is more than kin."

"It ain't. A kinsman's my kinsman always; a lover's my lover only when I choose. Oh, I know you think you've bought me like a mare, to keep in your stable and have out when you please. That's the way you treat your own females, but it isn't the way to treat me, my gorgeous one, though you're mortal slow at learning it."

"Will you swear to me as you only let Darius hug you 'cos he was kin?"

Hannah gazed at him pityingly.

"What a child you are! I likes you better when you're a man."

"Then give me a chance of being a man."

"I'm doing my poor person's best to learn you to be one."

"By driving me mad."

"By teaching you manners."

"Reckon my manners are as good as most men's."

"Your manners are Gentile manners, child, and strike a bit

rude to a Roman female. If you and me is to get on together you'll have to learn how to treat me in a polite fashion."

"Nannie—I'll do wotsumdever you like, so long as you let me love you. . . ."

He could not argue with her; he could not even bargain with her. He must, as he realized for the hundredth time, take her on her own terms, since she would come to him on no other.

Her eyes softened. His hands were stretched out towards her humbly, but the impression he gave was of vigour and strength. As he stood there opposite her, he had the bulk and beauty of a young god—or, in her own comparison, a Gentile prize-fighter, a cooroomengro.

He was bigger and finer than any of her own men, and as she had never had anything so splendid, so adoring and faithful, she could afford to forget that she had never had anything so stupid, so clownish and jealous. She moved towards him and smiled. She made no gesture, gave no invitation, but he knew that now at last he might touch her unrebuked. In a moment his jealousy was forgotten, his apprehension was gone. With a husky laugh, he seized her and clasped her to him, and her hardness seemed to melt into his passion as a rock melts into a wave.

§ 22

That summer was good to Bodingmares. Jim was justified in all his ventures. Not that these had ever approached recklessness, but at least he had broken out of the rut of his father's ways; he had not ploughed grass, but he had increased his hay acreage, and he had been fairly bold with catch-crops. The latter had especially flourished, and Jim had trifolium and Italian rye beyond his needs, so that he found himself selling to other farms.

Apart from the results of enterprise, he had been lucky in those ways which are beyond a farmer's contriving. Sun in the right month had prospered his hay; his corn, though a bit stalky, bore well in the ear, and his hops were free of the blight which had measled them for two years running. Encouraged on every side, he went forward to bigger adventures. He engaged a new hand—the first outside help that Bodingmares had had since James Fuller's lads were old enough to work. This man came with an excellent character from Hazel Street over in Kent, where he had worked as all-round labourer with a special knowledge of horses. Pookwell being occupied by Clem, he had to lodge at High Tilt, and tramp a mile and a half to and fro every day, since Robert refused to have him in his room; but such accommodation was usual in a district of small landlords and no building enterprise.

The plan of having Clem and Polly at Pookwell had worked most admirably. Clem was anxious to prove its efficiency by hard work and sacrifice, and Polly, eager to please both Clem and Clem's family, "did valiant wud the chicken," and certainly saved Jim several shillings a week. It was rather a strenuous life, and did not give the young couple much of each other's company; but neither of them had expected anything different, and their moments together between sunset and sunrise were doubly precious in view of the day's separation—and even the day had its broken comradeship, since Clem always ran home to Pookwell for his meals.

Jim was highly pleased with Clem and Polly, though he did not like all their ways—Clem seemed too readily, he thought, to adapt himself to a common labourer's existence after the yeoman glory of Bodingmares. But undoubtedly they were saving him money, and thus helping the farm in spite of their common ideas, and he showed his appreciation by giving them a half-holiday whenever there was no work for them to do.

Their loyalty and docility were enhanced by the opposing vices in Robert. Robert was not part of the season's progress, and had had little share in bringing it about. For the early weeks of the summer he had worked fairly well, though he was always out in the evening when the widening days did not necessarily bring work to an end at supper time. But after Clement's wedding he had seemed to go "all to pieces." He

absented himself from the morning's or afternoon's work without excuse or apology. His temper became vile, and he was
occasionally drunk. Everyone put this down to some hitch
in his friendship with Hannah Iden. Indeed, gossip of rupture
occasionally came up from the village, and put hope into
Jim's heart. But if any rupture did actually take place—
and there was reason to think that something of the kind
had really happened at least once—it was patched up again,
and Robert was received back into slavery.

The affair was now a common scandal, and Jim occasionally
found backs turned on him in the market-place or the public-
house. The general attitude, however, was one of commisera-
tion, which for some reason he found easier to bear. In the
decent saloon bar of the Royal George, or of the Eight Bells
at Salehurst, where yeomen drank a solemn glass in dignified
fellowship, Jim would expand on the subject of his brother's
villainy, his black ingratitude, his wickedness towards the
dead. . . . "If his pore fäather cud see him now. . . ."

The saloon bar voted Mus' Fuller a decent chap for keeping Robert at Bodingmares—he might easily get shut of him.
But Clem's wedding had given Jim a taste for playing providence to his brothers, and he liked to think that his long
suffering was all that stood between Robert and utter down-
fall.

"I've to remember my pore fäather," he said to Bream of
Little Moat, after an auction at Copt Hall; "fur his säake I
mun stick to the chap. Besides, wot ud he do if I got shut of
him? He'd go and täake up wud them 'Gyptians—I know it.
Fur tuppence he'd go on the road wud that baggage and her
cart. . . . Oh, I tell you, mäaster, as sometimes I've tar'ble
presentations, and see pore Robert selling baskets and clothes-
pegs on the north trade, wud all his self-respeck a-gone and
busted."

His brother was not as grateful as he might have been for
this forbearance. It was gammon to make out that he—
Robert—didn't do his work präaper. He hadn't missed a
day since the shearing, and the only reason Jim wasn't satisfied was that he wanted black niggers who'd work all day for

nothing, instead of honest white working men who saved their sweat with their brains.

Robert's finances were now in a horrible state. He was still working off old debts and at the same time involving himself in new ones. He had owed money to the landlord of the Woolpack, and had paid him off only to entangle himself with the landlord of the White Hart up at Burwash. Hannah was not his only source of extravagance—he was a lavish treater of stray acquaintance, and one or two friendships, otherwise in danger through the quarrelsomeness of his disposition, were maintained on a basis of propitiatory and reconciliatory drinks. He also played billiards and the noble game of darts. He liked to look smart and well dressed, to put his money on a winner, to read the evening and sporting papers, and lose no opportunity of proving himself a Dog. Besides, he was continually having to placate creditors with sums on account, or even, in the case of Porter of the White Hart, to pay interest—a hundred and fifty per cent. of Gentile usury. Beyond all this there was Hannah, whom he liked to take to the fair and to the pictures, for whom he loved to buy presents— shining and glowing pieces of jewellery or stuff, which he was generally overcharged for by shopkeepers aware of his eagerness and ignorance. He bought her a diamond ring on the instalment system, insisting that the diamonds must be real for a price of eight pounds, though she declared that they were not and that she knew the price of diamonds as a lord had once offered her some.

Unfortunately, Robert had now very few ways of adding to his wages. Clem was no longer available for purposes of borrowing, and he lost as much as he won over public-house games. True, he could have gone to the races with the gipsies as often as he liked, and their tips were generally good. But he had never been used to gambling in more than half-crowns, and the pounds he lost frightened him more than he was gratified by the pounds he won. Also he was not now on the best of terms with the Ripleys and their crew. He suspected them of jealousy and treachery. He would not take their tips, feeling that they might deliberately mislead him.

Darius Ripley was in love with Hannah; he was sure of it. He would like to clear Robert out of the way. And the dreadful part of it all was that he knew that Hannah was being turned against him by the very scandal that his love for her created. She had taken him on because she was proud to be loved by a yeoman, one of the oldest and most settled stock of the countryside where even the day-labourers looked down on her. But when that proud young chap had lost his character and dignity, when he was penniless and in debt, when his family had kicked him out, even though it was she who had disgraced and beggared and banished him, then Hannah Iden would have had enough—for that was her way.

§ 23

Late in the autumn of that year a further blot appeared on the soiled integrity of Bodingmares. An irreverent fate seemed to persecute Jim's respectability, and while granting him every kind of material prosperity to sour its gifts by some accompanying scandal. Fuller had not lived down the gossip and contempt aroused by Clem's mean alliance with Orznash, before Robert's disgrace reached its climax and brought Bodingmares still more shamefully into the talk of public-houses. And he had no sooner begun to fancy himself in his part of outraged and forgiving brother, than all High Tilt boiled over with the news that Mrs. Fuller was going to marry Wheelsgate, the postman.

This was quite dreadful. To begin with, she had been a widow just a year, and it would have been indecent for her to marry anybody no matter how rich and important after so short an interval, especially as everyone knew that she had not been quite happy in her twenty-three years with James Fuller. An appearance of grief would have been all the more becoming in her because everyone knew that the reality was absent. Also she had been light and flirtish ever since the first five months; she had been absurd in her blushing and excitement and return to youthful looks; she had given people cause to wag their heads and make ominous forecasts, so by all the

rules she should have disappointed them. But now everybody
in the parishes of High Tilt and Salehurst had "said it all
along."

Then to crown all, she had not chosen a wealthy suitor. She
could have had Pepper of Weights, a substantial man; Pix
of Little London, though at yeast ten years younger than she,
was infatuated with her, and his land touched Bodingmares
in the north by the river Dudwell. Arthur Powlard was a
widower, and had called twice with his daughter since Clem's
wedding. If Mrs. Fuller had taken one of these, then at least
she would have had something to show for her lapse, but she
had chosen just a common chap, a poor man, a public servant.
Wheelsgate was about fifty years old, and had worked as a
country postman all his life. He had saved a little money,
and was reported to be queer; in other words, he was fond
of reading and occasionally bought books. Mrs. Fuller had
a little settlement of her own, so that between them they would
be prosperous enough. They were taking a cottage outside
Salehurst, just where the road to High Tilt crosses the Rother
below Bantony.

There were tears in Elizabeth's eyes as she told her family.
"When I wur seventeen I married for a höame and a husband, and now I'm forty I'll marry fur love, surelye."

"Fur shäame, Mother, to spik lik that, and our pore fäather
dead scarce more'n a year. Your very weeds are hanging
from your head."

"Döan't think as I've aught to say agäunst your fäather.
He wur a good and religious man, as everybody knows. But
that sort döan't always mäake the best husband, and reckon
he wurn't a lively husband to me, as you might say. I äun't
miscalling him, but he wur more lik a Gospel Minister nor a
husband at whiles. Maybe I wur too young fur him; I wur
näun but a child when he married me, and you grows up different after you're married than you grows up a maiden."

"I döan't see as it mäakes things any better, your saying
all this about pore fäather," said Jim sorrowfully.

"Surelye it makes it better if my marriage wurn't a love-
marriage. It's ill turning from your true love after a year. But

my marriage wur the marriage of a young child. Now I'm to marry as a grown woman."

"Maybe," said Mary, "it's as dangerous to marry fur love as a grown woman as to marry fur money as a young child."

"I'm shocked and I'm grieved at you, Mother," said Jim, "fur howsumdever you may happen to feel in your heart, your doings look light in the parish, and it means more talk and trouble fur Bodingmares, just when folkses are starting to git used to Robert and his ways."

"You mean to say as you lump my marriage along of Robert's tedious goings-on? Then all I tell you, Määster, is that, if you're ashäamed of me, I'm ashäamed of *you*." And Elizabeth went out with a very bright flush on her face, which made her look ten years younger.

Clem and Polly took her part. Not that they were not inwardly scandalized, but she had been kind to them and had helped on their marriage, so in loyalty they were bound to stand by her. Robert was horrified and disgusted. His first thought was how it would affect his relations with Hannah, and he came to the conclusion that Hannah would dislike hearing her lover's family again in contempt. The lustre of Bodingmares would still further be dimmed in her eyes, and he thought that in that lustre alone he shone acceptably. Though it was pretty plain that Hannah valued him for his strength and beauty, for his size, for his vigour, big Robert seldom thought of his own desirableness; his love had brought him down to a humility in which he found it hard to think that Hannah could love him for his person alone. He felt convinced that he could not stand before her without money and dignity, and now money was scattering and dignity tumbling down.

Hannah was away when the gossip of Mrs. Fuller's choice first went round the village. She had gone with her tilt cart and her cousins Yocky Lovell and Jerome Bosville to Shovers Green, near Wadhurst, where there was a fair. The day she was expected back Robert went over to Blindgrooms. He would tell her the news himself, and see if she minded.

Contrary to custom, he found the kitchen full of people. There was Ambrose Ripley—Darius was absent—Tommy and

Sacky Carew, and Aurora Stanley, pure-bred gipsy cousins; and also less glorious relations such as Mary Dixter, Luna Devenden, Peter Criol, and other half-breeds named after the hamlets they came from. These were busy over the fire or round the table, and a savoury smell of roast pork mixed with the smoke that hung under the rafters.

Old Leonora Iden was plucking a fowl.

"Here's gorgy Bob from Bodingmares," she said as he came in. Everybody stared at him, and the dark eyes in the solemn, expressionless faces made him feel more than usually hulking and ill at ease.

"When is Hannah coming höame?" he asked Leonora.

"She's coming to-night, but she told me as she wasn't expecting her kind gentleman till to-morrow."

"I've a-come on purpose. There's summat I want to tell her. Wull she be long?"

"She will be long, and when she comes she will be busy. All the poor people are gathered together here for a little feast."

Robert could feel all the poor people's eyes upon him, boring through the smoke of the kitchen, and his sense of peculiarity and outlandishness grew.

"I'll go and meet her," he said, making an awkward dive for the door. "I reckon she'll be coming by the Mountpumps Road."

"I don't know what road she comes by, sweet gentleman, but she comes with her own people."

Robert was anxious to escape from the old woman, who hated him for his gorgeousness, and was doing her best, he knew, to mate Hannah romanly. He went out, ducking his head under the rafters, which, though convenient enough for the gipsies, threatened to knock out his brains as he towered among them.

It was good to feel the cold air on his cheeks and in his lungs. The December night was clear and full of stars. The Dipper hung over northern Delmonden, and the southern hills were blocked against a scatter of lights. There was no moon, but the starlight called the roads out of the darkness into a pale grey gleam, and in the flats below High Tilt's little gabled ridge the Rother wound like a silver string. Robert had never definitely heeded the beauty of the fields, by day or night, but he was unconsciously receptive of the evening's peace and freshness; the reek of the dirty kitchen, with the smell of roasting pork, was gone, and with the oppression of his lungs vanished a little of the oppression of his heart. He walked quickly along the Mountpumps Road—the shorter road from High Tilt to Ticehurst—his footsteps ringing on the frozen marl. He would meet her and drive back with her, though he would not go in to that outlandish feast.

But he had walked nearly to Ticehurst before she came in sight. At the throws outside the village he stood and saw the lights of her cart, swaying as the wheels lurched in the ruts, and heard her stock of kettles and saucepans clashing together. The small horse was dwindled by the piled vehicle behind him —heaped with baskets and basket-chairs and pots and pans and bedding. Out of its towering and lurching bulk emerged the paleness of hands and faces.

"Hannah!" he called sharply. "Is that you, Hannah Iden?"

"Who's there?" asked a man's voice.

"It's me—Bob Fuller. Wull you give me a ride back, Hannah?"

"There isn't room," said Yocky Lovell's voice. "Here we all are like fowls in a basket. Besides, it ain't fitting—Hannah rides with her bridegroom."

"Wot d'you mean?" panted Robert, who was hurrying along beside the slackened cart.

"I mean as there isn't room for you and me in this cart," said the voice of Darius Ripley.

"Hannah!" broke out Robert. "It äun't true. Tell me as it äun't."

"She can't tell you no such thing, brother," said Yocky, "for it's as true as what's written in the sky. Jerome and me have been together to see her married in Wadhurst Church."

"She was married by a clever priest," said Jerome, "who made it all as proper and let-no-man-put-asunder as if she was the finest lady in the land. She couldn't be more safely and

elegantly married if she was the queen. And now we're going
home to eat a porker her mother has killed."

"Let me get into the cart," gasped Robert.

"No, no, brother; it ain't fitting, seeing as she's another
man's wife, and as there isn't room for a cat's tail among us."

"Nannie . . . speak to me."

"Don't trouble her, brother. She's happy, and she's written you a real letter in the post that will tell you everything.
She didn't expect to have the honour of seeing you to-night."

Robert's breath was nearly gone as he ran beside the cart.
He could dimly pick out Hannah's shape, squeezed between
Darius and Yocky—the great wheel of her hat, and the lovely
droop of her shoulders under her shawl. With his last spurt
of strength he seized the rail of the cart, and tried to put his
foot on the turning axle. But a hand shot out of the dark
mass of bodies and baskets and crockery, and striking him full
on the chest sent him sprawling in the road. He was on his
feet again in an instant, but it was too late; the little horse
had been whipped into a gallop, and the cart went lurching and
dwindling out of sight.

§ 24

At first Robert thought that he would die. Surely no
one could endure such anguish and live. His wretchedness
was not only mental and spiritual, but physical; his heart felt
swollen, his throat and tongue felt thick, terrible qualms of
nausea made him weak, and his eyes and skin were burning.
For some hours he was in the hell of physical jealousy, the
blackest hell to which love has the key. He wanted to kill
Darius and to kill Hannah; he wanted to kill them horribly;
if they had been within reach he probably would have done so.
He pictured himself kicking out Darius' brains with his
nailed boots, and when he had done so he would hold Hannah's
face down in the water and mud of the ditch and smother her.
He felt her heaving and struggling under him as she suffocated.
. . . It was horrible, it sickened him, but he would still picture it, for the only other picture in his mind was that of

Darius loving her, and he could not, he dared not, look on that. . . .

To his surprise he found himself walking; he must have walked for miles, since he was nearly home. He had not passed through High Tilt, but had mechanically taken the bostal lane to Bodingmares from Scales Crouch. Round him hung the great black empty night; the fields were in the stillness of the small hours, windless, unstirred. A white, star-thridden mist muffled the Rother valley, and had crept up the fields to the pales of Bodingmares; it even lay in the yard, and the barn roofs and turrets of the oasts rose out of it. A strange, deep weariness fell on Robert, his limbs ached, and he was glad to creep upstairs to his bedroom and fall on the bed. There he found himself weeping, crying hopelessly.

His rage was dead, for his jealousy had temporarily burnt and exploded itself out. He could only weep for her cruelty and treachery. Why had she done this wicked thing? They had parted so friendly when she went to Wadhurst. Had she meant to do this all along?

He gulped and sobbed at the thought of her treachery. He had been honest with her, he had been true to her, he had given her everything she had ever asked him for, and a good deal more besides. His love had made her happy; she had said so. Yet here she was, turning from him to a little hound of a gipsy who had never given her any special devotion. Darius Ripley was a little black ugly chap with legs like a dancing-master's . . . a good light-weight boxer, that was all. That was a thick 'un he had given Robert in the chest; he still felt the burn of it. Why should Hannah go to Darius? Was it because her gorgy lover had lost his splendour by getting himself talked about on her account? . . . But that was her doing, damn her eyes! It was she who had brought him to scandal and trouble, and then shrugged away from his degradation. . . . He felt the fire of his jealousy once more creeping, and the knowledge made him turn again to his pillow and cry. He could not bear that again; he would go mad . . . and break things. Why had he not gone to Blindgrooms and killed Hannah and Darius, or let them kill

him? Should he go now? No, no! Killing people is tar'ble
. . . killing people you love is tar'ble. But he must go somewhere, he must have someone to help him in this horrible darkness, which was lit only by two pictures, one of himself killing
Hannah and one of Darius loving her. . . .

He slid off the bed and stood up with his head among the
rafters. The window was now a square of moonlight, and a
white light was creeping into the room. It showed him Clem's
dismantled bed against the opposite wall, and he suddenly remembered Clem, and his loyalty and his kindness. He would
go to his brother—he must—he could not bear to be alone.

Without waiting to think, he ran downstairs and out of the
house. The waning moon had come up out of the woods beyond
Boarsney, and seemed to be the visible heart of the cold that
lay like a clenched hand on the night. The fields shone
white between the silvered black of the hedges, and the shadows
were sharply and darkly bitten on road and grass. Robert went
through the yard into the home field, which spread lonely
hillocks under the moon, and then over the hard, frozen sods
of the turnip ground to the little backyard of Pookwell. The
house seemed wrapped in sleep; the dense shadows of its
thatched eaves were like lowered eyelids.

He went round to the front and found the door locked. He
beat on it violently; his passion broke the stillness of the
night and then was immediately swallowed up by it. He
knocked again and louder, and this time Clem's tousled head
came out of the bedroom window.

"Who's there?"

"It's me—Bob—let me in."

Clem's head retreated, and there were voices, then footsteps coming downstairs. The next moment the door opened,
and his brother stood before him in his night shirt, with round,
scared eyes.

"Wot is it? Wot's happened?"

"Hannah's guv me the chuck. . . . She's married Darius
Ripley. . . . Let me stop wud you, Clem, or I'll do somebody
in."

§ 25

The next day Robert had Hannah's "real letter." It was
brought down from the farm by Polly, who ran up to give news
of him. Robert was feeling better . . . his misery had reached
a drugging state. He had slept a little on Clem's sofa, and
though he could eat no breakfast had let Polly make him several cups of strong tea. He sat by the fire drinking tea when
she brought the letter in to him.

It appeared to be the joint production of several minds—
and hands. Hannah had had little practice in writing since
she left the council school, and this letter on a complicated and
delicate subject had obviously involved her in difficulties which
she had failed to surmount without help from her friends. It
ran:

"DEAR MR. ROBERT FULLER,—Hopeing this finds you well
as it leaves me at present this is to say that we had better
bring our frenship to a close. Seeing as Hannah was marred
to Darius Ripley in Wadhurst church by a preist. Dear Robert, I am sorry I did not tell you I was to do it but you wold
have made such a Hell of a row. I allways ment to marry
Darius as soon as his farther was dead and woud alow it him
wanting Darius to marry roman and Hannah only ½ roman
as her father was a christian in a workouse. But this cud
never have gorn on with you and me as I told you at the start
as my mother dosent like my going with Gentiles and I promised I marry romanly if Darius father wud have me and that
was always understood but not told you becos of your temper.
Well dear Robert I hopes you will not be upset. I have shone
you a thing or 2. Having no more to say I will now drore to
a close

"from your sinserely friend
                    MRS. RIPLEY AND HUSBAND.

"p.s.—There is no good your coming round as Hannah and
me will have started for the fare at Horsmonden early mornin
and if you meddles with her I will give you one on the boko."

The postscript was true. Evidently dreading the effect of her news on her lover, Hannah had arranged to be out of the neighbourhood before he received it. She and Darius had stopped at Blindgrooms merely for the wedding feast, and had set out at daylight for Horsmonden cattle fair. They would probably not be back for some time, as after the fair Darius was taking her to see his relations at Apuldram, near Chichester. So much was gathered from a visit to Blindgrooms and the gossip of High Tilt. All the village knew about Hannah's wedding, and all the village wanted to know what Robert Fuller made of it. They did not get the chance. For a couple of days he never left Bodingmares. Frantic bursts of rage and jealousy, in which he was savage and black with threats, alternated with hours of semi-comatose depression in which he sat heavy and stupid, a piece of cumbrous and depressing furniture in the new house of Polly and Clem. They kept him with them all that day and night, and the next morning he went back to the homestead, having been persuaded that a bit of work would do him good.

Jim was unexpectedly kind and forbearing. He was so genuinely relieved to see Robert delivered from bondage that he could endure finding Bodingmares again the focus of local gossip. He hoped to goodness that this ud be a lesson to the chap, and that he would now settle down respectable and marry some nice girl. Certainly he seemed to be working better and keeping clear of the pubs.

Robert had found that hard work brought him a certain measure of relief. It absorbed those violent energies of body which threatened every now and then to send him off murderously to Chichester; it also made him tired, so that he slept soundly, instead of dreaming of Hannah or lying awake thinking of her. Day by day he wore himself out with plough and spade, slept heavily at nights, and spent his few hours of leisure with Clem and Polly. They were kind to him and put on no superior airs—they made him welcome in their little kitchen after dark. Sometimes he felt a slight jealousy of their happiness, but being a purely mental jealousy, he found it almost agreeable by contrast with his feelings towards Darius and Hannah.

So the winter passed in hard work out in the hard fields, driving long graceful furrows with his plough, or caring for the ewes when their lambs were born in the days of rainy scud, or driving to the markets at Burwash and Etchingham and Salehurst and High Tilt. If the image of Hannah Ripley ever rose between him and the steaming flanks of his plough-horses, or of his trotting mare, or between him and the ewes' draggled fleeces and the little white, weak lambs, he would simply bend his back and clench his hands and be all back and hands and straining thighs till Robert Fuller's animal had saved Robert Fuller's man.

Sometimes of an evening he would go and sit with his mother. Her marriage had taken place before the ravens had done picking the carcase of Robert's love affair, and had not, there-fore, been quite so much gossiped about as Jim had expected. She had been married quietly and early in the morning, and only a few people had attended. There had been no wedding breakfast, but the bride and bridegroom had gone off for a real honeymoon at Eastbourne, which also helped Jim to hold up his head. Wheelsgate had turned out to be a more sub-stantial man than people supposed. He had comfortably fur-nished the cottage at Marsh Quarter, and Elizabeth had bright chintzes and polished metals, and new clothes in which she looked hardly more than thirty.

Robert had been very unkind and ungracious to her, but he was her son and in trouble, so she always welcomed him. Moreover, since his tragedy he had been much too beaten down to keep up his hostile attitude towards her marriage, and had postponed his financial emancipation for weeks by buying her a gorgeous pink satin eiderdown, which she said was far too fine to keep up in a bedroom where no company ever saw it, so had spread over the parlour sofa. Robert was proud and delighted that she should value his present so much, and every time he came to see her they would go into the front room to look at it and remark on its beauty and style and costly appearance.

So the evenings, which might have been difficult in their long passivity, were lived through by the help of his mother, or of Clem and Polly. His day could be endured till bedtime . . . then if he was tired enough to fall quickly asleep, all was well —and he generally was tired enough. Only sometimes the bounty failed him, and he would lie with his face rammed into his pillow, in a grief as abandoned as a child's and as motionless as an animal's.

§ 26

One evening in March when Robert went to visit his mother, he found Mabel Powlard sitting with her in the parlour. He did not recognize her at once, for he had not seen her since Clem's wedding, and then had scarcely noticed her in the midst of his sorrowful turmoil. Mabel rallied him archly on his bad memory, and Mrs. Wheelsgate looked shocked. She was inclined to be proud of Mabel's acquaintance, and thought a lot of her smartness and elegance. Mabel gave Elizabeth patterns and ideas for gowns, and took it for granted that she wanted fashionable clothes, and not just the sober, useful garments, remote from time, that the standards of the Rother villages decreed for her middle age.

Mabel was certainly a smart-looking girl. As she sat in his mother's parlour, with the flowery quilt and the flowery wall-paper and the flowery chintz and the family Bible, she imparted to Robert's flagging taste a savour as of salt and olives. She rasped and yet she stimulated. She brought the atmosphere of streets and shops and picture-houses into the stuffy little parlour of a country cottage. When he looked at her as she sat with crossed legs, showing her high, tasselled boots, he seemed to see the great flaring lights outside a cinema, and all the gay crowd of men and their best girls going up to take tickets. She was pretty, too—a trifle anæmic, perhaps, but he rather liked the delicate colouring of her lips. Her soft, reddish hair was pulled down fashionably over her ears, and had a little unnatural ripple in it. Her eyes were blue and rather prominent.

Mabel's way with men was also different from what he was used to. She did not giggle, but she talked a great deal, and her talk was full of flicks. Some of these he did not understand, and they irritated him—he told himself she was "clever" —but some struck him as very amusing, and somehow flattering to himself. Though she had not liked him at all when she sat beside him at Clem's wedding, it was her type to be self-conscious and sprightly in the presence of a man, just as another type giggles and is silent. This time she saw that she was making an impression, so was inclined to view him more favourably. Certainly he was very good-looking—a trifle too red in his complexion, perhaps (she wondered if it was true that he drank), and a bit clumsy and ignorant of the way to treat a girl . . . she felt she could not trust him to take the outside of the pavement if he walked with her in Bulverhythe, and she and her friends had agreed that you could not call a man a gentleman unless he did that.

They had not many subjects in common. Mabel did not like the country, and Robert's knowledge of picture-palaces was limited to High Tilt and Salehurst, where they never showed the newest films. He had not even made the best of his opportunities in these, but had used their darkness and privacy almost exclusively for love-making, so he had very little to say on Mabel's favourite subject—he knew none of the most popular actors and actresses by name, and could not even remember the titles of the pictures.

Harry Wheelsgate came in to tea at six, and afterwards Robert, in response to a hint from his mother, escorted Mabel to Salehurst station. He could not help being impressed when he found she had a second-class ticket—her father did not like her travelling alone third class.

"There's a very low kind of fellow about at present," she remarked with a sigh. "Not that I've ever had any trouble with them, but it doesn't do to trust any man in a third-class carriage. Sometimes they've the face to think that a girl is asking for it if she gets in alone. And, of course, some girls . . . but then I've never had any *need* to do that sort of thing, and wouldn't if I had. My friend Muriel said to me the other day: 'Ma belle'—that's what she calls me—it's French and means 'my beautiful'—only a play on the name, of course—'Ma belle, don't you think you're really too refined? A girl oughtn't to expect men to go *all* the way after her.' But I never could bring myself . . . and as for getting off with just anyone I happened to meet . . . in a third-class carriage, too . . . well, all I can say is that girls who do that sort of thing deserve what they sometimes get. Don't you, Mr. Fuller?"

Here Robert felt inspired to say that he shouldn't like to trust himself alone with her in a railway carriage. Whereat she bridled so violently that he thought he had offended her past forgiveness—and did not much care if he had.

§ 27

But evidently the offence was not very deep, for in a fortnight's time she was back at his mother's with some patterns for a blouse, and—so Robert was told—inquired after him most kindly. Indeed, so kind were her inquiries that Elizabeth had felt urged to manage a little tea-party for the following week. Mabel was coming to spend the day, and help Elizabeth make up her blouse with the material she brought from Bulverhythe; her father was coming, too—evidently his heart had not been wounded past repair by the widow's choice —and Jim and Mary and Robert were invited over from Bodingmares, and Polly and Clem from Pookwell, so it would be quite a party.

"Some people can afford this, I suppose," said Mary aside to Jim when she saw the well-laid table. Her stepmother's life at Marsh Quarter, with its mixture of comfort and obscurity, was exasperating to her, and her sense of decency was outraged by Elizabeth's quadragenarian flowering into silks and ribbons. Her attitude towards both Mr. and Mrs. Wheelsgate was very stiff, and she ate their cake with small, superior bites while calculating the cost of it a pound; but she was extremely affable towards Powlard and his daughter, though to the latter was due the encouragement, if not the inspiration, of Elizabeth's unseemly tastes.

"If you'll excuse me, wot an unaccountable smart hat you have on, Miss Powlard. I reckon as in Bulverhythe you git the very läatest thing."

"Oh, Mabel's a oner for clothes," replied her father.

"But I'm sure as you äun't extravagant," said Mary graciously, "extravagance being a thing as I cud never abide, and folkses putting themselves above their station, especially after they've a-gone and put themselves beneath it."

"And wot exactly do you mean by that?" asked Wheelsgate, smiling. He was aware of her spite, and in his state of fulfilment could afford to regard it humorously.

"Reckon my meaning's plain enough. Howsumdever, as I wur saying, Miss Powlard . . ." and she leaned towards Mabel with increasing amiability.

Clem and Polly sat silent. Mabel horribly scared them both, with her boots and her handbag and the powder on her nose. She made Clem painfully aware that his hands were not clean—you can't get rape dust out of your skin in one wash—and Polly blushed for the shortcomings of her wedding dress. It was uncomfortably tight—she had grown fatter since her marriage—but she had sustained herself with the thought that it was "middling smart," and here was Mabel making her feel all dowdy and common as well as uncomfortable. . . .

"I can't think why everyone's so stuck on her marrying Bob," she said to Clem as they walked home.

"It ud be an unaccountable good thing fur him to marry."

"But not her. She's sharp—she's hard—she's lik a spike."

"There äun't a girl aräound here as ud have him, surelye."

"But you'd never want him to marry Mabel Powlard, fur all that."

"If he döan't git married, and Hannah comes back. . . ."

"Maybe she'll never come back."

"More likely she will."

"Anyhows, I döan't see as it'll mäake it any better, Bob being married to Mabel. She äun't the sort as ull kip him from harm if he wants to go after it."

"Well, we döan't know yit as she'd have him if he asked her.
She mun have heard a gurt lot about his goings on, even though
she äun't lived here."

Polly sniffed.

"If she döan't mean to have him she's no right to go looking
and talking the way she dud—'Döan't you, Mr. Fuller?' after
every other ward, and her eyes all rolling about lik marbles."

"Maybe he'll never ask her."

"I hope he wöan't, surelye."

§ 28

It was some time before Robert discovered his family's in-
tentions with regard to him and Mabel. He had seen her
thrown into his life without thinking about it very much.
After all, it was good going about with a woman again. Hard
work and the kind company of his mother and brother were
not enough to push Hannah's dark image out of his head; he
wanted women's society, and had so far been unable to get it.
Milly Dunk had stuck her chin in the air and walked quickly
on when he said "Good morning" to her in Switesden Lane,
and Maude Willard had turned her back on him when one
day he asked her to go with him to the pictures. Therefore
Mabel's society was a flattery as well as a comfort. He could
see that she liked him; she herself had invited him to come
over and visit her at Bulverhythe. They had walked together
on the wide, brightly lit pavement, with the wind of a spring
dusk blowing behind them down the street; they had looked
into the shops together, and he had been aware that he was a
very smart young man taking out a very smart young girl.
Certainly Mabel was a "oner" in many ways. When in the
warm, glowing darkness of the picture palace he groped for her
hand, she pushed his away with almost a slap, and would not
take her eyes off the picture for all his longing. "Isn't he
handsome? Isn't she sweet?" said Mabel every other minute, as the actors and actresses rolled their eyes.

But when at ten o'clock he stopped with her at her father's
door, and they shook hands, there was something in Mabel's

face, tilted up in the lamplight, that he had often seen on the faces of other girls and knew the meaning of well. He bore no grudge, so kissed her at once, and the kiss intoxicated him. After his country loves, it excited him to touch the novelty of a powdered skin—Mabel's powder and scent were part of a new and very gripping charm. . . . When he let her go she was furious, and called him a beast, and said that was not the way to kiss a girl. Poor Robert, whose sentimental education had taught him no other way of kissing, stared after her forlornly as she marched up the steps and went in, banging the door. However, he knew by this time that her displeasure was not everlasting, and on their next meeting he was graciously taken back into favour, and, indeed, instructed in the art of kissing a refined young lady in a manner not shocking to her refinement.

When Robert discovered that his whole family, with the wavering exception of Clem and Polly, was set on his marrying Mabel, and was working all the social machinery of Bodingmares to that end, his first feelings were of indignation. So that was their little game, was it? Staking everything to make him respectable! They thought he would marry a girl like Mabel, all high heels and high notions . . . he, who knew what love was, as if the wild earth itself had taught him. . . .

Still, he hoped that Hannah would hear of his flirtation. His pride was stiffening in her direction, and he wanted her to think that his heart had not been desperately wounded, and that he, like so many men, had found a cure in a change. It was with such an idea that he had asked Maude Willard to go out with him, and made one or two other snubbed efforts at courtship. He loved Hannah as much as ever, and knew in his heart that he loved her, and still had his moments of despair; but it was inevitable that her continued absence should work a change in him, and make things possible which otherwise could never have happened. His love for her had always been highly concrete in its manifestations, and the images with which it was associated were one and all concrete and material. These images were now beginning to fade from want of fresh stimulation; their outlines were blurring into oblivion, and others, heavier, thicker, more real because more closely allied with his everyday experience, were beginning to blot them out. If Hannah came back, if one day he was to meet her on the marsh where the road crosses the river, or see her standing by the gate at Blindgrooms, or leading her horse up Mountpumps Hill, then back she would come into his heart and drive everything else out of it—because his heart belonged to her and she had signed it with her signature.

But Hannah did not come back. By the marriage customs of her race she belonged to her husband's people as much as to her own, and Darius's relations lived far away on Manhood's End, beyond Chichester. They were pure-bred gipsies, but had taken to house life in a cottage near Apuldram, and it was said that Hannah and her husband were to live with them for six months at least. However, she was sure to come back some time to visit her mother at Blindgrooms, and the Fullers were wise enough to realize that if Robert married he must marry before she came.

By this time the family had come to look upon marriage as his one hope of reputation. Marriage was the only cure known locally for the vices of extravagance and incontinence. A wife was supposed to provide an adequate counter-attraction both to the spendthrift entertainments of the public house and to the illicit delights of the twilight lanes, when love went hunting with the moths. Robert married would be in consequence Robert settled and respectable, all his shame and backsliding forgotten. Robert unmarried would remain a reproach and a disgrace.

The trouble was to find him a wife. No local girl would look at him. His reputation had not been any too clean before he fell in with Hannah—he had been regarded as a noisy, drinking sort, fond of losing his money over darts and shove-halfpenny, and both low and inconstant in his amours. His affair with Hannah had definitely outlawed him—he had loved her so shamelessly, publicly and helplessly, he had gone about with her gipsy relations, he had made it impossible for any decent chap, let alone a decent girl, to know him. The Fullers' only chance lay in a girl from "furrin parts," who had not properly realized his degradation. Powlard, of course, had a certain knowledge, but he talked magnanimously of a young fellow's wild oats, and obviously regarded the match with favour. He was impressed by the plumpness of Bodingmares, and foresaw a comfortable settlement for his daughter.

Affairs had now been brought forward to a certain stage where they had apparently stuck. Robert went often to Bulverhythe to see Mabel, and she came nearly as often to Bodingmares or to Marsh Quarter to see him, but Jim and Mary and Elizabeth looked in vain for further developments. It was now just as likely, too, that the developments would be in the direction of Hannah's reappearance, coming up like a storm out of the west to blast and wreck the carefully tilled field of Robert's courtship.

Who was hanging back—Bob or Mabel? Powlard undertook to sound his daughter, but Mabel was a "oner" at keeping her own counsel as well as at other things, and her father could find out nothing. Jim then undertook to convey a delicate hint to Robert, who told him to mind his own business and be hemmed to him, and that he—Bob Fuller—wasn't going to be druv.

Then the time came when Robert's invitations to Bulverhythe suddenly stopped, and a request that Mabel should come over and spend the day at Bodingmares was declined with frigid politeness.

"You've a-done it now," said Jim.

"I döan't care if I have," said Robert.

§ 29

It was June when Hannah came back. The hay had been cut in the low fields by the river, but the high grounds were still russet with sorrel and plantain and sainfoin waiting for the scythe. The lanes were dim with the warm dust that hung over them and mixed with the cloud of chervil and cow-parsley and fennel that filmed the hedges, making with it a sweet, stal scent of dust and flowers. Down by the watercourses the hawthorn had faded, and the meadowsweet sicklied the still air that thickened above the dykes and at night crept up as a damp, perfumed mist to farmhouse walls.

Robert met Hannah in the little lane that runs off the Sale-hurst road near Bantony. He was on his way to Haiselman's Farm with a message from Jim, and he did not know that Hannah had come back. Her shadow came round the bend of the lane, lying on the ruts and the dust and the wild gera-nium. He looked up to see who was coming, and saw her walk-ing towards him with a basket on her arm. It was a warm day, so she did not wear her shawl, and her free, strong figure —slightly coarsened, it seemed, unless his memory had re-fined it—was displayed by a green silk blouse fastened over her breast with a heavy brooch.

They were both taken aback. Hannah wished she had her husband with her; as for Robert, he was totally unfit for the occasion. He stood stock still and stared at her with his mouth open. His confusion restored her confidence.

"Good morning," she said, and passed him.

"Mornun," said Robert blankly. Then suddenly he realized that she was Hannah—his Hannah—the woman whom his love had held and lost, after whom his heart had cried all the winter through. He swung round and went after her.

"Is 'good mornun' all you've got to say after wot you've done to me?"

"I've done you no harm." There was a faint whine in her voice—she thought that he might fall upon her in this lonely, stuffy little lane. His face was very red, with the veins swell-ing.

But he did not want to hurt her. It surprised him to find that, after all his murderous impulses, his horrible thoughts of vengeance, now that he was alone with her and had her in his power all he wanted to do was to take her in his arms and hide his face in the soft hollow of her breast. She saw his weakness, and her own passed.

"You've no call to look so rude and black at me, Mr. Rob-ert Fuller. I only left you to marry, as was proper."

"I'd have married you, and you know it."

"It's ill done marrying outside your own people."

"But you dudn't play honest wud me, telling me naun."

"You'd eyes to see."

"How cud I see? You hid things—you went double . . . and I loved you so."

He stood before her in the lane, his cap pushed back from his forehead, his face flushed and faintly a-sweat with his trouble. He knew that he was breaking down before her, that he was pleading with her—though he had sworn that he would make her plead with him. But he could not help himself. The flood of his love had swept away every emotion that was not either spiritual or animal—a decent, civilized, sensible emotion like self-respect had no chance against it.

"Don't make me one of your vulgar scenes, Mr. Robert Fuller. Said I when I married Darius: 'Well, at least I've done with gorgy Robert's temper.' "

Her words cut him, and he gave a little gasp of pain. The hopeless thing about any appeal to Hannah was that she had no essential bedrock or bottom of tenderness which he could entreat. Such softness as she had was all on the surface, as the earth bears the loam and the clay over the hard rocks.

"Well, I must be going on," she continued. "I've bought a fowl for my husband's dinner, so I'll get home and cook it— that is, if you've nothing more to say."

"I never want to spik you another ward so long as I live."

"That's as you please, but as you had your mouth open I thought maybe you had something to remark. However, good morning."

As soon as she was gone his anger blazed out. He thought of going after her, throwing her down, and beating her with his stick. He would like to break her ribs, scar her beautiful back for life. . . . But it was no use imagining such things—he could not do them; directly he came up with her he would love her again, and reproach her and plead with her as he had done just now. How many times he had pictured this first meeting, and each time he had pictured himself as the avenger— he had scorned her, he had cursed her, he had threatened her, he had frightened her, he had murdered her . . . and then when the thing had actually happened all he could do had been to flush and sweat and stammer broken entreaties and reproaches. How she must despise him! . . . Oh, why had he ever met her? . . . Why couldn't he forget her?

§ 30

"Wot are you doing this afternoon, Bob?" asked Jim at dinner.

"Naun as I know on, säave as I said I'd go wud Pickdick and see how the hay's doing on the high snape."

"You can leave that. Pickdick knows hay, or ought to, at twenty shillun a week. I'd be glad if you cud go over to Bulverhythe and give Turner a call."

"Who's Turner?"

"Him wot's set up as a seedsman in High Street. I've got his cattylog here"—and Jim fumbled a mass of grimy leaves—"and I'd like to see—or fur someone as knows to see—one or two samples of hisn. There's awned wheat as I thought of putting into the Bugshull field when it comes out of potash this fall, and I thought as maybe the awned ud do better up by Bugshull than the red; you've got to be careful in them clays, and the whole was a bit too sedgy-leaved last time. You ask to see his oats, too."

If Robert had been at all sharp he would have noticed that Jim spoke with a very elaborate carelessness, and was staring at him hard all the while; he would also have noticed that Mary had stopped eating her treacle pudding and was staring at him too.

"And sinst you're in Bulverhythe," continued Jim with a rush, "you might give a look in at Powlard. Not one of us has bin there this dunnamany week, and maybe offence has bin given."

"I'm not a-going near un," said Robert.

Jim and Mary exchanged an anxious glance.

"It ud be silly to give offence," said the latter, "just now as the two families has bin brung together."

"Well, I äun't a-going to bring 'em any closer."

"We döan't mean anything personal to you, Bob; you mun

mäake your own choice. Howsumdever, you can't drop a nice young gal lik Mabel lik a hot potato."

"If you called now, it ud all be in the way of letting her down gently," said Jim.

Jim and Mary talked to Robert with their eyes fixed on each other, apparently drawing on a mutual spring of diplomacy. They had heard that Hannah Ripley had come back—Jim had been told so that morning by Bream of Little Moat—but they were unable to find out whether she had yet encountered Robert. Probably not, they thought, as she had only arrived yesterday. Bream had heard that she would not stop more than a week or two. Darius had bought a caravan and they were going to live on the roads, with occasional headquarters at High Tilt and Apuldram. This was encouraging news, for if only Robert did not entangle himself on this visit, the future would not be so thick with temptation as they had feared. Jim and Mary knew nothing of (and if they had known would not have believed) the loyalty of the gipsy wife and the chaste marriage ideal of her people, which would keep even a woman like Hannah, who before marriage had gone her own ways, the loyal helpmeet and servant of the man who had captured her at last. They had made up their minds that Hannah married was just as dangerous as Hannah single, and would not hesitate to bring Robert back to heel if it suited her convenience, as of course it would. As for him, he was tow to her flame, and as he had never loved her with a view to marriage, he would soon get used to the other man's rights.

The only thing to do, therefore, was to keep the couple apart. Robert must be sent afield daily to attend auctions and markets till Hannah was out of High Tilt. To-day a double opportunity arose. He could be not only sent away but sent into the neighbourhood of an eligible counter-attraction. Not that his present behaviour was promising; he swore with many emasculate Sussex oaths that he would not go near Powlard, and his brother and sister dared not rouse his opposition unduly by pressing him. However, he agreed to go to Bulverhythe and inspect the seedsman, so half their point was gained.

It was a hot afternoon, and the pavements of Bulverhythe
smelled of the June sunshine, but the sea-going streets were
fresh with the winds that sped up them from the sands
and the rocks. The streets were full of gay colours—bright
hats and blouses and parasols, moving to and fro before windows crammed with coloured fruits and glowing silks and
painted tins and toys. It made Robert's eyes ache, he felt
awkward and alone amidst all this colour and movement and
freshness. His heart was in a stuffy lane, throbbing before
Hannah as she stood there and spurned it. What was she
doing now? She was making tea for Darius Ripley, perhaps
eagerly waiting for him to come back from one or other dis-
honest appointment. Robert knew better than Jim; he knew
that Hannah could never by any possibility belong to him
again. · She had married Darius, so she would be true to
Darius and serve Darius all the days of her life. She was utterly gone from him; perhaps it was his own fault, and if he
had managed things better he could himself have been her
husband and kept her true to him for ever; or perhaps it was
as she had said, and she had always meant to marry Ripley
when she had the chance. Well, it didn't matter which—
she was gone and would never come back. But her being
gone did not prevent his wanting her. That was the dreadful
part of it. He was like a man interrupted in the middle of a
drink of water—his thirst is not taken away because the
pitcher is broken.

The seedsman did not think much of Mr. Fuller's acumen.
He seemed a dull fellow on whom one could safely land that
rather rotten stuff that had come in from Horseye. Robert
left him with his pocket full of little envelopes and his brain
humming with meaningless talk of "Barbachlaw," "Potato
oat," "Late and early Angus," "rape manure." Hang it all!
Was life to lose all its savour? . . . Once he used to enjoy getting the better of tradesmen, but now he didn't care who
made a fool of him. Oh why did his heart lie and burn in a
stuffy farmhouse lane while his feet beat the pavement in a
seaside town, and round him swept the sunshine and the wind,
and the girls with their pretty dresses and their meaning eyes?

He had not even the heart to follow up one or two opportunities that were given him. . . . More than one girl turned round with a friendly look towards the handsome, broad-backed, brown-skinned fellow, now knowing that his heart lay burnt in a farmhouse lane. . . .

Towards five o'clock he turned into a creamery and had some tea. It was a poorish place, with rather grimy marble-topped tables, but he had been attracted in by the cakes in the window. As he sat pouring his tea out of a teapot with a broken spout, it occurred to him how much better off he would have been taking tea with Mabel, in the cosy drawing-room over the shop. It was all very well to go about alone if you had the heart to invite strangers into your life whenever you felt lonely; a year ago he would have selected some girl from the crowd on the pavement, and brought her in here, or rather, stimulated by her requirements, to some better place. But now all the adventure in him was dead; the ruin of his one big faithful passion had brought down with it all the joys of casual acquaintance and promiscuous flirtation. He had no one to be faithful to, so he did not want to flirt.

Perhaps Jim was right, and he had better marry Mabel. He was in just the right frame of mind for marriage, no more spunk left in him. Oh, he used to be some sort of a fellow once, he used to keep the bar awake, he made the girls look out. . . . But now here he was drinking tea by himself in a third-rate creamery, while outside life streamed by him in colour and wind and sunshine—unwanted.

He couldn't go on living like this. He must have something to make him forget Hannah, something to fill up his empty heart that ached like a hollow tooth. He had been a fool to offend Mabel. Well, perhaps it wasn't too late to set things right. He had offended her before, and she had forgiven him. What if he went to see her after tea. . . . She might be angry, but he'd take his chance of that; and, after all, he didn't think she would be—not very angry. She liked the way he kissed her too much, for all that she made herself out so squeamish. He'd knock the squeamishness out of her . . . she should teach him to forget things. Married life is so

different from single life that a man's whole outlook is changed
. . . oh, yes, it must be so . . . even when one has loved
one's utmost before marriage. Old memories, old desires, old
torments are forgotten. Besides, one need not be so much
alone. . . . Not that he meant to ask her this evening—it was
too soon—but at least he could start by recovering the ground
he had lost.

The idea had flashed into his head like a piece of madness,
but the shock of it brought such relief that he found himself
adopting it as a reasonable suggestion. Anyhow, he would go
and explore the ground. He paid his bill at the counter, and
then took his place once more in the gay shift and dazzle of the
pavements. But this time he did not feel so much a foreigner,
for he had a purpose, an association. He would not tell Jim
that he had been to see Mabel, for Jim would flurry him with
obligations, and he wanted to feel himself free up to the very
last moment. That was still some way off; it would probably
take him some time to get back into his old place in her
favour, and perhaps he would never be able to make up his
mind to bind himself. But he was glad that he was going to
see her; the long afternoon had brought its reaction, and he
felt in a mood for her kisses. . . .

She lived in the west of the town. Her father's shop stood
at the end of a quiet terrace of genteel houses, the one plate-
glass window in their neighbourhood. The door was at the
side, at the top of a flight of steps. Robert ran up to ring
the bell.

The sunshine streamed upon him as he stood there, and the
south wind rushed up from the sea, full of the drawl of waves.
Something made him stop his hand as he lifted it to the bell-
pull. A soft, liquid quality had crept into the light, the shining of late afternoon; it swamped the sedate street and red-
brick houses with a queer, golden sense of adventure. Somehow the moment gripped him, and he stood motionless without ringing. Then by one of those perplexing, buried asso-
ciations which tangle thought, the moment linked itself with
another, nearly two years ago, when he had stood up in the
stuffy, lamp-smelling chapel at High Tilt, in response to some

strange appeal which he could neither understand nor deny. A
sudden fear shot into him. . . . Perhaps it was going to come
again. The south wind was full of danger, the sunshine was a
snare. . . . He felt as if something which had been pursuing
him had at last caught him up, and the fight was so intense
that it became almost physical, and unconsciously he edged
closer to the door. Then the wind, or the light that swam in
the wind, or the waves that drawled in it, or some response
to them all in his distracted heart, seemed to say, "Döan't
go in thur fur comfort, Robert; come to Me." . . . It had
happened again—the whole afternoon of sunshine, wind and
sea, colour and movement and youth in the sea-going streets,
had taken up the call that had come to him in the chapel long
ago. He felt the tears rush into his eyes, and he turned towards the sunshine with a new longing. . . . The next moment
his fear swallowed him up, and seizing the bell, he pealed it
with all his might; then, without even waiting for admittance,
opened the door and walked in.

§ 31

High Tilt was agog at the prospect of Bob Fuller's marriage.

"To think as any gal ud be such a fool as to have him,"
said Pont.

"She äun't heard," said Dunk.

"She must have heard. She's bin over here a dunnamany
times."

"But maybe she döan't täake things in," said Pix of Little
London; "she comes from the town, and she äun't see Hannah Iden, nor knows that no decent gal shud ought to touch a
man wot's bin wud a gipsy."

"She'll find out soon enough. I'm sorry fur her when she
gits spliced wud a tedious feller like Bob F."

"Maybe he'll reform and go straight when he marries. Most
chaps do it, and young Bob he döan't hang aräound the pubs
lik he used. Bill Willard said to me only yesterday as Bob's

drink seemingly goes wud his wenching, and ever sinst she guv him the chuck he's mostly bin sober."

"I döan't believe it. His bad ways are bred in his böans by now. Maybe, as you say, he's different from most chaps, and drinks when he's full of beans and loses the tääste when he gits low. Howsumdever, a wife ought to send his spirits up, and then we'll have him aräound agäun at the Woolpack, smashing glasses sääme as he dud that Saturday night last fall, do you remember?"

"Ho! Ho!" Everyone remembered, and many more such memories were added to the common stock before Bob Fuller dropped out of the discussion.

Jim Fuller had been plunged by his brother's news into a mixed state of bewilderment and beatitude. At first he and Mary could hardly believe it—that Robert should leave home swearing that he would not go near Mabel, even for purposes of talk and tea, and then should come back plighted to marry her, implied conditions of courtship unknown at Bodingmares.

"He must have chäanged his mind," said Jim, venturing on an explanation.

"Seemingly," said Mary with a sniff, and a toss of her head, "and maybe he'll chäange it agäun."

"He wöan't. I'm hemmed if I let him wriggle out of this. He's in fur it now, I tell you."

"I'm sure as I hope he is."

"It'll be our third wedding from Bodingmares since pore fäather's funeral, and the only one of 'em wud näun to be ashäamed about it."

"He mun kip straight till he's married, and not go scaring Mabel wud his ways."

"He'll kip straight enough, pore lad. He äun't got half the spunk he used. This marriage ull määke a new chap of him, and it ull give us a chance to höald up our heads at last. I tell you, Mary, I'm sorry fur that lad. I know as Hannah wur a bad lot and he's well shut of her, but reckon he loved her in his way, and he's bin in tedious poor heart since she's gone. It shows he's got some good in him that he dudn't go and soak and go quite rotten sinst she left him, but really lived a bit

better than when he had her. I tell you I'm glad as he's got
a nice gal as ull help him disremember his troubles and ull be
a credit to all of us."

"Well, anyways, it's one good thing as mother has done in
her life."

Mrs. Wheelsgate was justly proud of her achievement. She
felt that she had won regard from her stepson and daughter
besides saving poor Robert from a long, drifting misery.
Mabel was a good girl and a kind girl, she always spoke so
pretty and was so ready to help Elizabeth with her cutting
out, and was never shocked at her desire to follow the fashions
instead of the sumptuary laws of High Tilt—nor did she even
try to persuade her to copy the gowns "for matrons' wear,"
which Elizabeth had an uneasy feeling were more suitable to
her style and years than those so much more gay worn by the
slim and smiling girls on the other pages of "Monthly
Fashions." Certainly Mabel was very considerate and friendly
and good-natured, and would make a charming wife for pooi
Robert. Her only trouble was that she could not induce her
husband to give his opinion. "I'm sure, my dear, she's a very
pretty young lady," was all he would say before he put his
pipe back into his mouth.

The opinion of Clem and Polly wavered through many
arguments.

"I've always said," said Clement, "as marrying wur his only
chance."

"But not to a gal lik Mabel."

"Wot's wrong wud her?"

Polly pursed her lips.

"She äun't his style—she's a town gal. And he döan't love
her."

"Wot mäakes you think that?"

"Well, it's plain enough, surelye. His heart's wud that Hannah."

"But sinst he can't have her——"

"You talk so worldly, Clem, one ud think you believed your
own silly wards. You and me's bin married more'n a year
now, and reckon we shud ought to know wot marriage is.

You know as well as me as marriage äun't all sugar and smiles,
and as thur's things in marriage wot cud never be stood wudout loving each other."

"Surelye, child. But everything äun't the säame fur everyone, and wud you have pore Bob go single all his days because
he can't never git the woman he wants?"

"He can wait a bit, can't he? He äun't lost Hannah a
twelvemonth yit, and it's ugly seeing him disremember her,
horrid lot as she wur. I tell you it wöan't wark, being all
of a hurry lik this, wudout patience so much as to wait fur
love to go, to say naun of waiting till it cöames agäun. If
marriage is a sacrament, as I wur taught before my con-
firmation, reckon as you can täake it to your damnation
säum as any other."

§ 32

As for the bridal couple themselves, they, too, in secret
were a little bewildered. Mabel had never meant to have
Robert—she was aware that a match was being arranged
between them, and she had certainly wanted him to propose,
but she had made up her mind that she did not want to marry
him. He was not her sort; she wanted someone with more
polish and a little less virility; and he said such queer things
sometimes . . . you'd think he wasn't all there. So she
could not quite account to herself for her action in taking
him—especially after the way he had asked her. She would
never forget how he had burst into the room that summer
evening, and without any preliminary or explanation had cried
out: "Mabel, I'm sorry I stopped away. I want to marry
you. Be good to me, because I want you"—and then had
taken her into his arms with a strange, entreating gesture.
Instead of repulsing him, she had let him hold her, and something in her had melted . . . his warm, appealing arms, his
flushed cheek thrust against hers, his poor heart beating wildly
against her breast, had checked the impulse of anger and
denial at its first flash. He was so unlike his old, rough, com-
manding, clumsy self . . . and the new appeal in him woke
a new response in her—she had become soft and half maternal,

she had stood there and held his weight upon her shoulder.
She had that feeling with him sometimes still. Poor Bob!
He'd been through a lot, and no one understood him except
her. She had heard the outlines of his affair with Hannah,
but he had convinced her that it was all over now, and she
was not the girl to demand anything impossible of masculine
virtue before marriage. It had all happened before he knew
her. . . . She told herself that he would settle down nicely
when he was married. That sort always did; Mabel liked
a man to be a bit of a dog, as long as his dogginess was strictly
antenuptial. Besides, Robert's lapses were not so black in the
light of Bulverhythe street lamps as in the unenlightened
byways of the Rother Valley. After all, his were the small
sinnings of out-of-the-way public houses, small bets, small
debts, scandals of village sluts and tavern billiards. She
imagined that Bob would cut a poor figure in Leicester Square,
and with her superior knowledge of the world could afford to
smile at the shocked village which sought in its concern to
give her surreptitious warning. . . . "Now, if it ud been Hugh
Cousins, who was always up in London on the bust. . . ."

Having thus explained Bob morally, she would congratulate
herself on having engaged herself to a man of substance—
coming of an old family, too, as she told her friends. The
Fullers had been great people once, and had owned Bodingmares for hundreds of years. They didn't keep up much
style now, but people who were really well born could afford
to ignore appearances. She'd done better for herself than if
she'd taken Stanley Huggins. And Bob himself was rather
an old dear. She made up her mind to consider him as that,
and spoke of him in that way to Muriel and the others—it
seemed to suit him, since he was clumsy and rather stupid.
He jarred on her sometimes, but he was a good-looking, good-
hearted fellow, and she never regretted that she had taken
him—it was queer, but she didn't.

Robert, on his side, was pleased with Mabel. She had been
his refuge from a terror suddenly reinforced. Now that he
had her he could sometimes forget that he was lonely, and that

there were strange things prowling on his lonely way—dark shadows and queer lights that frightened his childish soul and sent it flying to substantial arms. He was glad he had asked her all of a sudden like that—though he hadn't meant to, not till he was running upstairs. She had been so tender and sweet when he had taken her in his arms; she had seemed changed and strong. And though she had never been quite the same since—after all, there had been no occasion—she had already given him a great deal of pleasure. She was a lovely little girl, with her soft, powdered skin and her fluffy hair and her dainty ways—not nearly a bad little kid. He liked taking her about; he liked people to see him with her; he liked Hannah to see him with her—not that Hannah ever had actually seen them together, but of course she must have heard. . . . She had left High Tilt now and gone off with Darius in their caravan to Rochester. . . . Oh, he was glad he had got Mabel, and he'd be good to her. He'd make her a fine husband; he'd hold her so close that she would shut out Hannah and her mournful shining, just as a penny will hide a star.

He was pleased, too, to find himself in favour with Jim and Mary and his mother—he would never have acknowledged that he valued their esteem, but he could not help being proud of it now that he had it again. Jim was behaving most generously in the matter of settlements; so, too, was Arthur Powlard. It had been decided that the young pair must be quite independent, and settle down on a small farm of their own. Mabel would have liked Robert to move townwards, but it was easy to see his unfitness for any kind of town life, and about this time a thirty-acre holding fell vacant near Bodiam. The house at Campany's Hatch was new, and could safely be called a villa by Mabel, while Jim inspected the land and the buildings and found them adequate. There were about ten acres of orchard and tillage, and the rest was marsh-land and grazing for sheep. Jim and Powlard agreed together to furnish and stock the farm, and the newly-married couple were to settle in at Michaelmas.

§ 33

The wedding took place at Bulverhythe, and was a grand town affair that frightened everybody except the town people. The reception was held in two palatial rooms at the Devonshire Hotel, and there was a crowd of guests—mostly Mabel's friends, shrill chattering girls, and arch young men who infuriated Robert by saying as they shook hands with the bride: "Wish you luck, Mabel, from a broken heart." The bridegroom's guests were inclined to knot together and gape at the rest of the company. Everyone was much impressed— the Fullers had done it this time. The bride wore a white satin dress and a lace veil, and there were bridesmaids with bouquets of carnations, and a wedding cake three tiers high, and real champagne that tickled the roof of your mouth and made you choke before you could swallow it.

Jim was best man, in a mood blent of triumph and embarrassment. Mary wore a new dress whose tight fit revealed a portly promise hitherto unsuspected, and made Pepper of Weights consider that there was still a way open for alliance with Bodingmares. Clem and Polly looked nearly as uncomfortable and pathetic as at their own wedding—Polly had covered her blue dress with a veiling of purple net, to make it seem like the new one she could not afford, and in the midst of the fashionable young ladies of Bulverhythe felt distrustful of the results that had appeared so marvellous before her little bedroom mirror and Clem's admiring gaze. Elizabeth looked young and alert beside her kind, silent husband, who seemed to add in that afternoon to the crowsfeet of critical humour that lengthened his eyes.

When the reception was over, and the newly-married pair had started for their honeymoon in the Isle of Wight, Bodingmares, Pookwell, and Marsh Quarter travelled back together to Salehurst.

"That wur a valiant wedding," said Jim, "summat fur us to remember all our days."

"Not that we'll disremember Clem's wedding, nuther," said Elizabeth, smiling at her younger son.

"Wot about your own, missus?" asked her husband.

"Maybe we haven't a-done wud weddings yit," said Elizabeth, with a sly glance at Mary. She had not failed to notice Pepper's behaviour that afternoon, and saw a chance of more match-making. But her step-daughter briskly disposed of the romance.

"Now, Mother, a-done do wud such silly talk. If you're thinking of that old Pepper wot you wudn't have yourself coming after me, you're larmentäable mistäaken, as is all I can say. He never looked at me till this afternoon, and then it wurn't me but my new body, as all cud see plain wot hadn't their eyes blinded by sediment; and as if I'd täake up wud a chap wot can't even tie his boot-laces in a decent knot. . . ."

"Bob looked middling fine in his new suit," said Clem; "you cudn't see whur the trousers wur altered."

"And Mabel!" cried Elizabeth. "Wurn't she wonderful in her veil!—just lik an angel."

"More lik a piece of cold fowl in the meat-safe," said Mary; "she wurn't looking her best."

"I never thought much of Mabel's looks," Polly felt encouraged to remark, "and she showed an unaccountable lot of her skin."

"You shut up," said her husband, good-naturedly; "you're fur ever talking back on your sister-law. Reckon Bob's showed his taste this time."

"Bob's done wonderful," said Jim, "really, when you think of wot he's done, and then of wot he might have done. . . . Well, it does mäake you think, that's all."

He leaned back in his seat, and his watch-chain expanded.

§ 34

Campany's Hatch stood far east of Salehurst and High Tilt, in the parish of Bodiam, close to where the Rother flows into the Kent Ditch below Ethnam. It consisted of a modern homestead, red-brick and rather gaunt, staring from a little bank into the drowsily flowing Rother, and a huddle of barns, mostly about a hundred years old, tile-roofed and tar-boarded. The Rother flowed past it through thick beds of reeds, and there always seemed to be a little wind moaning in the reeds and a queer moan on the water. Mabel heard it at nights, and sometimes she lay awake listening to it. It seemed part of the silence of the country night, which had awed and disturbed her when she came home after her honeymoon—a heavy silence, of which every creeping, sighing sound of night seemed an accentuation, just as the sprinkled stars seemed to accentuate the blackness of the country sky to eyes grown used to street lamps and the ruddy glow of a town.

The nights scared Mabel; they were so unlike the days. She had never imagined till then that the country held anything strange and terrifying. By daylight the fields looked dull and tame enough; she could see no beauty in them, nor in that stretch of marsh at the bottom of her garden, narrowing in the east as the hills of Sussex met the hills of Kent at the valley's turning, while the Rother drawled a sluggish stream between the reeds and pollards, with now and then a red sail upon it. "It's very ordinary country round here," she wrote to her friend Muriel, "flat and commonplace, as you might say, and everything so old. . . ."

How was it, then, that this ordinary, commonplace country put on by night so strange an air, making her feel an alien in a foreign land? Lying there in bed, in her flimsy, town-made night-gown, staring at the black, star-dazzled sky, listening to the sough of the reeds and the moan of the water as they wove themselves into the brooding, universal silence, she would feel strangely and terrifyingly lonely, a poor little exile from warm, lighted streets, adrift in the solitude of an unfriendly country. The common, homely fields seemed to take on a savage remoteness; the barns, with their familiar peaks and sprawls of roof, the woods that crept down to the marsh from Padgham on the other side of the valley, the familiar outline of Ewhurst Hill blocking itself against the stars, all held a dim threat of dislike and alienation. Even the man at her side, so familiar and commonplace to her now, by day her playfellow and companion and master, now seemed to take his part in the strangeness of it all, to lie a hundred miles remote from her, even though he touched her side. He belonged to this dark, unfriendly country, he was part of its clay; it had worked itself into him, his very skin smelt of its soil.

By day she laughed at herself for the fears of the night. The days were full of business and opportunity. She had not yet begun to find country life dull. She spent her mornings cleaning and dusting and cooking. Mabel was inordinately proud of her drawing-room (she reprimanded Robert smartly when he called it the parlour), of her tapestried suite and cretonne curtains and cottage piano. She loved dusting vases and ornaments that had been given her as wedding-presents, and she liked to lay her husband's dinner in the dining-room, and congratulated herself that she had already worked some improvement in his table manners.

The afternoons were less interesting than they ought to have been. Mabel did not go calling among her neighbours. One or two visits to other farms convinced her that they were a very common lot. She was disappointed that the better sort of people did not call; she had told herself that the villas and the vicarage would pay their tribute to Robert's ancient family. But the vicar did not call except as a vicar, and gave up doing even that after Robert had told him what he thought of the Established Church; the two maiden ladies from the cottage by the bridge never stopped their pony-carriage at Campany's gate, and Mrs. Simpson-Scott of Fowlbrook House actually seemed to think that she could have commercial dealings with Mrs. Robert Fuller while ignoring her socially, and came persistently to the farm for butter and eggs till at last she learned her mistake.

"We occasionally oblige friends," said Mabel loftily, "but we don't serve customers in the ordinary way."

Mrs. Simpson-Scott gaped at her, and that afternoon asked the vicar if he knew where on earth the new tenant of Campany's Hatch had picked up his wife.

Mabel saw that she was expected to frequent the society of ladies who wore aprons all the week, and on Sundays black capes trimmed with bugles and smelling strongly of camphor. She was expected to find relaxation in the gossip of stout, coarse-handed girls, who spoke of calves and chicken meal, and took hilarious delight in old American knockabout films if ever by some generosity or tenderness of the male they found themselves in the picture-house. She was indignant at this; she told herself that she had married a gentleman-farmer, and couldn't be expected to mix with people who made no claim to refinement. Not that her gentleman-farmer made any, but enjoyed himself with the husbands and fathers of the women she despised, though Mabel worked hard to bring him to a sense of his own greatness.

Her visits, then, were limited to the houses of her relations, and even here she found much to humiliate her. After all, Elizabeth was married to a country postman, and though the fact had not troubled Mabel as a friend it troubled her much as a daughter-in-law. As for Pookwell, it was a poor little place, and Clem and Polly were altogether common. They lived just like a labourer and his wife; she came in once to find Polly clearing up after Clem had had his bath in the kitchen. . . . No wonder Bob couldn't understand why he must never wash in the scullery sink. She didn't look down on them for being poor—oh, no, of course not; poverty was often quite refined—but they could have held their heads up and kept their hands clean, instead of sinking to the level of their surroundings.

Bodingmares was a little better. A second prosperous summer had resulted in new china and curtains, and Jim's good luck and success had won him respect as far as Bodiam. Mabel decided that she could safely call him a gentleman-farmer, and sometimes felt a little of his pride when he showed her his promising turnip crop, or his new steer, or spoke of the knowing and experienced cow-man who was coming to him from Churchsettle. Bodingmares was solid and reputable and flourishing, and inside it were the respectabilities of well-swept floors and clean sheets and copper pans. Of course there was much that offended—meals in the kitchen, and shirt sleeves, and farm men clumping in and out without any

realization of the gulf between them and their employers—
but on the whole Mabel approved of Bodingmares, and praised
it to her friends as "old-fashioned" and "quaint" and "really
a manor house, you know—belonged to the Fullers for hundreds of years."

So Bob's wife spent her days in small prides and small
efforts and small societies, and at night lay awake, chilled
and lonely, afraid of the darkness and silence of the country
in which she was a stranger.

§ 35

It never struck Clem and Polly to be jealous of Campany's
Hatch—at least, it never struck Clem, and if it struck Polly
she kept her own counsel. Robert had always been so much
the elder brother. . . . He had always had more money than
Clem, more freedom, more consideration, and now it seemed
only natural that he should be living independently on a nice
little holding, while Clem and his wife lived in a labourer's
four-roomed cottage and worked hard all day for others.
Besides, Mabel was a lady; not that Clem cared much for
ladies—the more he saw of Mabel the more thankful he was
that his own wife had no claim to such distinction—but he
would no more have thought of asking a lady to live in a
cottage like Pookwell, and scrub the floors, and wash her
husband's shirts and clean his boots, and chop her own wood,
than he would have thought of keeping a blood mare in a
farmhouse stall. She was a different breed of animal, and must
be fed and treated differently or she would go sick.

Mabel, on her side, did not think much of the married love
of Clem and Polly. He could not really love his wife, she
told herself, or he would not let her work for him as she did.
He did not even treat her with the consideration she had at
last trained Robert to show. He would sit in his shirt-sleeves
reading the paper, while she washed up the tea things, he
never opened the door for her, as she had so carefully taught
Robert to do, and he seemed to expect her to have his clothes
washed and mended, his house cleaned and his dinner cooked
all as a matter of course.

"Why don't you make your husband do that?" said Mabel one day when she found Polly chopping firewood.

"Clem's got his own work, surelye."

"But Robert would never let me chop wood. I might cut my fingers."

"Clem knows as I wöan't cut my fingers."

"But wood-cutting isn't woman's work. I should feel as if I was demeaning myself if I did it. That chopper's too heavy for you, and no wonder your hands are rough and hard if that's the way you use them."

"My hands are well enough," said Polly, beginning to be offended. "I'd sooner have an honest, working pair of hands than a pair of useless white 'uns," and her eyes rested for a moment on Mabel's.

"You mustn't mind my speaking," said her sister-in-law good-humouredly, "only I've got such good results out of training Bob that I thought you might find it worth while to try your hand with Clem. I never saw anything like the way husbands behave round here, expecting their wives to work for them from morning till night. I dare say it's just ignorance; they've never been taught how gentlemen ought to behave to ladies. But if one person is used to refined customs she can make a lot of difference in a place."

"I want no chäange, thanks," said Polly.

Mabel shrugged her shoulders, and they talked of other things till Clem came in, bawling cheerfully:

"Well, missus, whur's my tea?"

Certainly his behaviour as a husband was not up to genteel, town standards. He conformed to the traditions of the Rother Valley, where unselfish and devoted love was often hidden under superficial coarseness and indifference. But Polly, too, was the child of her neighbourhood and generation, and would not have had him changed. Indeed she would have been acutely embarrassed if he had sprung up to open the door for her, as Mabel expected a man to be always doing, or had taken to blacking his own boots or helping her with the sweeping and washing-up. He worked for her hard from morning till night, never allowed her to be put upon by his family, showed her consideration in all the fundamental things of their common life, where Mabel's standards would not have forbidden some tyranny; so she was glad that he should have his evening's rest, undisturbed by any domestic task, that he should enjoy his tub before the fire without undue qualms as to her trouble, and sit in his shirt-sleeves and smoke his pipe unrebuked by her refinement.

Both Polly and Clem were bitterly disappointed in her continued childlessness. Clem minded more for her sake than for his; after all, they had none too much to live on, and he was absolutely content with their present life together; but he knew how she had always loved children, how she had married him full of the hope of having a child. He had so often seen her with another woman's baby in her arms that it seemed cruel to think that she might never carry a baby of her own. At present he must be her child, and he submitted more and more to a maternal quality in her love, to a tender physical care for him, to something protecting and soothing in her caresses. She never complained or re-pined, and her acceptance woke him to a responsive sacrifice, so that he would often be clinging and gentle when he would have rather been passionate, putting the mother in her before the wife.

It could not fail to come as a pang to them both when they heard that Mabel was expecting a baby. She had now been married a little over a year, and she did not want a child.

"I don't like children," she said fretfully, "and I don't think I'm strong enough."

"You look middling strong, surelye," said Polly.

"Children mean trouble and expense, too; it seems a shame."

"I reckon Bob's pleased."

"Oh, Bob—of course he is. The trouble isn't his."

"But the expense is."

"He doesn't worry about that. As long as we've got enough for our clothes and to eat and drink and to keep the place going, he's satisfied. He never thinks of progress like me."

"Why, he wur telling Jim only last Wednesday as he'd a mind to buy them fifteen acres of snape wot are up at sale, ïf he does well with his oats this fall."

"That's not the sort of progress I mean; that's a very low idea. I want us to live in better style, with a servant—one who can wait at table. And now he goes and lands me with a child. I shall have to work harder than ever."

"Döan't vrother; he'll go on opening the door fur you, I reckon," said Polly maliciously.

§ 36

During the year that he had been married, Robert had seen very little of Hannah. She had come back to High Tilt on two or three occasions. Once Robert had met her, and had said "Good mornun', ma'am," in a very loud voice, and another time he had seen her in the distance, walking with Darius up Megrims Hill. But they had never done more than pass the time of day, they had had no conversation, and he did not know what she thought about his marriage.

Her occasional presence caused him no disquiet. His marriage had healed the wound in his pride; he could hold up his head; he had shown her that her power was broken. Moreover, High Tilt was five miles from Campany's Hatch; he did not run the continual risk of meeting her, and often, indeed, did not hear she was come till she was gone again. Besides, his marriage had worked a more sweeping change in his life than he had expected; it was not merely the intensification and domestication of an ordinary love affair. Mabel had a queer power over him, such as no other girl, not even Hannah had had in quite the same way. She ruled him through his comforts, and he paid her for all she did for him by doing what she wanted in small things. He obeyed her in trivial matters of fetching and carrying and lifting and opening— and his obedience was of necessity—while in bigger, more personal matters she submitted to his will.

On the whole he was happy. His farm interested him, and having been well started with stock and capital and experience.

had so far caused him little anxiety. He worked for himself
with a concentration he would never have worked for Jim;
besides, he no longer felt any temptation to go roving. His
instincts were satisfied, and he stuck to his fields with a faith-
fulness he had never shown to the fields of Bodingmares. His
interests were centred in that villainous red homestead and
its respectable barns; they no longer called him away from
his duties toward dim, unestablished desires. The unknown
adventure no longer piped to him from the horizon.

It was perhaps strange that he did not hear it call, for he
certainly had not yet caught it and brought it home. There
was no adventure about Campany's Hatch, no adventure about
Mabel—he had known all there was to know about either at
the end of a week. Not that Robert had ever consciously
gone hunting adventure. The call had always come through
a vague troubling of his senses, and he had run to obedience
no further than the nearest girl or public house . . . but even
that restless urge of his own manhood no longer drove him
now. It was satisfied and deaf. It had thickened and hardened above that depth of hungering sorrow which alone could
have answered the call from the horizon, as deep answers to
deep. His love for Hannah lay buried under the satisfaction
of his instincts by Mabel and Campany's Hatch. He told
himself that he loved Mabel—she was irritating at times, and
sharp words occasionally passed between them, but on the
whole she was a pretty, comfortable little kid, and his life
with her was like a drowsy rest after the storm of his life
with Hannah and the starving drought of his life alone.

At the beginning of their married life, when first he had
aroused her passions, Mabel asked him a great many questions about Hannah, as she had never done during the days
of their courtship. She seemed anxious to put her jealousy
to sleep, and with his help she had done so. He had assured
her that it was all over, that what he felt for Mabel was quite
different from what he had felt for Hannah—which was true,
though he would have told any number of lies to keep her
quiet. She had accepted his assurances, and soon all her
suspicions seemed to have passed. The gossip of High Tilt

did not travel, except in a diffused form, as far as Bodiam—Hannah's comings and goings were not known or watched. Mabel felt sure of her husband's love, and proud of him as he showed the results of her training in refinement.

But when she knew that her child was coming, a measure of this confidence seemed to go. The causes were, no doubt, partly physical, but also Mabel distrusted her husband because she no longer trusted her own looks. She told herself that she was "off colour," and did not expect Robert to care for her so much when she was looking ill as when she was looking well. She said it was a shame, and complained bitterly to her friend Muriel, since neither Polly nor Mary was sympathetic, and even Elizabeth could not understand how anyone could have Mabel's expectations without great joy.

Muriel agreed that it was a shame, and that men were all alike. She shared Mabel's disgust at the fact that her husband still spent many of his evenings at the King's Head, instead of sitting at home with her.

"The least he could do would be to give that up, and show me a little consideration now I'm so poorly."

"They're all the same," said Muriel.

"It's so lonely by myself—I get tired of sewing."

"Ma belle, if you'll excuse me, your mistake was ever letting him go out of an evening. A man has no right to spend his evenings in a public house once he's married."

"I couldn't stop him. Why, he was over at the King's Head only a fortnight after us coming here. He'd bad habits before he married, you know; but I must say I didn't expect him to keep them on. He says it's his only chance of getting to know the farmers round here, since I don't care for them always coming to the house."

"Does he ever see that woman he used to be so keen about?"

"No—of course not. Why do you ask? Who told you he was keen about any woman?"

"You did yourself, dear, when he was first after you. And there's been a lot of talk——"

"Not since he married!"

"No, no—but I was only thinking it was queer of him to be out so much. What does he do at the public house? I hope he isn't a drinking man."

"Oh, no—I can't say I've ever seen him the worse since we married, though he used to take a drop too much now and then before, I'm told."

"Then what does he do at the King's Head?"

"He meets the men, as I've told you. And he plays billiards and silly games like darts; and they have smoking concerts and meetings—Bob says he's going to join the Druids. Muriel, you don't really think as he's after anyone——"

"Of course not, ma belle. I only wondered why he went out such a lot, but now I quite see it's as you say, to meet the men. I'm sure he's faithful; he's got a faithful look about him . . . and it's only because men are all the same, so I couldn't help thinking—especially after all the tales there's been——"

"What tales? Not since we married?"

"No, I tell you—only the old ones. I've said again and again I'm sure he's all right. I believe, dear, you're getting fussy. You'd better not let him see—that ud be the very way to send him wrong."

But Mabel could not help letting him see. She was low and nervous, and Muriel's words took a morbid grip of her imagination. After all, it was very strange, Bob going out so much like that. She had always objected to it, but he would never alter his habits, even now when she was so ill and miserable. Of course there had been no question of any unfaithfulness during the first months after their marriage; she was quite sure that he had gone, as he had said, to meet the neighbouring farmers whom she did not like coming to the house. But now . . . now that she had lost her looks . . . now that she was tired and listless and—she acknowledged it, though she excused it—fretful? Perhaps he had taken up with someone else to while away the time till she was herself again—or perhaps he had gone back to that gipsy woman. This was worse to think of than the other; Mabel could have

borne an unknown rival better than a rival she had already
known the fear of. The thought preyed upon her, and she
was driven to voice it at last.

"Bob, do you ever see Hannah Iden now?"

He was reading the Sussex paper by the fire before going
out to his fields, and she had to repeat her words before they
reached him. He started a little.

"No, of course I döan't. Wot's määde you think of that
all of a suddint?"

"I dunno . . . it's your going out so often, and leaving
me."

He dropped his paper to his knee and gaped at her.

"But I only go räound to the King's Head—you said you
dudn't mind."

"No more I did till now—I feel so poorly. . . ."

Robert flushed. She was always spoiling with her frets
and lamentations his naïve delight in his approaching fatherhood. He could not understand why she was not as pleased
and expectant as he. But he answered her gently, for though
she vexed him, she appealed to his essentially male sense of
pity.

"I'm sorry you feel poorly, liddle creature. But I dudn't
know as you minded my going—I never stop läate, surelye."

"But the evenings are the only quiet time we have together."

"We have other times, and I only go wunst and agäun."

"You went three times last week."

"Well, we had the Farmers' Society's meeting, and wunst
it was the Druids, and t'other time I wanted to see Elphee
about them Portugal roots and thought I'd sääve myself the
trudge to Wassall."

"I don't really mind so long as you don't see Hannah."

"How can I see her? She äun't there fur me to see. She's
a score and a hundred miles away——"

His voice which had begun on a note of impatience ended
in quite a different key. He was conscious of it, and became
silent, biting his lips.

"Bob, you still care for her; I can hear it in your voice. . . ."

"I döan't care fur her; you mustn't be so foolish, kiddie, or you'll mäake me angry."

Her tears began to fall.

"I don't want to make you angry, Robert; I know you're telling me the truth. But I can't help worrying . . . you leave me such a lot . . . and I feel so ill——"

"You'd lik me to send fur a doctor?"

"No, no; there's nothing really wrong—only I'm tired . . . and lonely. . . ."

His annoyance melted into compassion, and he stretched out his arms to her. She came over to him, and leaned heavily against him, while her soft, scented hair trailed against his face, and her arms crept and tightened round his neck, holding his cheek against her cheek.

"I wöan't go out sinst you döan't lik it," he murmured. "I'll stop wud you sinst you're feeling ill."

"That's good of you, Bob; I knew you didn't understand how I felt, or you wouldn't have gone."

Her lips moved against his cheek, and he turned to her till her mouth was on his. Holding her close, all heavy with the burden of his child, he could for a moment forget how bittersweet she was, and stifle his longing for the other woman whose ghost she had called up.

§ 37

On a cold November day Robert was at Salehurst market, buying tegs. He had done so well with his marsh grazing that he felt tempted and able to add to his stock. A mellow satisfaction was upon him, which seemed to find its response in the yellow sunshine, gleaming on the lanes and on the drops of rain that hung from the twigs and thorns. The air was thick with a perfume of moist, trodden earth and sweet, rotten leaves. The cold had a stagnant quality about it; it seemed to hold all the country in a bath of chill sunshine.

No wind stirred; here and there a crimson leaf hung motion-less on the brambles, while the tufts of straw swept from passing carts by overhanging branches were unfluttered by any breeze.

Robert did his business more quickly than he had expected. He bought twenty black-faced tegs off a farmer from Iden Green and arranged for them to be taken to Campany's by his shepherd. They then went into the Eight Bells to have a drink. The bar was very full, and elbows were jostled while greetings were shouted over shoulders—as Boorman of Copt Hall caught sight of Pix of Little London, or Willard of Boarsney hailed the farmer from Gablehook, or the sunken squire from Harlakenden, who went to market with his own beasts, passed the time of day with Scales Crouch of Mount-pumps or Darwell Hole. It was a great gathering of farmers and cattle-dealers, and Robert soon parted from his first companion. He was glad to meet on his new footing of re-spectability and small prosperity the yeomen who had de-spised him in his unsettled days. He had a drink with Shovell and a drink with Pont, then suddenly he noticed that Darius Ripley had come into the bar.

It gave him a shock. He had not thought that Darius was in the neighbourhood, and none of the gipsies had been at the market. If Darius was here, Hannah could not be far off; anyhow, no further than Blindgrooms. Robert felt his heart turn sick; he had thought her four-score miles away, beyond Chichester, and here she must be quite close to him, per-haps at the very door. He nodded to Darius, who nodded and grinned to him.

The next minute he found himself growing restless. The bar, with all the broad backs and the broad vowels slurring from mouth to mouth, with the kindly reek of beer and fog of pipes, had become inexpressibly stuffy and tedious. He made some inane remark to Pont and Shovell, and edged away from them towards Darius.

"Good day," he said.

"Good day," said the gipsy.

"I dudn't know as you wur in these parts. Are you here to sell horses?"

"Are you here to buy one?"

"I äun't. But I know your game, surelye. You've a string of cobs at the back of this pub, I reckon."

"I've brought some good little gryes over from Hampshire, strong as any of your overgrown draymen in these parts. Would you like to look at 'em?"

"No. Is Hannah here?"

"She is outside this very same public-house. She could not come in because of the baby."

"The baby!"

"Yes, we have a fine brat—a Christian brat, called Gwendolen Aurora. . . . Good day, Mr. Beatup—yes, I've got some nice little nags in the square. . . ."

Robert was jostled away. He looked over the men's heads at the open door, then suddenly made for it. He knew that if he stopped to think he would stay where he was, so he didn't think.

He could see no one outside. He stood for a minute in the open doorway looking out into the street, where the wan sunshine lay spilt among the shadows of the gables, then a movement at his side made him turn his head, and he saw Hannah quite close to him, leaning up against the wall. She stood queerly motionless, a wrapped, brown figure, carrying her baby in her shawl, with the dead leaves drifted up round her feet. Her eyes were fixed upon him, and for a moment neither of them spoke.

Then he said "Good day" to her, as he had said it to her husband. She answered "Good day."

"Aun't you cold standing outside?"

She shook her head.

"I mustn't come in because of this little one. It is the law."

He had come close to her and stood staring at the baby. It was a very small baby, brown and wrinkled. It struck him that it looked more intensely "furrin" than either its father or its mother. On its wrist was a tiny bracelet, which accentuated this foreign look.

"How old is it?" he asked mechanically.

"Close on four months."

He could see her hand under the baby's body, and there was something strained and tender about it, something which spoke of a quality in Hannah which he had never been allowed to see. His gaze travelled slowly up from the baby to the mother's breast, and then rested fearfully on her face. . . .

His heart throbbed so loud that it seemed as if she must hear it. But he did not speak. He felt for a moment urged to voice his feeling, his longing for her a hundredfold increased now that he saw that she would have loved his child. But he kept silent partly out of hopelessness, out of the knowledge that she belonged to another man and to this child in her arms, partly out of what was not so much loyalty as acceptance of the fact that he belonged to another woman and to a child that was yet unborn.

He suddenly became aware that Darius Ripley stood behind them. One or two people had come out while he talked to Hannah, but his back had been turned and he had noticed no one.

"She's a fine brat, ain't she?" said Darius.

"Valiant," said Robert.

"Do you think she's like me or like her mother?"

"More like you, maybe," for the baby's smallness suggested rather the little husband than the wife, who was a large woman for her race—though by its face it would seem the child of neither, but some dim ancestor of them both.

"I'll take her now," said Darius, "and you can go and have a drink, my dear."

"Thank you, Darius," said Hannah graciously. "I will go in if Mr. Robert Fuller will go with me. I do not like going alone into rough company."

Robert took her into the bar and stood her a glass of six ale and some stout. He saw the farmers staring at him curiously, and that they spoke in each other's ears. But he did not care about appearances—his whole being was concentrated on savouring his few moments with Hannah. He did not speak, but stood staring at her while she drank her liquor, his own glass on the counter untasted.

"Well, I can't say as you're lively company," said Hannah as she went out, wiping her mouth on her shawl. "But I thanks you kindly for the refreshment. And now Darius and me must be moving on, for we have business in this place."

"Good-bye," said Robert sheepishly, looking at the ground.

"Good-bye, Mr. Robert Fuller, and pleased to have met you."

They went off up the street towards the market-place, and he set out for Bodingmares. He felt curiously tired, and when the farmhouse dinner was set he experienced a quite unprecedented distaste for food. Jim rallied him briskly, and Mary chose to be affronted, saying she knew that the beef-steak pie was a bit underdone, but not so much that he need grumble, and she was sure Mabel's pies must often go wrong in that oven, which wanted an extra brick as she'd told her a dunnamany times. He received their reproaches in silence, and struck them as unusually heavy and stupid. They came to the conclusion that he must have had a drop too much, just enough to make him sleepy.

He rode off in the early afternoon. The sky had cleared and pale lakes of shallow blue were spread round the sun, and seemed to be reflected in the light, giving the surface of the lanes, the roofs of the barns, the autumn patchwork of the fields a strange aqueous quality, as of the floor of a clear, shallow pond. Robert took the road that goes up from the Rother by Salehurst church, and then past Bantony and Churchsettle to Haiselman's Farm, Prawl's Farm and Bodiam. He went slowly, his mind thrown into a clear, sorrowful trance by the rhythmic movements of the horse under him, the clop and suck of hoofs in the thin mire that scummed the lane, and the creak of saddle-leather.

His memories grew in the pale light—sharp, regretful things on which the tears hung like rain on thorns. They were memories of this lane, of walks in it long ago, when, with his arm round her waist and her head against his shoulder, they had wandered up Silver Hill in the reddening twilight of the young moon, or had seen the brownish gleam of the harvest fields beyond the hedge, while the dusk slowly dredged the earth of light and spilt it in glowing sparks about the sky. He could feel her breath on his cheek, feel the warmth of her against his arm thrust under her shawl, and hear her loving words that were so few.

His thoughts of her seemed to swim in the watery sunshine of October; they were part of the autumn decay, of the memories of summer. . . . He wished he had not seen her standing there, with the dead leaves drifted up round her feet. She was gone, gone—she would never be beautiful and warm and loving for him again. . . . He must forget her—he had forgotten her—he had married a wife, he had begotten a child, he had established a house—then why had she come back? She was only a ghost. . . .

Suddenly he heard himself hailed.

"Hello, Mus' Fuller."

It was Elphee of Wassall and Crouch of Ethnam, both casual comrades of the King's Head, now on their way home from Salehurst in Elphee's gig.

"Never saw you at the market."

"I wur up in the square by the station."

"Did any business?"

"Bought a dozen tegs off Virgo."

"Bad day fur sheep, I thought."

"Tedious."

"You look as if you had a bit of a cold."

"I mun have caught cold, surelye. I feel all bunged up."

"Come and have a drink at the Red Lion—thur's naun lik a whisky fur kipping the cold out."

They were now close to the inn at the throws by High Wigsell. Robert would have been glad to get rid of his companions, but the next moment he reflected that a little cheerful society and a drink or two might keep out something beside the cold. There were still two miles to Campany's Hatch, and if they were to be anything like the first three . . .

§ 38

By the time he reached home he felt altogether jollier and better. He had had three drinks, and had talked a great deal about tegs and wethers and the price of wheat and the chances of tariff reform. Hannah's image had become fogged in his memory, and he had told himself several times that "wot wur done wur finished." As he rode up the farmstead drive in the thick sunless dusk his heart began to go out towards Mabel. It would be good to hold her in his arms again . . . after all, she was what he had got, while Hannah was only what another man had got. . . .

He found her waiting in the dining-room, where tea was laid. She had not yet lit the lamp, and her hair sprayed a queer golden light into the dusk; her face looked whiter and rather hollow.

"Hallo, my duck." He clasped her to him rather boisterously, and she pushed him off.

"Why are you so late?"

"Dudn't know as I wur lääte——"

"It's past five, and you promised me to come home directly after dinner. I've been waiting for you. Where have you been?"

"I'm sorry, kid." Once more his arm went out to take her, but she edged away.

"Sit down and have your tea—the kettle's boiling."

He sat down—obedient as she had made him in small things.

"Where have you been all this time?" she repeated.

"I wur up at the market, and bought a dozen good tegs off Virgo of Iden Green—then I went and had dinner."

"But that shouldn't have made you as late as this."

"I fell in wud Elphee and Crouch on the way höame, and we went into the Red Lion and had a whisky."

"Yes, you smell of whisky."

He felt vexed at her shrewishness—was this the way she received her husband after a daylong absence? Then he remembered that she was feeling poorly, and that perhaps she had fretted and grown anxious about him. He put out his hand and fondled her.

"Don't go pawing me at meals, Robert. I've told you it isn't manners. You haven't said anything about the market. How's Jim and Mary?"

He told her. It seemed to him that she looked very helpless and haggard. Was she going to be ill? Had anything gone wrong?

"You're looking unaccountable poorly, duck. Has anything upset you?"

"No, no. I feel perfectly well. Whom did you speak to at Salehurst?"

"Oh, Shovell and Cox and Pont and Willard."

"No one else?"

"Not that I remember, unless it wur Ebony."

"You liar!"

The words came in a low voice from between lips that seemed suddenly white and thin. Robert gaped at her.

"You liar!" she repeated, clenching her hands upon the table.

"W-wot d'you mean?"

"What I say. You're telling me a pack of lies. You saw Hannah Ripley at Salehurst market. You were seen speaking to her outside the Eight Bells."

"Well, wot of it?"

"What of it?—that's good. You'll make out as there was nothing in it, I suppose. Why did you tell me all those lies if there was nothing in it?"

"Thur wur nothing in it."

"Oh, you horrid liar!"

"Shut up. You stop calling me näames. I've a right to spik to whom I please."

"And then tell me lies about it."

"You'll drive me silly wud your lies. I don't tell more'n you."

"That's right—abuse me. You're in a temper because you're found out. You didn't think that you'd be seen and the news

taken to me. Now everyone ull laugh at me and say as my
husband's gone back to his——"

"Be quiet!" he thundered.

"But it's true," she whined. "You wouldn't have told me
you'd never met her if there'd been no harm in your meeting."

"I swear there was no harm."

"Then why did you tell me you hadn't seen her?"

"I dudn't tell you I hadn't seen her."

"You did."

"I dudn't."

"You did." She began to cry.

It was their first real quarrel. They had had bickerings,
but these had never worked up into anything serious. Now
the weather was definitely set for storms—Mabel was in a
morbid, depressed condition, anxious, strained and jealous,
while Robert was reacting from a day of shock and trouble,
imperfectly buried under three whiskies. This time her tears
did not touch him, as they had hitherto never failed to do;
they seemed to come so easily compared with his own.

"Adone-do wud your crying—it äun't no use. You're naun
but a cross-grained, tedious, jealous woman."

"And what sort of a man are you? . . . going about with
other women . . . while I have to keep at home . . . because
of your child that's coming."

Robert's fist came down with a crash upon the table, so
that the tea-things rattled and the cooling tea swished in the
cups. Mabel's eyes jerked suddenly wide and dry.

"Shut your mouth," he roared at her, "sinst you can't open
it except to spik lies. 'Go wud other women!' Oh, my Lord,
I've stuck to you better'n you deserve . . . I who went no
nearer another woman than to look at her baby."

His face twisted and his eyes filled with tears. Surely
he wasn't going to cry—no, not before Mabel . . . it was
that sudden picture of Hannah that had come—standing outside the door.

Mabel rose scornfully to her feet.

"I believe you're drunk—you've been drinking with that
creature. I'm not going to stop and listen to you any longer.

You're a beastly cad, and I shan't speak to you again till you explain and apologize."

"I've bin explaining ever sinst we started tea."

"Till you explain truthfully," she enlarged, and walked out of the room.

Something in her manner, contemptuous and disbelieving, exasperated him to fury. At least she should lose her self-respect as well as he. He sprang after her as she was shutting the door, wrenching it out of her hand. His flushed face and breath smelling of spirits gave her a sudden sense of terror. She ran down the passage and upstairs into her bedroom, locking the door in his face.

§ 39

For some moments Robert stood outside on the landing and exhausted his not very large vocabulary of abuse. Mabel maintained her maddening superiority of silence, and Bob was on the verge of kicking the door open and humbling her by physical force when a loud knocking sounded below. He was not so far gone as to be insensible of witnesses, and, smothering his feelings, went down to open the door.

It was a young fellow from Eyelid Farm, called with a bag of sharps, and all a-grin.

"Fine evening, äun't it—Missus well?"

"Middling well."

"I heard you talking as I cäum aräound—that's two shillun chäange, äun't it?"

"That's it. Good night."

"Good night."

Still grinning, the youth walked off. Robert stared after him with blackness in his soul.

"If I stay any longer in this house, I'll murder her."

He rammed on his cap and went out. The cool air was pleasant on his hot face . . . his face felt very hot and puffy; he wondered if it was true what Mabel had said and that he really was a bit on, as they say. He'd only had three small whiskies, but on a nearly empty stomach, and he had

been so terribly upset. . . . No, he didn't think he was drunk
—anyhow, the liquor was not in his legs, he could walk
straight, and he could see straight, too. He was only a bit
excited. It was that Mabel, that wretched girl—there was
something altogether goading and maddening about her; her
tears, her silence, her reproaches, her lies, had all been equally
exasperating.

He went into the King's Head. It was about half a mile
from Campany's Hatch, and seemed his best refuge at present.
He wasn't going back to Mabel; if he came within a yard
of her now he'd lay violent hands on her, and there would
be a row. This was worse than being alone . . . he'd have
been better off if he hadn't married her. For the first time
since his marriage, he had a definite reaction of regret, a
sudden longing for his free days, even though they had been
consumed by unsatisfied love. He still loved and was still
unsatisfied, and had into the bargain a spiteful yokefellow
who watched for his stumblings. Drat her! She was a bitch
—as he'd told her, as the farmer's son from Eyelid had heard
him tell her. Oh, damn!

He sat sulkily drinking a glass of gin and water. There
were one or two men in the bar, who passed remarks about
the weather and the crops, or asked him if he had done good
business at Salehurst market. But he did not feel inclined
to be sociable. He wondered who it was who had told Mabel
about his meeting Hannah, and exactly how much, or how
much more, he had told her. It was an added bitterness to
realize that he wished her accusations had been well-founded
instead of being just the jealous ravings of a woman who knew
nothing about the matter; who did not know that Hannah
could never be his, that she did not care twopence for him,
though he cared the world for her, that his love for her was
merely a hopeless aching, a hunger that could never be satisfied.

He had two more glasses of gin and water. They kept the
cold out—out of his heart. But drinking did not improve
his temper. The bar began to fill up as the hour grew later—
farmers and smallholders from the neighbourhood came in

for an evening glass and greeted him neighbourly. His answers grew surly and short; he did not want anyone to speak to him, and he felt that everybody must know that he had had words with Mabel—that boy from Eyelid must have told them. It was all crumbling—the illusion of his marriage and his respectability . . . the farmer of Campany's Hatch, a steady, go-ahead young chap with a pretty wife . . . seen making love to a gipsy outside the Eight Bells, and then heard calling his wife a bitch and threatening to break open her door. . . .

It was not like him to sit drinking in a corner by himself.

"Mus' Fuller döan't look lik a man wot's just bought a good lot of tegs," said Comfort of Lossenham; "found the itch in 'em, mäaster, now you've got 'em höame?"

"Wot d'you mean by that?" Robert's fist clenched menacingly on the table.

"Mean? Naun but wot I say, surelye."

The man looked surprised. "Wot's upset Fuller?" he asked Burch of Lomas.

"I dunno; he's got a sore head to-night. . . . Maybe a glass too much."

Robert caught the last words.

"That's it—you go abusing me. You may say I'm drunk. I äun't drunk. I'm sober."

"Surelye, Mus' Fuller, surelye," said Burch, anxious to keep the peace.

"Then wot fur dud you say as I wur drunk?"

"I never said as you wur drunk."

"You dud—I heard you. I know as you all talk bad of me, and say as I row my missus and go wud the gipsies. I know it."

"Mus' Fuller——"

The grave, respectable heart of the yeoman of Lomas was deeply grieved by such conduct in his favourite bar. Robert looked ready to fight anyone. The two farmers edged away from the table.

"It's true wot he's saying," said a young man who had just come in; "he's had a row wud his missus. Pilbeam of

Eyelid wur räound at Campany's and heard him hollering at her summat tar'ble."

"Dear, dear," said Comfort, glancing back at Robert, who to prove his sobriety had ordered a whisky.

"He shudn't ought to have no more to drink," said Burch in an undertone to the landlord; "he's had too much as it is. Maybe he'll go back and wallop her."

"I've never seen him the wuss for liquor," said the landlord, "though I'm told as he often got tight over in High Tilt. It's a shäame as he shud go to pieces all lik this. I wäonder whose fault it wur."

"Hers," said Comfort; "she's a minx."

"He äun't got a dove's temper nuther, I'll warrant. He sims unaccountable black to-night. And I döan't lik that swelled look he's got."

"I'll tell Daisy not to sarve him agäun," said the landlord.

"He'll mäake a row."

"Let him. I've my licence to think of, surelye."

So when Robert's glass came up again to the counter he was told that he had had enough for to-night.

"You're meaning I'm drunk?"

"I never said so. Only you döan't look well, and the liquor döan't act präaper in you."

"I'll drink wot I order and pay for."

"You'll drink no more in my public to-night. Come now, Mus' Fuller, pull yourself together and go home. If you've had a liddle tiff wud your wife you'll mäake it up better sober."

"Who says I've had a tiff wud my wife?"

"No one's said it."

"You said it, and it's a hemmed lie."

"Well, well, I beg your pardon—only you git off höame, Mus' Fuller. You äun't yourself to-night. Maybe one of these gentlemen ull see you part of the way."

"Whosumdever tries to go wud me, I'll land him one in the guts."

"Nobody ull go wud you—only be off!" The landlord was losing his temper.

Robert stood up and walked shakily towards the door. He had suddenly discovered that he had a violent headache and felt very sick. He would like a breath of fresh air.

"Mark you, I äun't a-going because of you," he said thickly.

Nobody said a word. The decent farmers round Bodiam were shocked at such behaviour from one of their number. Of course Robert Fuller had come into the neighbourhood with a tail of doubtful history behind him, but he had always behaved respectably, and though not exactly an engaging chap, had been on friendly terms with most of them. He belonged to the Druids and the Farmers' Club. . . . No one had ever dreamed of seeing him like this.

"I'm sorry fur his poor missus," a young man—the son of the tenant of Linkhill—whispered behind his hand.

The next minute he lay on the floor, with the blood pouring from his nose.

There was a muddle of cries and comments: "Shäame! shäame!" "Catch hold of un," "Fetch the police," "No, no, chuck him out!" "Put him in the road."

Robert lashed out furiously, but numbers overpowered him. He felt a blow on his cheek, just under his eye, and staggered. Then he found himself gripped by the scruff and elbows and ignominiously run out of the bar. A violent push sent him staggering across the road, and the door slammed to behind him.

For a moment he stood in the square of yellow light that came from under the taproom blind, and shook his fist and cursed. He did not know what he said, he was senseless with fury and drink. Then he turned and walked away. He did not care where he was going . . . he was going to Hannah . . . he did not know where he was going . . . the road seemed to pour under his feet in a grey stream, the hedges rose and fell like waves . . . lights came and glared in his eyes . . . a trotting horse, and cries of "Can't you see whur you're going?" No, he couldn't see . . . he stood for a moment and cursed them after they had gone by. Then he went on again . . . the road still slipped and flowed under his feet . . . he must be walking on water . . . like Peter walking to Christ . . . oh! his head suddenly crashed into something hard and solid in his way. He fell, and the last of his muddled consciousness went up in a blaze of light, followed by darkness.

§ 40

"I have loved thee with an everlasting love, therefore with loving kindness have I drawn thee."

The words were written in black letters on a clean sheet of paper that was nailed into his forehead. They were written in darkness on light. They were written in light on darkness. They burnt him up; he was a little cinder and he smouldered in them. Oh, how it hurt! . . . I am tormented in this flame. It is the love of God. I am a little cinder burning in it. Oh, oh, oh, how it hurts! . . .

"I have loved thee with an everlasting love, therefore with loving kindness have I drawn thee."

That was odd—for it was all quite natural, really—just a text hanging on the wall, and his eyes were open, staring at it. He had thought those words were inside him—that he was inside them—and all the time they were only hanging on the wall. It was a text—he might have known it—and quite a pretty text, too, with a robin in the corner, and some yellow flowers. He did not know they had a text in the house. He could not remember, his head ached so . . . and it must be nearly time to get up . . . he must pull himself together. Where was Mabel? She had got up already—he could hear her moving about in the room. . . . But that wasn't their room, it was quite different—different furniture and different paper on the walls. Where on earth had he got to?

"Mabel!"

"Bob!"

His name came in accents of tearful and relieved surprise. The next moment she was at the foot of the bed, between him and the text. Her hair was untidy, and her face marked with tears.

"Wot's happened?" he asked feebly.

"Don't worry, Bob. It's all right now."

"My head aches."

"I expect it does." There was an inflection in her voice which irritated some sleeping memory. He awoke still further.

"Whur am I? This äun't höame. Whur have you täaken me?"

"I haven't taken you anywhere. Don't get excited. The doctor said you were to keep quiet."

"The doctor? Then I've bin ill?"

"I should think you had."

"How long?"

"Nearly two days now."

"Am I in hospital?"

"No, you're in a private house. A gentleman found you lying in the road."

"Lying in the road? How on earth did I get into the road?"

"Come, Bob, you're kidding me. You must remember."

"I döan't remember naun."

"You don't remember going to the King's Head?"

"I've bin to the King's Head a dunnamany times. I döan't recall naun special about it."

Mabel looked at him carefully.

"They say you had too much to drink."

Robert's sensations bore out this verdict. But why should he have got drunk all of a sudden after keeping sober for two years? . . . He saw a picture—a curtain seemed to be pulled back far away at the back of his mind and showed him a queer little picture like a dream, of Hannah Iden standing outside the door of a public-house, wrapped in a brown shawl and carrying a baby . . . rays of light flowed out of the picture, lighting up dim corners, showing him things he had forgotten. He saw himself having tea with Mabel in the dining-room, with a queer dusk lighting up the cups and plates and her face that was haggard and angry . . . then he found himself on the landing outside her door, shouting abuse at her, wanting to hurt her . . . then he could not remember any more, and he didn't want to. He turned his head on the pillow and groaned.

"Go to sleep," said Mabel.

"But I want to know whur I am."

"I've told you. You're in a gentleman's house, in Goudhurst."

"Goudhurst! That's a hem far away. Wotsumdever did he bring me there fur?"

"He found you in the road at the bottom of Megrims Hill —you'd hit your head against a telegraph post. He brought you on to Goudhurst because he didn't know where you belonged, and he's some sort of a minister here."

"Wot's his näame?"

"The Reverend Beeman. He's got a nice house, and you're lucky."

"How dud you find me?"

Mabel became tearful.

"I had an awful night, with you gone off like that, and me not knowing what had become of you, and poorly as I was . . . it might have been bad for me. But early the next morning Mr. Crouch came round and said that the postman had heard a man had been picked up on the Sandhurst road and taken to Goudhurst, so I hired a motor-car from the inn —it cost me a pound."

Robert could not remember—and certainly did not want to remember—the extent of his misdoings. But a large, vague sense of guilt lay heavily and indefinitely on him, and he murmured:

"I'm sorry, Mabel."

§ 41

After that he slept for a little, and when he woke he could hear a man's voice in the room. It was a deep heavy voice, with a curious emphasis about it, as if every word were weighted with the speaker's dignity. "Yes," it said, "the blind—the cord is broken—perhaps a nail would be of use." Somehow the remark took on a deep significance, the silence trembled with it. Robert lifted himself on his elbow and looked round, but the speaker was standing right behind him,

and he could see no one. The movement caused him acute
pain in his head, and he fell back with a groan.

"Ah," said the voice, and a creaking footstep came solemnly
to the bedside.

Robert looked up and saw an elderly man with white hair
falling from a bald crown almost to his shoulders. He had
a large, heavy face, curiously unwrinkled for his age, with a
high pinkish colour on the cheeks. A little white bow was
tied under his chin, and he wore a careful suit of black clothes,
with a silver watch-chain across his waistcoat.

"Ah," he repeated with gathering emphasis, "so you are
awake."

"I äun't got the chanst of being much else wud all the
noise in the room," said Bob sulkily, for the pain had made
him cross.

The gentleman raised his eyebrows, or rather the part of
his forehead where they should have been. Then, having
conveyed rebuke, he proceeded:

"The blind is flapping, I fear. The cord is broken, but I
was telling your wife that a nail might be of use. Should you
object to the noise of one being driven in?"

"I döan't care," said Robert wearily, "reckon I've a middling beast of a headache."

"Do not repine, my friend. You 'ave deep cause for
thankfulness. If the Lord 'ad not guided my feet—or rather,
the hooves of my horse, since I was in my phaeton—to where
you lay abandoned—abandoned"—he repeated the word twice,
as if to emphasize both its literal and spiritual meaning—
"you might now be standing before your Judge instead of lying
in a comfortable bed in a Christian 'ouse."

He had spoken with just the same weight and solemnity
of the blind, but neither this nor his occasional difficulty
with his aitches could take away from the effect of his words
on Robert. The young man felt impressed, almost afraid—
as if he could really see his soul standing naked and abandoned
before his Maker.

"Reckon I'm grateful fur wot you've done, sir," he mumbled
sheepishly.

"I 'ave done nothing," thundered the old fellow, "but the Lord 'as done all. I am but His unworthy instrument. I am"—his voice dropped to an emphatic whisper—"a worm. And"—swelling again to thunder—"so are you."

Robert felt like it.

"We are both worms," continued the preacher with feeling; "we are all worms"— and his glance extended to include a resentful Mabel—"it is only through the goodness of the Lord that we stand upon our legs and call ourselves men. Those whom the Lord has justified may indeed call themselves men, but those whom He 'as not"—and his bright, childlike eye fixed itself upon Robert—"are nothing but worms, miserable worms wriggling in a ditch."

"Adone do wud talking of worms—you'll mäake me see 'em in a minnut."

"Doubtless. Such a state is, I believe, common to those of intemperate 'abits. But I want you when you see them to remember that you *are* one, and then the Lord's chastisement will not be wasted on you."

"I äun't got intemperate habits, as you say. . . ."

"My friend——!"

The preacher lifted one thick white hand, and the gesture, with a mournful smile, disposed of the lie.

"I äun't bin drunk for more'n two years," continued Robert aggressively.

"Shut up, Robert," said Mabel. "I'm ashamed of you."

"When I found you in the ditch," continued Mr. Beeman, "you were what is termed Blind Drunk."

"Well, I döan't remember naun about it."

"We will not discuss the subject further, since it is leading you deeper into your sins. I will only remind you that without are the dogs, and whosoever loveth or maketh a lie."

He turned impressively on his heel and went out. Robert lay and sulked for a bit. He was angry with Mabel for having taken the other's part against him.

"You might have stood by me, anyways—you're my wife."

"Well, that's cool—after the way you've treated me."

Robert wished he could remember how he had treated her.

Had he done something inconceivably dreadful? But that fragment of the past was lost, and he did not dare carry his questions very far in case they led to some awful revelation. So he said no more. A few minutes later a kind-looking woman of the servant class brought him a beaten-up egg in some milk, and Mabel went down to have her supper. Before she left him she asked him if he would like a book to look at while she was away, and Robert, who felt better and rather restless, said he would. There were four books on the dressing-table, but Mabel said they all looked very dull. Only one had pictures in it, and that was a Bible. The others were just sermons and a book of hymns.

Robert said he would have the Bible. He had always liked the Bible, though sometimes it scared him horribly, and pictures would make it still more interesting. Mabel handed it to him unwillingly—she thought it rather "soft" for a man to read the Bible, and was secretly alarmed by a tendency she sometimes found in her husband to be unashamed in matters of religion. Her prejudices were confirmed when she came back and found him sitting up in bed, with his elbows on the open Bible on his knees, and his fingers thrusting wildly about in his hair, while his blue eyes stuck out with horror. When she came up to him, he seized her hand:

"Mabel, it's tar'ble—look!"

On his knees was a picture of a falling city, all toppling and black and burning. Huge towers leaned this way and that, while flames shot out of the alleys and rose as high as the towers. Fire rained down from a black and thundering sky, while, lit up by the glare of the flames and the lightning, little knots of people ran about in confusion, stumbling in the cinders and fallen stones.

"It's hell," said Robert in a crushed voice.

"Well, what of it? It's only a picture."

"I never knew as it wur lik that."

"Don't be so silly. I've told you it's only a picture."

"But look wot's written, surelye."

Underneath the picture was printed in old-fashioned copper-plate:

"And without are the dogs, and the whoremongers and the idolators, and whosoever loveth and maketh a lie."

"Them's the very wards wot the Reverend used to me," said Robert.

Mabel caught the book away impatiently.

"And you mean to tell me you've sat gaping at that ever since I left you?"

"I opened the book anyhows, and it opened thur. Reckon them wards are fur me."

"Really, Bob, you're getting soft. You've had a knock on the head, so maybe it isn't your fault, but I must say that the ideas you get hold of sometimes make me wonder if you're half the man you look."

"You döan't understand."

"I dare say I don't. I was always brought up to keep religion in its proper place. If you're frightened of going to hell the best thing you can do is to behave decent, and give up drinking and telling lies."

"I don't drink and I don't tell lies."

"Give over, Bob, or you and me ull quarrel—and here comes Mr. Beeman."

The minister entered the room with an embracing smile, which Mabel returned in a chastened fashion. But Bob was too shaken and upset for any disguise. He had found Mabel singularly uncomforting, and turned eagerly to the man who, he thought, would be fitted by his life and vocation to re-assure him.

"I've had a präaper scare wud your Bible, sir, and I can't git it out of my head."

"I pray that you never may get it out of your head," said the Pastor benignly.

"Don't worry the gentleman, Bob," said Mabel with a cross nudge. But Robert was desperate.

"There wur a picture of hell," he continued, "and underneath it said wot you said to me—'wudout are the dogs and whosumdever mäakes a lie.' Not but wot I wur telling you the gospel truth when I said as I dudn't remember naun of wot happened before I got here."

"You need not seek to justify yourself, for there is One above that justifieth. My friend, I've not the slightest doubt that you were Led to see that picture and read those words, so that you might flee from the Wrath to Come."

There was a gleam in the old fellow's eye, and even his ponderous voice hurried and danced a little.

"I döan't want to go to hell," whined Robert.

"I tell him not to worry," broke in Mabel, "but to live decent and stop getting drunk and telling me lies about people he meets and says he doesn't—and then he'll be all right."

"But 'e will *not* be 'all right,' " and Mr. Beeman's voice became almost musical with triumph. "Do not think, my friend, to save your soul by the dead works of the legal conscience. You must put on Salvation—for the Just shall live by Faith."

"But how am I to do that? I'd do it lik a shot if I knew how."

"You will know in His appointed time, if it is His will to justify you. So far He has granted you one mercy—a sense of His wrath. You are afraid of hell, and rightly afraid. I will put up a prayer for you."

To Mabel's horror he knelt down by the bed and offered up a longish prayer, in which he asked that the heart of this poor sinner might be further moved and finally accepted. "Since Thou hast mercy on whom Thou wilt have mercy and whom Thou wilt Thou hardenest."

For some reason or other Robert felt a little comforted, and as he opened his eyes, which he had shut of custom while the minister prayed, he saw the text on the opposite wall.

" 'I have loved thee wud an everlasting love'—then maybe He wöan't send me to hell fur all that I've bin so bad."

"My friend, don't count on that. Those words are for the Elect. Whom He predestinates He justifies, and whom He justifies He also glorifies. Them indeed 'as He loved with an everlasting love."

"But couldn't He predestinate me?"

"Certainly He could, and I shall pray continually that He will."

"But if He döan't . . . shall I have to go to hell?"

"Ah, poor sinner, who are we worms to pry into the councils of the Almighty? The Scripture says that He has appointed some to honour and some to dishonour. We must trust 'is 'oly Word. And now I will wish you good night. I trust, Mrs. Fuller, that you 'ave all that is necessary for your comfort. If the blind should flap, I think that a nail would be of use. Good night."

§ 42

Neither Robert nor Mabel slept very well. Robert made that impossible for both of them. The pain in his head grew worse, and he became feverish, tossing from side to side, and muttering to himself in a kind of dream.

"Keep quiet, Bob," moaned the weary Mabel, but when she saw that he really could not help himself she grew compassionate, and got out of bed and wetted a handkerchief to lay on his forehead.

He muttered and moaned to himself, and sometimes she wondered if he was delirious, and whether she ought to fetch somebody, but every now and then he spoke to her rationally, and his eyes looked at her full of pain and understanding. Once he said:

"Mabel, I git such tar'ble dreams."

He kept dreaming of the black, burning city, and he was among those who ran hither and thither for ever and ever, trying to escape from the flames and cinders. Sometimes the city was as he had seen it in the book, at other times it was more poignantly familiar—just the well-known street of High Tilt, all seared and gutted with fire, with the flames running out from under the roofs of the Woolpack and the Royal George, and the smoke coming up in a black funnel from the oast house of Weights Farm, and all the windows broken, and the road littered with black spars and rags. That was worse, far worse, than the city in the book. Sometimes when he came into it, it lay calm and commonplace in a queer, sun-less afternoon light, and then it would all flare up like a fur-nace . . . or else behind one friendly window he would sud-denly see a little tongue of flame, and then it would be out under the eaves, and licking the door-posts, and he would be running from the Wrath to Come.

He woke up covered with sweat and gripping Mabel's hand.

"Oh, kiddie, kiddie—say summat comforting—I have such tar'ble dreams."

"I dare say you're a bit off your head, having knocked it," was all the "summat comforting" that Mabel could think of to say. But she was no longer impatient with him. She held his hand and stroked it.

" 'Wudout are the dogs, and the whoremongers and the idolators, and whosumdever mäake a lie' . . . oh, Mabel, I wur spikking the truth when I said thur wurn't naun up be-tween me and Hannah. I äun't no whoremonger nor liar. Oh, do say as you believe me."

"Of course I believe you," said Mabel soothingly; "I'm sorry we had that row, but I was feeling poorly and you'd had too much whisky."

"I'll never touch another drop so long as I live. But he says that'll do no good. . . . Oh, kiddie, reckon I'm in fur the Wrath to Come—and wotsumdever shall I do? Wot-sumdever shall I do?"

The next day he was worse, and the doctor had to be called in. He gave Robert a soothing draught, and said that he was on no account to be excited—an injunction which Mr. Beeman did not so interpret as to forbid his putting up several prayers at the bedside.

"I feel encouraged—deeply encouraged," he said to Mabel, "to see that he has at last awakened to a sense of sin. Now that has 'appened we may 'ope for more."

"I wish you'd let him alone," said Mabel ungraciously; "he'll never get well if you make him think about religion."

"That's just what I want him to think about without ceas-ing. Even if I knew it would mean the death of his body—

even then would it not be worth while, since it is the only 'ope for the life of his soul? I 'ave, besides, an inward assurance that he will find salvation."

"He's more likely to go off his head."

But Mr. Beeman was not dismayed. Before very long he had put himself in possession of most of the facts of Robert's stormy experience. Urged by fundamental terror and grief, young Fuller poured out not only the story of his love for Hannah Iden, but of his earlier aberrations and excesses—all those big and little things which he had not troubled about for years, which had all been swallowed up in his love for Hannah, but, now that the tides had ebbed, had returned to life like the world after Noah's flood.

Mr. Beeman's inmost man was stirred. He snuffed and pawed like a charger at the call of the trumpet. He had rarely, very rarely, had such a case as this. Sinners had seldom shown themselves so obligingly black and cringing. Here was a man who owned to having committed most of the worst sins—here was a man who, moreover, owned to having deliberately rejected the call of the Lord to repentance, a call miraculously given. Was there ever a more promising case of damnation? And yet was there ever a more suitable opportunity for the Lord to confirm the doctrine of Predestination than by showing His particular mercies to this black and derelict soul, which certainly had not concerned itself with the dead works of the legal conscience or outward forms of righteousness? Mr. Beeman did not fail to remind his Creator that here indeed was a chance that should never be missed.

The doctor soon discovered how matters stood, and advised Mabel to have her husband removed as soon as it became possible.

"All this kind of thing is extremely bad for him. I know Mr. Beeman means well, but he has peculiar religious views—very peculiar."

"He calls himself a Peculiar Baptist."

"The people round here call him 'Old Pope Beeman,' 'the Pope of Goudhurst,' and I believe he knows it and is proud of it. A very excellent man, but I've had trouble of this kind with him before. He has, of course, saved your husband's life, and I'm sure you must be grateful to him, but he is fast undoing his good work by troubling Mr. Fuller's conscience in this way. The patient is in a weak state and has had a severe blow on the head; I don't wish to alarm you, but I've told Beeman that if he isn't careful we may have trouble . . . religious mania, you know, is not uncommon with men of your husband's type. By the way, can you tell me anything about his family? Are they at all religious people—eccentrically religious people?"

"I believe his father was a bit queer that way. He used to read the Bible a lot, and think everything was wrong."

"Um . . . we must be careful. I've spoken to Mr. Beeman till I'm hoarse, but he's quite unreasonable—says it's a case of a soul to be saved, though how he's going to save the soul if he loses the intellect, I don't profess to know. However, you mustn't let yourself be unduly worried, Mrs. Fuller. I hope in a day or two he will be well enough for you to take him home, and then you can help him to forget all this. Let him have plenty of fresh air, plenty of good food, plenty to occupy him and nothing to worry him. And then when your hopes are fulfilled"—and he looked at Mabel very kindly— "I'm sure he will become happy and normal again."

§ 43

But the return to Campany's Hatch was not so successful as it should have been. Robert had got over the acute stage of his despair while still at Goudhurst, but he seemed to have lapsed into a settled brooding. It was not a favourable sign, the doctor said; the abatement of the violent symptoms into melancholy was likely to make recovery a slower business. He told Mabel that she must not put all the blame on Mr. Beeman. Probably Robert would have shown some signs of mental disturbance in any case; the nature of the accident, complicated by drink, heredity, and rather an unbalanced attitude towards religion, were enough in themselves to have excited a highly strung, highly sexed nature to the verge of mania. Mabel's attitude towards the preacher varied with her emotions. Sometimes she was furious to think of the havoc he had worked—even though he had done no more than direct and encourage tendencies; at other times she realized that but for him Robert might possibly be dead, and anyhow she could not help being impressed by his smooth and solemn manner, and by the dignity and order of his household. The old man was a widower, with a married daughter living at High Halden, and a housekeeper took care of his home. Nowhere had Mabel seen such burnished brass, such gleaming furniture, such excellence of linen. She could not fail to be impressed by the respectable comfort of it all, and she soon realized that the Reverend Mr. Beeman was a personage in Goudhurst and the neighbourhood. If men called him Old Pope it was not so much out of mockery as out of deference. Certainly he held the keys of heaven as tight as any successor of Peter.

It struck her that she might perhaps compound with him for her husband's salvation.

"I wish before he leaves," she said at supper the last evening, "that you'd tell Bob he won't go to hell."

"But, my dear friend, 'ow do I know 'e won't?"

"Of course he won't," said Mabel crossly; "why should he? He isn't half so bad as some."

Mr. Beeman threw his eyes up solemnly.

"My friend, my dear Mrs. Fuller, I only 'ope as you know not what you say. We are all the children of Wrath and doomed to hell till the Lord has mercy on us. If I saw in your 'usband any token of the Lord's favour, any sign that he had put on Salvation, then I'd tell 'im as plain as your nose. For the gifts and calling of God are without repentance. And now let me 'elp you to a little more of the Welsh rarebit."

Mabel and Bob drove off the next morning in a car hired expensively from the Goudhurst Hotel. Bob looked pinched and wan, and when Campany's Hatch showed its glaring homestead and mellow barns by the Rother stream, his eyes showed no greeting ardour. Mabel nestled up to him, murmuring:

"Won't it be lovely to be back home again?" But he only answered: "Yes, kiddie."

He did not take the interest in the farm and its affairs that she had hoped. During their absence, which had lasted nearly a fortnight, the place had been under the care of Crouch of Ethnam; but though Robert went round the barns with him the next morning, he seemed strangely lack-lustre and uninterested.

"He äun't got over it yet," said Crouch to Mabel; "he'll be himself agäun in a day or two, surelye."

Mabel forced herself to believe him. After all, Robert was still physically weak; she had followed the Goudhurst doctor's advice, and brought him home as soon as he was fit for the journey. If only Mr. Beeman had let him alone, it would have been well for him to have stayed longer in that comfortable, established place, where brasses shone and woodwork gleamed and linen was cool and white in the shadow of Predestination. But Mr. Beeman would not let him alone; he was even spiritually present at Campany's Hatch, under the outward form of three little black books: "Hart's Hymns," "Calling and Election, or the Sinner's Hope," by Richard Huntington, and "The Wonders of Free Grace," by James Weller. Robert would sit and read these in the evenings instead of the newspaper, and fragments of their wisdom drifted to Mabel over the pools of sleep in which at night she and Robert seemed restlessly to swim together. She was always conscious of her husband in her dreams—in them she seemed unwillingly to share his experience, from which she was shut out by day. By day he never spoke to her of his troubles, because he knew she could not understand them. She was annoyed, and she was sorry, and ashamed, and exasperated, and afraid, but she never understood.

The day after his return Clem came over to see him. The younger brother was shocked at Bob's pale, pinched face, the sorrowful stare of his eyes, which seemed fixed on some intangible horror beyond sight. The family at Bodingmares had never heard the exact story of his accident, or rather of the circumstances that had led up to it, and much conjecture was rife. It was even rumoured in High Tilt that he had "täaken up wud" Hannah again. But Mabel denied that. She and Bob had had a quarrel over Hannah, she acknowledged, but there was really nothing in it, and now that Hannah had gone away she didn't mind. Mrs. Wheelsgate had once been over to Goudhurst to see her son, and she brought back the news of his mental state, which Mabel also told of in her letters. Clem was therefore in a certain sense prepared, but he had not expected so violent a change, such an utter collapse of the old, swaggering Robert, whose swagger had moreover lately acquired the substance of respectability.

"It's the Lord wot's a-done it," he said to Clem. He did not treat his brother with the same reserve as he treated Mabel. They had shared too many confidences for him to withhold himself in silence now. They sat together in the little glass porch of Campany's Hatch, which concentrated the afternoon sunshine of November into a pleasant heat.

"I shud say as you'd a-done it yourself," said Clem, "falling about in the road. You're still a bit poorly in your head, I reckon. When you're stronger you'll feel differunt."

"I shan't," said Bob wearily. "Oh, Clem, I'm a sinner."

"Well, döan't vrother about that. Reckon it wur just a kind of bust out. Anyways, it's over now, and if you behave präaper, folkses ull disremember it."

"But all my life I've bin a sinner—outside the mercies of God. I've disobeyed His voice a-calling me—fur I know now as He called me at that meeting, when I stood up. . . . But I wur angry, thinking as He'd mäade a fool of me—and I dudn't want to be Säaved, and give up my beer and going wud girls."

"Do you want to be Säaved now?"

"Reckon I do—but it's too läate. I've sold my birthright fur a mess of pottage, and now when I say 'bless me also, O my Fäather,' it äun't no good."

"But wot's mäade you chäange räound all of a suddent?"

"It äun't all of a suddent. I've bin scared on and off fur a long time. . . . And then Mus' Beeman showed me as I wur bäound fur Judgment."

Clem remembered something.

"Did I ever tell you the dream I had wunst about pore fäather?"

"Wot wur that?"

"I dreamed as he said: 'I'm easier now the flaming Judgment's täaken away.' And then I looked and I saw a gurt Bible wud flames running out from under the covers."

Robert's eyes grew round with horror.

"A Bible wud flames. . . . But that's just wot it is, surelye. Fire's come out of the Bible and burnt me up. Oh, Clem, wot a larmentäable, shocking dream."

"It wur a good dream. Fäather said as the Judgment wur täaken away. Maybe that wur meant fur you."

For a moment a faint relief showed in Robert's eye, but the next it flickered out.

"No—reckon it äun't fur me. If I ever had a chance I turned my back on it. I wur angry at being mäade a fool of . . . and I wanted to enjoy myself. Oh, Clem, maybe I've done the sin agäunst the Holy Ghost."

He gripped his brother's arm in a throe of terror.

"Oh, I said as I'd sarve Him out, but reckon He's sarved me out instead—sarved me out and got the everlasting laugh of me."

The door suddenly opened from the house as Mabel came out to say that tea was ready, and Bob sank back into his usual silent state of trouble.

§ 44

December came, with mornings of cloud and rime, and yellow early sunsets, that seemed to drink up all the afternoon in a pool of glimmering, heatless light. The surfaces of the fields were frozen, but under those hard, thin sods there was a live softness, smelling of loam. In the pale sunshine that wandered in patches over the fields there was a continual gleam of water—of melting globes of frost upon the grass, or beads of rain on the thorns, or a dewy smother on the fleeces of the ewes. The world was never quite dry, and yet the drench of November was gone, and workmen stumbling awake to their windows at the first daylight streak, saw away over the woods to distant farms; for the mists no longer brewed in the Rother Valley or filled farmhouses with the smell of water and reeds.

Work slackened at Bodingmares, and Clem was able to go more often to Campany's Hatch. Also Robert occasionally came to see him at Pookwell, or to visit Jim and Mary at the big house. He was still in the black mood, but he was now becoming used to it and beginning to move in the midst of it like a pathetic automaton. Once more he went to market, he harvested his roots, he set snares for conies. Those who visited him casually from other farms said that Mus' Fuller had got over his trouble better'n he desarved. Only those who lived with him or knew him well were aware that the trouble had merely been driven in deeper. It was working itself into the bottom of his heart—he no longer struggled with it, as with a thing outside him; but in it he moved and worked and saw the world and had his being.

Mabel had no illusions about him.

"He's going mad," she said to Mary. "I've a feeling that we'll have him at Hellinglye Asylum before long. Oh, why did I ever let him go out that evening, in a tantrum as he was? I can't help blaming myself."

"I döan't see as it's your fault; a woman äun't to bläame fur all the silly things her husband does," said Mary, who had said "No" to Pepper of Weights. "You can't never tell wot a man ull do next in the way of silliness. I must say as I'm surprised, even at Bob."

"It isn't his doing—he knocked his head, and then that old fellow got hold of him and made him worse. Do you know, he came to us last week, and he said the sight of Bob made him happier than he's been for months. Funny ideas of happiness some people have."

"It's all along of having too much to do wud religion, as I've said a dunnamany times. Religion's well enough if you've got to mäake your living by it, lik a Minister or a Clergyman; but it's when you start mäaking, as you might say, a hobby of it that the trouble begins. Thur wur Bob's fäather, so religious that folkses cud scarce bear to live wud him, and reckon Bob täakes after him. Thank goodness it's passed over the rest of us."

Sometimes Mabel made efforts to reason with Bob; sometimes she implored him, telling him he was spoiling her life and the prospects of their child. Sometimes she tried to charm and soothe away his trouble. But it was all no good. They could not argue together, because in such matters they were strangers and spoke different languages. It was mere mockery to implore him to do what he had for so long tried to do in vain, and though her allurements were not dead, nor his passions, any passing moment of comfort had about it such an air of falsity that it was inevitably swallowed up in bitterness. Once she took him to chapel, where he had refused to go for some time, and it had seemed at first to do him good. He had been soothed by the Bible-reading and the prayers; but when the congregation stood up to sing "There is a fountain filled with blood," the sense of his abandonment had once more overwhelmed him, and when they came to the words:

> I do believe, I will believe,
>   That Jesus died for me,
> That on the cross He shed His Blood
>   From sin to set me free—

he could bear it no longer, and had flung down his book and left the chapel, outcast and reprobate before them all.

Clem was horribly worried about his brother, though he did not, like the others, think he was going mad. Poor Bob seemed to have nothing but trouble. First it was love, and then it was religion. You would not think that Bob was the sort of chap to trouble about religion, but he seemed just as unhappy now as in the days after he had lost Hannah Iden; he had just that same scared, wandering look. Clem had always had a deep respect for religious people, and often lamented his own unconverted state; but certainly Bob's religion did not seem to be doing him much good—though that was, he said, because he was not Accepted. Two years ago God had called him in the Throws chapel, and he had refused to come, and now when he wanted to come God would not have him. It was like when Clem had refused an invitation to the school-treat because he thought his father was going to Cranbrook fair that day and would take him with him—and then his father had not gone after all, and when Clem turned up at the school-treat the Minister would not let him in. That was what had happened to Bob, only with this difference—that his rejection involved no mere negative waiting outside, but fiery torments in an everlasting hell, whose horrors he had managed to communicate to Clem, so that Polly used to grumble because her husband always had nightmares after going to see Robert.

But of late Robert had said he did not mind about that kind of thing so much. At first he had been horribly scared at the thought of living in a city all flames, with everything eternally red hot, so that you walked about like a cat on hot cinders and dursn't sit down anywheres. . . . What he worried about most now was being cast out from the love of God. It was strange that Robert could find it in his heart to love God after all that had happened; but he said he did love Him and want to be near Him. Moreover, a change was noticeable in his life. He was much more gentle and patient with Mabel, even when she was most unsympathetic and irritating; he never got angry and cursed—even with the emasculate oaths of the South Saxon; he gave pennies to the one-eyed man who played the concertina at Salehurst and High Tilt markets, and he drank nothing but the solitary glass with which a farmer seals his business.

One would have said that Robert was getting quite good, but he did not appear any happier. He still went about with that stricken, appealing look in his eyes, which seemed to protrude a little more than they used, as if that remote horror which they gazed upon had dragged them out towards it. One day at Salehurst market it struck Clem that his brother looked wild; for the first time he seemed to see the trace of that madness which the others had sworn to long ago.

He stood close to a group of farmers who were discussing crops and weather and prices and Burwash Fair. They took no notice of him, for the Rother Villages had once again turned against Robert. The story of his last outbreak had gone the rounds with dramatic increase; he had got drunk with Hannah Iden at the Eight Bells, and then had finished up by fighting the bar of the King's Head at Bodiam; he had knocked two teeth out of a Bodiam farmer's head, and blacked another's eye; he had beaten his wife till the neighbours came; he had gone off after the gipsies, but had fallen drunk in the ditch on his way; he had been picked up by a Goudhurst minister and nursed through an attack of d.t.'s, which had been so violent that it had affected his brain and he was going melancholy mad. And serve un right, for Bob Fuller had turned to his vomit again like the dog.

He did not care, for he had quite lost his social instincts. Nevertheless, there was something pathetic about him as he stood there to-day, close to a talkative group of his fellows, but shut away from them not only by their judgment, but by his own. Clem's heart was sore with compassion. He went up to him and touched his sleeve.

"Come and have a drink, old Bob."

Robert shook his head.

"Come on," urged his brother.

"I äun't thirsty."

"Then döan't look so scared and downhearted. You äun't upset over them, are you?" And he glanced in the direction of the talking group.

"No, I döan't mind about them."

"Then, Bob, döan't look so——" He did not like to say "mad." But that was how Bob looked, and Clem could see that others were staring curiously at his brother. So far he did not think anyone knew the full complications in his story; Mabel had been too much ashamed for gossip, and the rest of the family had held their tongues either out of shame or tenderness. But it had begun to be rumoured that Bob Fuller was queer, and now more than one glance was thrown covertly or openly at him, as he stood there, big and cowed and clumsy, with his eyes all red and wild. Clem suddenly saw an urgent need for getting him away.

"Come höame and have a cup of tea wud me and Polly."

"I töald Mabel as I'd be back at four."

"And so you can be, surelye—leastways not more'n a half-hour läate. You'll just have time to sit wud us fur a bit and git comfortable."

"Clem, I feel as if my heart wur going to break."

"Döan't think of it. Reckon you'll feel better if you come höame wud me."

"I want to tell you summat. If God sends me to hell, it's because it's right. I desarve it, and He's only doing wot's good and right."

"Döan't spik of such things any more. Come along höame."

He took his brother's arm, and led him unresisting to the Ostrich, where he had left his horse. The Bodingmares cart was there too, with a calf in a net behind it. The animal lowed mournfully, for it had pushed its head through the net. Clem put things right: "Woa, then, old chap; it äun't fur long. Scarce three mile, and you'll have a suck of milk off Polly's fingers. . . ." He wished its eyes were not so like Robert's; it was partly the way they looked, and partly the way they stuck out.

Bob had gone to the stable for his horse, but when Clem had climbed up on the seat and was wondering why his brother did not appear, the landlord of the Ostrich came round the house:

"Mus' Bob Fuller's started, Mus' Clem. He asked me to tell you as he's chäanged his mind and gone straight home."

"Oh, durn him!" said Clem. He was glad that Robert had at least left the market, but he felt that he was not in a fit mood either for his own society or for Mabel's at Campany's Hatch. A quiet cup of tea at Pookwell with his brother and Polly would have done him far more good; it might have soothed him and sent him home in a more rational frame of mind. However, there was no use trying to overtake him, even though he had not got more than five minutes' start. He rode a strong horse, and Clem had only a grass-fed beast and the

weight of the cart and the calf besides. He would go over to
Campany's to-morrow morning; that was the best he could do.

§ 45

Clem reached home about three o'clock. For some time
he was busy with the new calf. He shouted for Polly to bring
it half a pailful of milk. She came up, her skin reddened with
outdoor work.

"So this is the feller," she said, as she rolled up her sleeve.
"How much dud you pay fur him?"

"Thirty shillun."

"That äun't bad. You needn't look so gloamy."

"I'm vrothered about Bob." And he told her how Robert
had looked at the market, and all that had happened.

"Well, Clem, you're a gurt owl," said Polly; "you shud
never ought to have let him go off lik that."

"I cudn't stop him."

"Then you shud have gone after him."

"How cud I, then—wud a seven stun calf in the cart behind
me. Bob wur on Stranger."

"Well, I hope as he'll come to no harm."

"How shud he?"

"By your own showing. You say he looked mad, and it
äun't säafe fur mad folkses to go off by theirselves."

"I wur only spikking figuringly. I döan't mean as Bob's
a looney, but he's vrothered summat tar'ble. I'd lik to git a
ward wud that öald Minister of Religion wot's guv him them
ideas."

"I wish as you hadn't let him go off lik that."

"How was I to stop it? I dudn't look fur him to dodge me,
or I'd have sent the boy fur Stranger. You döan't think as
he'll go raving, or harming himself, Poll?"

"He'll be right enough, surelye," said his wife, abandoning
censure at the contrite ring in his voice. "I'm only sorry
as he dudn't come to us instead of going to that selfish stick
of a Mabel; she döan't think of naun but herself and her
feelings, the ungrateful thing."

The five o'clock darkness fell, and work soon came to a standstill in the shadows of the barns and oast-house steeples, among which here and there a lantern shed a tricky light. Clem and Polly went home to Pookwell to their tea.

Like a good housewife, Mrs. Clem had damped down the kitchen fire with slack, and now she stuck in the poker, and up roared the flames, with a glow on the rafters. Clem sat down contentedly in his chair and lit his pipe. He watched the kettle boil, while she laid their tea. It was only bread and butter, for they could not afford to have brawn and pickles and such delicacies every day; but there was plenty of it, even for Clem's appetite, and they were both satisfied. Neither of them spoke much; it was the comfortable hour of silence; afterwards they would pull in their chairs to the fire and have a bit of a talk.

Clem was in the act of pouring his third cup into his saucer, when a footstep sounded on the garden path, and the next minute there was a knock at the door.

"Come in," cried Polly, for the door was on the latch, and Jim walked in with a yellow envelope in his hand.

"It's a telegram just come from Mabel. She wants to know whur Robert is."

Clem and Polly stared with open mouths at such a lordly form of inquiry.

"Bob shud ought to have bin höame hours agone," said Clem; "he started just after two."

"I töald you as he shudn't have gone alöan," said Polly.

"Maybe he's at some pub or other," suggested Jim. "But I thought as I'd come aräound and ask you, in case you'd found him here when you got back."

"Lemme see wot she says," said Polly. " 'Is Robert with you said would be home four very anxious Mabel.' That mun have cost her more'n a shilling wud the address. It's just lik her to telegraph instead of sending a man räound lik any sensible person."

"It's 'reply paid.' That means we mun send an answer back."

"Well, say 'No'; it's cheap, anyways."

"Fur shäame, missus," said Clem, "to be so down on her. I reckon she's larmentable scared."

"Why? 'Cos her mäaster äun't höame two hours after he said he would. She döan't know naun about men."

"Reckon she's brung up Bob to kip his hours, and, anyways, he döan't do any roving these times. I mun say as I'm a bit scared myself."

"Well, let's send her an answer back," said Jim. 'Bob left market at two know nothing about him.' Will that do?"

"It sounds a bit as if we dudn't care," said Clem. "Let's say as we're having a look fur him."

"Whur can we look?"

"I can run up to Haiselman's, anyways, and ask if they saw him go past."

"Well, let's send the answer fust; the boy's waiting. How'll this do: 'Bob started home at two making inquiries'?"

Clem and Polly thought that it did very well, so it was written out on the form and given to the telegraph boy at Bodingmares. Clem immediately set out for Haiselman's; he was terribly anxious, and reproached himself for the tranquil state of mind in which he'd accepted Robert's lonely departure. "If I'd thought as he'd be lik to do wuss than vrother, I'd have täaken Spongey out of the shafts and rid after un, surelye. But I let un go, and now his harm ull be my doing; reckon I döan't think of things as I shud ought."

No one had seen Bob at Haiselman's but then they weren't obliged to have seen him if he had merely ridden past in the lane. Clem's first enlightenment came on the way home when he met Shovell of Mountpumps riding eastward. It struck Clem to ask him if he had seen Robert.

"Yes, I've seen him, about three or four hour agone; he wur over by Delmonden."

"Delmonden!"

"Yes, riding out of the Parish."

"Did you spik to un?"

"I wished un good day, but he took no notice."

Clem was now really frightened. What had made Bob take the Kent road? He hadn't even set out for home, then. . . .

Was he going to Goudhurst to see Mr. Beeman? It was just possible. On the other hand, if he was really on his way to Goudhurst he would not have gone by Delmonden, which was a couple of miles off the high road; he would have gone by Hawkhurst and Gill's Green. . . . Where could he be going like this alone, riding off alone from his wife and his brother and his friends? Perhaps his mind had given way under the strain of its own black ideas, and he was mad, wandering about aimlessly in the lanes and fields . . . or perhaps he had resolved to kill himself. He would hang himself or drown himself in some lonely place. . . .

Clem hurried back to Pookwell, where he found Polly anxiously waiting for him. She had repented of her hard words towards Mabel, and was eager to atone for them by going over to Campany's Hatch and comforting the poor terrified wife.

"Reckon she'll be half out of her mind when she gits our telegrapht. We mun go to her, Clemmy. It äun't right fur her to be alöan."

"Wot time is it?"

"It's only just gone seven; we can be there before eight if Jim lets us have the trap."

"He mun give us Nimrod, then; Spongey ull never do it so quick."

"Of course he'll give us Nimrod; he wurn't out but an hour this marnun. Anyways, you go and ask him."

Clem went off to Bodingmares, and came back with Nimrod in the trap. Jim, as a matter of fact, was glad that they were going over to Campany's Hatch, for Mary had pointed out to him the harm that might come out of Mabel's being left solitary in a state of nerves and hysteria—such as alone could have accounted for such unprecedented action as a telegram—and if Clem and Polly had not undertaken to go and see her, he would have been tormented all the evening through by an uneasy feeling that he ought to have gone himself.

The night was fine, with one or two big scattered stars in the black sky. The roads were hard with the recent frosts, and Nimrod was fresh from an afternoon in his stable. So it was well before eight that Clem cleared the white gate-posts of Campany's drive, and lurched up the marl and gravel track towards the house.

"She'll think it's Robert," said Polly. "Cry out to her as it's us, Clem."

"She knows Bob äun't got the trap, silly—and there she is at the door. Hallo, Mabel—has Bob come höame yit?"

"Döan't ask her out lik that, you owl. We thought we'd come over and see you, Mabel, as you seemed vrothered a bit —or you'd never have sent a telegrapht, surelye. There's näun to fret over. I've known Clem be four hours läate."

Clem's eyes and mouth opened wide as he lifted her down. He wondered what she would say next.

"I'm glad you've come," said Mabel. "I'm at my wits' end." Her voice sounded tired—it drooped and had a strange weak quiver in it. She stood leaning against the doorpost, wearing her husband's overcoat. She had evidently been down the drive again and again to look for him.

"Cheer up—he'll be in to his supper, I'm certain sure. And, Mabel, it ud be middling kind of you to git us a cup of tea. Reckon it's cöald driving."

Clem put a rug over Nimrod, and they all went into the kitchen, where the kettle was boiling over in a subdued, disheartened way. Polly helped Mabel get the tea, while she talked cheerily of the general errancy of husbands, their late hours, and unaccountable habits. Mabel seemed to take heart a little—the occupation, the company, the talk, all made her feel less blind and helpless in her trouble.

"I dare say I'm silly worrying like this—it's being alone all day and Bob behaving so funny as he's done for the last six weeks."

"He's bin läate before, surelye."

"Not since we came home from Goudhurst."

Clem said nothing. He could not put on Polly's easy affectation of cheerfulness. She was pretending, of course, for he had told her about Bob's being seen over at Delmonden, but she was trying to keep Mabel's spirits up for the sake of Mabel's child. That was just like Polly.

"Maybe he's doing some business at a farm—cäame up sudden on his way back."

"Not likely—and I can't think of any business that ud take him all this time. Oh, there's no good your talking, Poll. I'm sure he's up to some harm, and I can't bear it—I can't bear it."

She laid her arms on the table and burst out crying. Polly tried to soothe her, but the short reaction of comfort was over, and she sobbed and cried hysterically.

"Oh, it's all too cruel—I've had such a ghastly time . . . ever since my marriage . . . oh, if I'd known it ud be like this . . . there was only just a little happiness . . . at the beginning . . . and now it's all terrible . . . if only I knew where he was . . . but I'm sure . . . I'm sure . . . he's with that woman."

"Mabel!"

Both Clem and Polly shouted her name together.

"You döan't mean it!" cried Polly indignantly. "Oh, Mabel, I'd never thought it of you. You döan't tell me as all this time you've—as all this is because you're jealous."

"What else am I to be, when he stops out to all hours, after he'd promised me to be home? I know he still loves her —I know he still wants her—oh, I've seen it in his eyes, ever so many times, when you all thought he was only worrying about religion. It's Hannah he wants, not God—and it's only 'cos you're such fools that you don't see it."

"It äun't true," said Clem, crimson with anger. "He never gives her a thought. You shud ought to be ashäamed of yourself, spikking so—and you may live to be sorry. Shovell of Mountpumps saw him riding over by Delmonden this afternoon. I pray as he äun't gone mad, or drownded himself, or hanged himself on a tree."

"Delmonden! What does that show but that she's somewhere over that way? Why should he ride four miles to Delmonden to hang himself? He could do that anywhere. No —that shows me plain—I know—I'm sure—he's after her, and you'll never make me think different. You're all blind—

blind. You don't care tuppence for me . . . how he deceives me . . . it's only him you think of, who's led me such a life, who's——"

"Be quiet!" said Clem. "Thur he is, surelye."

They were all silent. A horse's hoofs could be heard thudding and sucking on the marl of the drive. They came quickly nearer, and stopped at the door.

Mabel turned pale, and for a moment looked as if she would faint.

"It may be just anyone——" began Polly. But the next moment the house door opened, and then the door of the room.

"Bob!" cried Clem, as his brother came in.

Robert was hot and dishevelled; his coat was plastered with mud down one side, and dead leaves and grass were sticking to him. His hair was all rough and sticky under his cap, and in general he looked as if he had had a fight with somebody."

"You beast!" cried Mabel, and broke into fresh tears.

"Bob," repeated Clem, going up to him. He grasped his hand, and then was suddenly conscious of a change in him. This was not the desperate and mournful Bob who had ridden off alone from Salehurst market, but a man who had marvellously regained confidence in himself, who no longer went on all fours, but stood upright. Clem was suddenly struck by a terrible suspicion that perhaps Mabel was right, and that he had been with Hannah after all. . . .

"I'm sorry I'm läate," said Robert. "Döan't cry, Mabel. I'm sorry, kid."

His eyes were shining, there was a ring in his voice, and about his entire disreputable appearance an air of confidence and self-possession which seemed to point to nothing but a successful love affair. Clem's doubts grew stronger.

"Whur have you bin?" he asked.

"Over by Scales Crouch—nearly to Seacox Heath. I'll tell you about it afterwards."

"He's bin with Hannah," sobbed Mabel.

"No I äun't," said Robert, but quite without resentment.

"I don't believe you. You've told me so many lies."

"Well it äun't a lie this time, so döan't git upset, my dear."
He went over to her, pulled her head against him and kissed
her, though she shrank from him. He was more than ever
like a man in love, whose overflowing love spills itself upon
every surrounding object, however unresponsive and mean.
But somehow Clem could not help believing him when he
said he had not been with Hannah.

"What made you stop out like that, then?" asked Mabel sul-
lenly. "You've scared me to death, and Clem and Polly too."
"I'm sorry I scared you. But I met a friend."
"You've got some fine friends—they're always bringing
trouble. Who was this one?"
"The Lord Jesus Christ."
Mabel broke into loud sobbing.
"Oh, that beats it—that beats all! You're as mad as a
March hare—not fit to be out alone. Oh, I shall die of the
shame of you. . . ."
"Hush, Mabel—hush," said Polly. She put her arm round
her and tried to make her rise. "Come upstairs wud me.
Reckon you'd lik to go to bed—it's läate and you're tired,
surelye."
At first Mabel tried to push Polly away, then she suddenly
yielded. Sobbing bitterly, she went off upstairs, and Robert
and Clem were left alone together.

§ 46

For a while neither of them spoke, then Clem said:
"Well, Bob—wot's happened?"
"I've got Salvation."
Clem said nothing. He remembered an earlier occasion
on which his brother had "got Salvation"—with indifferent
results. But he could not ignore the change in him now. The
very way he sat at the table, the way he moved, the way he
spoke, told of some wonderful event, some experience that
had wakened into strength and life the tortured shadow of a
man who had ridden away from Salehurst. Clem fumbled for

his pipe, took it out, filled it, and lit it slowly, then handed his pouch to Bob.

"No thank 'ee. I've done wud that. I'll never smoke nor drink so long as I live, please God."

Clem was a little taken aback. A religion which made an offence of one's harmless and comforting baccy and occasional pint could not be regarded altogether as a blessing, and he had a moment of rejoicing in his own unregenerate state. However, as he stared at Bob he could not help realizing that he would be very happy all the same.

"Clem, you'd never believe all that Lord's done fur me."

"You'll tell, surelye?"

"Reckon I will—oh, Clem, reckon I'm the Queen of Sheba and the half was not told me."

"I hope as you've got shut of all them tar'ble ideas of yourn. You döan't look now as if you wur scared of hell."

"Reckon I äun't scared. Wot is hell to God's Elect? I'm säaved, and Satan ull never git me."

"How do you know? I döan't mean as I'm doubting, Bob. But you mun tell me wot's happened. You looked down enough at the market, surelye. Wot mäade you ride off all alöan?"

"I felt as if I mun git off somewheres by myself, or my head ud bust. I döan't want to hurt your feelings, but I felt as if I cudn't abide your talk. My head seemingly had hammers in it, and my heart too. Reckon I wur präaperly upset. I thought as I'd go höame, and then I thought as I'd go and see Mus' Beeman, and then I thought, 'It's all no use, he can't tell me naun to comfort me; I'm lost and I mun know it.' Then I thought I'd go and hang myself."

"Bob, I was afeard as you'd do that."

"You need never have bin afeard, fur I'd never have done it. I'd have got maybe forty year more hell that way, and that ud have bin präaperly silly. I rode near up to Seacox Heath thinking of it, and I saw how unsensible it ud be. Then I saw as the only sensible thing to do wud be to go and git drunk, and then git höald of a gal and have a good time. I mun git all the pleasure I can out of life, sinst I can't be any wuss than damned. That wur sensible, but I found—it wur queer—but I found as I dudn't want to do it. I knew as I cud have got no happiness out of drink or gals—not even out of Hannah—the only thing I wanted wur God, and sinst He wudn't have me, thur wur naun I'd täake instead. Then I went and tied old Stranger to a gëate near Mopesden, and I climbed over into the field, fur I felt all mazed and tired, and I laid down on the grass among the dead leaves that had come over from the wood, and reckon I mäade myself präaperly dirty, but I dudn't care. All I cud think on wur God, and I thought 'He's wonderful. He's the wonderfullest thing thur is, and if I cud feel I wur Chosen of Him, thur ud be naun else I'd want beside.' Then I think as He's true in all His ways and righteous in all His works, and as it's right and präaper as I shud go to hell if He'd sooner it happened; and I said, 'Lord, Thy will be done. I döan't know naun. I'd go to hell to please Thee.' Then I said 'Amen' to my own damnation."

He stopped, and with his bright shining eyes looked straight at Clem, who was sucking violently at the stem of his extinguished pipe.

"I said 'Amen' to my own damnation," he repeated, "and then it all happened. It wur lik a shining, silver light, and it seemed to come all over me, and my heart went light wud peace and gladness, and then summat in me seemed to say, 'I have loved thee wud an everlasting love, therefore wud loving kindness have I drawn thee.' And then I seemed to melt for joy, and I kneeled up on my knees, and I took my Bible here out of my pocket, and I said, 'Lord, I reckon I'm lik Gideon and want a sign. Please give me a sign.' Then I opened the Book—and wot do you think I saw?—why, them very säame words: 'I have loved thee wud an everlasting love, therefore wud loving kindness have I drawn thee.' That wur three times I see them, and three times is true. That wur the text hanging on the wall when I wur in Mus' Beeman's house, and he said them wards wur fur the Elect. So sinst God sent them to me, reckon I'm one of the Elect, reckon I'm one of God's Chosen. I'm säafe, I'll never go in fear of hell no more. Oh, Clem, when I think wot I wur—a very worm and no man, as the Scriptures say—and then I think how He has accepted me, not fur any legal works of mine, but all through His Free Grace, I reckon I'll give all my life to Him, to sarve Him and love Him, and reckon as I'll never drink nor smoke nor grumble at Mabel as long as I live."

"You spik just lik a Preacher, Bob," said Clem admiringly.

"It's the Gospel's on my tongue. Oh, Clem, reckon I cud bust the pläace up wud love and joy. Reckon I mun go now and tell Mabel wot I've töald you."

"I'd leave her alöan at present," said Clem warily; "she's middling tired. You can tell her to-morrer."

"Maybe you're right. Anyways, I can talk to you—and Polly when she comes."

Clem was afraid that Polly might not be quite sympathetic, but when at last she came down from Mabel's room, having left her asleep, she listened to Robert's story—which he never seemed weary of telling—with unwonted graciousness. After all, his look and manner gave a better account of him than his poor, clumsy tongue. His tongue could only tie knots in the English language and scatter broadcast the jargon of Calvinism, but his eyes and his voice conveyed a less tangled wisdom—in them he carried his experience undefiled by his poor attempts to express it. Clem was glad that Bob had found comfort and peace, even if he called them by queer, mouth-filling names. Polly could not, perhaps, go as far as Clem; but evidently she was glad to see her brother-in-law so changed for the better; and when she went away, she gave him a sisterly kiss along with her injunction "not to wäake pore Mabel, but leave it till to-morrer."

"Well, wot do you think about it?" asked Clem as they drove home.

"It's early now to see how it'll wark. But I can't help wishing as he hadn't got hold of such a Salvation sort of religion."

"He wur always that way of thinking—it wur pore fäather's way, and reckon it's a good way, though I never cud täake to it präaper myself."

"I döan't want to say naun agäunst him—pore Bob; I guess he's had his bad times, and I'm middling glad as he's out of them, fur a while, anyhow. But he's a queer chap, mäaster, and I can't help thinking as he'll find as much trouble on his way to God as ever he found on his way to the devil."

PART II

PART II

§ 1

THE following days of that Christmas time were for Robert a period of humble and wonderful happiness. His whole life was changed by the removal of the shadow that had darkened it. When he awoke in the morning he wanted to shout and sing, when he had eaten his breakfast he wanted to go out and tell everyone how good God had been to him; often when he was out at work he would feel, as he told Clem, as if a bucket of light had been upset over him, and still grasping his spade, or the handle of his plough, he would fall on his knees, and give himself up to an ecstasy of love and thanksgiving. His whole mind and heart had been yielded to the new experience; he could think and speak of nothing else, and things which had been but common things till then became suddenly glorious and divine.

This transformation showed itself most clearly in his human relationships. He loved everyone as he had never loved before. He loved Mabel till his love felt like a great, white fire that would burn her up; he loved his mother and brothers and sister, and his step-father and sister-in-law, and was continually doing them small acts of kindness; he loved all the farmers round Campany's Hatch, the men he met at market or at auctions or at work from day to day. They all shone in the new light, they were all made in the image of the God who had delivered him, through whose bounty he now walked the fields in peace, for the Flaming Judgment was taken away . . . "and there shall be no more curse."

The only flaw in his joyful mysteries was his inability to share them with others. He made no effort to keep them to himself, he held back no sweet secret, he was always ready to tell the story of his conversion to whoever was willing to listen, and soon it was well known throughout the parishes of Salehurst and Bodiam and High Tilt. But no one seemed able to see the light that he saw or feel the warmth that he felt. As a matter of fact, the tendency was to regard him either as an Outrage or as a Joke. To many there was something decidedly humorous about Bob Fuller in a state of Salvation—Bob who would not set foot in a public-house, though everyone knew he had been chucked out of the King's Head, blind drunk, scarcely three months ago—Bob whose tongue now rolled with Scripture as once it had rolled with oaths—Bob who would take you solemnly apart and with protruding blue eyes tell you the story of his Conversion, he who used to have the biggest collection of smutty stories in the district . . . you really couldn't help laughing. Others, however, saw more disgrace than humour in his state. They were shocked and disgusted to see the man who had been Hannah Iden's lover, who had been picked up drunk out of the ditch at Megrim's Hill, now telling everyone that he was saved, that he was a Chosen Vessel, the Elect of God. It was an outrage to their sense of decency—they smelt cant.

"I likked him better when he wur an honest sinner," said Pix of Little London.

Bob did not find his family much more sympathetic. Jim and Mary saw him again an enemy to their credit.

"Wotsumdever ull Bob do next?—that's wot I'd lik to hear," said Mary; "fust it's a woman, and then it's drink, and then it's the devil, and then it's God; reckon he's tried every way to disgrace us as he knows."

"I've a-done wud Bob," said Jim; "he may do wot he pleases, I äun't a-going to vrother about him no more."

"I've naun agäunst religion in its präaper pläace, but the pläace fur religion is Church on Sunday, just as the pläace fur your dinner is the table at dinner-time and not all over everywheres all times of the day. Even the fowls know as they shudn't ought to lay their eggs sääve in the boxes."

"I can't help thinking as pore fäather's at the root of this.

He brung us all up to think serious, and now Bob's thought himself upside down."

"He hasn't stuck to fäather's ideas. He won't put his head into fäather's Church at the Throws, saying as the minister's an Armenian, though heaven knows as he is as English as me and you."

"Well, he's his own mäaster now, so he can be, as they say, a law unto himself and a fool unto himself—I shan't meddle."

Robert found his mother a little kinder than Jim and Mary. She would let him sit with his arm round her and tell her of his wonderful deliverance, and when he urged her to seek deliverance too, she would say, "Yes, dearie," in her soft, contented voice. But he knew that all she really felt was gladness that he was eating and sleeping better now, and no longer had that tar'ble worry on his mind. She was shut up, he told himself, in the comforts of her home, and the love of her husband—she did not realize that she was poor and blind and naked.

As for Clem, though he was by far the most sympathetic of the family, he also caused him the most sorrow. For Clem's eternal state meant even more to him than his mother's or Mabel's—and there was no use pretending that Clem was saved. He had never gone through any experience remotely resembling a conversion, and though he was alone in treating Robert's experience with respect, he evidently understood it no more than the others. He was just a happy, contented, hard-working, clean-living, well-behaved Vessel of Wrath—who enjoyed his wife and his pipe and his beer and his dinner all unheeding of the claims of a jealous God. Bob's arguments and exhortations were all in vain.

"I'd be säaved if I cud, surelye. It äun't as if I'm standing out agäunst it—it's only as it döan't happen."

"Then you shud ought to be in grief and trouble, banging your head and calling yourself a sinner. But you look lik a young horse out at grass . . . reckon you döan't care tuppence about the Wrath to Come."

"I'm hem sorry, Bob—leastways, if you're vrothered. But

seeing how things are, maybe it's as well as I döan't sim to
mind. Reckon I äun't the sort of chap wot them things
happen to, and I've no right to expect anythink wonderful lik
you and pore fäather."

Clem and Polly were indignant at the attitude Mabel had
chosen to take up. As soon as she had got over the relief of
having once again a rational and good-humoured husband, her
ingrained antipathy to religion asserted itself. She looked upon
Bob as "soft," and she was disgusted with his new ways—
his total abstinence, whether of glass or pipe, his awkward
righteousness which always made him explain and expose the
worst side of his stock at markets, and drive bargains that
sent the other man home either gloating or guilty. She was
miserable and shamed when he insisted on saying grace before
meals, when he knelt down night and morning by the bedside
and said his prayers like a child, with his hands folded before
him.

"I thought I'd married a man," once she taunted bitterly,
"and now it seems I've married a Young Man—a Young Man's
Christian Association."

Robert bore gently with her tongue, and this made her
angrier still. She had always covertly worshipped his arro-
gance, even though she had trained him to submission in small
things—his doggishness, even though that had fallen short
of town standards. Her experience in Bulverhythe had taught
her to associate religion with weedy young men who played
halma and had Pleasant Sunday Afternoons, or with young
women who looked as if their hats had been dropped on their
heads by a passing aeroplane. The meekness of her husband's
tongue made her forget the strength of his young body, which
seemed to grow in vigour now that it was delivered from the
burden of the mind. His love for her, also, seemed to have
taken on a new quality. It was more diffident and beseech-
ing; it had glamours and ardours for which she could find no
response, and doubts and hesitations for which she had nothing but contempt. With a bitterness which soon began to
show in the lines of her soft face she realized that his chief,

almost his only desire towards her was to see her as he was, to make her as visionary and ridiculous and soft as he.

"I believe you'd make me as big a fool as yourself, if you could," she said one day, when he had rebuked her for wanting to go to the pictures.

He looked at her with imploring tenderness.

"Mabel, I cud never be happy fur ever in heaven if you wur being miserable fur ever in hell."

"I should hope not!"

"But I may *have* to be," said Robert pathetically.

§ 2

Towards the end of January Robert's son was born. Mabel would have preferred a girl, for "they're so much nicer to dress," but Bob was delighted—he saw himself being born again, just as he had been born again in the meadow outside Mopesden Wood. He made endless happy plans for the baby's future—plans which, needless to say, included his salvation at an early age. Unfortunately certain of these plans involved difficulties with Mabel. To begin with he insisted that the child should be called Nathaniel, instead of Arthur Clement, which were the names that Mabel and the rest of the family had chosen.

"It means 'given of God,'" said Robert seriously, "and reckon that's just wot he is, and we mun call him after God's ward better'n after his uncle and grandfather."

"But it's a horrid, vulgar, common name," mourned Mabel. "I never heard of a refined person being called by it. Besides, if you *must* call him that, can't you call him the others too? Father, for one, will be regular hurt if you don't, and people often have as many as three names."

Robert's chin came forward dogmatically. "I döan't höald wud folkses having a string of näames. They dudn't in the Bible, surelye. We döan't read there of folkses having more'n one näame. Anyways, I wöan't näame my child after a heathen king and a popish saint."

"Clem wur näamed after the Bells of St. Clement's, if it's him you're miscalling," said Polly, who was sitting beside Mabel, with the victim of the conversation cuddled very close in her arms.

"I wöan't have my child näamed after a church of the Crown of England, neither."

"No, you'll name him after a Baptist chapel," snapped Mabel; "it's nothing to you that if he's called Nathaniel no one ull ever take him for a gentleman."

"I döan't want him täaken fur a gentleman; I'd sooner he wur täaken fur a Christian."

"Oh, you're no good!" and Mabel began to cry.

A look of infinite pain came into Robert's eyes. He stooped and gently patted her hand. She snatched it away.

"Döan't be so vrothered, Mabel," comforted Polly; "reckon you can call him 'Nat'; it's a middling nice näame and it suits him präaper."

But Mabel was not comforted, and her distress increased when she realized that her baby was not even to be given his vulgar name in the orthodox and respectable manner. Bob refused to have the child christened.

"Wot shud he be christened fur?—wot can he know of Christ?"

That part of the problem did not trouble Mabel. All she knew was that, even if you went to chapel, you had your child christened in Church, in order that he might have god-fathers and godmothers who should supply him properly with silver spoons. A child who had never been christened, who had no godparents or silver spoons, was a mean child indeed, and Mabel swore fretfully that Robert was not acting fairly by his helpless offspring. Then, to crown all, Robert went off to Mr. Beeman's at Goudhurst and was christened himself. He called it a Believer's Baptism, and came home with flushed cheeks and shining eyes; but Mabel cried for half the night, and felt somehow as if her husband had stolen her baby's baptism.

"Half the country ull have the laugh of me," she complained to Clem and Polly. "Everyone wonders when the christening's to be and whom I'm having as godparents, and then it's my husband who goes and gets christened. The fool!"

Polly was in this case inclined to sympathize with her. She resented the idea of Baby being cheated out of his silver spoons. They evidently formed no part of a Believer's Baptism, judging by the unendowed state in which Robert had come back from Goudhurst.

"Can't we have him done wudout Bob's knowing?" she asked her husband.

"No," said Clem, "it wudn't be seemly—and we mun respeck Bob's convictions."

"Bob's got some valiant convictions, as you might say, and I döan't see why a pore liddle innocent child shud suffer fur them."

Polly sometimes seemed to forget that she was only her nephew's aunt. Her feelings towards him were so much more motherly than his mother's, that she had an occasional way of talking as if he was hers instead of Mabel's. Curiously enough, for about two days after he was born, she could hardly bear to look at him. The little crumpled thing in the shawl in Mabel's arms made her heart ache with the thought of her own childlessness—for now she knew that there was no good hoping any more. She who loved babies so much was never to have one. She could not bear to look at Mabel's, so lukewarmly greeted, so lightly prized. Then slowly the bitterness had passed, she lost a little of her longing to say "Mine"—it was so sweet to hold and fondle little Nat even though he was not hers, to dress and undress him, to give him his bath, to soothe him when he cried, to give him his bottle—for he was a bottle-fed baby, for reasons that Mabel thought more urgent than the doctor—and listen to the uncouth noises he made in the process. For Polly's intents Mabel was the ideal mother—she did not mind how often her sister-in-law came and played with Baby, or took him out or bathed him. She, who was so jealous where her husband was concerned, seemed to have no jealousy in the matter of her child, and Polly who, if she had been a mother, would have kept her child to herself as fiercely as her husband, marvelled at Mabel's attitude, but was thankful for ˙

§ 3

Though both Clem and Polly agreed that Mabel did not deserve to have a baby, they found that Robert was a kind and loving father, if you could only make him give up some of his notions. He was devoted to little Nathaniel, and infinitely patient with him. When he cried at nights he would walk up and down with him in his arms, without pining for his own healthy sleep, never grumbling, never ruffled, though in addition to the baby's cries he had Mabel's tossing complaints that her night was spoiled and it was a shame that they could not afford to have a servant to take charge of the child. Sometimes by day, too, he would play with him, and his face would take on almost a young and playful look, which was neither like the old Robert who loved Hannah Iden nor like the new Robert who was grave with his sense of Particular Mercies. Clem and Polly thought that perhaps the baby would make him less "queer"—his fatherhood would make him more like other men, and his religion would cease to be something Particular and Elect and Separate, but would become absorbed in his everyday life and a part of common experience.

But Clem and Polly did not quite realize the power that was driving Robert. He had yet to show them the love of God, not as a diffused inspiration, but as a concentrated and explosive force, boxed up in the inner chamber of his heart, the big thing in the little room which must inevitably blast its way out, even if it broke his heart in the process.

One market day in spring Clem, who was busy in the fields and had no buying or selling to do, did not go to High Tilt till the afternoon. In the afternoon he put on his black coat and his bowler hat, and went off to the village just to watch the stock and prices. It was not a very full market, as there was little movement in sheep at that time, and when Clem came into the square at the back of the Royal George such people as there were seemed all gathered up in one corner. An auction must be in progress, for all he could hear was one voice lifted above a general silence. Then he suddenly saw that the speaker was Robert. What could he be selling? . . . With a cold creep of his skin he realized that Robert was not selling—he was preaching.

For a moment Clem stood motionless. He was appalled, and then found himself suddenly angry. What right had Bob to go and make a fool of himself like this? There he stood, in the midst of a ring of farmers and farm-hands, many of whose respectable backs Clem recognized, holding forth in his loud, blurry voice, which his brother knew would twist huskily in and out of a maze of words till at last some frayed tangle of a statement was flung down, complicated by one or two knots of Bethel jargon. Clem's humble respect for Bob, whether as man or as theologian, had been modified, not so much by recent events as by the self-confidence which had grown out of his own marriage and heightened experience. Anyways, it wurn't seemly of Bob to stand up and preach, all in the open lik that, him not being taught. Clem was shocked, and not only on his own account. He foresaw trouble for the preacher: "Reckon he'll put everyone agäunst him; reckon they're laughing at him now—I can see it."

This was not quite true. Bob's congregation was too astonished and too respectable to laugh. It stood round with expressionless features—indeed there seemed to be more emotion concentrated in its backs than in its faces. As Clem drew nearer he began to distinguish his brothers words: "Salvation . . . reprobation . . . silver light . . . Particular Mercies . . ." all the stale, familiar expressions that he had heard over and over again. But when he came right within earshot it struck him that Bob was not, after all, talking so badly. Anyhow, he was plainer and easier to follow than when he had held forth to Mabel and Clem and Polly in private. For one thing, no one attempted to argue or interrupt, his words poured unimpeded over the silence.

"So that's how it all wur, and that's why I'm here, begging you, praying you to täake warning by me, and give up the

warld and its wickedness, and lay hold on Him. Oh, open
your hearts to receive His mercies, that He may säave you
from hell and the Wrath to Come. Reckon I'm a tedious,
poor worm, and yet He has chosen me. Hallelujah! Oh, receive His promise—there's no need fur you to vrother about
dead warks; He just holds out Salvation to you lik a cup of
tea, and all you've got to do is to täake it and be thankful.
Reckon I wurn't säaved by the dead warks of the leggal conscience, since I did naun säave the warks of darkness. But
now He's mäade me one of His saints in Light. . . ."

He seemed to have reached the ebb of his inspiration, but
struggled to make some sort of a formal ending.

"Give Him your old broken hearts, so as He may give you
new ones. Thur äun't no other way . . . it äun't wot föalkses
do . . . nor wot they believe, nuther. . . ."

"Then wot is it, mäaster?"

He had been interrupted at last, by the younger Shovell.
The power which he had held over them was beginning to
crumble, and after Stan's question came an outbreak of shuffles
and murmurs.

Robert stared at his interrupter with perplexed eyes, then
he caught sight of Clem on the outskirts of the crowd. He
made a movement towards him, elbowing past Pont of Udiam
and a farmer from Mountpumps way.

"I've a-done," he said thickly. "I've given you God's ward
and you mun täake it. I've said all the Spirit gäave me, and
you mun do wudout any finish up or fine Doxology. I äun't
a preacher, I'm just a pore sinner wot the Lord has säaved."

Clem took his arm, and tried to nod carelessly to various
acquaintances as he walked off. He was still a little angry
with Bob, but his first thought was to get him out of danger—
whether of any retaliation or of his own starting off again.

"Bob, do you think as thur's any good in spikking lik that
to a lot of föalkses wot döan't care a mouldy root?" he ven-
tured diffidently, when they were some distance from the group
which still remained clotted, though no longer in silence, round
the place where his brother had stood.

Robert made a clumsy, desperate gesture:

"Wot mun I do?—how can I help it? If the Lord says
'Speak,' can I höald my tongue?"

"But need you spik to so many? Reckon they're just an
idle, listening lot; they'll never care or do naun. I'm not
saying aught agäunst your having a ward in season, but——"

"That wur how I started, surelye—a ward in season, and
it led to many wards. Willard of Boarsney—not the öald
man, but young Alf who is even as Bethesda and Chorazin—
asked me to come and have a drink. And I töald him as I'd
a-done wud the devil's poison, as he shud ought to know.
And sinst he asked me why, I töald him the story of my
Salvation. And whiles I wur a-telling, others came räound me
and start listening, and I wur all fur shutting up, but the
Lord said, 'You spik and tell of all I've a-done fur you, and
I will give you a mouth and wisdom.' So I spuck, and the
Scripture was on my tongue. And then I saw 'em all as
sheep having no shepherd, and my heart yearned upon them,
even upon young Alf Willard who'd started it all by his mock,
and upon Leslie Cripps who's never paid fur them roots he
had off me, and never will, surelye, sinst he knows as I
wöan't take the law of him. Howsumdever, he's a sheep having
no shepherd, and I'm sorry fur him from the bottom of my
heart."

Clem said nothing, for Bob seemed acutely distressed; he
went with his chin sunk forward, and in his eyes there was
an angry, tender yearning, which made his brother feel almost
shy. So they walked up High Tilt Street in silence.

§ 4

Needless to say, the episode created a proper stir, and not
in the village only, for the news of it was carried to distant
farms by yeomen and tenants who had gone to market. As
in the general matter of Bob's conversion, outrage and humour
were the predominant emotions. That he, Bob Fuller, should
dare stand up and preach the Gospel in the village that he had
so often scandalized, at the back of the very pub where he
had so often got drunk or had chucked about his money in

debts and bets to buy presents for Hannah Iden, that he should take upon himself to tell other men, who had always been respectable, how to set about saving their souls—it was enough to make any decent fellow sick.

Others, however, found it the funniest thing he had done yet. They would never forget his red face as he stood there among them, how he had flapped and floundered, how he had made a fool of himself, how he had made them laugh—when once he had gone away and they had got over the surprise of it.

There was also a small number which had been impressed —Bob had not spoken so badly, he had meant what he said, surelye. Maybe it was true that he had really been converted. It was certainly wonderful to see him going about so respectable, with his clean and gentle tongue. Not that he had done it for very long, to be sure—it wasn't six months yet since he had been found drunk in the ditch on Megrim's Hill. . . . Howsumdever . . . well, wot did Mus' Vine of the Throws Chapel think of it, anyways?

In default of any pronouncement from authority, an enormous amount of discussion went on among the different parties till Bob and his salvation were finally submerged in an outbreak of foot-and-mouth disease at Wadhurst. In time definite opinions began to be associated with definite public-houses, and there was something in the nature of a schism between the Royal George and the Woolpack, the former being talked over by Pepper of Weights to the doctrine of indignation, the latter under the guidance of Cox of Haiselman's vaguely committing itself to the statement that "maybe there mun be something in it." The more ribald spirits leavened indiscriminately the lump of the serious-minded, and those were troublous times for landlords who wished to keep order and solemnity in their bars.

Clem naturally heard a good deal of the gossip. Jim, in an agony of shame, forswore public-houses for over a week, and, anyhow, people would not have discussed the matter before him. But Clem was different—nobody troubled to change the conversation when his good-humoured, freckled face appeared; indeed, he was appealed to by all parties to "do summat wud Bob"—either in the way of making him hold his tongue or of explaining the matter further.

"He'll bring himself to trouble if he goes in such ways," said Pepper of Weights. "You mun think of your brother Jim and stick by him fur a whiles. You always go sticking by Bob, whether as it's heaven or hell as he's bound fur, and I mun tell you here as we wöan't täake any more preaching from a chap wot's bin a byward in the Parish fur looseness this five years. So it'll be fur his good as well as everyone else's if you mäake him höald his tongue."

"I can't do naun wud Bob, as you might know," said Clem disconsolately. "And, anyways, I can't tell wot he means next. Maybe he'll never preach another ward. Reckon he just got started by young Willard asking him a question, and the best way to mäake him höald his tongue is fur you all to let him alöan."

"But there's foalkses about as ud lik to hear more," said Dunk of Shoyswell, who was a disciple of Cox. "He spöake but ten minnut, and it wur all the säame: 'Let the Lord säave you säame as He säaved me.' Well, we'd lik to hear more wot he did to be säaved and wot we mun do."

"Bob says you döan't have to do naun to be säaved," said Clem. "I döan't quite mäake him out thur, surelye. Howsumdever, it's all got to do wud having things imputted on you. Bob's got good brains, and he goes more into the warkings of Salvation maybe than us."

On the whole, however, Clem agreed with Pepper rather than Dunk, and was desperately anxious that nothing should happen to "start Bob off agäun." For about a week it looked as if his anxiety was groundless. Robert's first public testimony, as he called it, had not been quite so God-blessed as it might; he was well aware of the indignation and suspicion it had aroused, he had not in the least enjoyed making it, and hoped devoutly in himself—though he would not have acknowledged the same to anyone—that the Lord would not again require such an effort of him.

But at the end of the week, Clem calling with Polly at Campany's Hatch to see the baby, was met by an indignant and tear-stained Mabel, who protested that it wasn't fair, it was too bad, and that the old chap ought to be stopped from meddling—she'd die of shame . . . as if all this hadn't been bad enough. . . .

It transpired that the Reverend Mr. Beeman, having heard of Robert's testimony, had invited him to speak at Goudhurst Chapel the following Sunday afternoon. Being Pope of Goudhurst, he could answer for his deacons, and, moreover, he guaranteed—in the old-fashioned, sloping handwriting of the letter Mabel indignantly flapped—that the preacher would also be much refreshed in his own soul.

"I ask you," said Mabel, "I ask you. . . ."

It was all she could say for some time, till she had had another good cry. She annoyed Clem and Polly exceedingly, but they could not help being sorry for her. It certainly appeared as if fate had tricked her into marrying Robert under false pretences.

"He'll be no better than a minister now . . . to think that I should ever marry a man who went about ranting in chapels . . . it isn't fair, I tell you. And he'll make such a fool of himself, too. Why, Bob can't speak English, to start with . . . and he gets in such a mess with his sentences . . . and him excited too . . . oh, he'll be in Hellinglye yet!"

"But, Mabel dear," soothed Clem, for Robert's sake, "I reckon this is better than spikking anyhows at market. If he gits a tääste fur spikking prääper in a Church, it'll be all to the good, surelye. Maybe he'll do well, and määke you proud of him."

But his thoughts were not so courageous as his words, and when Bob came in that evening he took him apart and tried to reason him out of the new project.

Bob was obstinate, or, in his own language, he was "led."

"It's middling queer, but that very morning at breakfast, before I got that there letter, just as I wur drinking my second cup o' tea, I had these words powerfully impressed on my soul, 'Behold I shall send thee forth unto the Gentiles.' Then the letter cääme, and I saw the Lord's hand plain. Wot mun

I do? Maybe He wants to mäake an instrument of His pore worm. Anyways, I mun tell föalkses wat He's a-done fur me, whether they listen or whether they wöan't, and I reckon Mus' Beeman wudn't have asked me to preach in his chapel if he hadn't thought I'd bring a blessing wud me."

Clem saw that Bob had been touched in his vanity. Mr. Beeman's letter of thankfulness and encouragement had removed his doubts as to the success of his former venture. He was like a child who is told that it has done well and has no self-criticism to make it doubt the verdict. The adverse comments which had reached his ears were now all so many utterances of Satan, of the wicked and the reprobate who sickened and trembled to hear the pure Gospel preached. "Young man," the old Pope of Goudhurst had written, "I look upon you now as a chosen vessel of the word of God. Maybe He has a great work for you to do for Him in His poor, distressed family."

§ 5

So on a warm March Sunday, when the hedges were brushed with green bloom, and the willow catkin made creamy splashes in the brown of the woods, Robert went off to Goudhurst—on foot, since he must not ride his horse on the Sabbath day. He wore his black clothes, and they made him very hot, but he was anxious to look as much like a preacher as possible, which was difficult with his brown and ruddy skin and his sturdy, ploughman's frame.

He was to spend the night with Mr. Beeman—it was the longest parting he had had from Mabel since their marriage, and he wished their good-byes had been more affectionate. But Mabel was still sore and cross. No gentleness would melt her, no warnings shake her; she put herself in painful opposition to the Word. Robert had a terrible feeling that she might be lost—indeed, it was very difficult to think who, if any, of his family circle was likely to be saved; they were one and all either hostile or indifferent. Robert's own safety seemed a doubtful blessing if he was to enjoy it alone, or in the unrelieved companionship of Mr. Beeman. But at the roots of his heart was an instinctive faith in the God Who had shown him mercy in the field, and would one day equally show mercy to those he loved, saving them in their own despite. After all, if Robert's own sins had been unable to send him to hell, his mother's worldliness and Mabel's frowardness and Clem's ignorant content might prove insufficient to withstand the Everlasting if somewhat Particular mercy.

It took him nearly five hours to walk to Goudhurst. He followed the high road as far as Gill's Green, then turned into a maze of little creeping lanes by Furnace Farm. He was in Kent now, among the high hills that are like chequer boards with their fallows and ploughs and woods. The lane went twisting down to the Furnace Stream, and then up again by Tubslake and Three Chimneys, till he could see Goudhurst above him on the crest, its line of roofs spiked with oasthouses and windmills.

He was beginning to feel tired, for he had done all the farm's duty before he started. Moreover, it was very hot; his boots were powdered with dust, and the dust had fanned itself over his broad black back. He took off his hat, and mopped his forehead round which it had dug a trench with its hard rim; he suddenly felt that it would be good to turn out of the lane, and lie down on the earth-smelling grass of one of those big, quiet fields, just where the shadow of the hedge was lacy on the edge of the sunshine . . . to smell the earth, and feel its sweet, living strength as he lay on it, holding him up like the Everlasting Arms . . . while round him the primrose leaves uncurled, and the spotted leaves of the field orchid broke the green film of their bract, and the warm daisies breathed out a scent that was the caught essence of spring heat and honey. It would be good to lie there and watch the meadow's conversion, to see spring doing for the Goudhurst fields what Free Grace had done for Robert Fuller. . . . He sternly pulled up his thoughts, the heat was making him dream; and lately he had detected in himself a growing libertinism of thought, which was continually throwing up images such as this. It was the devil, trying, in mind as in body, to tempt him out of the narrow lane into the wide

meadow. He distrusted a yearning for the beauty of the
fields which had lately grown up in him. Of old times he
used never to think twice about the country and the fields
and the earth, but since his conversion he had had several
temptations of this kind, temptations to turn to mere beauty,
which made him all the more distrust them as the devil's game,
striving to turn him from the Creator to the creature, from
human, immortal souls to the earth which shall wax old as doth
a garment and as a vesture shall be folded away and changed.

Thus wrestling with himself he came to Goudhurst, tired
of body and vexed of mind, and in no very good mood for
the afternoon's doings. Perhaps this was partly responsible
for his want of success. Anyhow, his preaching was a failure.
When he found himself in the stuffy, bare little chapel, with
the big brown blinds pulled down over the windows to keep
out the sun, and a blue-bottle droning through the scrapings
and shufflings and Amens of the congregation, his tongue
seemed to swell big and clumsy in his mouth and at the same
time his heart to parch and shrivel in his breast. He felt
as if the chief wonder of his message had been left outside,
and tried in vain, during Mr. Beeman's opening prayers, to
drag it indoors—he could not relate it to anything inside. . . .
On the contrary, it seemed to call him out, to stand in the
doorway just where it swung ajar and a little breeze crept in,
and call him out to the fields and the young woods which
were saved by the mercies of spring. He gripped his hands
together till the knuckles stood white out of the coarse, earth-
grained brown. . . . It was hard to be tempted now, just
when he so wanted to show the Lord's power. . . . Oh, doubtless the Lord had some good purpose in allowing him thus
to be tempted and humbled.

When he stood up to speak, his uneasiness grew. He found
his task far more painful than that of haranguing a score of
farmers at High Tilt market. These few old men, with one
or two stern young ones, these rough-hewn, suppressed women
and girls, were more like a jury than a congregation. Also
their interruptions confused him. An old man close under
the pulpit ejaculated "Glory be to God" at regular intervals,

irrespective of anything Bob was saying; while there were occasional and more or less appropriate mutterings of Amen. Robert found himself unable to think of any of these people as sheep having no shepherd; perhaps the hard breathing of their shepherd and Pope at his elbow prevented this. Anyhow, he was unconvincing, stuttering and stale; all the time he was thinking of himself and not of them, which made him painfully aware of his own shortcomings and their lack of appreciation. Also, he spoke only for fifteen minutes, which in itself would have damned him.

When the ordeal was over, and, after a closing hymn, he had gone back to Beeman's house, he braced himself for trouble. He felt sure that the old man would be disappointed, even reproachful; he might think that Robert's failure was due to lack of preparation, or—since preparation was usually a secondary matter with those who trusted in the Spirit— to lack of Grace. Mr. Beeman had certainly expected more edification; he had not failed to point out to the Lord that in this converted sinner, once the scandal of three parishes and now their glory, He had an opportunity of an effective mouthpiece that ought never to be missed. However, though he was continually reminding his Creator of His opportunities, he took no offence when He refused to profit by his assistance. "It is the Lord, and He 'as done whatsoever seemeth best to Him," he would remark, and feel rather magnanimous. Neither was he less magnanimous towards Robert than towards the Lord:

"Reckon you did your best, dear friend, and it wasn't your fault that you wasn't given utterance."

"I tried to do the säum as I did at the market, surelye— just tell föalkses wot His Mercy has done fur me."

Mr. Beeman lifted the teapot so solemnly that Robert found it difficult to dissociate it from his words.

"What people want, my friend, is a savoury discourse, in which the general precepts and tenets of salvation are gathered together under several heads and applied as honey to their souls. This afternoon you were addressing saints, so there was no need for you to enlarge on the terrors of hell, seeing

that all whom you saw had crossed the line and were bound
for their certain 'ope in Zion. I give thanks unto the Lord
that there is not a member of my congregation over fourteen
who isn't saved. There are many ungodly and sinners in the
town . . . other sheep 'ave I who are not of this fold, but of
the lot you saw every one of them 'as found grace."

Robert felt suitably abashed.

"Reckoned they döan't think much of me."

"They take my word, of course, that you are converted.
But one or two, who spoke to me after the meeting, have fears
as to your doctrine. I mention no names, but one devout
soul smelt Antinomianism in your discourse to-day, and others
grievously suspect Wellerism and High Haldenism, while one
—I'm sure the accusation is quite unfounded, and merely
mention it to warn you—accused you of being a Gardnerite."

Poor Robert's eyes grew round with horror—he had no
notion what these heresies were, and felt vaguely that he was
committed to every one.

"Some also," continued Mr. Beeman, "complained of your
grammar. I myself noticed that you used one or two expressions that are generally affected by the vulgar. If I were
you I should make it a matter of prayer."

"Yes, sir," said Robert humbly.

He felt utterly abashed, and when tea was over he made
some stumbling excuses, and said he must start for home at
once. He could not face the prospect of a night under that
roof with the woe of evening chapel and the solemn offices of
supper and breakfast—those rites with which the Pope of
Goudhurst satisfied his suppressed ceremonial instincts, putting
into his meals what his convictions forbade him to put into
his worship.

§ 6

Robert set out sadly in the cool of the day. The sunshine
was aslant, and seemed to move in great solemn strokes of
light over the hills of Goudhurst and Horsmonden. The val-
leys were cups of coolness, with a brush of dew on the grass,

and here and there the brown woods were lit up with kindling gold. On the high, light-swamped meadows the cows pastured in the rake of the sunset, while the breeze, which was not so much a breeze as a pulse on the air, brought the sound of the bells from steeples of "the Crown of England" across the hills.

His strapping frame had quite recovered from the morning's fatigue, but none the less he walked wearily, for his mind dragged. His naïve elation in his call to service had dropped into a black and bound depression. He saw himself definitely rejected—not as a soul, nothing could shake his assurance of that—but as a servant. He told himself that for his sins the opportunity was denied; he was to be treated like David, who was not allowed to build the temple because he was a Man of Blood. The privilege had entailed on Solomon, whom Bob could never consider a good substitute for the eager and loving, if bloodstained David—perhaps because he could not dissociate him in his mind from the Old Firm of Solomon Solomons which he had encountered in all its glory at every race-meeting of his unsanctified days, with a diamond ring on its finger and a diamond pin in its tie, and unfailing wisdom wherewith to get the better of uninstructed Gentiles. It was painful to think that Solomon Solomons might be allowed to preach the Gospel while Robert Fuller was not, though Bob now humbly acknowledged himself as a man of blood. Had he not broken a front tooth for Hoad of Linkhill scarcely six months ago?—and though Darius Ripley was only a potential Uriah, certainly Hannah had been a very definite Bathsheba.

He spent five miles in "applying" the story of David to himself, and had ended by renouncing his pretensions in favour of young Nat, whose place in the scheme he now saw more clearly, when he came to the high road again by Gills Green. The sun had dipped behind the wooded hills of Twissenden, and the sky was a soft grey, blurred in the west with rose, and pricked here and there with a star. The grey of the sky, with its flushing freak of light, seemed to wash over the fields

—all colours were wiped out, and the roofs and barns of Tanyard Farm merged into the dimness of the meadows and the huddled trees.

Robert became aware of a man before him on the road— a dark figure stealing shadowless ahead. He drew even with him, and the man said "Good night."

"Good night," said Bob.

"It's a fine night," said the man.

"Yes, middling fine."

"That's good for me, since I'm sleeping out in it."

"Whur are you bound?"

"I'll be fetching up at Battle Union some time to-morrow —do a bit of stone-breaking for some skilly and a bed. That's how I go—padding the hoof from Union to Union, with a doss in the fields now and then if it's warm. I'm sloping along Newhaven way—thought maybe there'd be a bit of work for me at the dock."

The dim light was just enough to show him ragged and unshaved—his clothes gave out a rank odour of stale beer.

"Got a fag on you, Mister?" he asked after a pause.

"No—I döan't smoke."

"Whoo!"

"I gave up all them sinful, worldly things when the Lord changed my heart," said Robert, gulping the words out with an effort, as part of his obligation to testify in season and out of season. He expected ribaldry, but the tramp heard him with deference.

"I had a brother got converted once," he said, "up at Huddersfield, and really it was beautiful to see him keeping off the drink for as long as it lasted."

"It cudn't have bin a true conversion, or it ud have lasted fur ever."

"Well, my brother didn't know that. He's got converted twice since, once by the Salvationists and once by a sort of monk—the first time the Wesleyans did it. He's a kind as converts easily, you might say. But then we were a religious family—when I was a little shaver I used to go to a Sunday school up Bordesley way, and I could tell you the names of the books in the Bible all off in a string."

"If you'd git God's ward into your heart as well as into your head you'd be surprised at the things it ud do fur you."

"Would it stop me wanting drinks as well as wanting fags?"

"I never touch a drop now."

"Um . . . but maybe you didn't go as far as me. I'm a frightful chap for the stuff when I can get it. Sometimes I feel sorter sorry, for it's at the bottom of all my trouble. You see, I——"

The tramp told Robert his story—a common, drab sort of story, of drink and the kind of dissipation that goes with drink up Bordesley way. It was not unlike Robert's own story, but with more drink and less woman in it, and the end of it was unlit by that kindly light which had shone upon Robert's dark page. Bert Slater had lost one job after another, and now had been for a year on the roads. He was rather down on his luck, he said, at present, but the warm weather was coming, so he hoped things would improve. Still, it all made him feel sorter sorry. . . .

The darkness that crept down on them over the fields gave them a queer sense of intimacy and closeness as they trudged together on the dim, forsaken road. When the tramp had finished his story Robert told his own, from his boyhood to the day of Particular Mercies—but he was no longer hortatory and admonitory, he was just one man talking to another. In the darkness he could not see his companion's face, scarcely his figure—he had merely a general impression of raggedness and slouchiness and filthiness, the latter chiefly dependent on his sense of smell. This allowed him to speak differently from the way he would probably have spoken in the light, and the words relieved his overcharged soul and at the same time seemed to interest his companion.

"It all sounds good," said the tramp. "Makes you sorter feel as there's Somebody up there. If only I could keep off the bloody wooze . . . but it's having to go so long without it that makes me so bad when I do get it. I sometimes think that if I could count on my quart a day regular. . . . However, I used to get that easy enough when I was with Banks and Son, and I lost that job 'cos I was always too blotto to turn up on Mondays. . . ." He shook his head perplexedly at his own shortcomings.

It was now close on ten o'clock, and they were nearing Hawkhurst.

"I won't go into the village," said the tramp. "I'll doss out under the next haystack. Where are you going, matey?"

Robert had made no definite plan. He had vaguely meant to walk on home, but now he realized that if he went straight to Campany's Hatch he would arrive in another hour, and have to knock up Mabel and explain his quick return.

"I suppose you wouldn't stop and have a bit of supper with me," said the tramp, "and then we could finish up our talk, and I'd find you a warm place for a nap, since I don't suppose you're used to sleeping out."

Robert was not, but his robustness did not shrink from the venture, even in March. The brooding Sabbath of the fields called to all in him that was tired and sore and disheartened, and did not care to face the complaint and discouragement he would find in his own bed. . . . Also he felt drawn towards his unknown, half-seen comrade. Smarting from the mockery of the froward and the judgment of the Elect, it was good to find someone who neither mocked nor judged nor questioned—and though it seemed unkind to share Bert Slater's probably insufficient supper, he could make up for it by treating him to breakfast at the Royal Oak to-morrow morning.

So a few minutes later Robert and the tramp found themselves under the comfortable lee of a haystack in a field near Cockshot Farm. Slater had in his pocket two slices of bread, which time and friction had resolved almost into two handfuls of crumbs; he also had a piece of lard which Robert could quite truthfully say he did not want and leave to his hungrier comrade. When they had finished eating they sat and talked to each other in long, coiling sentences and ruminative pauses, till the rising of the Waterbearer over Standen Street made Bert Slater declare that it was time to turn in.

Robert said a prayer for them both before they lay down in the hay, and was comforted by the fervour of the tramp's Amen. A strange, sweet peace had dropped on him at last—he had forgotten the rubs and humiliations of his Sabbath, they seemed somehow to have merged into his bodily fatigue, which was slowly throbbing into rest.

But though he rested in body and mind he did not sleep till it was nearly dawn. The night seemed awake . . . it was full of a living scent of earth and grass, which mixed strangely with the musty dry scent of the hay. There was a continual flutter and whisper in the hedge, queer muffled sounds came from the next field . . . later he knew that it was the sheep munching . . . above him in the black sky the stars hung like lamps of fire, seeming wonderfully close and low. He watched the Plough slowly turning over Delmonden, and the sky seemed full of the same peace as the fields, and the same sense of waking. . . .

He slept just when the rich blue of the darkness was turning grey, and when he woke the sunrise was darting through the palings of the lane, falling on his closed eyes and open mouth, so that he tossed himself awake and sat up with his hair full of hay. Slater was up and performing a toilet scarcely less elementary than that of a sheep. He was grateful for Robert's suggestion that he should breakfast with him at the inn, but he sorrowfully declined it.

"It's the smell of them pubs . . . the very sawdust on the floor. . . . Oh, I'd have my nose in a mug before you could stop me. Heigho! You'd better buy me some bread and cheese, matey, and start me off with that. . . . No, don't give me any money—it ain't safe. I've been thinking a bloody lot last night . . . you've made me think with all the things you've told me . . . good things they were . . . and I've thought this, that if only I could keep off the wooze may be I could live decent and get a job again, for as I've told you I come of a religious family, and sometimes it hurts me when

I pass a church and hear all the people singing. . . . I've half a mind to make a try and see what I can do."

"You might start and täake the pledge," suggested Robert.

"Have you taken it?"

"Only to my God."

"That wouldn't be much use to me. . . . But look here, I'll take it to you if you like. I'll make a promise to you not to touch any strong drink or liquor for a month—I dursn't make it longer, but if I can keep off it for a month it'll be something."

It suddenly occurred to Robert that the pledge was one of the Dead Works of the Leggal Conscience, but poor Slater was so eager, and looked so desperate an object in the clear, stripping daylight, that he felt unable to refuse him. After all, he was still outside the Covenant of Grace, still under the Law, so perhaps it was right that the law should be his school-master, as Scripture said.

The tramp felt that his undertaking would be more binding in writing, and there was some difficulty about paper and pencil; but in the end Robert found the stump of a pencil in one of his pockets, and offered the fly-leaf of his Bible for the entry.

With the licked head of the pencil and much hard breathing it was written: "I, Albert Slater, have taken the pledge not to drink any strong drink or liquor for one month from to-day, God helping me," and was signed "Albert Slater" and "Robert Fuller."

Robert put the Bible back into his pocket and went with his disciple into the village, where he bought him some bread and cheese and a bag of bull's-eyes, having heard that the latter were a useful antidote to the craving. They parted at the throws beyond High Wigsell, and it did not occur to either of them to make any plans for meeting again.

§ 7

It was rather awkward that the spirit of truth forbade any temporizing with Mabel when she asked for an account of his day, and what had brought him back so early. "I gather you just made a fool of yourself," she said unkindly, "and perhaps this'll teach you to live like the gentleman farmer you are instead of the minister of religion you're not."

When she heard about the episode of the tramp her indignation fairly scorched him.

"You mean to tell me you slept out with a common tramp . . . to think that my husband should ever do such a thing! . . . Oh, I'm ashamed of you—you can't help going with the dirt."

Robert heard her abjectly. He shrivelled in the flame of her words. Something was struggling at the back of his mind, urging him to seize and shake her, put things straight between them once more, show her his manhood and the shame of her shrewishness, but he thrust it away, feeling that it belonged to the godless past; he fled from it into utter abjection, for in no intermediate state could he be safe, though he knew that she despised him for his meekness.

He turned back to the duties of the farm, hoping a little that he would not again be called upon to leave them for the adventures of the Gospel. After all, since he was so stupid he could lead a life of prayer at home . . . and perhaps he would end by changing Mabel's heart, and Clem's, and Polly's and his mother's—somehow Mary and Jim had dropped out of the scheme of salvation.

But Robert was not to be left in peace. A few days later he had a long letter from Mr. Beeman, urging him not to be disheartened by the seeming failure of his first attempt, but to wrestle with the Lord, who it appeared was anxious that he should preach the Gospel while at the same time taking every opportunity to thwart and discourage him. "It is the debt you owe Him for the mercies He has shown you. Blessed be His Holy Name."

Those were the words that compelled Robert—he could not resist his own gratitude. Though he certainly now had cares a-plenty, nothing could make his life less than immortal diamond. The past—even the past of his happiest times with Hannah—was nothing but darkness compared even with these present times of loneliness and disappointment afield, of disagreement and estrangement at home. Every morning, when he knelt down to pray at the bedside, he knew that he had something for the lack of which all his former life now seemed drab and worthless, and which, if he were to lose it, nothing—not the most perfect human love in his home, not even the love of Hannah restored—could ever make good to him.

So he could not find it in his heart to refuse to proclaim the mercy that had been shown him, especially when the summons came from Mr. Beeman, who had been so kind to him, and was incidentally his Confessor, and Pope, and Infallible Church. The minister offered to instruct Robert in sound doctrine, so that he should not again stagger the faithful with leanings towards Gardnerism, or High Haldenism, or any other enemy of true Calvinism. Robert was not a good subject for instruction. His rather literal mind proved a leaky craft in the toppling seas of Whitefield and Calvin; his intelligence nearly foundered among the waves of justification and imputation. But he managed to keep afloat with the aid of the text in which all Particular doctrine lies coiled up like a rope: "Whom he did foreknow he also did predestinate, whom he did predestinate them he also called, and whom he called them he also justified, and whom he justified them he also glorified."

This text was found acceptable by the congregation scattered among the Rother villages of Sussex and the 'dens of Kent. Robert preached on it in the Particular Baptist chapel at Horsmonden, and was accepted with the text. He could point to himself as foreknown, predestinated, called, justified, and glorified, and with his gratitude seemed to surge up a new confidence, that caused his words to flow, instead of dripping slowly over his parched tongue. Mr. Beeman was pleased with his disciple, and praised him at the Pontifical High Tea which followed.

"Now you've been instructed, you've got the 'ang of the Gospel better, and folks can listen to you with edification. It gives you the jumps if you feel the preacher ain't sound. Not that I 'old with the new presumptious ways of teaching

Gospel ministers in colleges and other 'aunts of learning. It the Lord calls you, He will not fail to teach you what you ought to know, and it's taking the matter out of His hands to go and learn it at a college."

On his way home Robert informally repeated his sermon to a knot of women and little girls by the well on Light Foot Green. Though his chapel experience had been so much happier this time, he still could not get rid of the idea that the Elect sat as a jury, and felt that he would like to preach for a change to somebody who wasn't saved. The women and little girls were obviously not saved, or they would have been attending some place of worship on Sunday evening, instead of gossiping round a well. As he began to speak their mouths dropped open and remained so till he had finished addressing them. By that time a few of their male belongings had come out of the neighbouring public-house, and the close was animated by some witticisms, which Robert perfidiously found more welcome than the Amens and Hallelujahs of the justified.

He went on, wondering if he had done any good, but feeling that at last he had preached to publicans and sinners.

§ 8

Robert's new life had now entered on a new stage. He had become, in spite of himself, a preacher—not a regular preacher, for he was still a farmer all the week, and did not add the letters G.M. or Gospel Minister when he signed his name, as Mr. Beeman did; nevertheless, he was a preacher, who had his definite sphere of labour in the villages round Goudhurst. About half a dozen chapels and meeting-rooms were "affiliated" with the Goudhurst chapel, and over these old Pope Beeman held sway. With the exception of High Halden, where a lively schism existed, his power was absolute—he could any day he liked order the regular Minister to stand aside and admit some Chosen Vessel to his pulpit. On one Sunday Robert testified before the Elect at Frittenden, on another at Bethersden, and again at Biddenden and Boars Isle.

Mr. Beeman always accompanied him, and on the way home, or at tea or supper afterwards, would give him the benefit of his criticism. Under his guidance Robert's address lost much of its first naïve fervour, he acquired little hypocrisies and pomposities, and on the whole he was approved of by the Particular congregations in South West Kent. They cavilled and criticized, but they decided among themselves that he was no doubt a God-blessed young man and knew how to apply the Word. He had not so far succeeded in learning grammar, though he had taken Mr. Beeman's advice and made it a matter of prayer, but his blunders gave a pleasant sense of superiority to those of his congregation who were in a position to notice them.

When his regular ministrations were over, either on Sunday evening or Monday morning, he would go home by some rambling way—by Harlakenden, or Mayshaves, or Kalsham Green, or Gablehook—and address stray groups on village greens, or from the churchyard steps, or outside the public-house. Once he even stood in the doorway of a forge at Omenden, and while the iron clinked on the anvil and the bellows roared, told the smith of the day which shall burn as a furnace. . . .

Robert loved this irregular ministry, as he could never love his more ordained and imposing duties. It belonged to the casual nights he spent under the stars—soft purple nights of June, when the horns of the yellow moon burned above the woods, and the air was warm, and thick with the smell of hay. He associated it with the sweet, straggling sunlight of late afternoon or early morning, with village wells, and cool deserted lanes; and his heart went out to these few stray stolid folk as it never went out to the chapel congregations. He made no wonderful stir among them, either for good or evil. The inhabitants of West Kent are not an excitable race, and Robert was not stoned at the cross-roads, any more than he was thronged by repentant sinners. A few stray witticisms or an occasional cup of tea were the only tokens that divided the sheep from the goats.

But in spite of the fact that he addressed open mouths rather than open ears, he was not discouraged. His preaching was a relief to his own soul—overburdened with its gratitude to the Precious Blood. He felt drawn in love towards these stolidly straying sheep, and enjoyed the occasional tokens of their goodwill. He was beginning to find in his new life more and more of self-expression, more and more of relief from the anxiety and loneliness and care of his home. It did not occur to him that a measure of his happiness was due to his closer association with the fields, to a growing communion with the earth, which was a part of these Sabbaths.

The rumour of him spread, of course. Those who listened to him in stolid silence, found their tongues fast enough after he was gone; and though his official testimony was limited to the Beemanite chapels round Goudhurst, the wild growth of it straggled as far as High Tilt and Campany's Hatch.

"Bob said at Peening Quarter as it döan't matter wot you do so long as you're sääved." . . . . "Bob said at Gablehook as Salvation's lik a cup of tea, and you've naun to do but take it." . . . . "Bob said he loved Mus' Pitcher of Ramstile lik his own sheep." . . . "Bob said in the public at Heartsap as they wur all God's poor family." . . . . "Bob said at Iden Wood . . . . Bob said at Bugglesden . . . . Bod said at the Brognes . . . ." There was no end to what Bob said, it appeared.

People were growing accustomed to him in his new righteousness. There was little of that burning indignation which had raged when memories of the old Bob were fresh in the mind of Bodiam and High Tilt. He was beginning to drop out of the life of the district. On Sundays he was generally away at Goudhurst, and his week-day leisure was never spent in a public-house; so his contact with his neighbours was limited to the day's work, and Campany's Hatch had now few enterprises to bring its owner to market.

Indeed the farm was ill-served by the määster's zeal for souls. Robert had engaged a boy to do odd jobs, and to help

Mabel on the days he was away from home. But these continued absences from a one-man holding could not fail to be
disastrous. Mabel was town-born and unskilled, and also had
her baby and housekeeping to look after, and the boy was not
an efficient substitute for Robert either in strength or experience.

"He'll have the plääce in the auction-market soon," said
Jim, "leaving it lik that, sometimes fur six days in the month.
I call it wicked—valiant liddle bit of gräound as it is . . .
and Powlard and me set him up thur, thinking as he'd mäake
a good thing of it."

"He's messed his hay 'cos he wouldn't cart on Sunday,"
said Mary; "there's no sense in him even when he's at
höame."

"Bob's been the gurt trouble of my days—bad or good; and
now as he's started wud this new nonsense——"

"You're right in calling it nonsense, and it äun't seemly,
nuther. All this preaching's no better'n being sick; he's swallowed more gospel than he can kip down, so he just goes
and is sick. I say it äun't seemly, and I'm sorry fur pore
Mabel who has to put up wud it all."

Mabel was sorry for herself. She hated being the wife
of a strolling preacher, she hated being left alone every other
Saturday night, she hated seeing the farm neglected. She
felt, moreover, that her friends must despise her—married to
a ranter, a travelling Y.M.C.A. What a fate to have overtaken Mabel Powlard, who used to go out with some of the
smartest boys in Bulverhythe. Even the old days, when she
was jealous of Hannah and Bob spent his evenings at the pub,
had been better than these.

She sometimes paid him out for his week-end absences by
going away herself when he was at home. Her father took
her part against him, and she knew that she could always go
to Bulverhythe for a night when she pleased. Robert so
bitterly felt the punishment that she went rather often. On
these occasions she either left the baby with him or with Polly
and Clem. Robert sometimes felt called upon to rebuke her
for being an unnatural mother, whereupon she would retort

by calling him an unnatural husband. . . . It seemed as if
the Particular Mercies were breaking up his home.

So the summer dragged through. There were days of sweetness, of tender, yearning contemplation; and there were days
of bitterness, of difficulty and jar and fret. Sometimes, too,
Robert would begin to be troubled by doubts—as to the certainty or even as to the reality of his new experiences. As
the blessedness of his contemplative moments increased, bringing with it a fuller, more poignant sense of union, so in the
intervals between them, when his spirit dropped back exhausted from the heights, the memory became more dim, the
certainty less glaring, the heights so remote that they seemed
almost imaginary. . . .

Sitting in the sunshine with his baby in his arms, lying
awake in the tremulous dawn beside his wife, or working for
them both in the warmth and peace of the August fields, he
fought sorrowfully to win back those moments that had
brushed him with their glory as the wing of a passing bird.
. . . He would tremblingly revise the past and see himself
unworthy, he would try to count the souls he had saved and
find not one; all the toil of his body, all the travail of his
soul, would seem mere fruitless effort in a world which was
beautiful only in the occasional reflection of a far-off God,
as a pool catches the sun for a moment and then remains daylong scummed and cold. Sometimes a kind of despair would
seize him and urge him to yield, to go back to the certain
pleasures of a pipe and a public-house and a placated Mabel,
to give up this quest of what might be only a dream. . . .
But then swiftly he would either remember himself in the
days when he had those certain pleasures, and yet was in the
shadow of death, and thrill once more with gratitude to the
goodness that had called him into light; or else the doubt would
pass into a sudden passionate certainty, and the world and
all in it would fall away, leaving him alone with his love.

§ 9

At the beginning of September Robert had a Call to Shadoxhurst, a village some miles east of Bethersden, and outside

the Beemanite obedience. Hitherto his ministry had been straitly confined to those villages where his protecter held sway, but it would seem that his story had travelled beyond the pale of his labours, and that they of Shadoxhurst were at least anxious to see how he looked. Mr. Beeman urged him to accept the call; he saw himself treading into Shadoxhurst on Robert's heels. His appeal was reinforced by Scripture, for Bob, on consulting his Bible, "turned up" the text: "The land of Zebulon, and the land of Naphthalim, by the way of the sea, beyond Jordan, Galilee of the Gentiles; the people which sat in darkness saw great light; and to them which sat in the region and shadow of death light is sprung up." This could be looked upon as nothing less than a Divine command to go to Shadoxhurst, and he wrote his acceptance to the deacons.

The journey would be a longer one than the others, and though he could have gone by train on Saturday night as far as Frittenden Road, he decided that here was a wider opportunity for his irregular testifying than any he had yet had, and decided to go on foot, starting in the morning. His way would run through some of the old ground, by Tubslake and Gills Green, and then through Benenden into strange lands—Starvenden and Pale Mill, Little Wad and Witters Oak, where the people who sat in darkness had never heard how Free Grace had found Bob Fuller in the field outside Mopesden Wood.

Mabel was very angry when she heard of this decision—so angry that she refused to help him with his spelling in his letter to the deacons.

"I never heard of such a thing—leaving the farm for three whole days, as if it wasn't bad enough leaving it for one. It's nice for me, having to do all the work on Sunday."

"Thur's unaccountable liddle to do these times, kiddie. I'll have had all the apples picked by then, and thur'll be naun but the chicken to see to, and you've got Podgam fur that."

"He's a fine lot of use, I must say. The chicken, or even you, have got more sense than him. I have to go tearing after him all day. . . . And there's baby too. . . . I call it a

shame, Robert, I really do. If you *must* go to Shadoxhurst,
why can't you go by train instead of mooning about the country on foot?"

"Mabel, I'm telling you, dear, as my gurtest joy äun't
to preach in the chapel, whur seemingly everyone knows the
Gospel better'n I do; it's to preach it in the highways and
hedges, as the Scripture says, and compel them to come in.
Thur's men as have never heard of the Free Grace, and I
want summat tedious to mäake them know wot I know, so's
they can be wot I am."

"Then I'm sorry for their wives."

He looked at her without speaking, and something in his
goodly, ruddy face, with the blue eyes full of trouble, appealed to a side of her that was dying fast. Her heart began
to beat quickly, and going up to him she put her arms round
his neck, dragging him close. . . .

"Bob, come off it. . . . Why must this be between us? We
used to be happy together once. If you've simply got to be
religious, can't you be it without all this fuss and trouble?
Sometimes I feel as if I couldn't stick it any longer . . . you
going away like this . . . and loving so many things better
than me. . . ."

"I don't, kiddie," he murmured tenderly; "I just love you
as I always dud, but when the Lord calls me I mun go, and
whur He calls me I mun go . . . fur He's bin so good to me,
Mabel—gooder nor you can think."

"I don't see any goodness in taking you away from your
wife, and making a fool of you, traipsing about the country
. . . and the place ull fall to pieces, you going off like this,
and you lost the best part of your hay because you said God's
Word wouldn't let you cart on Sunday. . . . And never the
comfort of a pipe or a glass at the pub. . . . Oh, Bob, *has*
God been good to you? You ask it to yourself now—solemn.
If all along of Him some day you find you've lost your farm
and your money and your—and your wife, will you still say
God's been good to you?"

"Yes," said Robert, "I wull."

He did not push her and his temptation from him, but held

her close to his heart, while his eyes stared over the soft, straying feathers of her hair, out through the open window towards the greenish star-pricked sky behind the orchard. She was crying now, sobbing with all the fret and grief of the past year, which had found only a partial vent in reproaches and peevishness. Her marriage had been a failure, an utter disappointment. . . . She had married as she thought a gentleman and a rake, and he had proved himself but a common fellow, and had finally turned teetotaller, Biblereader, Psalm-singer—all she hated and despised most. Her heart was laden with the bitterness of her disillusion; she had no hope nor pride left.

"Döan't cry, dearie," said Robert; "döan't vrother. I can't believe as the Lord ud ever let you go from me, and as fur the rest, hasn't He promised that as many as shall lose houses and lands fur His sake and the Gospels, shall find 'em agäun in the warld to come, wud life everlasting?"

"I don't want them in the world to come," sobbed Mabel; "what use ud they be to us then? I want them now—with the kid growing up and all. I wonder you don't care for his sake if you don't care for mine."

"I do care fur you both, but the Lord will provide. I mun trust the Lord. Howsumdever, I tell you wot I'll do, Mabel. I'll ask Clem to come over on Sunday. He döan't mind wot he does on the Lord's day. He can look after the chicken fur you and see as Podgam does his wark. And I'll ask him to bring Polly too; she'll be company fur you, and maybe she'll mind baby fur a bit."

"If I'm not to have my own husband, I don't want anybody. Besides, they can't get away except on Sunday, and I'll have Saturday and Monday all alone. Oh, it's too cruel."

Neither words nor caresses could bring them any nearer an understanding, and on Saturday morning Robert set out with a heavy heart.

§ 10

The air was faintly thickened with September, and held in its stillness the smell of apples and burning weeds. The hills of Kent across the Rother were covered with patched, warm colours—the pale stubbles, and the golden brown of corn yet standing, the rich, yellowish green of the hop-gardens against the dark bice of the woods, the red twist of the little clay lanes between the hedges, and here and there a speckled crop of farmsteading.

Robert walked towards them over the grassy ruts of the marsh road; behind him lay Sussex in a huddle of wooded hills, before him the Kentish windmills hung motionless sails in the sunshine. The Rother had taken its southward turn under Bodiam Bridge, flowing past Udiam and Churchsettle down to Salehurst. The boundary between Kent and Sussex was now the Kent Ditch, sunk deep among the fields and choked with thorn and alder.

He crossed it near Peter's Green, and then set off up the little narrow, chalky lane to Sandhurst, toiling in the short noon swelter up Megrim's Hill. It was on this very road that he had been found lying drunk and unconscious a year ago. If he had not been straitly taught otherwise he would have thought it a happy adventure that had thus laid him low; for if he had not quarrelled with Mabel and got drunk at the King's Head and fallen into the ditch and been picked out by Mr. Beeman, then he would not have known the Everlasting Mercy, the wonders of Free Grace. . . . Oh happy sin that had been so happily forgiven! But he must not think that; perhaps if his Calling and election had come to him some other way, less catastrophically, he would not now have to make such a struggling response . . . travail abroad and trouble at home. He might have loved God comfortably . . . though that was wrong, too. . . . It was doubtful whether you could ever be really comfortable under Grace. . . .

So Robert's thoughts flew in shreds till he came to Four Throws, and felt called upon to speak there to some road-menders who were eating their dinner under the sign-post. These were joined by two women who had been gossiping across a cottage fence, and then by several children on their way home from school at Hawkhurst. Robert's appearance, his sturdy figure and ruddy skin, with the rakish look which his cap and clothes and little moustache gave him—for he had given up trying to look like a Gospel minister—won for him a certain success of curiosity. He had not spoken before at Four Throws, though they had the rumour of him from Hawkhurst and Newenden, and his congregation was glad to have seen him at last so that they could compare impressions with the other villages—"a stout feller, but wud some middling queer notions," they said of him.

He spoke only for ten minutes, then put on his cap and went on. He did not stay to watch for any effects; his experience taught him not to expect these. He had once dreamed of marvellous conversions, of voices suddenly raised with his to give glory to the Lamb, of Pentecost on a village green. But now he had learned to accept an outward failure, to sow the word as he sowed the grain in the furrows of his black March fields, knowing that what he sowed should not quicken except it die. . . . Here and there a question would be put to him, some doubt, some fumbling experience, shown him, but usually any comment he received would be in the way of ribaldry—the ribaldry that enlivens the bar of the Wheatsheaf or the Crown.

When he left Four Throws he took the little lane that runs by Gun Green and Furnace Mill, down into the valley of the Benenden stream, through many ash woods—then up past Scullsgate and Nineveh to the high road at Crit Hall. The day dipped with him down into the valley, and he came up into a red sky and a wild, raking sunset which sent the big shadows swimming over the fields, shadows of woods, shadows of barns, and the big steeple shadows of oasts, running before the thick red light that poured from the hills of Swattenden and Coarsehoarne.

Robert spoke again in Benenden Street, on the green outside the church. Being Saturday night, he had rather a good hearing. Indeed the entertainment he provided conflicted rather dangerously with those in progress at the Ewe and Lamb across the way, where the farmers' benefit society was having a sing-song, and by the church at the end of the green, where a Harvest Thanksgiving was just going to start. The landlords of both were inclined to be resentful—the publican told Bob to chuck it or he'd show him how to mäake a noise, and the parson suggested that he should come into the church and strengthen his gratitude to the Lord who had redeemed him by the contemplation of vegetable marrows and other tokens of a bountiful harvest.

"They are the meat which perisheth," said Robert, "and you ask me and these pore sheep of your'n to chuck labouring fur the bread of life, but go and disremember our starving souls wud seeing all the stuff we've gotten fur our bodies. I tell you, my friends"—turning once more to the stragglers on the green—"as thur's tedious liddle sense in giving thanks fur the wheat if you're yourself one of the tares wot are to be burnt in unquenchable fire, or sending in a valiant marrer as gurt as a pig to lay on the minister's desk, when you yourself's naun better than the nasty burdock you picked out o' the marrer bed."

The church bell tanged through his words, and a husky song came through the open door of the Ewe and Lamb. Gradually his congregation melted away, either through the square red doorway of the inn, or the golden lozenge-shaped doorway of the church. The doors shut, the red light and the golden light were gone, only the orange circle of the harvest moon hung in the dim blue sky. Its beams seemed to be cut off by the thick, stubble-smelling air. No light from it straggled through the sky, or to the earth. Robert could scarcely see who was left to hear him. He had a dim impression of some children straying towards him from the corner of the green, but as they came nearer he saw that they were a flock of geese. . . .

§ 11

He slept that night in the high corner of a field by Dockenden. He was now growing accustomed to the fields at night, and no longer lay awake listening to the silence, but slept refreshingly with his head in the cool grass. Once he woke and saw that the moon had set and that the Sign of the Ram hung over him, a scatter of light on the dark meadow of the sky. The sky felt very near, just in that moment of waking, as if he could touch it with the swing of his sleepy arm, and rake down the shimmering stars of the Lamb of God into the field beside him. Drowsily content, he turned over, burrowing his face into his sleeve. . . .

He woke in the full flush of the dawn, with the sunlight pouring on him through the hedge. It was about six o'clock, and he had still many miles to go. So he rose and made the toilet which was so much shorter than his prayers. He had some bread and cheese in his pocket, the remains of his supper last night, and before he left the field he breakfasted, washing the stale stuff down with mouthfuls of water from a land-spring in the grass, water that tasted of soil and wood and rain.

He struck out across the fields, for he was still in familiar country, and hoped to reach the Tenterden road between Mockbeggar and London Beach. As he walked up Tenterden Street the echoes of Tenterden chimes went down it, singing, "My lodging is on the cold, cold ground." The street was full of people on their way to Church, but luckily Robert did not feel the need to gather himself a congregation. For one thing, there was not time, he had still some ten miles or so to walk through new country, for another he had for a brief respite ceased to feel the strivings of the Word. In his heart was a sense of rest, just as in his body there was a sense of well-being, brought about by his long healthy tramp and his night in the open air. He felt strong and happy, with a curious sense of detachment even from spiritual things. He was convinced that the Lord would bless his testifying at Shadoxhurst—anyhow he did not, according to his custom, give a thought to what he was going to say. Such forethought-edness would have been highly disrespectful to the Holy Ghost, Who would undoubtedly impress on Robert's mind both his discourse and the Scripture for it.

He left Tenterden by the Ashford road, and for some time his way skirted the Upper Levels of the Rother, known as Shirley Moor. Here the Marsh is made by the Highknock Channel and the Reading Sewer, creeping southward towards the Isle of Oxney. Great stretches of green level spread towards the South, melting into the golden fogs that veiled the Lower Marshes of the Kent Ditch and the Fivewatering. Sussex was smeared into the sky—there was no distance, only the marsh with its pollards and reedy watercourses.

At Brook Street he left the road and the marsh, turning northward by Boldshaves and Tiffenden. He was in new country now, about twenty-five miles from home—the land of Zebulon and the land of Naphthalim, Galilee of the Gentiles. But he had walked the last few miles quicker than he had expected, and saw that he would be at Shadoxhurst a full hour before three, when the service began. So when he passed a little chapel at Colliam Green, and heard singing inside, he went in.

There were only about ten people in the congregation—one or two old men, an old woman with a sweet, mournful face, a few middle-aged women, a vacant-looking boy, and a girl in a kind of invalid chair. The pastor was about to administer the Lord's Supper, and Robert felt drawn to stay, to be worshipper before he went away to be evangelist. The atmosphere of the little chapel was friendly and peaceful, unlike so many he had been in—the walls were brown with much sunshine, and time and sun had mellowed the wood of the pews and the minister's desk.

Bob asked the minister if he might stay and partake, and on furnishing proof of his conversion was allowed to do so. So he stayed in that little sun-swamped room with those few strangers of the unknown village, and ate and drank in memory of Dying Love and in token of Love Risen and Alive towards God and man. It was over in a little more than an hour—the prayers, the reading, the preaching. Then the old men walked out with bowed heads and eyes that seemed to search the distance, the women set off briskly for their homes and their husbands' dinners, the vacant-looking boy wheeled out the girl in the invalid chair—the little company scattered, after shaking hands with each other and the stranger.

Robert felt as if he would like to stay—for the first time he experienced the attraction of a holy place. He, who was now beginning to feel at his ease only when he worshipped in the open air, would have liked to kneel through quiet hours in one of those mellow pews where the wood was warm with sunshine, and feel in himself the peace of many prayers, the strength of many communions, not his own. But the minister and a deacon were waiting to lock the doors—for the rest of the week the little House of God was to be a locked casket with its hidden treasure.

§ 12

Robert found the Elect at Shadoxhurst very much as the Elect of other places. The fact that they were not Beemanites was merely a matter of jurisdiction, not of faith, and was due to a very natural wish to call their souls their own. They were eager to assure him both of their orthodoxy and their good will; no one, they told him, could for a moment question his action in coming to preach at Shadoxhurst—now, if he had preached at High Halden, or at Ebony, where the minister had "gone over" to High Halden, taking most of his congregation with him, there would have been scandal, for High Halden and Ebony were in flagrant schism, whereas between Goudhurst and Shadoxhurst there existed a spiritual bond all the closer because it was without any material restrictions. The Beemanite rite was strictly followed, with the exception of the hymns, for Shadoxhurst in a moment of Progress and Enlightenment had discarded Hart's Hymns which were still used at Goudhurst in favour of the more advanced and modern Moody and Sankey.

When the afternoon's ordeal was over he had tea with the head deacon and his family whom he thought very worldly, because the girls talked to each other about blouses and the father himself seemed less interested in church matters than in crops and politics. Robert, who was used to find the tea-table merely a more intimate and searching continuation of the pulpit, was shocked at all this secularism, which he also considered highly unsuitable on the Lord's Day. He declined an invitation to stay the night, and left soon after five, setting out in the direction of Witters Oak.

As he tramped away, passing the locked tabernacle at Colliam Green, it struck him that he was missing a priceless opportunity by walking through so much new country without leaving a crumb of Gospel. He had come a long way merely to preach to the Saints, while all along the road were sinners who had probably never heard of the Particular Mercy. Since he was now so far from home it would not be a bad plan to write to Mabel, who would probably get the letter on Monday morning, and tell her that he would not be home till Tuesday night or Wednesday.

It struck him that Mabel might be a little annoyed at his staying away five days when she had already objected to his staying away three, but at present Mabel seemed so much farther away than the Gospel . . . the thirst for sinners was upon him (the Saints never failed to produce this effect), and he pictured himself scattering the precious Word in strange furrows, proclaiming Free Grace at foreign crossways where every road led into the unknown. . . .

The post office at Witters Oak was open just before the dispatch of the evening post. Robert bought paper and stamp from the girl in charge and wrote his letter at the counter, with no anxious speculations as to its effect on Mabel, such as a more lively imagination might have given him.

"I feel much refreshed in my soul, and am, dear Mabel, your loving husband, Bob."

Having now set himself free, he walked off towards Haffenden Quarter, turning south by Dogkennel and Witsunden. He testified on the green at Wagstaff, and there won the brightest laurels of his experience, for when he had done, a stalwart farmer came up and clapped him on the shoulder, saying he had never heard such good words; no, not in Church nor in chapel nuther. He was on his way to the latter with his Bible under his arm, but Robert's good words had so powerfully impressed him that he saw the uselessness of seeking salvation by legal works, and would rather wait for the Election of Saints. He persuaded Robert to go home with him to supper and talk of the matter further; he even asked him to spend the night at Childrens Farm, but Bob's rejoicing spirit longed for another night of freedom, and he left his convert, having commended him to the Lord. The farmer was the first fruits of his missionary career, if he excepted the tramp on the Hawkhurst road—as he ruefully felt bound to except him.

His spirits were high as he set out towards Dashnanden, though he could see that the fine weather of the last week was breaking. Rags of cloud flew low before a south-west wind, and behind them the stars jigged like lights through the rents in a curtain. The moon put an angry yellow light into the clouds and the sky and into the blot and huddle of the fields below. The air was no longer thick and still, but rainy and swift, clear as flying water.

But in spite of it all, and a few regrets that he had not taken the comfortable shelter of Childrens Farm, Robert sang as he went along:

> "Oh, let me sing Thy beauty, Jesus,
>   Like sunshine on the hills—
> Oh, let my lips pour forth Thy sweetness
>   In joyous, sparkling rills."

His heart seemed full of the words and the love they expressed. The God of his redeemed soul and of the flying night felt very near, and his hunger for Him seemed about to be satisfied . . . that was the greatest joy that he had known —a hunger that was part of satisfaction and a satisfaction that was still sweetly hungry . . . he could not imagine anything more lovely, not even the perfect satisfaction that he had learned to expect in heaven:

> "Longing for home on Zion's mountain,
>   No thirst, no hunger there."

As he came near Castwisell a drop of rain fell into his singing mouth, and then the rain began to fall thickly, patter-ing with a heavy rustle in the hedge and the oak trees by the way. The wind woke and shrieked, and there was a sudden grip of cold upon the night. Robert saw that he was to be cheated of his outdoor sleep—now that the weather had changed his love for such a thing seemed almost ridiculous, and he craved for warm blankets and a roof. No doubt he could find a doss at an inn, though he knew that most village inns were mere drinking places, with seldom more than a couple of bedrooms to let to those who did not mind the fleas—which Bob did not.

He saw lights at a cross-road, and found an inn sooner than he had expected. It was the Crown at Castwisell, a small unpromising looking place, but with a cheerful red light streaming from its bar window. Robert had not been into a bar since he had disgracefully left the King's Head at Bodiam; his attempts at the conversion of bars had been one and all delivered from the doorway, which provided a double safety both from inward temptation and outward attack. He entered this one with something like a thrill; the rub of sawdust under his feet, the smell of beer and pipes, and rumble of husky voices all brought so many stirring memories . . . of the days when he had roused the pubs round Saleshurst. . . . The place was full, as it was near closing time, and scarcely anyone seem to notice him as he came in from the wet.

The barmaid was favourably impressed by the handsome young fellow she saw shouldering his way towards her, and felt both surprised and disappointed when he asked for a glass of lemonade. The surprise became alarm and the disappointment disgust when, as she handed him the mean liquid, he remarked: "Now is the accepted time; now is the day of salvation." Robert had lately been struck by the idea of "giving Scripture" to any stray acquaintance of the lane or counter. So far the results had not been encouraging, but his whole experience as an evangelist had taught him not to expect anything so Dead and Legal as results.

The barmaid not seeming responsive—indeed she had turned her back—he took his refreshment to one of the side tables. He sat there rather moodily, wondering if he should get his bed, or if in the meanwhile he ought not to testify to this most unsympathetic assembly, when a man suddenly slid into a chair opposite him and said:

"Hallo, mister!"

"Hallo," said Bob.

At first he did not recognize the fellow, then he realized that it was Darius Ripley, who had grown a big black beard.

"I didn't know you," he apologized.

"Not with my new chin—and yet I knew you, even with your new heart."

Robert started, and the gipsy laughed.

"When my wife tells Gentiles things like that," he said, "she says it's the Dookerin Dook or Spirit of Fortune and gets their silver money. But I just tell you it's the talk of eighteen villages."

"Wot's the talk?"

"That you've become a Gospel-engro and speak good words. Maybe you'll speak some to the poor people."

Robert did not answer. In his mind was a picture—of a tall woman, leaning against the wall of a village inn, with a child in her arms, and the dead leaves drifted up round her feet. . . .

"Where's your wife?" he asked.

"My wife's at Catherine Wheel, bikkening or selling clothes-pegs. She'll be back to-morrow with the two brats."

"Two!"

"Yes, we have two brats now. Wouldn't you like to see my wife and the two brats?"

Robert felt uncomfortable. He had a feeling that Ripley was "after" something—though exactly what, it would be hard to say. He disliked and distrusted him, but at the same time he was intensely relieved to find that he could think and speak of Hannah without a pang. For some months he had been wondering what would happen if he were to meet her again; now he saw that he had nothing to fear—even that wild, sweet spirit could not come back into the heart where the Strong Man Armed kept His goods in peace.

"You might come and speak a word or two of Gospel to

the poor people," continued Darius in his whining, lilting voice. "We love good words, and have heard many—my wife once taking the brats to Church."

Robert suddenly had a vision of himself converting the whole tribe of Ripleys.

"Maybe I'll come and have a look at you to-morrer. I'm sleeping here to-night."

"Sleeping where, mister? Eighteen villages knows as you love a doss in the dry field, but the field ain't dry to-night."

"I shall sleep here—at the inn."

"But you can't sleep here. They have only one spare bed, and that's let to two commercial gents, as I happen to know, having sold a dawg to one of 'em."

"Maybe they'll let me shäake down in the bar."

"Not after a threepenny lemonade. That ain't their sort at the Crown. But I tell you, mister—how much was you going to pay for your room?"

"Maybe half a crownd."

"Well, I'll let you sleep in our caravan for that—the whole caravan, for my wife and the brats and I sleeps in the tent on summer nights, it being more romanly. But you can have a doss in the caravan for half a crownd, and pay us a shilling for your breakfast."

Robert did not feel strongly attracted by the offer, but inquiries at the counter unexpectedly revealed Darius in a state of truth—the one bed belonged indeed to the commercial gents, and no conveniences in the way of a shakedown on the floor were to be expected by threepenny lemonades. Meantime, the landlord was ominously banging doors and windows and wiping up spilt liquor, and outside the rain sheeted across the lamplight. . . . Robert made up his mind to accept the gipsy's offer. Of course it was a swindle—half a crown for a mattress in his dirty caravan, which must have some substantial drawback, or he and his family would be sleeping in it themselves. . . . Still it was satisfactory to know what really was at the back of Darius's mind—and it would be only for one night—and Hannah was not coming back till to-morrow morning . . . not that she mattered.

The gipsy's reasons for vacating the caravan became obvious in a quarter of an hour. It was not merely that the place was alive in every seam—Darius and his family were used to little discomforts of that kind—but it was letting in water badly. A piece of sacking had been nailed over the worst leak, but it soon became saturated, and the rain dripped through, making a big pool which spread to the corners. Moreover, Robert was not alone—Darius had let another mattress to a half-bred gipsy-boy, who lay curled up like a dog when Robert came in, and a pile of dry straw and fern was covered with what at first sight appeared to be a mass of rags but on inspection was revealed as an old woman. Even estimating that the other lodgers were not, like Robert, paying hotel prices for their accommodation, there must have been, in theatrical language, quite five shillings in the house. Bob felt inclined to resent Darius's money-making activities, but he was too tired and sleepy after his long tramp—he must have walked quite fifty miles since Saturday morning—and the night outside was too utterly fierce and wet for him to make much protest. After all, he was hardly bred, and not so fastidious as Mabel would have liked . . . he huddled up on his mattress, and, fighting for sleep, he won it.

It seemed hours later that he woke, in reality it was probably not more than twenty minutes. He heard a child wailing and a woman's voice. Some altercation was going on just outside the caravan, where Darius's tent was pitched, and suddenly Robert became aware that Hannah must have come home and was pleading with her master to let her in. Evidently Darius was angry with her for turning up like that in the middle of the night; Robert could hear him calling her a lady-dog and other more exotic names. In the end, however, he relented, for the wailing of the child—or rather now of two children—and the woman's shrill defensive voice became muffled by canvas and eventually whimpered into silence.

A great stillness hung on the night, broken only by the drip and trickle of rain, and Robert lay awake, thinking how two years ago he had tossed and groaned and sobbed at the thought of Hannah with Darius, and how to-night he lay peacefully, with them there together not thirty yards away. . . . It was wonderful—this aspect of his conversion impressed him more than any other. His love for Hannah had been so fierce and dominant a passion that he was humble and awestricken before the greater love that had subdued it. One would have thought that if his love for Hannah had been taken away there would have been no Robert left. . . . And yet here he was, praising God.

> "Lift ye then your voices
> Swell the mighty flood—
> Louder still and louder
> Praise the Precious Blood. . . ."

Tears of happiness and exultation gathered in his eyes, as he turned his cheek once more to the mangy pillow.

When he woke again it was daylight—a grey daylight, full of pale rain. The rain pattered and sang on the roof of the caravan and trickled and gurgled in its seams. The pool of water on the floor was soaking the edge of Bob's mattress. He sat up and stretched his powerful young arms, throwing back his head. The boy and the old woman were gone, and from outside came a fine smell of cooking.

He opened the door and looked out. At first he saw nothing but rain, then he began to take stock of the encampment, such as it was. It consisted of another caravan very like the one in which he had slept, and crammed with chairs and baskets and brooms, stowed away out of the rain; also a couple of brown tents, from one of which came the savoury smell. He felt that he must at all costs have a wash and a shave, so he went into Darius's tent to ask for a bucket.

At first the interior seemed to be solid; what with smoke and human beings its contents were resolved into one indistinguishable mass. In the middle was a brazier over which Hannah—he realized with a shock that it must be Hannah—was frying a rabbit. At first he thought it was the dim, reeking atmosphere that magnified her, but a second look made

him painfully aware that she had grown very stout. Not
only was she a nursing mother, but she seemed altogether to
have broadened and coarsened; she had become typical of
her race, where the women, if they do not shrink and shrivel
into middle age, grow inexpressibly sloppy and coarse. Her
eyes still looked at him much as usual from under the dark,
untidy thatch of her hair, but her face was both lined and thickened. He recoiled. Could this be Hannah who had been so
sweet and slim in his arms once?

Her voice broke up his memories:

"Good morning, Mr. Robert Fuller. Darius told me you
was here."

"I slept last night in the caravan."

"You've come to preach the Gospel to us?"

"Wull you listen?"

There was a sudden catch in his breath at the thought of
Hannah having the Gospel from his mouth.

"I like to hear good words."

Meantime she fried the rabbit, stooping over the brazier
with the red glow on her face, showing up pitilessly the net-
work of lines round her eyes and mouth and the growing
heaviness of her chin. Bob stared at her, and his heart was
too full to speak. It was full of a queer tangle of feelings—
the realization that he found Hannah's ugliness attractive,
just because it was a part of herself, her ugliness . . . and
yet his love for her was dead, so what was there in him that
survived her loss of beauty? . . . There was also a second
realization—that all the linked events which had brought him
to the camp at Castwisell were just the workings of Divine
Providence, willing that he should convert Hannah and bring
her to the Lord, that she should learn from him good who
once had learned evil. . . .

The new sense of this mission almost overwhelmed him.
Hannah's soul suddenly became more to him than all the
souls over which he had yearned—his mother, Mabel, Clem,
all the poor folk at cross-roads and village greens. . . . He
would have sacrificed them all as the price of Hannah's re-
demption. His eyes suffused with tears; he wanted her so

for Christ. . . . At the same time he felt bashful and reluctant; he could scarcely find words to tell her the good tidings. . . .

He did his best during breakfast, while she and Darius sat opposite him with their dark, shining eyes. The breakfast was hardly worth the covenanted shilling, for the rabbit was badly smoked, and Robert, for some strange reason, could eat almost nothing. When the meal was over, Hannah sat nursing her baby. She evidently did not resent being preached at for three-quarters of an hour.

"There's no denying, Mr. Robert Fuller, that you speak good words," she said, "and it's really and truly wonderful, since in the old days you spoke such bad ones."

"I've töald you wot's happened to me; it's the Lord's Everlasting Mercy wot's chäanged me all in a flash from red as scarlet to white as snow. You mustn't think as it's any warks of mine."

"You're highly modest, mister," said Darius politely; "I've heard eighteen villages speak of your goodness and holiness. It is very civil of you to tell us such pleasant things, and we have been much entertained at our breakfast. You will come and sleep in our caravan another night?"

"I mun go and preach the Ward."

"But you will come back to-night? We'd be pleased to hear more. We should like to change from red to white like you, shouldn't we, Mrs. Ripley?"

"Indeed we should. I always had a very high opinion of Christian people, and my eldest brat is a Christian person, but not the younger, for I have been told that it is not true, after all, that christening saves a brat from smallpox."

"No, our youngest brat has been vaccinated, which does better than christening. He will never have the smallpox my Uncle Wenzelow died of. But when he dies he will not go to heaven. The eldest brat will go to heaven, but perhaps she will go there sooner than is pleasant."

"No baptism can git you to heaven," began Robert, and Darius had some difficulty in bringing him back to the original starting-point of the conversation—his plans for another night at Castwisell. It was still raining and might not clear, and the caravan was a beautiful, lovely caravan; no inn could provide such princely accommodation at such a humble price.

Robert felt indignant with the little thief, and inclined to spurn his swindling suggestions. But he realized the solemnity of the task before him. He was now convinced that he had received his "call" to Shadoxhurst simply and entirely for the purpose of his meeting Hannah and showing her the way of salvation. If he left her now, he had disobeyed the divine command. So he promised to come back for supper. By then, he trusted, the weather would have cleared, and he could spend the night in a field.

§ 14

His intention was to sweep a circuit round Castwisell, testifying in half a dozen places. He had found out from Darius a little how the country lay, and tramped off in the direction of Ihornden, where there was a hamlet.

But he did not go any farther than Hareplain, the little hill above the Hammer Stream. He felt more tired than he had ever felt before in his life; he wondered why he should be so punished for a matter of fifty miles; and as the weather had cleared a little, he thought he would sit down and rest. So he sat on the trunk of a tree beside some gorse bushes, and watched the mist drifting along the Hammer Stream and against the hill.

The clouds were still low, but they no longer flew before the wind; instead, they seemed to move in a solemn march along the horizon. The sky was like a smoked plate, and against it the woods were black, ragged and smeared with mist as if drawn with smudged charcoal. Only the gorse at his side seemed to hold a colour as of fire, burning on the hill.

He leaned his elbows on his knees, and thrust his stubby, ill-shaved chin deep into the palms of his hands. His eyes stared out towards the slow-moving clouds of the horizon, but he did not see them. He saw instead the gipsy camp at Castwisell, with the two caravans looming through the rain, and the brown humps of the tents, and the red glow of a brazier shining through the door of one of them like an angry eye. Then he saw Hannah stooping over the brazier, all blowsy and untidy, with her youth and beauty gone, but still Hannah. Then he saw her nursing her baby while he spoke to her of Eternal Life. Her eyes had never changed like the rest of her; they were still those shining dark greedy eyes, more the eyes of an animal than of a human being, since their beauty and their wildness seemed to have no roots in a human heart, but to belong to some impersonal quality of the wild and harsh and lovely earth, or of nature in some petty, savage mood, when she strews the ditch with little corpses. There was nothing so big nor yet so little as humanity in Hannah.

But her wifehood and her motherhood had tamed her, they had made her conform at least to the outward shape of tenderness. It was this tenderness, though it might not be more than a shadow, which had made her so tragically sweet a year ago when she had stood with her baby outside the Eight Bells at Salehurst. Without it she had been joy and wonder and passion, but with it she was something more, for tenderness had given her a part both in life and in pain.

He flung up his head and squared his shoulders, clasping his hands between his knees, but he did not get up off his trunk and go on to Ihornden, as it was now high time for him to do. He could not preach the Gospel when his thoughts were full of Hannah. He must lay the ghost in his heart before he could hope for utterance. Something told him that the only way to do so was not to see her again—to give up all thought of going back to Castwisell—but to tramp resolutely through the southward villages home. He was still weak, in spite of the Divine strength; his love for Hannah had not died with the old Adam in him, but was also mysteriously part of the new man who lived in Christ. If he did not see her, he was safe enough, but if he saw her—even with her youth gone and her beauty marred and her passion tamed— he still wanted her, because she belonged to a part in him which had not changed, which he saw now had stayed unmoved through the earthquake of his conversion . . . one of "those things which cannot be shaken," as the Scripture says.

Yes, undoubtedly if Bob had any sense he would now go home, and realize that he was not fit, and would probably never be fit, to trust himself in the presence of Hannah Ripley. He would never again be puffed up at the thought of the love he had conquered; perhaps, indeed, his present state of humiliation was a punishment for his self-confidence in thinking he had conquered it, who was a very worm and no man. . . . But there was one fatal objection to the scheme, and that was his knowledge that he had been brought into Kent simply for the purpose of converting Hannah. She who was his great danger was also his great work, and if he turned away from the work out of fear of the danger, what would the Lord think of His unprofitable servant?

It was true that Hannah did not look a likely candidate for election, but it was essential to distrust appearances, and even if he did not succeed in impressing her with the divine message now, he might sow the seed which should sprout on some future occasion. The sense of his mission deepened upon him. He saw Hannah as God's special desire and care, and himself as God's instrument. He saw a triumphant opportunity to show his thankfulness for his own election, and also to make a partial reparation for the year in which his love for her had been sin. The sin seemed to be all his now; to his exalted memory it was as if he had led her astray; and now he was to lead her back, so that they two who had been together in darkness should now be together in light.

He dared not refuse his commission. After all, the Lord who had given it to him would give him strength to perform it; and he did not love Hannah as he had loved her once, with stormy selfish desires. Perhaps it would be a help— this falling off in her looks. . . . Oh, poor, poor Hannah! He wondered if she had suffered, if pain had drawn the lines on her face and taken the ease and slimness out of her body. He found it hard to think that she could feel pain, who had given so much. . . . But those who are without Christ must always be in pain, as he knew well. . . . He would never forget those dreadful months that had gone before deliver-

ance. He must lead Hannah into the fold of the Lord's flock,
both for her sake and out of his own gratitude to the love
that had redeemed him. Then he would go on his way, and
never see her again.

§ 15

After all these exalted and grateful feelings, it was strange
that he should find himself totally unable to preach that day.
He managed at last to drag himself to Ihornden, but he could
only loiter, without words or thoughts. He walked a mile or
two out of the village, and coming to an inn, went in and
had some bread and cheese and a cup of tea. He took his
Bible out of his pocket and opened it beside him on the
table. Its thumbed pages opened at the words, "I have loved
thee with an everlasting love; therefore with loving kindness
have I drawn thee." He flushed with exultation; these very
words had been the seal and earnest of his own conversion.
They were for Hannah now; God was calling her with the very
same words that He had called Robert. He loved Hannah
too with an everlasting love, she was His Elect and precious.
. . . Bob shut the book with trembling fingers.

He roamed about during the afternoon in the neighbourhood
of Ihornden. He still found himself unable to speak, though
he went to Catherine Wheel, and prayed earnestly for the
Spirit. He wondered if it was a sign. . . . Was the Lord
displeased? No, not with those blessed words in the Book.
It must be the divine will that now he had found Hannah he
should preach the Gospel to her only. He would be given
utterance to-night. He wished it was time to go back to
Castwisell. But it was still early. A sudden, almost uncon-
trollable longing for a pipe came over him. He went into a
wood, and lay down in a dry place under the reddening hazels;
but he could not rest, though he felt very tired. How slowly
the hours passed! . . . His heart was beating violently, and
the pulses in his brow and throat were hammering.

At last the restless day sank into twilight. Large clear
spaces showed themselves in the sky, like lakes with stars

sprinkled in them. The clouds went in a great scud over the zenith, sweeping the lakes of stars. The moon had not risen yet, but a queer glow was in the open spaces of the sky. As Robert walked towards Castwisell it began to rain—first a few flying drops, then a great downpour. When he reached the caravan the night was all one inky storm.

Hannah was cooking a savoury supper of mushrooms and chicken. She was still in her outdoor things, having just come from her business of clothes-peg selling, with which she had doubtless combined other business more profitable but less reputable. She wore a long plush coat, with an apparently sable "dolman," and a big hat with feathers as in the old days. She grinned cheerfully at Robert, and he saw that she had lost a front tooth. Time was certainly paying her out for her long defiance of him, now that at last he had her at a disadvantage.

"Good evening, Mr. Robert Fuller; have you converted many sinners?"

Robert shook his head sadly and sat down.

"There's only one sinner I want to convert, Hannah, and that's you."

"I'm not a sinner. I was married in church and have my lines; anyways, I'll trouble you to call me Mrs. Ripley."

"I'm sorry," said Robert humbly, "but if we say we have no sin we deceive ourselves and the truth is not in us."

"That's a good piece out of the Bible, ain't it?"

"It is, surelye."

"Then I don't mind your telling me a good piece out of the Bible. But the Bible's not always civil—and I'd have you civil to me, Mr. Robert Fuller."

"Reckon I'll always think high of you, Ha—Mrs. Ripley."

"That's right. And now I hope you will have a bit of supper with us and tell us some more good and civil words."

Darius had come into the tent.

"It's one shilling and ninepence we asks for the supper," he whined, "being poor people, and having pervided a chicken, which is dear meat."

Robert knew that the food had either been stolen or had

died of old age, but he was anxious to keep friendly with Darius, so—as terms were strictly cash—he handed over the coins. But he would have liked to kick the gipsy, for he felt that the little villain was simply trying to make all the money he could out of the Gospel. He evidently looked upon Bob's preaching as a personal indulgence for which he would always be willing to pay. But for Hannah's sake he must be tolerated, and if anything would buy Robert a few hours in which to fight for her precious soul, then the price would be forthcoming.

The fowl had evidently been stolen, for it was juicy and tender. After it they ate a great many apples, sitting round the fire while Hannah nursed one child and gave the other some sips of fowl and gravy. It was a homely, rather sordid spectacle. The red glare of the brazier fell on their bodies as they sat round it, and made visible the thick reeking atmosphere of the tent, which had now a fresh ingredient in the steam of three sets of damp clothes.

Robert had eaten a fairly good supper, but he still felt nervous and unsure of himself, and during the meal their talk—what there was of it, for there had been big gaps of silence —had been just of ordinary things. When Hannah had put the babies to sleep, wrapped up in her shawl at the back of the tent, Darius said he would go out and have a word or two with his Aunt Truffeny Lovell, who occupied the other caravan. She was a wicked old woman, he said, who would not keep herself clean, and in other ways was apparently in need of nepotic advice.

Then Robert discovered that he did not want to be left alone with Hannah. He had counted on Darius being with her when he wrestled for her soul. He should have taken up his burden during supper. . . . He got up, and said he would go round to the inn, but Hannah caught his arm.

"Ain't you going to speak good words to me, Mr. Robert Fuller?"

He could feel her touch on his wrist after she had taken away her hand. He swallowed violently.

"I'd sooner spik to you and your husband together. He

mun be säaved along of you. And thur's your Aunt Lovell,
too——"

"You'll never put anything good into her, nor into Darius
neither. He couldn't do with such things, having to sell
horses and dawgs. I'm just a poor female who hasn't her
living to get. There'll be no harm in my learning what's
good."

Robert thought of the clothes-pegs and the chicken, but
her lies—like her worn face and her gross body—only made
her more appealing. He could not sit comfortable inside the
Kingdom of Heaven, with Hannah outside the door, selling
clothes-pegs and stealing chickens and telling lies. . . .

He sat down beside her on a pile of rags, and her face in
the red glow of the brazier seemed to him like the face of a
soul in hell, of a soul perishing at the bottom of a gulf from
which his love alone could save her . . . no, not his love—
God's love. Her eyes looked up at him, as she squatted
with her arms round her knees, and as he looked down into
them it was as if he was looking down into a gulf—a gulf
of darkness and sin and loss, the gulf in which he himself had
been until the Everlasting Mercy found him. At all costs
he must drag her out, with her singed garments smelling of
fire. . . . But suppose instead he fell in himself, suppose instead of his pulling her out she pulled him in with her. . . .
Her eyes seemed to be dragging him down.

With almost a physical effort he turned his away, and once
more scrambled to his feet.

"No, I can't spik to you; it mun wait. O Lord, this äun't
the präaper time, me being but a weak human man."

He did not know what he was saying, he only knew that she
had caught his arm again and was pulling him back beside
her.

"Don't go away, child. Aren't you going to give me the
good word? Are you afraid of me? I haven't changed."

He turned to her in anguish.

"Oh, Nannie," he said, "God loves you. He's never stopped
loving you once, for all you've turned agäunst Him and the
cruel things you've done——"

Then he knew that he was merely declaring his own love for her and calling it God's. The thought made him tremble with shame, and his eyes filled with tears. Through the tears her face looked up at him as from the bottom of a pit. . . .

His last power suddenly broke, he fell on his knees beside her, and, taking her in his arms, covered her face with kisses.

§ 16

It was all over in a second. Suddenly he had a wild animal in his arms, who fought him with kicks and scratches and loud angry screams. He released her as violently as he had taken her, and saw the doorway full of heads—Darius's, the unclean Mrs. Lovell's, and some children's heads which he had not seen before.

Hannah sat on the ground, rocking herself and sobbing. Robert could feel the blood trickling down his cheek, where her nails had dug five angry furrows.

Darius came into the tent.

"What's happened?" he asked furiously.

There was no answer.

"You're a fine Gospel Minister. I leave you alone ten minutes with my wife, for you to teach her how to be good and go to Heaven, and then you start this sort of game."

Robert could not speak. He was quite without words and almost without thought.

"What's happened?" asked Darius, taking his wife by the shoulder.

"He's a beast," sobbed Hannah, "a wicked beast."

"I've done her no harm," stammered Robert, finding voice at last.

"No harm!" shrieked Hannah. "D'you think it's no harm to be messed about by you?" and she would have flown at him again if Darius had not held her back.

"You're a swine," he said to Robert, "a common swine, and eighteen villages shall know it, Mr. Gospel Preacher."

Bob turned white.

"It'll be gorgeous news for all the folk you've preached at

to be told that you can't be left alone with a man's legal, certificated wife. They'll be pleased—they'll say, 'This is a fine Gospel and a damn-fine Gospeller.' "

The tent was full of noise. The commotion had wakened the babies, who were crying loudly. Hannah was still sobbing, and Mrs. Lovell was jabbering incomprehensibly.

"Haven't you a word to say?" continued Darius. "I thought you was full of 'em. Don't you know what it'll mean if I tells everyone in the Hop Country that you tried to steal my lawful, certificated wife—seduce her, as is said by them what uses fine language? Don't you know what it'll mean to your trade? Don't you know as you'll never be able to lift up your head or your voice again?"

But Robert knew only one thing—that he had fallen from grace.

"You can't speak a word. You're ashamed of yourself, and it's the only good thing I see in you, you gorgy swine. Maybe if you're ashamed I shan't be so hard on you as I might feel disposed, being a lawful, legal husband."

He looked searchingly at Robert.

"He's half a fool," said Mrs. Lovell. "You'll have to speak plainer, Darius."

"Hold your tongue, you old mare," said her nephew; "and you listen, Mr. Robert Fuller. I'm not a hard man, and I don't want to spoil your trade as a priest or minister, so maybe I'll not tell anyone about the beastly way you've behaved."

"Tell if you like—I deserve it—and it mäakes no odds to me. I can't never preach the mercy of God no more."

"You can, if nobody knows your private habits. And I shan't ask a lot of you, I ain't a blackmailer, and I knows you ain't rich. If you pays me five quid to buy my wife a new hat and shawl and make all straight and comfortable, then we'll call it quits."

"Wot?" said Robert sharply. Something had penetrated his thoughts.

"I say, as it can easily all be settled for a small sum. Hannah ull forgive you, and my Aunt Truffeny Lovell ull hold her tongue, and my nevvies Tom and Benedict, and myself

Darius Ripley ull hold our tongues.   And you'll pay us five
quid one week from now, and we'll call it quits."

"You'll be a fool if you don't do it, gentleman," said Auntie
Lovell.   "I call five quid nothing for what you've done.   The
other gentleman had to pay ten, and he scarce got hold of
Hannah properly. . . ."

"Hold your tongue, you old bitch," shouted Darius.   But
it was too late.   Robert's slow mind had leaped at last, and
the next minute his body leaped.   Without a word he flung
himself upon Darius, and bore him down struggling to the
ground.

"Help! Help! Police! Police!" shouted Auntie Lovell.

Hannah screamed loudly.

Robert and Darius fought on the ground, rolling over
and over.   The gipsy was wiry and well trained, but Bob
was a bigger man, and his hands had a strangling grip upon
Darius's throat.   He would probably have killed him had not
the fight been interrupted by two men who, driving by in a
gig, had heard the screams and hurried to the spot.

"He's murdering my husband," shrieked Hannah.

"Shoot him!   Shoot the mad dog!" cried Mrs. Lovell.

Robert was seized and pulled off Darius, just as he had
nearly choked the breath out of him.   The gipsy lay unconscious on the ground, with a thin stream of blood running from
the corner of his mouth.

"We'd better send for the police," said one of the men.

There was a chorus of tears and protests from the gipsies.

"You needn't trouble, mister.   We ain't spiteful.   We don't
want the police."

"I dare say not," said the first man grimly, "but I think
they ought to look into this.   You drive off to the throws,
Mr. Gain, and I'll stop along here wud this lot."

"Think you'll be all right alone?"

"Oh, I'll be right enough.   There's only women and children—and this fellow, who doesn't look as if he had much
fight in him now."

Robert was huddled on the earthen floor, blood and tears
on his unspeakably dirty face.   His hands were clasped before

him in the attitude of prayer. But he did not pray. There
was no use. Neither prayer nor repentance nor love nor faith
could help him now, who had trampled under foot the Promises
of God.

§ 17

Clem and Polly had been to tea with Elizabeth Wheelsgate
at Marsh Quarter, so it was not till fairly late that they found
Mabel's telegram. The telegraph boy had pushed it under the
door, and they both jumped as if they had found a snake on
the mat.

"That must be Mabel!" cried Polly. "No one else sends
telegraphts. Oh, wotsumdever can have happened now?"

Clem picked it up and opened it gingerly.

"Come at once in dreadful trouble Mabel."

"Oh, wotsumdever can that be?" cried Polly.

"Whur's Bob? He mun be at höame now. He wur coming back Monday."

"She döan't say wot it is, but I reckon it's Bob's trouble,
or he'd have come aräound."

"We mun go and see. I can't mäake out wot's happened
the way she puts it."

They did not wait to change their clothes, but set off at
once, Polly in her tight blue dress—which had undergone a
fresh metempsychosis with the help of an old lace gown of
Mabel's—and Clem in his black coat and small, ridiculous
bowler. They did not even go over to the farm to fetch the
trap. By striking across the fields Clem calculated that they
ought to reach the Bodiam road in about twenty minutes,
just in time to catch the carrier's cart on its way back from
Ticehurst.

They managed this successfully, and arrived at Campany's
Hatch in a little less than an hour. The place seemed deserted as they walked up the drive, but when they came to
the house they saw the boy Podgam dawdling behind a barn.

"Is your mäaster in?" asked Clem. "Whur's your missus?
We've just had a telegrapht."

Podgam came forward, a grin struggling on his face with a look of proper concern.

"Missus is indoors, surelye; and mäaster—he's in jail."

Clem and Polly stared with their mouths wide open.

"I thought maybe you'd have known. They know at Ethnam and at Gurt Wigsell, and it's all over Peter's Green."

"Döan't stand talking to him, Clem," said Polly, "but come in quick and see Mabel. Döan't scratch your head lik that."

"I'm vrothered," said Clem.

"Well, come in and see Mabel. Maybe it äun't true."

"It's true as Gospel," put in the boy; "he's bin had up for murdering Darius Ripley."

"Murdering. . . ."

"That's wot they say at Ethnam, but at Peter's Green they say it wur for kissing Mrs. Ripley. . . ."

Polly seized Clem by the arm and dragged him towards the house. Mabel was at first nowhere to be seen, but after they had called her once or twice she came out of the scullery, her face puffed up and disfigured with crying. When she saw Clem and Polly she began to cry afresh, but the tears would hardly come from her swollen eyes, they merely oozed and dribbled, and when she spoke her voice was nearly gone.

"Oh, you've come at last. . . . I don't want Jim and Mary . . . I shall die of shame."

"Wot's happened? Is it true that Bob——"

"He's in jail at Headcorn."

She tottered and fell back against the door. Polly caught her in her arms.

"Come into the kitchen, and I'll mäake you a cup of tea."

Once in the kitchen Mabel sank into a chair and covered her face. She was utterly broken, her spirit and her self-respect were gone together. She sat rocking herself, with her hair all rough, and one great hank loose on her shoulder. She had no softness or beauty left; even her characteristic "refinement" seemed to have deserted her. She looked crude and degraded. Clem stared at her without speaking. He was horribly scared at her grief, and yet he wanted to know about

Bob . . . what had happened to him? . . . what was this dreadful thing he had heard? . . . if only Mabel would tell him. . . . He would have liked to ask her, but at present he felt, as he put it, all gummed up. The only person who had any presence of mind was Polly, and she expressed it not in words but in action, scurrying about with the kettle and teapot.

Mabel began at last to sob and mutter:

"Don't stand gaping at me, you fool," she said to Clem. "Can't you do something? Oh, this'll kill me. I know it."

"But wot'll I do? Wot's happened?"

"I've told you. Bob's in jail . . . for assaulting Darius Ripley, when he . . . when he . . ."

A burst of hysterical, tearless sobbing choked her words. Polly began to lose patience.

"Can't you kip yourself quiet, Mabel, and tell us just wot's happened? Maybe Clem can do summat, but he can't do naun if he scarce knows half."

"Don't you understand?" sobbed Mabel; "you must be pretty thick. That beast of a Bob has been caught—caught— caught out—with Hannah Ripley, and now he's in prison for assaulting her husband when he—he found them together."

Clem and Polly stared at each other in utter bewilderment.

"It can't be true," cried Clem. "Bob ud never do such a thing now he's Säaved."

Mabel gave a laugh which was even more unpleasant than her crying.

"That's it . . . now he's Saved. Oh, he's enjoyed himself many a time—now he's Saved. You bet!—going off for those week-ends."

"But, Mabel, you döan't mean . . . you know fur truth as he wur at Bethersden and Biddenden and all them pläaces."

"Yes, but we don't know—at least we didn't know—what he was up to on the way. Now perhaps we've an idea why he wouldn't go by train, and took such a mortal time getting backwards and forwards . . . and perhaps we guess where he slept of a Sunday night."

"Hold your tongue," said Clem angrily. "I döan't believe

it. Bob's bin straight from the day he got Salvation. His way äun't my way, but it's a straight way, and I know he's kept to it."

"Then how d'you account for his being in jail—all along of his row with Darius over Hannah Ripley?"

"Has it bin proved? Has he bin tried yit?"

"He's to be tried to-morrow. But it's all quite plain. I heard it from Policeman here, who'd heard from the police at Headcorn. Darius is in the Union Infirmary over there— Bob's nearly killed him."

"But they mayn't have quarrelled about wot you think. Reckon thur's a middling lot of things as Darius wants bashing fur."

"That's it—you stand up against me, as you always do. I tell you everybody knows that Darius caught him with his wife—Ugh! I could be sick. . . . You'll just be shown up as a fool if you believe different. Bob spent Sunday night with those dirty gipsies . . . it's proved, it's well known—and on Monday Darius came back sudden, and caught Bob and Hannah so as there was no mistake . . . and then Bob went for him, and would have killed him if he hadn't been pulled off . . . that's what they're saying everywhere, and if you don't believe me you can go and see for yourself."

"And I wull go, surelye. We'll all of us go."

"I shan't. I'll never set eyes on Bob again. I've done with him."

"Oh, Mabel . . ." and Polly began to cry, her tears spilling into the cup of tea that she carried to her sister-in-law.

"I've done with him," repeated Mabel sullenly. "I've stood enough. Oh, it was pretty bad when he turned all soppy and religious, but now I know he only used his religion to cover his beastliness . . . he used it so as he could go messing after Hannah. Look at this——"

She took a letter out of her pocket and handed it to Clem. It was Bob's unfortunate letter from Witters Oak.

"I have made up my mind," read Clem, "to come home slow by Sissinghurst and Dashnanden and other foreign places, seeing as the Gospel must be preached to them also, so may not be back till Tuesday, and hope you won't mind."

"There—you see the sort of lies he tells! Always the Gospel when he's plotting to get with Hannah. Don't tell me this is the first time he's done it. I bet you he's been unfaithful to me a dozen times and called it the Gospel. Oh, the damned hypocrite! Oh, I'd sooner he was the softest, soppiest Y.M. that ever was rather than the beast he is. I thought I was ill-used then, but now—Oh, it isn't fair; I've been put upon all through. He only married me to help him forget her, and when he found he couldn't, he took up with her again—you know he did, that time he met her at Sale-hurst and then came home and was such a brute to me. And when he saw I wasn't going to stand any nonsense, he went and invented his religion as an excuse for getting away from me and going with her. Oh, I see through it all now; he's a hypocrite and a canting scoundrel, and I'll not see him again as long as I live."

"Mabel," said Clem, "you know as all that äun't true. I can't believe as Bob's done anything wicked. Anyways, I'm going to Headcorn to see."

"And I'm going back to father at Bulverhythe."

"Mabel, you can't!" cried Polly. "Wot'll happen when it's all cleared up, as it is sure to be, and Bob comes höame and finds you and baby gone?"

"It won't be all cleared up—you take my word. Anyhow, he was found with Hannah, and that's enough for me."

"Well, I call you a tedious cruel girl," sobbed Polly; "pore Bob to have his höame all busted up because of some fool's mistääke that's bin määde."

"Most like them 'gyptians have played him a trick," said Clem. "Darius ud be jealous and want to sarve him out for wunst being so set on Hannah."

It was an unfortunate remark. Mabel burst into a storm of crying, and staggering to her feet went groping to the door.

"Clem, you gurt owl!" cried Polly. "Mabel, he means naun säave wot's over and done."

"Nothing's over and done. He never loved me . . . it was always her . . . and always will be her. . . . I'm going to father—now—to-night."

She fumbled for the door handle, being too blind with tears to see. She had made herself quite ill with crying, and as she groped and staggered there, was suddenly and violently sick.

Polly ran up to her.

"Come wud me, Mabel. Döan't vrother any more. You can't go to-night, anyways; you've mäade yourself ill. Come and I'll help you git to bed, and Clem and I ull stay the night here, and to-morrow fust thing he'll go to Headcorn."

"And I'll go to Bulverhythe."

Polly saw the uselessness of trying to argue with her as she was now. She half led, half dragged her up the stairs to the room where Robert's child lay sleeping. At the sight of his little dark head among the white mass of pillows on the big bed, Polly's heart suddenly became tender and savage. She stooped over little Nat, her breast heaving passionately, and one or two tears fell upon his face.

"I'll leave him behind with you, if you like," said Mabel. It was a piece of diplomacy on her part.

"Wull you?" asked Poll, eagerly and incredulously.

"If you like. Father doesn't care for kids, and I know you'll look after him all right. . . . And I don't want to take Bob's child away from him if he wants to keep it; but I'll never go back to him—never—never. I've finished with Bob —and I wish to God that I'd never begun."

§ 18

Clem set out for Headcorn in the very first train running on the Rother Valley railway. Even so, he arrived only just in time for the trial before the county magistrates. Bob was being led into the dock just as Clem at last succeeded in making his way into the court house. The sight of his brother was a shock to him. During a nearly sleepless night and the long jolting journey, none of the various eventualities which had occurred to him had taken into calculation any possibility of Robert's guilt. But now when he saw him—that unshaved, haggard face, those dreadful eyes—his guilt suddenly became one of the chances with which he had to reckon. Bob would not look like that if he was merely the victim of circumstances, of a misunderstanding, of a revengeful trick. He would know that he could vindicate himself, that a set of gipsies were not formidable accusers. Of course, Hannah's share in the matter would make it very hard for him; she might even have subjected him to severe temptation. But that circumstance was not enough in itself to account for his abject appearance, nor the possibility that his earlier relations with her might be exposed at the trial. After all, he had no character to lose; he had never posed as anything but a converted sinner. The tale of his misdeeds had been told by himself from many a village pulpit, from many a village crossways; he could not object to its repetition here.

Yet there he stood like a man smitten, with bowed head and hanging jaw, and terrible red-rimmed eyes that seemed to be staring at something unseen and horrible beyond the court house wall. . . . Clem remembered that that was how he used to look in the days before his conversion, when he felt convinced that he was damned. He took no notice of what was going forward; he made no answer when the chairman of the magistrates addressed him. He just stood there looking —damned.

The question was put whether he would plead guilty or not guilty, and Clem knew that Bob's answer would settle the matter definitely as far as he was concerned. But Bob refused to plead at all, he refused to answer the magistrate's question. He just stood there dumb and stricken. Accordingly his plea was entered as "not guilty."

The evidence was next taken. Darius Ripley, Hannah Ripley and Truffeny Lovell were witnesses, as well as the two farmers who had stopped the fight. Darius's throat was bandaged, and he looked pale and shaken—he was allowed to sit while he gave evidence. None of the gipsies looked comfortable in the witness-box, they were too used to finding it an ante-room to the dock. When Darius had finished his evidence, and the accused was asked if there was any question he wanted to put to the witness, it was obviously a bad moment both for Ripleys and Lovells. But Robert had no questions to ask.

Thus encouraged, the witnesses became less nervous, and a fine story came out against the prisoner. Darius Ripley had met him at the Crown at Castwisell, and, as he was unable to find accommodation for the night, invited him to sleep in his caravan. The invitation had been repeated for the following night, Fuller having spent the day preaching in the neighbourhood. After supper Ripley had occasion to leave him alone with his wife, and a quarter of an hour later heard loud screams. He ran to the rescue and found his wife struggling with the accused. On his entrance Fuller hurled himself upon him and would have killed him but for the timely arrival of Mr. Boorman and Mr. Gain. Hannah bore out her husband's evidence. She had known the prisoner in Sussex some years ago, she said, and he had objected to her marriage. Mrs. Lovell and the two farmers then gave their accounts, and there seemed little more to be said. Certainly Bob did not say anything.

Clem sat bolt upright, gripping his bowler with both hands between his knees. This story could not be true . . . and yet he saw painfully how true it might be—poor Bob, confronted with sudden temptation after long self-denial, tired and tried with the failure of his married life and his bungling efforts as a preacher, and brought back again into the power of his life's great love. . . . It was not so strange that he had fallen—though Clem did not believe that the circumstances were just as the gipsies had given them—but it was very cruel. For now whatever man did in the way of punishment Bob would punish himself without forgiveness. Clem could read that on his brother's face. He stood there a man to whom man's judgment is nothing, since his own heart has condemned him. He had no wish either to accuse others or to excuse himself. He had already been accused and found guilty before a greater Judge; it was nothing to him if Headcorn Petty Sessions made him white or black.

The magistrates consulted together and gave judgment through their chairman. They found the prisoner guilty of a very grave offence. He was lucky in not finding himself arraigned for attempted murder, with a chance of being sent into penal servitude. The magistrates were taking into consideration his position as a preacher, and all that his loss of character would mean to him. But they could not let him off with a lenient sentence. Though this was his first appearance in court he did not bear an unblemished character, and he had been found guilty of a brutal and cowardly crime. He must go to prison for six months.

Robert made no sign. He did not seem to care—hardly to understand. A constable touched his arm, and he went out of the dock, to make room for the next item of the magistrates' busy morning.

§ 19

Clem asked and was granted permission to see Bob before he went to Maidstone Jail. He was with his brother for about ten minutes, in the presence of a constable. Robert looked much the same as he had looked in court, but he seemed less oblivious of his surroundings. When Clem came into the room his eyes lit up for a moment, then darkened. For a time neither of them could speak, and they looked at each other in silence.

"Well, Bob," said Clem at last, "all this is unaccountable sad and I'm middling upset about it."

"So am I," said Bob.

"But I've come to tell you not to vrother, sinst I mean to stick by you."

His brother said nothing, and Clem felt disappointed.

"Dud you see me in court?"

Bob shook his head.

"I wur thur, though. I come along to Headcorn by the fust train, having heard about you last night."

"Does Mabel know?"

"Surelye. She sent a telegrapht to Poll and me. Poll's with her now."

A slow flush darkened on Bob's cheek.

"She'll never spik to me agäun, I reckon."

"Döan't you fear—we'll bring her räound."

"There äun't no cause fur her to be brung räound. Why shud she spik to me? I'm lost."

"Oh, döan't you say such a wicked thing."

"It's true. It's in the Scriptures: 'If we sin after that we've received the knowledge of truth thur remaineth no more sacrifice fur sins.'"

"But, Bob, it dudn't all happen as them Egyptians said. I know as you wurn't as bad as all that. Why dudn't you ask Darius questions when the gentleman said you m'ght?"

"I've got no questions to ask of nobody. God is my Judge, and He has condemned me. It is a fearful thing to fall into the hands of the living God."

"But dud you truly määke free wud Hannah?"

"Surelye, or I shudn't be here now. After all the tender mercies of God to me I turned lik a dog to my vomit agäun ... 'Oh, of how much punishment shall he be worthy who hath counted the blood of the covenant, wud which he was sanctified, an unholy thing, and done despite to the Spirit of grääce.'"

"Döan't say such things."

"I mun say them. They're my judgment."

There was a few moments' awkward silence. They sat staring at each other. Or rather Clem stared at Robert, for Robert's gaze was vacant and remote.

"Six months wöan't sim so long," said the younger brother huskily at last, feeling it best to concentrate on the concrete aspects of the tragedy. "I'll mind Campany's Hatch while you're a-gone, and see after the kid ... and Mabel. ... Reckon you'll be back in time fur the spring sowings. ..."

His voice trailed off helplessly—Bob seemed so far off, in a hell beyond his reach. Clem could do nothing for him—

even if he performed the highly improbable and kept his home together, it would not really matter to Bob.

"Döan't look at me lik that," he said hoarsely.

"I were wondering if you'd do summat fur me."

"Surelye. I'll stick by you, as I've said."

"Wull you write a letter to Mus' Beeman at Goudhurst, and ask him to come and see me? Maybe, sinst he's a minister of the Gospel they'll let him come. . . . I want to spik to him . . . thur's just a chanst as he can show me light . . . you mun do it, Clem."

"I'll do it, surelye. But—but, Bob, d'you think Mus' Beeman's lik to be any comfort to you? Reckon he mäade you tedious miserable a year agone."

"I mun see him—he's a man of God, and he has God's ward in him. Promise you'll ask him, Clem."

"I've promised. But . . . old Bob . . . it justabout breaks my heart seeing you vrother over these things, when you've such a lot to put up wud besides. Maybe it wurn't right and präaper fur you to kiss Hannah, but reckon it wurn't much —no more'n many a man ud do, and has done, I guess. And as fur bashing Darius—there's no cause fur you to be so upset and low over having done wot wur no more'n he desarved."

"You döan't understand," said Bob. "I haven't sinned as the heathen which know not God—but I've sinned agäunst the light. I'm one of them of whom it says 'it wur impossible to renew them agäun unto repentance.' Fur one morsel of meat I've sold my birthright, and now I am rejected. I tell you agäun—'there remaineth no more sacrifice fur sins.' "

"I can't mäake out your doctrine, Bob, and thur's no sense pretending that I do."

"You'll have to go in two more minutes," said the police constable.

"Give a message from me to Mabel," said Bob; "say as I ask her pardon, and I desarve as she never forgives me; but I hope she will fur her own sake."

"Yes—I'll tell her. Polly and I are having the kid wud us."

"Mabel's going away, then?"

Clem flushed at his mistake.

"Fur a bit—but never fear, we'll have her back by the time you come."

"Döan't you go pressing her. I've mäade her mighty miserable, wot wud one thing and another . . . it'll only be sense of her to kip away. And tell Jim and Mary, too, as I'm sorry . . . and mother. . . . I've brung 'em all a tedious lot of trouble."

"Döan't spik of it, Bob."

"And you, young 'un—I'm mäaking you unhappy."

"Oh, no, no—naun—döan't you vrother."

"Good-bye, then."

"Good-bye."

§ 20

Clem left Headcorn forlornly in the afternoon. His trouble had brought him to the actual pitch of not wanting any dinner, and he moped miserably about the town till it was time for the train to go. His only comfort came from a few minutes' conversation with a large policeman in the station road. The policeman had seen Clem in court and knew he was the brother of the wild-looking preacher who had been run in for assault, and had been given a sentence which the police, who knew the gipsies, thought remarkably hard and undeserved.

"They're a nasty lot," he said to Clem, "and I know there was a sight more to that business than came out in court. Your brother was naturally a bit upset, having his character to lose, and wouldn't take the matter up as he should have done. There's a strong notion as that Ripley's got money out of chaps for trying to get off with his wife. These gipsy women, they'd never look at any man but their husband, but they'll make a pretence if he tells them, just as one of our women who's bad enough ull make more'n a pretence. But the gipsy bullies are cleverer than ourn. The wife screams, and in they pop—having been listening outside—and kick up a row, and then offer to hold their tongue for five quid. We

had a chap up for that sort of thing last year—a man called
Devenden from the Quarter country—but it couldn't be proved
against him, and he got off."

"Do you think that's how it happened wud Bob?"

"I dunno—maybe. It struck me as likely, seeing as Ripley
ud have known he had a character to lose, and him having
been friendly with Mrs. Ripley once. I'm sorry we can't
prove it. However, the little blighter didn't get off. He was
run in as he was coming out of court. The police at Chichester have been after him, and, as soon as they heard we'd
got our hand on him, so to say, they phoned over about it,
and it'll be Mr. Darius who'll stand in the dock to-morrow."

"Wot fur?"

"The usual—dawg-stealing; and his wife and old Mrs.
Lovell ull git it too, for fencing—or receiving stolen goods."

"I wish they cud hang the lot," said Clem, delivering himself of the most vindictive sentiment he had expressed in his
life.

"You must look at it this way—them gipsies is like animals, and you can't hold them responsible for their doings as
you would ordinary human beings. I've seen a good deal of
'em, there being plenty in these parts, and always in court
for something or other. There ought to be some place where
they could be put away all together, so as not to do us any
harm. Ordinary folk can't reckon with 'em, as their minds
work so different from ours—so we're always being had. I'm
sorry your brother was had—I know what that sort of trouble
means in a decent family, and he looked a stout chap too,
though maybe not quite right here, was he?" and the policeman touched his forehead.

"He took to religion a bit queer, but he wur a good feller,
though you mayn't think it."

"And why shouldn't I think it? I know as even a good
feller often can't help looking at a pretty girl. Not that Mrs.
Ripley was a pretty girl. Good Lord! She wasn't the sort
as ud get *me* off the narrer path of virtue."

"He used to care for her years ago before she married—he
cared very much."

"Pore chap. Is he a married man himself, by the way?"

Clem nodded.

"And she'll take it hard, I reckon. Women always do . . . however, he'll have got his religion to comfort him. And reckon six months in quod won't do him any harm—if only you can persuade him not to take it to heart too much—the disgrace, I mean. Look here, you tell him there's something us police knows better than the chaps that are in prison, and that's the chaps that ought to be and aren't. These laws of our'n . . . they was made to get scoundrels off. Oh, the villains I've had my hands on and then had to let go on account of these laws of our'n which was made to protect the weak and helpless——"

The policeman digressed into reminiscences and reflections —in the midst of which Clem had to leave him to catch his train. He was sorry, for he found him comforting; but he must not wait—having heard the worst that had happened at Headcorn, he must now go and hear the worst that had happened at Campany's Hatch. The little train—a string of ancient South-Eastern coaches hooked to a toy engine—heaved itself out of the station, with Clem crouched miserably in the corner of a third-class smoker, chewing an unlighted woodbine.

He reached Bodiam about tea time, and hurried to Campany's Hatch. Polly saw him from the window, and when he reached the house he found her standing in the doorway with the baby in her arms.

"She's gone," said Polly.

"He's got six months," said Clem.

They stood staring at each other in silence.

"I cudn't kip her," said Polly at last. "I tried to mäake her stay till she'd heard fur sartain sure, but she wudn't, and now I äun't sorry. Six months! . . . pore soul!"

"It's hard," said Clem; "it's tar'ble. I've a feeling as she'll never come back."

"We mun git her back somehows. It ud be too bad fur him to come höame and find her a-gone. . . . Not but wot she has reason, if it's true about him and Hannah."

"It's part true, anyways."

"Then Mabel wöan't never come back."

Clem said nothing. They had gone into the kitchen, and sat facing each other across the bare, scrubbed table.

"A gal lik Mabel ull never live wud a man who's bin in jail," continued Polly; "and she's that jealous of Hannah—you'd think as she'd go off her head. Oh, mäaster, wot mäade him do it?"

"He stopped two nights along of her and Darius at Castwisell, and reckon it all got too much fur him to bear—he and she wur left alöan together, and he dud but täake her in his arms."

"Is that all?"

"That's all, fur she struck out, and Darius cäame in, and then pore Bob went fur him, being mad seemingly."

Polly wiped the tears off her face.

"It's all middling sad, Clem."

"Middling sad."

"I suppose as how Bob's loved Hannah all this time?"

"That's it, I reckon."

"I can't bläame him, nuther, when I think as how it ud have bin if you and me hadn't bin married and yit had loved each other just lik we do now. . . ."

Clem nodded gravely.

"Sims to me as Bob's life's lik a green apple tree—he's picked his fruit lik other men, but it's bin hard and sour instead of sweet. Love and religion—they're both sweet things, folks say, but with Bob they've bin as the hard green apples."

Polly took up her hat which was hung on a chair.

"We mun be gitting back höame—I sent ward to Jim as we'd be back to-night."

"What about Nat? Has Mabel left him to us?"

"Yes—just fur a time. Her father döan't care fur kids."

"Nor does Mabel, nuther."

"Anyways, I'm glad to have him. I've always longed to have a baby in the house."

Clem pulled her to him with a fondling arm, and together they looked down at Robert's baby.

"Oh, mäaster, I wish he wur ourn."

"So do I, both fur our säakes, and fur all the good he's
ever lik to git out of his parents. Howsumdever. . . ."

§ 21

During the next six months Clem was busy keeping his
promises to Robert. He even wrote to Mr. Beeman and
asked him to go and see him, though he had great qualms
as to what the result of such a visit would be. He wrote
to Bob at the end of three months, as he understood he
was allowed to do, and told him all the news which was good.
He said nothing about Mabel, for there was nothing good to
say. She was still at Bulverhythe, defiant and broken, keeping house for her father, and going two or three evenings a
week with her friend Muriel to the pictures, where she found
a sort of consolation in watching the sorrows of the film
heroines and heroes. Once or twice she came over to see
the baby.

"I suppose I'll have to take him back with me soon," she
said, "but father never could do with kids in the house."

Nothing that Polly or Clem could say would make her
change her mind about returning to Robert. Her face would
grow hard and set when he was mentioned.

"I've finished with him. If you only knew what I've been
through, you wouldn't ask me to go back. First that woman
and then religion and then that woman again. And now
he's in jail, and everybody knows what for . . . oh, it's
nearly killed me. He's messed up my life—if I hadn't married him I could have married Stanley Huggins and had a nice
little house in the town. But he would marry me—just to
help him forget her. . . . And now here I am married and nobody's wife, for I'll never live with him again, and yet he's done
nothing that I can divorce him for . . . except break my
heart."

It was just like Mabel to talk about divorce, thought Clem
and Polly, just as it was like her to send telegrams. However, they could not really feel set against her, even after
what she had said about Bob, for they knew that it was true

that she had suffered, and the fact that she did not suffer graciously did not make her suffering any less dreadful.

"Then, Mabel," said Polly, "sinst you wöan't be höame when Bob comes, and sinst your fäather döan't want kids aräound, maybe you'd let us kip baby till Bob comes back, just to give him a bit of a welcome."

"Oh, yes, you may keep him, since you're kind enough to be bothered with him. And of course he's Bob's child—I can't take him away from him. If Bob wants to have him . . . he gets more like Bob every day."

She looked almost angrily at the child, who was crawling about the floor. He was a fine, sturdy little fellow, and certainly had Bob's high colour and blue eyes, though his hair was still quite fair. Clem and Polly adored him ridiculously —at night he slept between them as if he was their own child, and all day long he was with one or the other of them, receiving a love and notice that had been given him only spasmodically by his real parents. They told themselves that they must not forget that he was not theirs; they taught him to say "dada," so that he might welcome back his father when he came, but at present he would shout it whenever he saw Clem, which produced the wrong effect entirely.

About a fortnight after Robert went to jail Clem and Polly had moved into Campany's Hatch. At first Clem had tried looking after the place from Pookwell, leaving Podgam in residence, while he himself tramped over every morning; but this had soon proved impossible, and early in October they moved into the bare red farmhouse among the old barns by the river. Jim engaged a new hand in Clem's absence—Bodingmares was now thriving more prosperously than ever, and he had a hired shepherd and a hired cowman as well as his brother and Pickdick. But Jim's spiteful destiny decreed that the year of his greatest prosperity should also be the year of his deepest humiliation. He took no pride in his rich acres, nor in the price that his heifers fetched at Battle fair. The heart of his achievement was broken, since on his family had fallen the blackest taint that was known in the Rother villages—the taint of prison.

He was anxious that Bob should not come back to the district, that on his return from prison he should go to some new place where his relations shouldn't "git the splash of his muck."

"It ud be easy enough to sell wot's left of the lease of Campany's Hatch, and the live and dead stock should ought to bring in a good penny. Sinst you're writing, Clem, you might say as it ud be a präaper thing to do. It's the only chanst of our being able to hold up our heads agäun."

But Clem refused to say anything of the kind. He did not want his brother to think that his world was crumbling to bits in his absence. If Bob had lost his wife he might as well keep his farm, and anyhow he was not to know that his relations —or some of them—did not want to see him again. So he stuck loyally to Campany's Hatch, doing the best he could for its rather seedy acres, trying hard to accustom himself to the shoddy new house, which seemed so bare and unhomely after the low rafters and sweet-smelling walls of Pookwell.

But shortly after the New Year Robert himself relieved him of his charge, for he wrote to Clement then—his only letter. It was not much of a letter; it contained no news of himself, and was made up chiefly of bald statements of things he wanted done before he came back. One of these was to get rid of Campany's Hatch—"but ask Mabel first, but I know she will not care." He seemed to accept quite definitely the idea that Mabel would never live with him again, and Clem wondered if she had written to him, or whether he merely went by his knowledge of her character. He seemed anxious that she should not be forced or persuaded in any way: "Let her do what she likes about me. It is her turn now."

So Clem and Jim made arrangements with a firm of auctioneers for the selling up of Bob's stock and tools and furniture. Mabel was asked if she would like to keep any of the last, but she said she would rather not. The walnut sideboard, which had nearly filled the little dining-room, and the bedstead with brass knobs which had done the same for the bedroom, no longer gave her any housewifely thrill. She did not want furniture of her own now that she lived with her father, and she thought it better to live with him in her present ambiguous position. Everything to do with Campany's Hatch seemed bound up with unhappy memories—she did not want to see a stick of it again.

So Clem spent a depressing day while the auctioneer, with a mixed crowd at his heels, went up and down and in and out of Campany's Hatch, knocking down fowls and pigs and tools and furniture to various farmers and householders of the neighbourhood and a few dealers from village furniture stores. All that night the younger brother's dreams rang with the auctioneer's unending patter—"ten and six I'm bid—eleven shillings shall I make it?—ten and six I'm bid—ten and six once—ten and six twice—ten and six for the third and last time—Gone!" The sale realized a fair sum—nothing much, but enough, with the disposal of the lease, to set Bob up very humbly in a new district where he could make a fresh start.

In spite of the way he had stuck to the farm while he thought there was a chance of his brother's wanting it, Clem saw the wisdom of this abandonment. Opinion against Robert in the neighbourhood was very strong. Those who had laughed at him and those who had been outraged by him and those who had said "there mun be something in it" were all banded together against him now. Popular opinion condemned him as a ranting hypocrite, who had been properly exposed at last, and everybody "had said it all along."

"The long and the short of it is," said Shovell of Mount-pumps, "that you can't gather grapes off thorns or figs off thistles, nor the gospel off Bob Fuller, nuther."

"He wur black," said Pepper of Weights, "and he'd have us call him white—but the whitewash is all off now."

"Mark my wards," said Pont of Udiam, "as when he gits out of jail he'll be back in the pubs agäun."

"He's a low, tedious, lousy lot," said Pepper, "and it's the only one good thing them gipsies have done—a-showing of him up."

Certainly Bob would have had a hard time of it if he had come back to hold his own by the Bodiam river. He showed his sense in wanting to cut adrift. If only Mabel could have gone with him and helped him start his life again. . . . But that was his own fault, and probably he could never be happy with her again any more than she could be happy with him. Clem wrote and asked his brother to come to him and Polly at Pookwell when he left Maidstone. Then they could look round them and think a bit—anyways, Bob would not feel so strange coming to a place he knew.

§ 22

When in the swale of a March day Clem drove to the station to meet Robert, he realized for the first time that he was a little afraid of his brother. For six months Bob had been shut out of his life, shut away into a new set of experiences. What had they done to him? It was impossible to tell, for he had had no news except that inexpressibly bald letter. But Clem could guess a little of what Bob had been suffering in the Kentish prison town. It would not have been so much the pains and humiliations of imprisonment; Bob was not a sensitive subject, either in mind or body, and though he might have pined a bit for the fresh air, ought to have come through six months' hard labour pretty well. Neither, Clem felt instinctively, would his misery concentrate on the loss of his home, nor on the fact that he had lost his brief reputation and would not be able to preach again—at least, not for many years. The heart of bitterness seemed to lie in those words his brother had spoken to him at Headcorn, "There remaineth no more sacrifice for sins." Robert had been convinced of his eternal damnation. He had lost the God he had loved and served so gratefully, and there remained for him nothing but a fiery looking forward to judgment. During those months in prison, how would that idea have worked? Would Mr. Beeman have done anything to remove it? Would his heart have purged itself of fear? Or would the fear have broken his heart? Clem did not know—that was why he was afraid.

There were only a few people on Salehurst Station when the

little Rother Valley train drew in. Bob came out of a coach
at the back, and walked towards Clem and shook hands without a word. What Clem noticed most about his brother was
that he looked extraordinarily clean and tidy. His clothes
smelled a little of some fumigation, but they were carefully
brushed.

"Hallo," said Clem. "How are you?"

"Hallo," said Bob.

"I've got the trap wud Spongey. You'll be pleased to come
to Pookwell, Bob?"

"Surelye."

"We've got a new bed and a washbowl and some hooks in
the other upstairs room. And we've got the baby too, as I
töald you when I wrote."

"That's valiant," said Bob.

Clem waited for him to inquire after Mabel, but he did not,
so to cover up an awkward silence, the younger brother said:
"We've got bacon fur supper wud mashed potatoes."

"That's good."

"And mother said as she'd look in fur a bit afterwards."

"She shudn't ought to give herself the trouble; I'll go
aräound and see her."

"Oh, she liks coming to us."

They beguiled the drive to Bodingmares with suchlike careful
conversation. It struck Clem that his brother did not look so
shattered as he expected, and he felt a little cheered and reassured. It was difficult to read the look in Robert's eyes, but
anyhow it was not that desperate, stricken look he had seen at
Headcorn. . . . Perhaps Bob was a little thinner than he
used to be; that was what made those queer lines on his face,
from nose to mouth, stand out so remarkably. Clem had not
noticed them so much at first, but now when the yellow, watery
sunset came streaming over the fields, with a few rods of yellow rain slanting across the light, Bob's face suddenly showed
all lined and aged. There were lines at his mouth and eyes
and between his brows . . . the skin on the cheeks was quite
fresh and firm, it had not wrinkled; those lines had just dug
and scored themselves across his youth. . . . Clem was glad

when the sun dipped behind the hedge and Bob's face became once more just a rather young and rather wooden one.

Polly was waiting for them at Pookwell with the baby in her arms.

"Here's dada," she said, when the trap drew up at the gate, and running down the path, she bundled Nat into Robert's embrace before he could hold out his arms to Clem.

"He's growed," said Bob.

"Well, wot else shud he d̄ in six months? He's a valiant child, and weighs more'n two stun. Clem put him on wud the weights this marnun."

Young Nat gave a wriggle in the unaccustomed arms, and Bob handed him back to Polly just before he began to howl.

"He'll git used to you in a day or two; he can't help it just at first. They dōan't remember at that age. As soon as he's more accustomed like, you can have him to sleep along·of you at nights, but he mun stay wud us for a whiles yet, or he'd holler and kip you awäake."

Polly was more free in her talk than Clem, whose attitude towards his brother was rather that of a careful housewife towards a cracked plate. Polly even spoke of Mabel while they were at supper, just mentioning her by name. But Robert showed no emotion. He ate his supper quietly, without much talk, eating what he was given, but by no means showing the zest and thrill that bacon and mashed potatoes should have aroused in his breast. Afterwards he helped Polly clear away and wash up the things. He seemed humble and grateful in his attitude towards her and Clem, but he said no more about it than about anything else.

Mrs. Wheelsgate arrived soon after eight, and they all sat round the fire, trying to talk of indifferent matters. At first Elizabeth had been inclined to sentiment; she had cried a bit when she kissed Robert.

"Now, Mother, dōan't fret fur me," he said.

"But you're looking thinner; your clöathes hang loose."

"I weigh a päound more'n when I went into jail."

She said no more, but dropped her hands from his shoulders with a bewildered gesture. Then they pulled their chairs

in close to the fire, for the March wind was beating round
the house; the weather provided them with some conversation
on the price of coal and the underwood that Dunk was cutting
over at Shoyswell. Then Polly talked about the baby, and told
his grandmamma of his latest doings. She managed her share
of the proceedings best; Clem was obviously embarrassed, and
Mrs. Wheelsgate looked bewildered and lost. The strain was
ended only by the party breaking up for the night.

Clem walked home with his mother, and when he came back
found Polly just lighting her candle for bed. Robert still sat
by the fire, and when Polly went out of the room, he suddenly
seemed to remember something, and getting clumsily to his
feet, he went and opened the door for her. Polly, unaccustomed to gallantry, made her first blunder:

"Oh, Bob, that's wot Mabel larned you, äun't it?"

"Surelye," said Bob in an extinguished voice, going back to
his seat.

In the middle of the night Clem was wakened by a peculiar
sound. For a moment he lay listening; it came from the next
room, and had a curious monotony about it, so that at first
he scarcely recognized it for the sound of sobbing. But as his
sense cleared, he knew. Robert's bed was close up against the
wall; he probably did not realize that only a foot of lath and
plaster divided him from Clem and Polly.

Soon Polly woke up and heard it too.

"Oh, mäaster, wot's that?"

"It's Bob."

"Mäaking that row; it can't be."

She listened a moment, then whimpered a little herself.

"Oh, Clem, the pore soul; I can't bear it. You mun go to
him."

Clem slid out of bed, then changed his mind.

"No, I wöan't go. I know he'd sooner I dudn't."

"But you can't let him grieve lik that. Go and täake baby
to him."

"No, missus, you can't understand. We wurn't never meant
to hear that. He döan't think as we're just by the wall."

He got back into bed, and soon afterwards the sobbing

ceased. Perhaps Bob had heard them talking, though they had spoken carefully in whispers for fear of waking the boy.

§ 23

The next two or three days passed uneventfully. There was no more sobbing at night. During the day Robert worked hard, both in the house, where Mabel had taught him to be handy, and in the fields, where he helped Clem. He seemed to like work—to find some sort of relief in it. At first Jim did not like seeing him about his land, or rather he did not like other people seeing him there. He tried to make Clem persuade Robert to go away——

"He mun määke a fresh start whur the föalkses döan't know what he is. If he äun't got enough tin I döan't mind helping him a bit."

"If he goes, Polly and I goes too," said Clem.

"Now, döan't be a gurt owl," said Jim, who could never have got another man to do Clem's work for Clem's wages.

"I äun't going to let Bob go off by himself the way he is now."

"Wot way? He's right enough. He shows it less than some ud think präaper."

"I know better'n you wot he feels, and I tell you as he äun't fit to go off alöan by himself. I'm willing to go wud him anywheres, and so's Polly."

"Well, I'd sooner he stayed than you went. After all, he döan't do much harm aräound here."

"Harm! He does a man-and-half's wark, surelye."

"That's new fur him, anyways. Reckon they larned him to wark in prison."

Clem said nothing, and Jim, fearing that he had offended him—for he was that prize among workmen, a man who is at once valuable and unconscious of his value—made a propitiatory surrender.

"Well, tell him he can stay—and wark fur me fur twenty shillun a week and his board, wud you."

"I'll tell him," said Clem, "and I'll tell him, too, as he can go if he likes."

But Robert much preferred to stay. He clung to Clem and Polly as his only friends, and at the same time he saw the unkindness of pulling them up by the roots and transplanting them into some new district. As for himself, all places were alike. He cared nothing for the eyes coldly staring or the eyes turned away that he met on the few occasions he went out on the road. He knew that Clem felt no embarrassment or shame on his account, and as for Jim, he could make up to Jim by hard work and loyal service for the disgrace he brought him; after all, he need not go much afield, or meet anyone to whom he would be an offence.

So it was settled that Robert was to stop at Bodingmares, for the present anyway. Clem and Polly experienced much secret relief, for though they would willingly have gone with him into furrin parts, they loved their little house and their work on Jim's farm, and would have felt forlorn indeed in new surroundings. As for Jim, once more he had taken Fate's trick with a noble action. He found that his forgiveness of Robert —for such it came to—had done more to wipe out his disgrace than any amount of righteous indignation. His action in receiving Robert back as a worker into his fields was applauded throughout the parishes of Salehurst and High Tilt. Mr. Vine brought a delicately veiled reference to it into his sermon at the Throws Chapel, and every bar in two villages declared that Jim Fuller of Bodingmares was a decent chap.

Robert was appropriately grateful, and showed his gratitude by never going near the homestead or presuming that his toleration as a hired servant included his toleration as a son of the house. But this avoidance was partly due to his fear of Mary. His memories of her tongue of old times made him disinclined to meet her now. However, it was impossible that he should be a regular worker on the farm and never see her.

One day he was so thirsty that he felt he must go to the house and ask for a drink. Probably only a servant would be there.

But when he knocked the door was opened by Mary.

"Hallo!" she said. "So there you are! Wot do you want?"

"I'm thirsty," Robert mumbled sheepishly.

Mary looked at him in silence for a moment, opened her mouth to say something, and then thought better of it.

"Which ull you have—beer or water?" she asked instead.

"Water, please."

"So you haven't got over that? I'd a-thought you'd have started a new sort of religion after all this."

Robert said nothing.

"If I wur you," said his sister, "I'd tääke a warning and git shut of all this teetotal rubbish. When the fowls döan't lay after Molassine wot I do äun't to give them more Molassine but to määke a chäange and try Thorley's. That's wot you shud ought to do wud them notions of yourn. The first lot dudn't, so to spik, määke you lay, so you mun try another kind. D'you mark my wards?"

"Surelye."

Robert was turning away.

"Well, sinst you've come for a drink of water, thur äun't much sense in your going off wudout it. Come into the scullery and I'll find you a cup."

Not long after that, when the hop-spraying kept Clem and Robert and Pickdick late in the river garden, Jim asked them all to come into the house for a bit of supper. Bob saw that he was to be tolerated under the family roof, but he did not abuse the toleration. He never went near Bodingmares unless he was asked, and even then he occasionally refused. He preferred keeping close to Pookwell, and going to see his mother about once a week at Marsh Quarter.

Clem and Polly worked hard to make him happy. They were ashamed of Jim and Mary, whose words and faces made impossible what their actions allowed, they were ashamed of Mabel, who neither came nor wrote, they were ashamed of the respectable farmers of the neighbourhood, yeomen and tenants, who would give poor Robert neither recognition nor fellowship. Not that he seemed to want either, but Polly had a deep conviction that a little society would be good for him, and

Clem would have liked to take him with him to market and see if he could get back any of his interest in the movements and prices of stock.

Robert seemed grateful for their efforts. He was always gentle and soft spoken now. He praised Polly's cooking when he saw that he was expected to do so, he was invariably ready to help her in the house, chopping wood, washing plates, carrying coal, doing all the odd, dirty jobs that it had never occurred to Clem to do. Polly "did not know herself," as she put it. As for Clem, he found his brother invaluable; he was greedy for work, and would have liked to fill his whole day with it. Every morning, before they were up, they would hear him coming down to light the kitchen fire. He had his baby with him at nights now; the child had taken to him at last, but it had required a lot of persuasion. Little Nat had found something terrifying in this big, strong, sad father, who never laughed or sang to him like his other father, who never threw him in the air and caught him again, and who sometimes held him so clumsily and closely.

Clem and Polly understood the baby's feelings. Sometimes they could not help being scared of Bob. He was so different, he was so utterly unlike the swaggering, rather villainous Bob of the old days; he was so unlike the sullen, obstinate Bob who had married Mabel, or the exalted, apocalyptic Bob who had preached the Gospel in the 'dens of Kent. This silent, gentle, hard-working, humble creature was a stranger to the brother who had known him all his life. He could not think that this was the same Robert who used to brag about his drinks and his bets in the big low bedroom at Bodingmares. . . . What could have changed him? It seemed to Clem that he must have been through some terrible new experience. . . . He was like an extinguished lamp.

Once or twice the younger brother tried to win his confidence, but he bungled the matter, chiefly through his own fear. They discussed the future, the improbability of Mabel's return, Bob's financial position, the care of the child. . . . But Clem knew that his brother's tragedy lay in none of these things. He knew now that he was living, working, talking, sharing his daily life, with a man in despair, whose own life was nothing but an extinguished lamp.

"Git him to talk to you, Clem," said Polly, anxious for Clem's sake as well as Bob's, for Clem was beginning to have sometimes a look very like Robert's in his eyes.

Young Fuller shook his head. "He wöan't talk, he wöan't tell me, and I justabout can't ask him."

"But it may be naun."

"Does it look lik naun?"

"It may be only some notion he's got."

"He's got a notion as his soul's lost fur ever—that's the notion he's got."

"But he never talks about religion now."

"That's just wot tells me, surelye."

§ 24

One day, when Robert had been back with them about three weeks, Clem took him to Ticehurst market. He thought that the change would do him good, and at Ticehurst they were not likely to meet so many of his judges. They spent a fairly uneventful morning inspecting sheep, and had only one unpleasant encounter—with Bream of Little Moat. Bream had come to Ticehurst to sell a horse, which for various reasons he thought he would be able to dispose of more easily among strangers. He was therefore annoyed to see little Clem Fuller standing there with his stick under his arm, and beside him Clem's notorious brother Bob, whom it was an affront to bring among decent people.

If Bream had belonged to more exalted circles, he would have conveyed his disgust by such subtle methods as failing to see Robert though he stood before him, but his circumstances had fitted him only for the cruder forms of self-expression.

"Hallo," he remarked, "have you come to preach us a sarmon?"

It was Clem who flushed and countered.

"Hallo," he said, "have you come to sell us a spavined hoss?"

"Now you mind your wards, or you'll land yourself whur your holy brother's just come out from."

"I'll land you in the muck first." And Clem clenched a violent fist.

"Adone do, Clem," said Bob; "döan't git yourself in trouble. His wards döan't matter naun."

"They're true wards," said Bream.

"Surelye," said Bob.

Bream was taken aback by such submission, and could find no suitable retort before Bob had dragged the bristling Clem away.

"We mun go höame now," he said; "thur's naun else to do now we've seen the tegs, and I wöan't have you fighting wud chaps because of their spikking truth."

"It wurn't truth. It wur just low sneers as any decent feller ud be ashäamed on. I'd lik to smash his fäace."

"You kip cool, youngster," said Robert in a voice that reminded Clem of the old Bob.

They were walking home, as the trap was wanted for other things that morning. Neither of them spoke again till they were out of the village. Then Robert said:

"I döan't want you to be always täaking my part agäunst folks; they're mostly right in wot they say."

"They äun't right. They're just a dirty, canting lot."

"No, that äun't it quite. You mun put yourself in their pläace and think. I've bin thinking myself, and I see now how bad it must all have looked. Thur wur I, racketing about and giving scandal all aräound. Then all of a suddent I start preaching and saying I'm sääved . . . reckon it wur middling decent of folks not to call me a hypocrite straight off, as only some of 'em did. Then they hear as I'm in quod—that I've nearly killed a man because he found me mäaking free wud his wife. . . . It's only natural as they think dirt of me and say as I wur shamming all the time."

"But, no matter wot they think, they shudn't ought to spik so. They mun let you alöan after all you've bin through."

"Their wards döan't hurt me. I tell you, young 'un, I care

fur naun. Now I've lost God, wot difference d'you think it
mäakes wot I lose beside?"

"But, Bob, you döan't mean that surelye? You haven't
lost God. . . ."

"If I haven't lost Him, that's because I never had Him."

"But that äun't true. You wur so holy and pious as you
guv me the shivers, and wot you say is 'The gifts and calling of
God are wudout repentance.' "

"That's just about it. The Elect can't fall from Grace; and
sinst I äun't in Grace now, I never wur in Grace."

"But how do you know you äun't in Grace now?"

Bob gave a queer laugh.

"You mun have mäade a mistäake one way," continued
Clem, "and it may just as well be about now as then."

"It äun't my own judgment now. I've bin shown clear whur
I stand. I töald you as Mus' Beeman had bin to see me in
jail."

"Well?"

"Well, we talked it all over and over, and I töald him all—
everythink as I cud remember—and after he'd thought and
prayed, he said as he'd come pretty well to the conclusion as
I'd never bin in Grace——"

"The old put!"

"Höald your tongue. He's a man of God."

"But how's the likes of him to know whether you wur or
wurn't in Grace?"

"He can read the signs. Wot he says is this: I might have
done wot I done wud Hannah and Darius and still bin in
Grace. But then I'd have known it; I'd have had the Spirit's
assurance in my heart, saying, 'Who can lay anythink to the
charge of God's Elect?' But I dudn't feel that. I felt all in
darkness and as if I'd lost the marcy of God. If I'd bin in
true grace I'd have known as naun cud täake the Lord's marcy
from His saints—even their sins. So because I felt all outcast, then it showed as how either I'd fallen from Grace or
else I'd never bin in Grace. Seemingly by the true doctrine
it can't be the fust, so it mun be the second."

"Well I never—I never in all my days heard such notions. And wot does he määke of all your preaching, and your gitting converted lik that?"

"We know as Satan can appear as an angel of light, and reckon that's wot he dud to me, deceiving me to think as I wur Sääved when I wur just a poor child of wrath. And even from the fust, Mus' Beeman says as thur wur things he cudn't määke out. Fur one thing, utterance wur never präaperly given me—I never cud preach a true refresher . . . the folk at the chapels wur always grumbling about me . . . and then, if you remember, I never cud win a single sinner to Christ; thur I'd stand spikking and pleading myself hoarse, and not one ud be moved to lay hold on Salvation. . . . Mus' Beeman said as sometimes when he spuck the sinners ud be leaping out of their seats and spinning in the air wud their feelings of Particular Mercy . . . he'd have a row of 'em groaning on the floor . . . and me, they'd do justabout naun fur me but gape."

"But, Bob, I've heard you say as Salvation's like a cup of tea, and you've naun to do but put out your hand and tääke it. Reckon you shud ought to know if you've had it in your hand or not. Thur can't be any mistääke about holding a cup of tea."

"That's just it, kid, that's just it"—and Bob's eyes glistened tragically—"I took the cup of tea in my hand right enough, and I had a tääste of its sweetness, but it wurn't never meant fur me; and now it's bin tääken away."

"Then all I can say is that God's sarved you a wuss trick now nor ever He sarved you in the Throws Chapel, when you testified wudout meaning it."

"It wurn't a trick. Reckon He offered me Salvation full and fair that time in the chapel, and reckon I määde a mock of it. And thur wur another time too I never töald you of . . . outside Mabel's house. . . . Oh, reckon I've despised and rejected the free gifts of Grace! So it's only right as the Lord shud let me think I have His marcy and then tääke it away, just to larn me to mock His treasures."

"Well, I can't say as it sims fair. Reckon if God's good as you say, He'd never do such a thing, and if He äun't good, you're well shut of Him."

"He *is* good," said Robert.

"Then he can't have a-done this, surelye."

"You spik as one who know naun of Grace. Döan't you see it's all in Scripture? Reckon I'm the sheep wot never went into the sheepfold by the door, but clomb over the wall, and the säame is a thief and a robber. Reckon I'm the man wudout a wedding-garment, who'd never bin asked to the wedding, and yit he went in, wudout ever cleaning himself, and the Lord said, 'Who is this wudout a wedding-garment? Cast him into the outer darkness whur there is weeping and gnashing of teeth.' . . . The trouble is that I can't disremember the bridegroom's face."

He turned away his eyes, and for a moment seemed to be fighting with himself. Then he continued:

"That's the tar'ble part of it. I seen God once, and I can't forget Him. It wudn't be so bad fur me now if I'd never known Him, never loved Him, never thought I wur His friend. . . . But now I've tasted and seen how gracious the Lord is—and yet I'm cast out from Him for ever."

"I döan't believe it," said Clem indignantly, "I döan't believe it, and you döan't präaperly believe it yourself. If you're so sartain-sure as you're cast out, why do you go on living good as you've never lived before—all kind and quiet and such a help to me and Polly, and forgiving Mabel and Jim and Mary and all that lot wot döan't desarve it? Döan't it show as down in your heart you still believe God loves you? Or else you wudn't be so middling careful to please Him."

"You döan't understand. I try to sarve God, as you say, because all I've got left of God is to sarve Him. That's the only thing I can do fur Him now, and it's the only thing wot can't be täaken from me. . . . I mun kip that liddle bit of Him . . . it's all I've got left."

"Then all I can say is——" But he said no more.

§ 25

During the days which followed Clem and Robert were silent
on the matter so urgent to them both. They went about their
work in silence; that burst of confidence on the Ticehurst road
seemed to have exhausted their resources, and for nearly a
week their intercourse was limited to talk of crops and stock
and the different jobs of their day.

But Clem, anyhow, was thinking deeply. He was trying to
find out if there was anything he could still do for Robert.
Evidently he himself could not persuade him; he was not clever
enough to meet his brother in argument, and he did not know
enough, or perhaps care enough, about religion. He could not
understand how it was that after the way, according to Bob's
notions, God had treated him, he could still love God and want
to be near Him, and pine after Him day by day. But doubtless
a really good and religious person would understand, and perhaps be able to persuade Bob that he was not outcast after all,
but Foreknown and Predestinate and Justified and all those
things that he wanted to be.

The trouble was that Bob would listen to nobody. He
would not go and see Mr. Vine, or Mr. Brackpool, the rector
of the parish, as Clem suggested in his desperation. He would
listen to nobody but Mr. Beeman, and Mr. Beeman had already spoken. It struck Clem that the only chance for Robert
was if by some miracle the old Pope of Goudhurst should find
out he had been mistaken. . . . Would it be possible to make
him eat his words? It was not likely, but the more he thought
about the matter, the more he realized that Mr. Beeman alone
could bring his brother any relief. Surely if he knew how
miserable Bob was, he would change his mind and speak comfort. . . . Anyhow, it wouldn't be a bad plan if Clem were
to take an afternoon off and go and visit the minister at Goudhurst, and see if something couldn't be done.

He did not much relish the prospect. He had never met the
old man, and did not like what he had heard of him; moreover,
he felt awkward and shy of such a mission. Also, he could
not help realizing that it was not likely that Mus' Beeman

would agree to alter his decision or make any further, more comforting pronouncement. Still, it was the only thing to be done; he could not watch Bob's heart slowly breaking day by day without making even a hopeless effort to save him.

He had not Bob's reasons for tramping the fifteen miles between High Tilt and Goudhurst, so he set off comfortably enough by the first afternoon train from Hawkhurst, and arrived at his destination about four o'clock. The outside of the house impressed him; it was so white and clean, with green shutters, new-painted, flung back from the broad windows, and a bell and knocker so beautifully burnished that he scarcely dared touch either of them.

When at last he screwed up the courage to ring, the door was opened by a stout, comfortable-looking woman in a starched white apron, who gave him a welcoming smile when she heard his name, and left him to wait in a spick and span little hall while she went to tell the minister. So this was the house whence judgment proceeded. . . . Clem looked round at the green walls and the big vase full of spreading hawthorn set on the beautifully polished table, and found it hard to think that in this place Robert had learned the mysteries of Wrath which were his torment now.

The housekeeper came back and said that the minister was at his tea, but would be very pleased if Mr. Clement Fuller would join him.

Gingerly depositing his hat on the floor—since the surface of the table looked too exquisite to receive it—Clem trod after her into a low sunny room, which seemed full of a gleaming white cloth. On the cloth were laid out plates of bread and butter, of jam, of watercress, of spring onions, and of lemon cakes. Clem's eyes glistened—before they were swept through the increasing splendours of the tea-table up to its crowning or chancellor effect in a large pewter tea-tray with an enormous black teapot, before which, like some high priest of the ceremonies, was stationed a venerable old man in black, whose scalp seemed to have shared in the general polish of his surroundings, and whose white hair fell from the sides of his head almost to his shoulders, in striking contrast with his face, which was the rosy unwrinkled face of a young child.

At first Clem could not help being impressed by his venerable appearance, but the next moment he hated him; that smooth unlined old face made him think of Robert's young face all scored and dug with lines. . . . This was the man who held the keys of his brother's heaven—and had shut, and no man could open.

"Good afternoon," he said stiffly.

"Good afternoon, Mr. Fuller. Pray be seated. I take it that I 'ave the honour of a visit from the brother of Mr. Robert Fuller of Campany's 'Atch."

"He döan't live thur now; he lives along wud me."

"Ah, yes. I remember now that he told me he meant to give up the farm. Pray let me give you a cup of tea. This is real green tea, Mr. Fuller, such as you have probably never tasted before. It is now very rare, but I remember when I was a lad it was drunk by all better-class families. The lower classes drank the black tea, such as is most common nowadays."

Clem took the cup speechlessly. He was beginning to feel a little of this man's effect on Robert. There was something in that deliberate, heavily modulated, half cultivated old voice that seemed positively to smother. His pronouncements automatically became oracles. Just now he had pronounced on green tea, and Clem found himself staring at his cup with submissive reverence.

"A pleasant day, is it not?" continued the oracle, and Clem felt that a new article had been added to the creed. "I take it that you came by train—or perhaps you are transacting business in these parts."

"I came to see you about my brother," said Clem.

"Ah, yes. Um . . . and 'ow is your brother?"

"How d'you expect 'im to be?" said Clem, desperately resorting to rudeness to jerk him out of his submission.

Mr. Beeman shook his head sorrowfully.

"The story of that young man is one of the saddest that I've ever encountered in the course of a long ministry. Won't you take one of those bread-and-butters?—and I recommend a little watercress."

Clem helped himself, but let the food lie uneaten on his plate. A sudden distaste for the whole meal had possessed him —it was not like tea.

"I visited him in prison," continued the old man, "as perhaps you may be aware. The journey from here is exceedingly toilsome. I had to change at 'Awkhurst and again at 'Eadcorn, and the connexions are most inconvenient. But I remember the days when there was no railway here nearer than Salehurst—so we must not grumble."

"Wot I've come to spik to you about is wot you said to my brother in prison. I want to ask you—maybe he dudn't git your meaning quite clear . . . but Bob's got a notion in his head as his soul's lost, and he says you töald him."

"Ah, my dear friend, that was a very sorrowful occasion— I well remember it. The life of a Christian pastor is full of cares, and it was very grievous for me to have to tell the young chap I'd made a mistake about him—or rather had been taken in by Satan."

"Then you dud tell him he'd lost his soul."

"I told him I could not consider him in Grace."

"That wur it, and it's bruck his heart. Oh, if you cud see him now, all struck down wud sorrow, you'd pity him . . . and I've come here to ask you to send him a message, to let me tell him as you say it äun't true as he's lost, that he's in Gräace right enough—and reckon he'll believe you and be a chäanged man, and happy agäun—leastways as happy as a man can be wot's lost everything on earth. It's only a liddle thing fur you to do, but it'll mäake all the difference to Bob. You just let me tell him from you as he äun't going to hell."

"My dear young man, you are asking me to change the counsels of the Most 'Igh."

"In wot way?"

"Well, it ain't for me to say if your brother's Saved or lost. I can but read the signs, and if, according to them, he's in Grace—then I don't know what Grace is."

"I döan't know wot you mean by in Grace and out of

Grace and all that. I reckon Bob's a good chap—better'n most of us."

"You can but read the outward man; God alone readeth the heart."

"He'll see naun in Bob's heart but wot's good."

"Do not speak so blasphemously. Bob is a worm. You are a worm. I am a worm. Besides, the conclusion of the matter ain't whether your brother does or does not do right with his legal conscience, but whether he is or is not in a state of Grace."

"I döan't know wot you mean by a state of Grace. . . . All I know is that Bob's a good chap, that he's given up a lot and put up wud a lot, and gone preaching the Gospel . . . and as fur wot he did wud them gipsies, reckon he wur tempted, and it äun't fur me and you to judge him."

"You are yet without the light of sound doctrine; you do nothing but tell me what your brother has *done,* when we are told that all our righteousness is as filthy rags. It is a shocking thing to see a poor worm boast of its filthy rags, when it should be on its knees begging pardon of God. Let me give you another cup of tea."

Clem thrust his hands into his hair. He seemed powerless to argue with this calm, benevolent old man who had a terrible faculty for making a cup of tea and the day of judgment seem equally portentous. Also, though he was used to Bob's doctrinal expressions, he had never really fathomed their meaning, and was quite at a loss in this marsh of theology. "In Grace"— "out of Grace"—what did it all mean? . . . He watched Mus' Beeman as he pontificated behind the tea-tray, and a kind of helpless fascination came upon him. He felt unable to fight for Bob any longer.

"I am sorry," said Mr. Beeman, lifting the teapot solemnly, as if it were a monstrance. "I am sorry that I cannot give you any comfort for your brother. If he was in a state of Grace he would be the first to know it, and the fact of his reprobation is not known to him merely through my poor words but through his own interior witness—there is no Abba Father in 'is 'eart."

"But if you'd only say. . . ." Clem pleaded abjectly, his eyes fixed on the teapot.

"Young man, I have told you before that I can't change the counsels of the Most 'Igh."

"But pore Bob——"

"I am deeply grieved for your poor, unfortunate brother. But I ask you—can I 'elp it? From the first we were taken in by Satan; though I will say I had my suspicions, even from the first. Your brother was a great disappointment to me in many ways—he never took properly to Salvation. The saints didn't feel at 'ome with him—they couldn't get the feeling of the Lord speaking through his mouth. Many's the time I've wrestled with the Spirit on his account, wondering what the matter was . . . and now of course it's plain. He never was in Grace. He, and me as well, had been deceived by Satan disguised as an Angel of Light."

Clem could not speak. He sat as if paralyzed, his eyes fixed on Mr. Beeman's teapot, which he still held aloft, and which seemed in some strange way to join in his condemnation of Robert.

"Your brother never was quite at 'ome with us," continued the minister; "he'd go trusting to legal works such as converting sinners, and it was through legal works that he fell, for he tells me that he had a notion he was meant to convert the young woman as all the trouble was about. He didn't wait upon the Lord. Then I never could feel quite sure about his doctrine—there wasn't a heresy going about that he didn't seem to get some splash of"—it seemed to Clem as if the teapot shared its owner's look of shocked suspicion. "One of my deacons said to me: 'You mark my words—that man ull end as a Gardnerite'"—the teapot shuddered. "Well, his hour came—'e was weighed in the balance and found wanting —Mene, Mene, Tekel, Upharsin. If he'd had real Assurance, if he'd truly been in Grace, not all the onslaughts of the wicked one could have shaken him out of it. Even when the whole thing was shown up and he got sent to jail he could still 'ave 'eld 'is 'ead up, knowing as he was the Lord's Chosen. But did 'e 'old 'is 'ead up? Did 'e say: 'Who shall lay any-

think to the charge of God's Elect?'—I ask you. No, 'e didn't.
He just went flat like a bust bag. Why?—because 'e knew
'e was lost—and there remaineth no more sacrifice for
sins, but a certain fiery looking forward to Judgment"—the
teapot suddenly shot up on Mr. Beeman's uplifted arm, and
for a moment became an almost celestial object, thundering
judgment and doom. Then Mr. Beeman lowered it and poured
Clem out a cup of tea.

"So that's settled," he said. "I'm sorry I can't give you
any comfort, Mr. Fuller. But perhaps you may find it Elsewhere."

"I döan't want any comfort if Bob's got none. I döan't
want to go to heaven if Bob äun't thur. . . . But I can't believe as God ud let him be täaken in lik that—at the fust, I
mean."

"He had led a very wicked life, and had put himself in
Satan's power. You never can tell what the devil will do with
his own."

"I can't see as Bob wur so tar'ble bad. Reckon he was a
bit wild at times, but then a lot of chaps take a glass too much
now and then; and as fur Hannah Ripley, he loved her . . .
you can't say as it wur his fault as love dudn't come to him
säafe and präaper as it comes to most. Anyways, I döan't
see as he's done aught to desarve all this."

Mr. Beeman smiled almost pityingly.

"There you go again—talking about 'deserve.' I tell you
it's not what we deserve, but what the Lord decrees."

Clem suddenly rose to his feet, and pushed his cup away.

"I mun go höame," he said, "fur it's plain as you'll never
help me."

"Willingly would I 'elp you—right gladly would I 'elp you
—if the power were given me from on 'Igh. But it ain't.
It is the Lord's will, and we must bow down before His judg-
ments."

He ushered his visitor into the neat little hall, where the
petals of hawthorn were dropping on the polished surface of
the table—and here suddenly Clem got back his courage.
Escaped from the stupefying ritual of the tea-table, he was

able to shake off that queer smother of oppression which had settled on him. His heart burned with indignation against this old fellow, who benevolently condemned poor Robert to life-long misery, accepting his doom with calm self-satisfaction. He hated his smooth, venerable old face, his well-kept, polished hall, his august and plentiful meals—all the ordered and prosperous surroundings from which he dealt out the Wrath to Come.

"Then you wöan't chäange your mind about my brother?" he said almost truculently.

"My friend—it isn't my mind, it is the Lord's."

"It äun't!" cried Clem thickly; "you're telling lies. I döan't believe—I'll never believe as Bob's done anything to desarve wot he's having now. He's a good chap; he does the wark of two men, and he lights our kitchen fire every morning. The Lord ud never condemn him; and as fur his having bin in jail, it's naun—reckon he dudn't do anything half so bad as wot you're doing wud your wicked lies . . . wot I pray you'll answer fur one day, and täaste a liddle bit of wot my pore Bob has to swaller."

He choked with grief and rage, and the old, unruffled voice answered him:

"You are very violent, young chap—very violent to an old man. But I wish you no 'arm. I bear you no ill-will. I know in 'oom I 'ave trusted. Pray mind the scraper—you are about to fall over it. . . . Ah, I was afraid so. I 'ope you are not 'urt."

§ 26

Clem did not tell Robert about his ill-fated expedition to Goudhurst. It would have only made matters worse. He managed somehow to explain his half-day's absence, and Bob never asked many questions now. The burden of life and work was taken up with an added sense of hopelessness. Robert toiled behind the plough in the spring sowings, he drilled with aching back in the turnip fields, he bound and sprayed the hops that were beginning to weave their first tendrils round the poles. He cared for the new-born calves and the lambs that raced round the fields at the merry time of sunset. He helped thatch the Dutch barn, he dunged the orchards. He was perhaps even a little quieter than when he had first come home. He often sat through a meal without speaking a word. There might have been some fresh lines on his face, and some of the old ones were a little deeper. But some of the high colour he had lost in prison was coming back, under the thick dark sunburn that the weather was putting on his cheeks. He ate well and he slept well; he once told Clem that he sometimes had painful dreams, but these turned out to be painful only in their waking, since in them he was back once more in the love of God, happy and safe.

Every week he put a bit of money by for Mabel. It was not much, after he had paid for his board and the keep of his child, but he was pleased to think that it would buy her one or two small luxuries she might not otherwise be able to afford, such as a new hat or a visit to the pictures. She was well provided for both by her father and by her marriage settlements, but since it so obviously pleased Bob to do this for her, neither Clem nor Polly tried to dissuade him.

Mabel received his offering in silence—a silence that had not been broken now for weeks. She seemed to have dropped out of the life of Bodingmares and its offshoots of Pookwell and Marsh Quarter. Yet they could not quite feel that she was gone—she had belonged so inextricably to them in spite of her queer hostilities and furrin ways. Now and then Clem thought of writing to her and asking her to come and see Bob, but the contemplation of a letter invariably palsied him —besides, he did not know whether Bob wanted to see her again or not.

Then a day came when Robert had to go into Bulverhythe to see the dentist. He had a bad tooth which ached very much at nights, and they thought he had better go and have it out.

"Since I'm in Bulverhythe I'll go and have a look at Mabel," he said quite calmly at dinner before he started.

"Wudn't you write her a letter fust?" suggested Polly.

"I'd sooner call aräound and just ask her if she'll see me—she can say 'No' if she döan't want to."

"You shud ought to tääke Nat wud you, then."

But Robert shook his head.

"I only want just to spik to her and see how she's doing."

Clem had arranged to go with him to Bulverhythe. He knew that Bob did not like being left much alone, and he could do some business at the sadler's while his brother was at the dentist. He found, after they had started, that Robert wanted him to go with him to see Mabel.

"You might see her first, Clem, and ask her if she'll see me—she always thought well of you, and maybe you can määke her let me come in."

Clem felt convinced that the interview with Mabel would be just as fruitless and depressing as the interview with Mus' Beeman; but Robert did not seem to expect much from it, though his heart was set on it, so his younger brother agreed. They met at about five o'clock at the corner of Mabel's street, and went together up the steps of her house.

Mabel was at home, and craftily they sent only Clem's name in to her by the servant. Yes, Mrs. Fuller would see him . . . and Clem found himself in her drawing-room, in the midst of a suite of tapestried furniture, a piano, and many ferns in ornamental pots, while Robert waited uneasily in the hall.

"Hallo, Clem," said Mabel. "I was wondering if you'd ever come and see me. Have you had your tea?"

"I döan't want any, thanks," said Clem hurriedly, feeling that in its very different way Mabel's tea would be just as damnable as Mus' Beeman's.

He sat opposite her in silence for a moment or two, staring at her with those round, yellowish eyes which Mabel had always found disconcerting. He felt that he ought to break it to her gently that Bob was in the house, and it was just because he was so anxious to be diplomatic that he finally blurted straight out:

"I've brung Bob to see you."

"Where is he?" cried Mabel.

"Outside in the passage. He wants to see you summat tar'ble."

"I don't want to see him."

"Please let him see you, Mabel—just to spik a ward."

"He's come to ask me to go back to him."

"He äun't—he wöan't."

"I wonder he's got the cheek to come, after the way he's treated me."

"He's middling sorry fur all he's done bad—and he thinks he's lost his soul—and he's just had a tooth out."

Mabel looked more relenting. She still had it in her power to pity Bob physically, and the thought of the lost tooth touched her. For the lost soul she cared no whit—his soul had always been a disturbing factor in a purely physical possession . . . if it was now lost, so much the better. But she had loved Bob's strong white teeth, and was sorry that one of them was missing.

"You'll promise me he won't try and make me come back to him? And there's no good his trying to make me take the kid, either. I can't have him here with father, and I must stop with father now because of what people will think."

"He wöan't ask you back, and as fur the kid, he's set on him—leastways, as much as he's set on anything. May I tell him to come in?"

"Oh, very well . . . I suppose I can't help it."

Clem opened the door, and summoned Bob, who came in and stood before Mabel.

He stood upright, with a queer air of self-possession about him, though he was humble and silent. To Mabel he gave a new impression of dignity. She had never seen anything dignified in Bob before, he had always been a bit clumsy, he had always failed to be impressive either as a sinner or as a saint; but to-day he had a spice of dignity, though she could not tell exactly in what it lay.

"Hallo, Bob," she said, with the edge off her self-confidence, "how are you?"

"I'm very well, thank you."

"I hear you've just had a tooth out."

"Yes, one at the bottom."

"Did it hurt?" asked Clem.

"Naun particular. He put some stuff into the gum."

They were all three looking anxiously at each other. None of them wanted to be talking like this about Robert's tooth, and at the same time they were dreading the time when it should be exhausted as a topic of conversation.

"I wunst had some stuff put in," said Clem, "but it hurt tar'ble all the säum."

Nobody said anything more for a moment. Three pairs of eyes wandered covertly. It was finally Mabel who had the courage to break away.

"How's the kid?"

"Doing valiant. He gain a päound last week."

"You don't mind keeping him for a bit longer? I can't take him yet awhiles."

"I'll keep him as long as you like. I döan't want to be rid of him."

Mabel flushed.

"He always was more your child than mine. He's growing like you too; he's not like me."

"He's a stout liddle chap," said Clem.

"Well, we aren't likely to quarrel over him anyhow. I know you think I'm an unnatural mother—and I dare say I am, but it's not all my fault."

"No, it äun't," admitted Robert.

"I'm glad to hear you say that. I know Clem and Polly think I was a beast to leave you . . . but really it was getting too thick."

"I'll never ask you to come back," said Robert, "though if you'd come I'd be unaccountable glad."

Mabel shook her head.

"There's no good thinking of it—I'll never come back. It isn't only what's happened. . . . I never was the right wife for you, Robert."

"I'm sorry," he said humbly, "but I reckon you're comfortable here—got all you want—and I'll always manage to send you a bit."

Mabel laughed mirthlessly.

"Oh, yes, I dare say I'm 'comfortable'—I've got nice furniture, and a piano. . . . But if you think it's any better fun for me than for you, being married and living separate like this—all alone and yet not free. . . . We might get a separation order, I suppose; you can keep the child——"

"Maybe that ud be the best thing to do."

"Oh, döan't do naun in a hurry," put in Clem.

"It won't be doing much," said Mabel, "and we'll be just the same as before, except as it'll all be settled and on a legal footing, as father ud say. He's been wanting me to get a separation . . . but sometimes I wish you'd done something I could get a divorce for, and then we'd be free, so that if we wanted to marry anyone else, we could."

"Do you want to marry anyone?"

"No—not now, at any rate; I've had enough to last me a while. . . . But there's always fellows around . . . and it's awful being like this, neither one thing nor the other. At one time I felt sure that now I'd left you, you'd go with Hannah——"

"I cud never do that."

"What? Don't you love her any more?"

"Yes, I love her right enough," said Bob naïvely, "but, fur one thing, she döan't want me—she's got her own husband—and besides . . . well, all that's over."

He stood stockish, with rather a stupid look on his face. Mabel began to wonder what had made her think him dignified.

For a few awkward moments they stood looking at each other, none willing to make any movement to end the interview, and at the same time all aware that, for any practical purpose, it was over.

"Well, maybe we mun be going," said Clem at last.

"Yes—perhaps—good-bye," said Mabel.

They shook hands all round.

"I'll write," said Mabel to Bob, "when I've talked to father about the separation order."

Bob mumbled something, and the brothers went out hurriedly, nearly falling over their sticks. Mabel sat down to the piano, which she could not play, and picked out with one finger the opening bars of the Waltz Dream; they could hear her as they walked away up the street.

"Well, that wurn't much use," said Clem.

"Still I'm glad I seen her," said Robert.

They said no more about her till they were home, and not very much then—only just enough to let Polly know what had happened. Robert was quieter than ever at supper and afterwards. He seemed to be brooding deeply. When he had helped Polly as usual with the washing up, he went out into the warm dusk, smelling faintly of hawthorn, and leaned over the gate.

He stayed there while the darkness fell and drowned the dim gleaming gold of the buttercup fields. The air thickened as it chilled, smudging the few faint stars that were hanging round the chimney of Pookwell. Down at the rim of the eastern sky, above the woods, there was a wan kindling, showing that soon the May moon would rise and call the buttercups, and the chervil, and the roads with the feathery dust, out of the darkness into her white peace.

Robert saw ghosts in the lane. They were the ghosts of his old self and Mabel and Hannah, adrift under the stars. He could see Bob Fuller ranging round the pubs, drinking, and playing darts and billiards, and startling the old men— he could not think that Bob Fuller was himself. He saw Bob Fuller and Hannah Iden slinking together between the hedges, through the little lanes with their shadows, to the Rother marshes spread under the moon—and the moan of the river and the dancing silver on the reeds . . . and the moan of love in Hannah's throat, and his own heart beating and breaking for joy . . . that was himself right enough; he saw no stranger there. . . . Mabel came, provoking, enticing, repulsing, disappointing, suffering, repining, eating her own heart out. . . . Poor Mabel!

He was startled by a footstep at his side. It was Polly.
"Me and Clem are going up to bed—when'll you come in?"
"I'll come now."
The horn of the moon showed above Bugshull Wood, and
the pale light was on Robert's face. Polly looked at him
critically. She was sorry for him—tedious sorry—but she
couldn't help being a little angry with him too, because she
knew he was making Clem unhappy.

"Bob, it's silly of you to go mooning by yourself. You
mun stick indoors wud us and kip cheerful."
"I döan't know wot mäade me come here."
"Nor I nuther. And now sinst I'm spikking to you, Bob,
I mun say as you shud ought to do your best to kip cheerful—
leastways to look it—fur Clem's säake. He's unaccountable
vrothered about you."
"I'm sorry."
"Well, you try and be in better spirits. I know you're
troubled, but it'll come right. You've got stuck on a lot of
ideas wot äun't got no sense in them, and Clem's gitting all
the trouble of them too. I tell you he scarce slept a wink
last night, and the night before he was tossing all over the
bed—and sometimes he looks all sad and gloamy, him who
used to be so satisfied."
Bob looked abashed.
"I'm middling sorry, Poll. I'm a bit upset, but I didn't
mean to vrother you and Clem."
"Then you try and look more cheerful. I tell you it'll all
come right. Döan't think me hard-hearted, Bob, but I can't
help worriting about Clem, when I see him so chäanged and
gloamy."
"I'll do my best."
"Reckon you will—I know you're a good chap. And now
let's go in to bed—you'll find baby nicely asleep."

§ 27

Baby was indeed nicely asleep. His head showed a small
brown patch above the turned-back edge of the sheet. Robert

stood looking down at him for a moment before he set the candle on a chair and began to undress. He undressed slowly, for he had grown curiously vague and slow in some of his actions of late. He stood for some time with his collar in his hand, looking out of the window, which was uncurtained. The moonlight was flooding the garden, the dark clumps of the lilac bushes and the sods of the cabbage ground below. Up into the midst of it rose a pyramid of white blossom—a young cherry tree flowering late. The whiteness stood out against the grey illumination of the bushes and the darkness of the shadows—it seemed to hang on the air. Robert stood staring at it abstractedly.

His head ached a little—he had had a good deal of pain in his head of late, though with more consideration than Polly gave him credit for, he had said nothing about it. He was, moreover, in a state to which he was also growing accustomed —a state of heaviness and bewilderment, which was accompanied by a queer mental alertness, apparently working under the thick outer paralysis. . . . He stood for some minutes holding his collar in his hand, staring out at the hanging whiteness of the cherry tree.

He was thinking of Mabel—how she had stood in the middle of that drawing-room in the Sea Road at Bulverhythe, with the tears spilling out of the corners of her eyes. He remembered what she had said—she would never come back to him —after all, he did not want her to come back. . . . He didn't really love her; it was merely that she seemed to belong to him in some queer sort of way, to be part of his flesh. . . . If she were with him now he would only be making her unhappy—just as he was making Clem unhappy—and Polly— everyone.

Oh, it's no fun living with a man in hell, and Mabel was more comfortable in the Sea Road at Bulverhythe, with her father and her furniture and her piano . . . and yet she had said she was not happy—"living separate and yet not free" . . . she had actually wished that he had taken up with Hannah, so that she could divorce him—that was a lot for Mabel to say.

He put down his collar on the chest of drawers and, taking
off his coat, hung it carefully on a nail. Then he sat down
on a little low chair by the bed, and began to unlace his boots.
He did not get far with them—his eyes were still fixed on the
moonlight and the hanging cloud of cherry blossom. The
stillness and beauty hurt him—he could not tell why; but
they seemed to reproach him. Perhaps it was because these
quiet moon-flooded nights were part of memory, and all his
memories reproached him now. They were like children saying: "Why did you give us life?"

He slid from the chair to his knees beside the bed. It
was from force of habit, because he never prayed now. There
was no use importuning the Lord Who had condemned him.
Shall not the Judge of all the earth do right?—and Robert did
not want to trouble Him with his useless prayers and entreaties,
since he felt that such must be painful to One who was, in
spite of appearances, the God of love. . . . The waves of his
trouble seemed to spread from his heart in circles that en-
gulfed first Mabel, then Clem and Polly, and at last mysteriously lapped the footsteps of the Judgment throne. Anyhow,
Bob felt, Jesus must be sorry he was condemned. . . .

He hid his face in his hands, and became very still. It was
Polly that he saw now, standing there and looking at him re-
proachfully: "You mun kip cheerful and not vrother Clem."
Oh, he knew he was a kill-joy—he knew he was spoiling their
lives. But he could not help it. Such grief as his could not
be hidden. And yet Polly was quite right—it wasn't fair
that Clem should get unsettled and depressed because of him,
because of his kindness to him, just because he had been good
to him when everyone else had turned away. He had faced
the neighbourhood's disapproval by taking the outlaw under
his roof, he had risked losing favour with Jim—he had stood
by Robert when everyone else, even his own wife, had forsaken him. . . . It was not the only occasion he had stood
by him—as Mabel's husband, as Hannah's lover, Clem had
always been on his side. He had always been Bob's best
friend; and now his brother was repaying him by making him
wretched; for it was not only Polly's words that had shown

him a change in his brother, though with the inevitable selfishness of grief he had somehow accepted that change. He had been unable to help noticing Clem's growing depression—naturally it was not cheerful to live with a man like him.

If Robert had any decency he would make up his mind to go away, and hide his misery in some furrin place. But the thought was intolerable—the companionship of his brother and sister-in-law—the small bustle of their day—the fact that he was hardly ever left alone—all combined to make his life just bearable. Away from them, lonely and among strangers, he would have lost his last prop—he would rather die. Yet, as long as he stayed, Clem would be unhappy—it was impossible to expect him to be anything else. He ought to go away—but he could not; for one thing, Clem would never let him—for another, he'd rather die. . . . Well, why not?

He lifted his head sharply from his clasped hands. The moonlight was in the room now, and the horned moon hung in the square of the little window. She was very white and dim—there was none of the glassy radiance of winter, nor the burnished splendour of autumn. She was just white, like a blown petal of the white tree which seemed mysteriously to hang among the shadows. She lit up the face of the child sleeping in the bed, and he stirred and moaned, flinging one arm outside the sheet. Robert put it back, and the baby half woke: "Mumma—dada——" he murmered at Robert's warm touch.

Well, why not? . . . The baby was no reason—he scarcely knew his father. That murmur of sleepy love had been for Clem and Polly. He would perhaps for a day or two ask questions about the queer man who had been with him for a little time and then had gone . . . but he would not cry when Clem and Polly told him he would never come back. He would love them, who had been so much more of father and mother to him than his own, and they would take care of him and teach him and bring him up a happy child—he needn't worry about the baby.

Of course Clem and Polly would mind—they would mind

summat tar'ble. But it would not be any worse for them than having to watch him now, and as time passed they would get over it. His memory would not be the continuous burden that his living presence was, and in time they would come to talk about it as "all for the best." Then there was Mabel —his death could not possibly bring her any sorrow. Perhaps one or two of those tears would run so oddly out of the corners of her eyes . . . but then she would remember that she was free, that there was to be no more semi-detached life for her, that she could marry again if she wanted—one of those chaps that were always around. Certainly he seemed to owe it to Mabel to take himself out of her way, and there was no other way to do it but this. He had given her enough trouble— why should his spoiled life go on spoiling hers?

The more he thought of it the more he saw that it was the best thing to do. The best thing he could possibly do would be to go out quietly and drown himself before people were about. Of course he knew that it was wrong—"thou shalt not kill." But he felt he had no right to scruple at any wrong-doing which would be a deliverance to those who still had their lives to live and their souls to save. His life was lived and his soul was lost—it could not make any difference to him what he did, he could not be more than damned. Indeed he might be better off in hell than he was now, since perhaps the pain and horror of the burning city might keep him from thinking such a lot about the love of God. . . .

His mind was practically made up, except for a faint protest of fear. For some reason he hated the thought of the physical struggle of death—it loomed larger than the terrors beyond it. Also he found that he shrank piteously from the thought of leaving Clem. After all, his brother represented so much sympathy and comfort, and their parting would be for ever. There was no thought of a happy reunion to soften the wrench of farewell. Clem would go on living his happy life till his time came to go to heaven—as would Polly and Mabel and Nat and all of them—he would never see any of them again. For during the last months Robert's circle of wrath had narrowed imperceptibly, till at last it held only himself—everyone else he saw basking in the warm rays of God's love, he alone was cast out—for his sins—as he deserved.

He stiffened himself—his scruples were now only selfish and must be overcome. The best thing to do was to act at once. "What thou doest, do quickly." The first faint glimmer of dawn had come into the sky. He must not wait, or people would be about. Should he not go out at all, but hang himself on the hook behind the door as old Mus' Piper of Copt Hall had done ten years ago? No, that would be horrible for those who found him—Mrs. Piper had fallen down in a fit. He had much better drown himself—that made the least trouble of all, and people said it was an easy death to die . . . queer that he should mind the mere physical act of dying so much. He had better drown himself in the pond. The Rother was scarcely wide enough—he might lose his self-command and struggle out; but once he had walked into the middle of Bodingmares pond . . . like most men of his class and neighbourhood, he could not swim, so all he had to do was to find a sufficiency of water. But the cows drank in Bodingmares pond, and if his body wasn't found quickly he might poison the water for them. He shuddered at the thought of the kindly, sweet-mouthed cows he had milked and tended drinking their death through him. . . . He must leave a paper with directions where to find his body—also there were one or two other things he would like to say . . . and bits of things he would like people to have.

He rose stiffly from his knees and hunted for pencil and paper. There was a pencil in the pocket of his coat, but he could not find any paper—he must use the flyleaf of the book Clem had lent him—a story called "The Crofton Cousins," which Clem had given him years ago as a prize in the Sunday school, and which he let Robert take up to bed with him in case he was awake and miserable during the night. It seemed a pity to write on it—but he would only write in pencil, so Clem could rub it out.

There was not much to write, for the testator had very little to dispose of. The money realized by the sale at Cam-

pany's Hatch had been given to Mabel, and owing to her claims
he had saved nothing from his wages. He had a pair of new
boots which he wanted Clem to have—they would be much
too big for him, but he could stuff paper into the toes; and
he wanted Mus' Beeman to have his Bible. His watch and
chain, which had belonged to his father, he left to Polly for
the baby. He then put the book on the dressing-table, laying
a brush across it to keep it open.

Colours were now beginning to creep out of the dawn—
pale, lightless colours, green, violet and rose, faint and dull
in the sky and in the garden. The cherry tree no longer hung
in the shadows, but lifted its white blossom from the dark
delicate stem. Robert's throat tightened. Those white spines
lifted into the soft, flower-scented dusk seemed still for some
unaccountable reason to reproach him—they were like Aaron's
rod, bearing buds and blossom.

He turned back into the room, and put on his coat. His
Bible lay on the chair by the bedside, and he took it in his
hands. The Flaming Judgment . . . should he look and see
what it had to say?—it never had a message for him now.
He opened it mechanically: "Who hath taken his counsel
against Tyre, the crowning city, whose merchants are princes,
whose traffickers are the honourable of the earth? The Lord
of Hosts hath purposed it, to stain the pride of all glory."
That was the sort of thing he always hit upon if he opened
the book now—it had no message for him. He idly fluttered
the leaves, and they rolled over, thumbed and greasy with the
agony and ecstasy of months. What was this on the flyleaf:
"I, Albert Slater, have taken the pledge not to drink any
strong drink or liquor for one month from to-day, God helping
me."

That was the chap he had met on his first missionary
journey—on his way home from Goudhurst. He wondered
what had happened to him—he hadn't thought much of him
since. Had he kept that pledge? He would never know . . .
that was the chap who had first taught him to sleep out—he
remembered that doss under the haystack by Cockshot Farm.
He had had many nights in the open since then . . . oh,

that was the summer he could not bear to think of—that wonderful summer of the lanes and fields and villages. He had felt the love of God in his heart, filling him with joy—he had been the man without the wedding garment enjoying himself at the wedding, during the brief time that elapsed before he was cast out.

He put the Bible down. Mus' Beeman would perhaps value it, and be sorry for him occasionally—Mus' Beeman whose wedding garment was so exceedingly starched and white. . . . He stood looking down at Nat. Should he kiss him? No—he might wake up. He had better go off with as little ado as possible. He wished that the dawn and the soaring cherry-tree did not make him feel so sad . . . he would be away from them soon . . . away from their reproach. The little wind was rising and shaking the leaded panes of the window.

§ 28

He took his boots off to go downstairs, then sat on the doorstep and put them on again, laboriously lacing them up as if he had not only two furlongs more of life. The dawn had now begun to glow—it was no longer white like the cherry-tree; first the sky kindled in long ruddy slats, then an amber light trailed up the Rother marshes, and burned on the river . . . the wind rose again, shaking the trees.

Robert went out into the field at the back of the house. From the top of it he could see the homestead of Bodingmares among the haystacks and barns. The moment before sunrise was so intensely clear that he could see the very tiles, worn and mottled with age and weather. In the strange sunless gleam and the utter stillness it was like some mirage, some house in a dream. Beyond it, a little to the east, was a clump of willow and alder, surrounding the pond; and far away, but clear with that peculiar watery clearness which means rain in the Rother Valley, he could see the Kentish hills, checkered with fields and sprawled with woods. Then suddenly the sun rose and swept up the fields in a soaring light—the watercourses gleamed, the windows of farmhouses burned, the wood seemed to change colour, and the subdued chatter of birds among the trees swelled into a song. A blackbird's liquid note sounded close to Robert in a hawthorn tree, for some reason it seemed to fill him with a heart-breaking surprise. . . . The sense of reproach grew; he had thought till then that Clem was the only living thing he would be really sorry to leave, but now he saw that the wrench was also to be with this quiet country of the Rother Valley, which all his life had been so much to him and yet so strangely little.

As he walked across the big field in the sunrise, with his shadow running before him towards death, he found himself wishing that he had loved the country better. As a boy and young man he had preferred the public-house to the fields, and had sought the lanes on summer nights only for the sake of some girl that he hugged. . . . Then when he had done with public-houses and girls he still had not turned to the fields—because he mistrusted them, because they were the creatures and he sought the creator. Yet the mistrusted earth had been his comfort all through that wonderful year . . . memories came to him of footprints in the white dust of Kentish lanes, of big fields tilted to the sunset, of ponds like moons in the night, of dim shapes of villages in a twilight thickened and yellowed by the chaffy mist of harvest, of the spilt glory of big solemn stars, the mystery and the wonder of sounds at night—sounds of animals creeping, sounds of water, sounds of birds. . . .

The procession of his thoughts moved fast under the heavy crust of bewilderment. Outwardly he still went stupidly, almost brutishly, to his ignoble death in a farmhouse pond; but inwardly his mind was seething, full of memories, desires, tangled ends—which were now beginning mysteriously to be sorted by some hidden process working gradually nearer the surface.

The pond was about two furlongs from Pookwell, cupped in some alders and sallows. The big yellow flags were opening now among the reeds, and a yellow light gleamed from the sunrise on the surface of the water. It was all lit up and aflame, and, as Robert looked down on it from the field, it seemed to join in the reproach that had first come to him on the hanging whiteness of the cherry-tree, and now seemed to come from every tree, from every lane, from every hedgerow, leaf and flower, from the hidden song of the birds, and the fanning, flooding sunrise.

"Are you going to drown yourself, Robert Fuller? Are you going to be dead whilst we're alive? Is your body going to be green and slimy at the bottom of that pond? Aun't you going to milk the cows this morning? Aun't you going to light the kitchen fire? Döan't you want to see the sun any more? Aun't you going to dress your baby? Maybe he'll wäake up and cry now he's alöan."

He stood at the edge of the pond, looking hunted and ashamed. The reproach seemed to swell all round him, from the fields and from the sunshine—the reproach of beauty crying after the blind.

"All your life I've bin here fur you to see, and you've scarce ever looked at me till now; and now you look—and you're gone, surelye."

"But I döan't want you—I döan't care how beautiful you are. I döan't want naun wudout my God."

"I am your God. Döan't you know me?"

The fields and the farms and the sunrise were calling him now with the voice he had heard in the Throws chapel—the voice that had tormented and delighted and enraged and made a fool of him for years.

"I am your God—döan't you know me? Did you think I was away up in heaven, watching you from a gurt way off? Didn't you know that I've bin with you all the time?—that every time you looked out on the fields or into your kind brother's eyes or at your baby asleep in his bed you looked on Me?"

Robert's temples were hammering, and the big pulses in his neck were throbbing heavily. The deadening weight of stupefaction seemed gone—and instead of it he could feel his heart breaking. . . .

"Why do you run away from me and hide like a stupid fox that döan't know its own earth? Why wöan't you look and see how beautiful and homely and faithful and loving I am. You can't get away from me. Even if you go down into hell, I am there also. I'm a part of your sorrows, as you're a part of Mine."

"But, Lord, you've cast me out."

"How could I ever cast you out? I'm plighted to you wud the troth of a mother to her child. You lost Me in the mists of your own mind. . . ."

On the slime at the edge of the pond there were the marks of birds' feet—tiny claws impressed on the soft sand. . . . Robert looked at them and trembled. Then he lifted his face to the sky, so that the sunrise fell on it, pouring out of the clouds, striking up from the broken ripples of the pond. His face was all smeared and dabbled with the sweat of his agony, and it shone in the sunrise, catching it like the water, till it was transfigured and gleaming.

"O Lord!" he cried, "O Lord!"

§ 29

"Clem, Bob's never lighted the fire."

Polly's grumbling voice came up the stairs to Clem as he hitched on his trousers.

"Maybe he äun't down yit."

"It's gone six."

"Reckon he'd sleep sound, after gitting that tooth out."

Clem strode across the two feet of landing, and opened Bob's door. The room was full of sunshine, spilling over the bed, in which the baby lay contentedly awake, waving his arms.

"He äun't up here—he mun have gone out."

"Well, it's the fust time he's disremembered the fire, and he's never brung my coals in, nuther."

Something smote Clem.

"I'll help you," he mumbled, and went downstairs.

He carried in Polly's coals for her and helped her lay and light the fire, then he undertook to watch it while she ran up to dress the baby.

A minute later he heard a scream:

"Mäaster!"

"Wot is it?"

"Bob's a-gone and drownded himself . . . he's written it here. . . . Oh, wotsumdever shall we do?"

Clem ran upstairs, trembling and sick. He found her standing by the chest of drawers, holding a book in her hand. The fly-leaf was scrawled over with Bob's disorderly handwriting.

"I don't want to make you miserable any more, so will drownd myself. It is an easy death. So do not grieve for me, dear Clem and Polly. But I have pains in my head——"

"Oh, it's like wot they always say when they do it in the newspapers," cried Polly hysterically.

Clem stood with his arm round his wife's shoulder, leaning on her with all his weight, so that she had to prop herself against the chest of drawers.

"Oh, döan't tääke on so, pore soul," she comforted; "reckon it's all fur the best. He's happy now . . . he says we're to have Baby . . . and he's a-gone and left his Bible to Mus' Beeman. . . ."

"Then he can go and tääke it to him himself!" cried Clem furiously, "fur thur he is coming in at the gëate."

"Who? Mus' Beeman?"

"No; Bob."

Clem dashed down to the door, shaking with fury and excitement. Reaction had swung him from grief to rage, and for the first time Robert faced his brother crimson and spluttering with indignation.

"Wot d'you mean by it?" shouted Clem, "wot d'you mean by scaring us lik this, and then walking in at the gëate as if naun had happened? Reckon you'll brëake our hearts wud all your ways."

Bob stood staring at him with his mouth open.

"Come in, Bob," said Polly tearfully. "You mun tääke off your clothes sinst they're wet."

"They're bone dry," ejaculated Clement.

"I'm sorry," stammered Bob; "I'm middling sorry fur the

fright I've guv you. I dud my best to git back in time to
stop you seeing wot I'd wrote."

"Then you didn't never drownd yourself!" said Polly.

"Reckon I didn't. I went out to drownd myself right enough,
but when I got there the Lord showed me His beauty."

There was a short, heavily charged silence. Clem and Polly
looked at each other.

"He showed me as all the warld wur His, and me along
wud it, and as how He'd never let me go . . . and as all this
vrother of mine wur just as when you wääke up wud your
head under the bed-clothes on a sunny morning and think
it's night."

"Then you mean to say . . . you're telling me, Bob, as you
döan't believe any longer as you're lost?"

"Twur I as lost Him, not Him wot lost me—reckon He
wur thur calling after me all the time, and I wudn't hear,
being that silly. . . . It's more lik fur a sheep to bite her lamb's
head off, or fur a woman to throw her child out of the winder,
than fur Him to cast out my soul. Oh, I've bin in hell . . .
but He wur thur too, along of me, and I never knew it. . . ."

"Then, does this all mean as you've bin converted agäun?"
asked Clem dubiously.

"Reckon I wur convarted more'n eighteen months ago—
leastways I guv myself to God then, and though I sinned He
never cast me off. But all the time I'd some tedious silly
ideas in my head about Him, fur till this very morning I
thought as He wur an angry God, a Flaming Judgment, as
you might say. But now I see as how He's love . . . and
He's beauty . . . He's in the fields määking the flowers grow
and the birds sing and the ponds have that lovely liddle white
flower growing on 'em . . . and He's a lot more homely than
föalkses ud think. . . ."

Clem noticed that his brother's hands were trembling, and
he stood with his chin lifted, in one of those moods of exalta-
tion which used to be common of old, but now had not visited
him for months.

"Wot showed you this, Bob—all of a suddint?"

"I dunno. I just stood there, and something seemed to

git broken in my head—and then I thought all different. I sim to hear a voice spikking to me—not a tar'ble voice, nor a voice lik a minister's, but a sort of voice lik wot they have in these parts, all quiet and rough. And it said as God äun't shut away from us up in heaven, but He's down here—He's in the fields wud the young corn and wud the animals caring fur their young, and He's in you and me—thur äun't no gitting away from Him. . . . And then I thought of the Scripture wot says, 'If I go down into hell, Thou art there also,' and I saw as that ways I cud never go to hell, sinst the only hell I wur scared of wur being wudout God."

"Well," said Polly briskly, "you might have thought of all that a bit earlier, and säaved yourself and everybody else a lot of trouble. Howsumdever, sinst you've come to your senses, so much the better, and you mun help me git the breakfast now."

Robert obeyed her readily. Clem remained standing in the doorway, staring into the lane without seeing. For a long time he stood leaning against the door-post with his arms folded over his chest. Once he lit his pipe and let it go out again. When Polly had called him twice, the second time rather roughly, he went in to breakfast.

At breakfast Bob held forth in still greater detail on his wonderful experiences. Reticence had always been but a fugitive quality in him, and he enlarged on his adventures at the pond side till only the limitations of language, especially his, prevented Clem and Polly from knowing as much about them as he did. This new set of experiences was about as unintelligible to them as the old, but they saw that he was now happy, that he had passed out of his despair, so they were thankful—and as sympathetic as they knew how.

"I feel as if I cud justabout never pay Him back fur all He's done fur me," said Robert. "Reckon I mun tell all men as He's a God of love and everythink lovely."

"Now, Bob," said Clem seriously, "you mun let other people alöan. You can't go every time you're converted preaching the Gospel about the pläace."

"But reckon I preached a hard Gospel the fust time: I

preached as Christ died fur the Elect, and as everyone else ud
burn in hell. Reckon I wur täaking away God's character all
the time, and I mun go and mäake it right agäun."

"You let it alone fur the present, anyways."

"But I can't let it alone when I've spuck agäunst His love.
I mun go and tell Mus' Beeman, too, as he's bin mistäaken."

"You may go and tell Mus' Beeman anything you like—
I'll give you a day off to do it—but you mun let other föalkses
alone. Fur one thing, they wöan't stand it from you at present;
you mun remember as the neighbours are all set agäunst you,
Bob."

Bob held his tongue, but Clem still felt rather anxious about
him. His brother's tendency to make a scandal of everything
that happened to himself, good or bad, must be reckoned with,
and he knew the dangers of that thrilling exalted mood, which
he could see Bob was in now, in spite of the differences.

"We mun kip an eye on him fur a day or two," he said
to Polly afterwards. "He's that stuck on telling everybody
everythink."

"He'll be a middling gurt owl if he goes and starts all that
agäun."

"That's wot I'm saying—the whole neighbourhood's set
agäunst him, as is only natural; they wöan't stand no more
of that from him."

"Surelye—and dud you hear as Hannah Iden's back?"

"No—is she?"

"Yes, her and Darius. Maudie Pont töald me; if Bob sets
eyes on her, maybe we'll have all that started agäun too."

"Bob's shut of her, I'm certain sure."

"I äun't. You can't be certain sure of anythink wud a man
like Bob. I shudn't care fur him to see too much of her even
now."

"You think lik a woman, missus—you think as one of us
can never git präaperly shut of one of you. But I tell you
Bob's a good feller, and though I wish as his religion wur a
bit quieter, I reckon it's a good religion and ull kip him
straight."

"Then it ull do now wot it dudn't do before. Howsumdever,

I'm glad he's got his spirits back and sees things a bit more natural. Fust he dud naun but grieve 'cos everybody wur going to hell except himself, and then he grieved 'cos nobody wur going to hell but him; he sims to have settled things more reasonable now. But as you say, we mun kip an eye on him, and it wouldn't be bad, I reckon, if he stopped by me this morning and picked over the fruit fur the jam."

§ 30

Clem was glad to leave Bob with his wife. He would be too busy that morning to keep an eye on him, and he could trust Polly to see that his brother did not make a fool of himself in any way. If only Bob would behave himself and keep quiet, things might take a turn for the better now. Anyhow he was happy and rational again—more rational than he had ever been since his conversion. If only he would go on like this, perhaps in time, when she saw what an improved man her husband was, Mabel might think of coming back. . . .

Thus Clem's imagination painted some glowing pictures that morning at his work, and during a tramp he had to make into the village, to see Pepper about a horse—pictures which were one and all darkened when he came back to the farm, and found Polly waiting for him there.

"She's come after Mus' Robert," said Pickdick. "I said as you'd a-gone into the town, and maybe he wur wud you."

Clem groaned.

"I haven't seen the chap. Why cudn't you have kipt a better eye on him, missus?"

"I did but run out to see after the eggs whilst the water wur boiling, and he wur picking over the liddle green gooseberries—then when I come back, he wur a-gone, having got through wud the picking; so I thought maybe he'd be up at the pläace."

"He äun't bin aräound here this marnun," said Pickdick.

"Then I can't think where's he's a-got to."

"I can, surelye," said Clem with another groan.

He had remembered that to-day was Salehurst market.

"Whur, then?"

"He's a-gone to Salehurst, lik the hem fool as he is. He'll be telling them all about this new conversion of his'n. Bless my soul, missus—why cudn't you have looked after him?"

"I did but go out five minnut—and I never thought as mortal man cud have picked over them gooseberries so quick."

"Well, I mun to go after him, anyways; föalkes wöan't stand his preaching at 'em after all that's happened—maybe they'll do him some harm."

"Wait and have your dinner, mäaster."

"No—I'll go now, and mäake him behave sensible if I can. He's lik a child some ways, is Bob, and I'm afeared he'll git himself into trouble."

He started off at once. The day was hot, but he walked fast, and had soon reached the cross-roads outside Salehurst. It was only one of the smaller markets, and so far he had not met anyone, but at the Throws he saw a trap coming towards him. The driver hailed him from the distance:

"That you, Mus' Fuller?"

"Surelye, Mus' Cox."

"I wur driving out to fetch you—your brother's started his preaching agäun, and I'm afeared as there'll be trouble."

"I wur just a-coming after him myself."

"Then jump in and I'll drive you."

Clem put his foot on the wheel and sprang up. Cox turned the horse's head towards Salehurst.

"I knew as you wur the only chap as cud stop him, so I thought as I'd go fur you at wunst. I did my best, but he wur set on gitting up and telling 'em all some wonderful new thing as had happened to him; he never seemed to think that föalkses wöan't stand that sort of thing from the likes of him—begging your pardon."

"Bob's a valiant chap," said Clem, "but he äun't got all the sense that he might."

"Seemingly he's got religion agäun," said Cox. "I'd bin töald as he'd a-done wud all that sort of thing, having a notion as he wur lost. But now he wur saying as God's showed Him-

self to him agäun as the God of love and I know not wot else
beside. Folkses wöan't stand it."

"Had they begun to play up rough?"

"Oh, only a few that wur hollering at him. . . . But them
Egyptians are about agäun; I cud see Darius Ripley there
listening, and you know as Darius said as he'd git even wud Bob
Fuller for gitting him seven months in quod?"

"I never heard it; and anyways Bob didn't git him locked
up—it wur fur dog-stealing."

"Yes, but if Bob hadn't mäade all that row and brung in
the police, Ripley ud never have bin caught. It wur Bob's
trouble wot showed the police where he wur. Reckon if there's
any skylarking, Darius ull mäake it wuss—and there's other
Egyptians about too."

Clem looked scared.

"D'you think they'll—they'd never do him any harm?"

"Oh, döan't you vrother—all they'd do at the wust ud be
to give him a ducking."

"I döan't want Bob to git a ducking."

"Maybe we'll be in time to stop it—not as we can do anything if the trouble's begun, but if they're only jeering and
hollering, and you git Bob to give over. . . ."

"He wöan't give over fur me. . . . Wot's that?"

"Where?"

"Down on the Marsh—yonder—it's lik a lot of folkses running."

"That's it—that's them. Reckon we're too late, and they've
got your brother."

He pulled the horse up violently, and they both jumped
out of the trap. They had just reached the bridge at the foot
of the station hill, where the Rother runs under the road and
turns northward towards the River Dudwell. Two or three
furlongs away a little eddying group of people was moving
over the marsh. The centre was very close, a dense dark
mass, but the edges sprayed and scattered, contracted and expanded, changing its shape from a circle to a long ellipse.

Clem had never run so fast in his life—he left Cox, who
was a trifle unwieldy, far behind. He caught up with the

crowd while it was still some way from the spot where the
Rother spreads and deepens for Bugshull Mill. They were
evidently bound for the mill-pond; Clem could hear no cries,
but a confused murmur, and a heavy, running sound . . . as
when the Salehurst United charge up the field at a football
match and the Etchingham goal goes down before them. . . .
At first he experienced a certain relief to find that they were
so few; after all, the respectable farmers of Salehurst market
would not take part in such an orgie, even though they might
allow it—but as he drew even with them he realized that it
would be about as hopeless for him to tackle twenty men as
two hundred. Their numbers were made up of the rougher
elements of the market—gipsies (among whom, however, he
did not see Darius), young rowdy labourers and farm-boys,
and one or two of the smaller farmers' sons.

"Stop!" cried Clem. "Stop!"

No one took any notice, and he could only run beside the
others, panting and imploring. The centre was just a closely
knotted mass—there was no struggle; evidently Robert was
submitting to his fate, either as a matter of policy or, more
likely, of conscience.

"Stop!" gasped Clem. "Let him go. He äun't done you
no harm. You're a hem set of bullies."

"You höald your jaw," said Stan Shovell, running near, "or
maybe we'll chuck you in after him."

"Adone do, Mus' Clem," broke in Cox, who had now
reached them. "You can't meddle. They wöan't do your
brother any harm if he goes quiet."

"They'll drownd him."

"No, they wöan't—they'll only give him a bit of a ducking,
as ull do him all the good in the warld, between ourselves."

"Oh, Lard!" panted Clem. "Oh, Lard!"

They had reached the pool at last—the sheet of water that
holds the reflection of Bugshull Mill and its Lombardy poplars.
The wheel was not working, so there was no danger of Robert
being sucked under and drowned, but Clem was frantic at
the thought of what was to happen. He suddenly caught
sight of his brother, a stumbling dishevelled figure . . . and

then, to his horror, Robert began to struggle. The sight ot the stretch of cold water of unknown depth filled him with mortal fear.

"Lemme go!" he shrieked. "Lemme go!"

Clem made a plunge towards him, but was seized and held by Cox of Haiselman's and Stan Shovell. He fought them both, friend and foe, with the same fury. Then suddenly there was a big splash, and he became still.

Silence hung for an instant. Everyone was staring at the place where Robert had vanished. The water spread in ever wider eddies. . . .

"He's drownded!" cried Clem.

But the next moment Robert appeared, standing up to his waist in water, a ludicrous figure with his hair dripping in his eyes, and the water pouring off him as he choked and gasped.

There was a loud burst of laughter from the men on the bank.

"Now, Robert Fuller—preach to us about the goodness of God."

"Are you Sääved?"

"He's washed, anyway."

"Pull him out and chuck him in agäun."

"No—he's had enough."

"Three times is the dose."

"Git höald of him wud your stick, he can't run away."

"No, let him stay thur and preach to us."

"He says God's in everything. Have you found Him in the water, Bob?"

Robert opened his mouth.

"He's going to begin."

A torrent of blood suddenly poured from Robert's mouth.

"Lard, you've hurt him!"

"Help him to shore—we mun't kill him."

"It's naun—it's only his nose bleeding."

"No—it's coming from inside. He shudn't ought to have fought so."

Robert struggled slowly through the water towards the bank,

seized two tufts of grass to pull himself up, then fell forward unconscious, still half in the water.

§ 31

He was brought home in Cox's trap, propped up between him and Clem. He said he felt better, but by the time they had reached Pookwell his face was grey. Leaving him with Clem and Polly, Cox drove off to fetch the doctor.

Clem helped his brother take off his wet clothes and get into bed. Certain movements seemed to give him great pain, and Clem was afraid that something was broken inside him. His own anxiety and compassion were still clouded with rage; he felt that he would never be able to lose the impression he had had that day of his fellow-men, that he would never again be able to greet any of them civilly at market. It is true that Bob's executioners had been only a handful of riff-raff, but the respectable farmers and tradesmen had stood by and allowed them to do as they liked; they could almost certainly have stopped them if they had wished, but—with the exception of Cox—they had not wished, they had probably been glad to see Bob Fuller punished. . . . "A ducking ull do him all the good in the warld"—even Cox had said that.

"Döan't look so wild, kid," said Bob, as Clem put the sheet over him with tense, trembling hands. "Reckon it wur all meant fur a joke. I cud see as most of 'em wur just horse-playing all the time."

"A valiant joke—säum sort of joke as a dog has when he worries a sheep."

"Well, it's a joke wud him, anyway."

"How are you feeling now, Bob?"

"A bit queer. . . . I've got a pain."

"The doctor ull be here in a minnut."

The doctor came and examined Bob. A couple of ribs were broken, and there were some internal injuries besides. The pain was becoming more and more unbearable every minute, and before he went the doctor gave him something to make him go to sleep.

"D'you think he'll git better soon?" asked poor Clem when they were out of the room.

"I'm afraid he's very badly hurt. Of course I can say nothing for certain—he's young and he's strong—but I think I ought to prepare you for things going badly."

"Do you mean as he'll die?"

"He is in very great danger. Will you and your wife undertake to nurse him? I'll send round the District Nurse in the evening—there may be need for injections."

Clem sat down miserably on the stairs.

"Cheer up," said the doctor, "he may pull through."

"It's a shäame—a hem shäame."

"I quite agree, and if I were you, when he comes round, I'd try and find out if he knows who the chaps were who knocked him about like this. Someone ought to go to jail for it. I suppose you didn't see much?"

"No—only the outside lot. I saw one or two just as they wur all mäaking off, after Bob wur took bad, but in that mess you cudn't tell wot wur happening, surelye."

The doctor wondered whether he ought to suggest that the patient's wife should be sent for, but he knew the situation was delicate, so left it to young Fuller.

Clem talked it over with Polly, and they decided to send for Mabel at once. In spite of all, she was still Bob's wife, and the whole of tradition demanded that she should be at his bedside now. So Mabel received one of those "telegraphts" of which she was so dashing a sender, and the next morning saw her at Pookwell, very hectic and tearful, but quite soft towards Bob, who had captured all her physical pity now.

He lay in a curiously broken attitude under the bed-clothes —somehow his attitude suggested a body utterly broken. There were two red, hard spots of colour on his cheeks, and his eyes were brilliant and restless.

"Hallo, Mabel . . ." he said when he saw her, but seemed unable for further speech. She sat by him for about ten minutes, holding his hand, then rose to go when the doctor came, kissing his hot cheek before she went.

During the next two days he was kept very much under the influence of drugs, for the pain was great. In one or two lucid intervals he spoke to Clem. Once he said:

"It'll be good fur Mabel if I die—I never thought of that when I chäanged my mind about drawnding myself . . . maybe I shud ought to have thought of her, but my heart wur that full I cud think of naun but how beautiful it wur to live in the lovely warld."

Another time he apologized to his brother:

"I know as you and Poll dudn't want me to go out and spik to folkses about wot had happened to me . . . but when I wur sitting there wud the sun all shining on me and the liddle green gooseberries in the plääte . . . and outside the blue sky and the white and yaller flowers . . . then I thought as I mun go and tell everyone as God is love and as all things lovely are a part of His love . . . and how it äun't true about wrath and hell and all them scaring things. . . . He said: 'Consider the lilies'—that just means 'look at the flowers—daisies and oxeyes and milkmaids and such. . . .'"

Clem could not extract any information from him likely to lead to the arrest of his assailants.

"Reckon it wur one of their rough jokes . . . lik a lot of calves. . . . I didn't notice no one in particular—and reckon it wur a bit my own doing. . . . I shudn't ought to have fought so . . . but I wur so tar'ble scared of being drownded."

When, at the end of the second day, it became pretty certain that he would not live, Clem asked him if he wished him and Polly to keep the child, always supposing, as was most likely, Mabel did not want him.

"Surelye—you mun kip him. He's more your'n than mine."

"Bob—you döan't want—shud you want me to have him brung up in your religion?"

Robert was silent for a moment, looking out of the pale sky, translucent with a dying sunset. Then he said slowly:

"If you know of an easier way to God than mine, you mun show it to him."

Clem felt something hard and thick rising in his throat. He put out his hand, and laid it over Bob's—all brown and calloused, but now strangely helpless under his own.

"Oh, Bob, it sims unaccountable hard as you shud die in the middle of the month of May."

"Reckon it sims hard, seeing as I'd got back my täaste fur living, as you'd say . . . and, Clem, I feel tar'ble queer, wud this pain and the stuff the doctor gives me, and all . . . and I döan't lik dying—it scares me. But I've a feeling as if I go to the Lord God I'll only be going into the middle of all that's alive. . . . If I'm wud Him I can't never lose the month of May. . . . Oh, when I think of how He called me all those years agone, and I running away all scared lik a silly sheep—and saying as I'd sarve Him out . . . oh, reckon it's He that's sarved me out—caught me and sarved me out, and got the everlasting laugh of me."

And feebly from his sick-bed Bob joined in the laugh of God.

Clem read the Bible to him now and then, but he was not able to stand much, and towards the end—on the third evening —he was quite unconscious, under the influence of the merciful drug. Clem and Mabel and Elizabeth and Polly with little Nat in her arms were in the room when he died. But he saw none of them. It was dusk, and the warm mist of May hung in the garden, the trees and the flowers standing stirless in the grey light. Robert lay in the bed, his face towards the window, breathing heavily. Suddenly there was a faint tremor, the breath for a moment became more natural, and he murmured some indistinct words that sounded like "queer dreams" and "shadders of trees on the road." Then his breath gathered itself into a deep sigh . . . and stopped.

§ 32

He was buried in the graveyard of the Throws chapel, where his father lay. The funeral took place early in the morning, for the family did not want "a lot of folk staring aräound." The secret of it was well kept, and no one was at the graveside but the relations.

Naturally, local opinion against Robert had a good deal relented. He had a better reputation dead than ever he had had alive. This may have been due in a measure to the fact that he had said or done nothing to lead to any arrests among his persecutors. He had died game, if otherwise ignobly. There was an inquest, of course, but it led to nothing but a verdict of "Manslaughter against some person or persons unknown." None of the witnesses who stood up and blundered their way out of the net of the Coroner's questions would acknowledge having laid hands on the deceased. "It wur just a lot of chaps larking round, and you cudn't see wot wur happening, surelye." In the end the Law dismissed Robert's death as a practical joke—"a lark that went too far" was the heading under which the local paper reported it.

The evening before the funeral Clem and Polly had lined the grave with late primroses and cuckoo-flowers and buttercups. They were still fairly fresh when Bob's coffin was lowered down on them, with two wreaths of white composite and black jute, one from the widow and one from the rest of the family. These represented an almost sentimental generosity, since they were to be buried with him, for Jim was anxious that Bob's grave should not be made conspicuous by funeral adornments—"maybe later, when folkses have disremembered a bit, then we can put up a stöan." So the two masterpieces of the artificial florist's art went down into the grave like some old-time offering to the dead—"from his eversorrowing Widow. Not lost but gone before," and "With fondest love and sympathy from Mother, Jim, Mary, Clem, Polly, and Little Nat—Daddy's gone to be with the Angels."

It was a dull morning, with pale lifts of light in the grey sky. The hawthorn stood out with an almost luminous whiteness against the low clouds, and the buttercup fields were bronzing with the early sorrels of June. A soft wind panted up from the Rother, bringing with it mysteriously the scent of water.

Mr. Vine stood at the head of the grave, and offered up the prayers, which included everybody except Robert. Mabel stood next to him, her weeds flying out in the wind. She looked very smart and pretty in her weeds, which had been bought expensively in Bulverhythe. The tears were running out of the corners of her eyes . . . for some obscure reason she grasped a Book of Common Prayer. Polly was crying too, but Clem's eyes were quite dry; he seemed to have cried all the tears that were in him during the four dreadful days between Robert's death and burial . . . now he had only one emotion left—anger at Mary, because she had not bought new mourning, but was wearing the old, tight things she had worn at his father's funeral . . . she probably did not think Bob worth spending money on. Clem and Polly were recklessly clad from head to foot in brand new blacks—instead of his usual bowler Clem wore a soft-brimmed hat, in which, with his woolly hair, he looked like an Italian organ-grinder . . . he stood fumbling and pleating it in his black kid fingers as he glared at Mary, whose jacket was held over her aggressive bosom by a huge, funereal-looking safety-pin. . . .

. . . And in that grave lay Bob, who had sat on his bed in the big, low-pitched room and told him all the secrets and adventures of a Man's life . . . that was Bob who had been the scandal of the Woolpack and the Royal George, who had wagered in shillings and drunk in quarts . . . who had gambled at Lingfield races with the gipsies, and borrowed Clem's money . . . and loved Hannah Iden. . . . And Clem had watched Bob being slowly beaten to his knees by that power he had once challenged till there was nothing of his old pride and glory left, till he finished as the servant of the little brother he had taught and despised. In this dust the Man had ended, to this lonely bed the Lover had come. . . .

His thoughts had travelled away from Mary and her short-comings, and came back to find the party at the graveside dispersing. This time there were no funeral cabs; they all walked back in groups and couples—first went Mabel and Elizabeth, then Jim and Harry Wheelsgate and Mary, and last of all Clem and Polly, a little uneasy in the company of Mus'

Vine, who walked with them as far as the street. He talked about the weather and the crops, as if poor Bob, who was uppermost in all their minds, had become somehow indecent as a topic of conversation—and Clem knew that at home, too, they would be talking of the weather and the crops, and Bob would never be mentioned among them except with a lowering of the eyelids and the voice.

"Yes, you'll soon be able to cut in the river field. . . . I hope the sorrel won't be the plague it was last year. . . . Good-bye."

Mus' Vine shook hands with them at the entrance to the village, where his cottage stood. He held their hands a little longer than was necessary, to tell them that he sympathized; and spoke of the crops only because he was not quite sure whether they would like to speak of Bob. . . .

When he was gone Clem put his arm into Polly's. The others were far on in front.

"Oh, Poll . . ." he said.

"Döan't you fret, my dear."

"I can't help it . . . when I think of him . . . how he used to go up this here street wud his hands in his pockets . . . and the check breeches as he always wore."

"Reckon you're thinking of him as he wudn't lik you to think."

"Maybe."

"He'd sooner you thought of him after he'd larned better ways."

"He wur a decent chap, Poll. I know as people here are set agäunst him, and as even his own folk haven't much to say fur him . . . somehow, wotsumdever he did, living or dying, he cudn't help mäaking it shocking . . . but he wur a good chap, the best I've known."

"Surelye," said Polly, "if Bob had only had sense he might have come to be a saint and martyr—who knows? He had the makings of one! but he had no sense—if he'd had sense he'd be alive now."

"Reckon he did wot he thought right."

"That's why it's a pity it wurn't sense. Howsumdever,

döan't you fret over him, my dearie. We've got his liddle boy at home, to be the joy and comfort of us both."

Her eyes lit up, and she drew Clem's arm closer against her heart. Then they mended their pace, for a thin shower was spattering in the dust.